"A great storyteller with a gifted and individual voice."   —*Charles de Lint*

"Smith's writing, evocative yet understated, gracefully brings to life his imagined realms."   —*Quill and Quire*

"Smith paints his worlds so well that you are transported within a paragraph or two and remain in transit until the story ends."   —*Broken Pencil*

"His stories resonate with a deep understanding of the human condition as well as a characteristic wry wonder... Stories you can't forget, even years later."
—*Julie Czerneda, award-winning author and editor*

"An extraordinary author whom every lover of quality speculative fiction should read."   — *Fantasy Book Critic*

"Smith is definitely an author who deserves to be more widely read."
—*Strange Horizons*

"Sadly under read, Douglas Smith is deserving of an entire 'Science Fiction You Haven't Read…But Should' article all to his own, and you'll likely see it one day."
—*Digital Science Fiction*

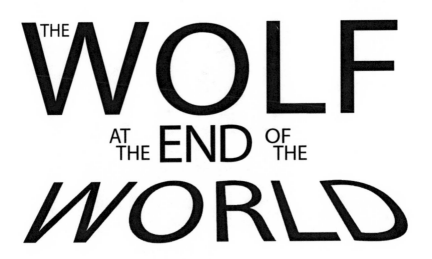

THE WOLF AT THE END OF THE WORLD

Douglas Smith

Lucky Bat Books

A Lucky Bat Book

The Wolf at the End of the World
Copyright 2013 by Douglas Smith

Cover Art by Jean-Pierre Normand
Cover Design by Brandon Swann

Introduction
Copyright © 2013 by Charles de Lint

ISBN: 978-0-9918007-3-5

Published by Lucky Bat Books
www.LuckyBatBooks,com

First Edition September 2013
10 9 8 7 6 5 4 3 2 1

To my family.

Acknowledgements

Although this is a work of fiction, it takes place in our modern world and I needed the help of many people to ensure that I got the important things right. I'd like to thank those people here.

Thanks to Chief Anita Stephens of the Chapleau Ojibwe First Nation, as well as her mother, Theresa, for their hospitality at the Blue Heron Inn and for their help with my questions on Ojibwe stories, traditions, and culture. Thanks to Monica Bodirsky, History Program Coordinator/Editor at the The Native Canadian Centre of Toronto, for her help answering my many questions on Ojibwe spiritual beliefs, ceremonies, and traditions.

Thanks to Constable Marshall Canning for his tour of the Chapleau OPP premises and for his assistance with police procedures and how the OPP operates in a small northern town, and to Margaret Coulter, Senior Constable, Nishnawbe-Aski Police Service, Chapleau Ojibwe Detachment, for her help on First Nations police forces. Thanks to Mayor Earle J. Freeborn of Chapleau for his insights into a small northern community, and to Cam Robitaille for acting as my guide into the bush and helping me get the flora, fauna, and weather right. Thanks to Dr. Douglas P. Lyle, MD ("The Writers Medical and Forensic Lab" http://www.dplylemd.com) for answering my questions on DNA sampling and testing, and to Bob Yap of Ontario Power Generation for his help with hydroelectric dams.

If there is anything that I have wrong in this book on any of the above topics, the fault lies with me and not with any of these people who were so generous with their time and help.

Thanks also to Candas Jane Dorsey and Sandra Kasturi for their editorial input to the first draft, and everyone at Lucky Bat Books for their work on the production of this book, with a special nod to Jeff Posey and Louisa Swann.

Finally, thanks to Charles de Lint for his wonderful introduction and for his encouragement throughout.

INTRODUCTION

BY CHARLES DE LINT

Nishiyuu, Heroka, & Douglas Smith

IN MARCH 2013 I was driving north on Highway 105 with my brother-in-law Paddy. The 105 starts in Hull—just across the river from Ottawa—and goes all the way to Grand Remous where it T's at the 117. But we were only going as far as Gracefield where I was having some work done on my car at a garage on the highway.

It's about an hour's drive. It was cold, the skies were grey and spitting snow. Just outside of Kazabazua, we noticed a straggling line of people walking on the other side of the road. It took me a few moments to realize who they were.

Two months ago, seven Great Whale Cree (six young adults and an older hunter) left Whapmagoostui at the mouth of the Great Whale River, on the border of the Cree and Inuit lands in Quebec's James Bay Treaty area, and started south in support of Idle No More. They called the 1500-mile trek "The Journey of Nishiyuu" and by the time Paddy and I saw them, the group numbered almost two hundred and they were stretched out along the highway for about a mile or so.

Most of them were young Natives, many of them living close to the original walkers, so they'd come a good distance themselves. They came from Chisasibi, Waswanipi, Missitissini, and other communities in Cree country, and further south from Algonquin communities such as Kitigan Zibi near Maniwaki. Many of them wore white hooded wool parkas with embroidered designs in bright colors. Some wore boots, some just running shoes. Some had staves, decorated with feathers and ribbons, a few carried flags from their respective reserves. They looked tired, but determined.

They were still headed south when I returned driving my own car and I had the urge to get out and walk with them. My heart lifted to see them there—making their point with a peaceful demonstration of heart and hope.

You have to know that it was -40C when they left their home. They had to start out on snowshoes, and some days it was simply too cold to allow their food to defrost so that they could eat. Honestly, I'm surprised they made it through their first week, but they pushed through every hardship, determined to succeed.

It took them another week or so to get to Ottawa. My wife MaryAnn and I went up to Parliament Hill to cheer them on the last leg of the journey. We followed them in through the gates and joined a crowd of hundreds. There was drumming and welcomes called out over the loudspeaker system as the walkers settled in the stands behind a small stage with banners proclaiming "Honour Your Word" and the cameras of the press crowded in front.

Chiefs spoke, greeting and praising the walkers, then the walkers themselves spoke in Cree, explaining what had started them on this journey, what they hoped to accomplish.

But just before that, there was a magical moment when an eagle appeared in the sky over the crowd and circled a few times to our cheers and the pounding of drums before it flew on over the river and disappeared from sight.

It reappeared later in the afternoon—still magnificent—for another circuit of the sky above the Hill, but nothing could quite replace that initial fly-by. You could feel the spirits paying attention. You could almost hear the low murmur of thunder coming from the Gatineau Hills, across the river and beyond Hull.

And everything else faded away for a long moment—from the city going about its business behind us and anything that made us individual.

For a moment, we were all one.

I REALIZE THIS MIGHT SEEM a long and unrelated preamble to my introducing Douglas Smith's newest novel, but there were many moments while reading *The Wolf at the End of the World* when I felt that same magical moment that I did when the eagle made its first regal appearance at the end of the Nishiyuu Walkers' journey.

And the walkers weren't simply supporting the Idle No More movement. Their journey was also a way to draw attention to their culture, to the stories and legacy of the Cree, and the plight in which the present-day Cree people find themselves as governments and big business roll over their cultural needs.

Doug tackles these same issues in *The Wolf at the End of the World* and that's what gives the novel its heart, especially since he does it in the best way possible. There are no lectures. The novel never stops for a long discourse. These matters are simply part of the story, in the same way that the plight of the Heroka shapeshifters is, and the machinations of the clandestine government agency that is the Heroka's enemy.

There are interesting parallels between the Native characters and the Heroka. The fictional government agency has no more empathy for the shapeshifters than the real government had—and unfortunately, it appears still has—for our Native peoples. The Cree have long been the gatekeepers of the North; the government would prefer that they were no more than a footnote in history.

But politics aside, what makes *The Wolf at the End of the World* such an engrossing read are the characters and Doug's wonderful prose, a perfect blend between matter-of-fact and lyricism. I can't remember the last time I read a book that spoke to me, so eloquently, and so deeply, on so many levels.

HAVE YOU EVER HAD that sense of déja vu when meeting someone for the first time but you feel like you've known them for ages? Of course you have. I like it when it happens because as a writer I live a fairly solitary life, but as I go out on a book tour or to a convention, I'm suddenly thrust into the middle of an unfamiliar social whirl. It's very handy, and comforting, in a situation such as that to have that immediate connection with someone else.

I get it from books, too. From the first page I know—sometimes it's only a feeling before I've even cracked open the cover—that this book is going to be a friend. It's going to stay with me.

That happened the first time I read the original manuscript of *The Wolf at the End of the World*. At this point I was only familiar with Doug's short stories, and yes, a few of them were about the Heroka, and yes, I got the same feeling from those particular stories, especially "Spirit Dance" which went on to inspire this novel, but not with the same intensity.

When I found out there was a novel-length manuscript about the Heroka, I knew I was going to love it and cajoled Doug to let me read it. Happily he did. I've now read *The Wolf at the End of the World* a couple of times and know that I'll be rereading it in the future because it's that sort of book. Richly layered and deeply resonant.

An old friend, from the first time you read it.

IN CLOSING, let me just mention that to my shame as a Canadian, Prime Minister Harper couldn't be bothered to be there on Parliament Hill to welcome the Nishiyuu Walkers. He was in Toronto that day, welcoming a couple of Chinese pandas to the zoo—but we all know that big business and money always trumps spirituality, especially when it comes to politicians.

I doubt he'll read The *Wolf at the End of the World* either, but if he ever did, I can tell you which side of the arguments Doug raises in his novel that Harper would be on.

It wouldn't be the same as mine.

—Charles de Lint
Ottawa, Spring 2013

PART I:

"DRAW TO YOU THE WOLF AND BOY"

"Of old, men were placed here on Earth by the Powers in this wise: they were pitied and befriended by every kind of thing, by as many things as are seen, and by things that are invisible. They dreamt of every kind of thing. Even the animals taught them things. That is why the old-time people had Manitou power."
—*Louis Moosomin, Cree, blind from childhood*

CHAPTER 1

MARY

EVERYTHING HAD GONE WRONG, and now Mary Two Rivers was running away. Away from the dam site, away from the damage they'd done, stumbling through the bush in the dark, trying to keep up with Jimmy White Creek and ahead of the security guards. And the dogs. She could hear dogs barking now.

What had she been thinking? Why had she gone along with Jimmy and the rest of them? She was an A student. She was going to university in the fall. She had plans, plans to get off the Rez. Plans that didn't include jail.

Hanging a banner over the dam to protest the loss of Ojibwe land was one thing, but then somebody had poured gasoline on one of the construction vehicles and lit it on fire. And she'd let herself be part of it.

Just because Jimmy had a cute smile and cuter butt—a butt that was getting farther and farther ahead of her as she struggled to keep up. She was a bookworm, not an athlete, and the ground was starting to rise. Jimmy was heading for the west ridge overlooking the still dormant dam and its reservoir lake. She didn't know where the other kids were. Everyone had scattered when the guards appeared, and she'd followed Jimmy. Or tried to.

"Jimmy!" she cried in a desperate whisper. "Wait up!" She didn't know these woods anymore. If she lost him, she doubted she'd get far before the guards caught her.

Jimmy stopped on the hill ahead of her, chest heaving, breath hanging misty in the chill October air. The moonlight caught his pale, sweating face, and in that moment, she wondered how she'd ever thought he was handsome. "Mary, you gotta keep up," he panted, his voice breaking. "There's a path through the trees on top of the ridge. We'll lose them in there and cut back to the Rez." He started up the slope again, not waiting for her.

Forcing her trembling legs to move, she kept climbing. Jimmy disappeared over the top. Half a minute later, she scrambled up the last few yards. She looked around. Jimmy was nowhere in sight.

The tall jack pines stood closer here, the undergrowth thick between them, their high tops touching, blocking off the cold light from the waxing half moon. Whatever path Jimmy had taken was invisible, hidden by darkness.

She was alone and lost.

She sank to the ground, shaking. She was going to be caught. She was going to jail. What would her parents say? Their dream was for her to get a degree, to beat the odds of being born on the Rez. Their dream....

She swore softly to herself. *Her* dream, too. She stood up, anger conquering her fear. They would *not* catch her. Sucking in a deep breath, she let it out slowly to calm herself as she looked back down the hill she'd just climbed.

The dam and its dark captured lake lay in the distance below. Five burly figures were climbing the bottom of the hill. But worse, ahead of the guards, two gray shadows leapt over the rocks and brush of the slope. The dogs would reach her in less than a minute.

Turning back to the forest, she listened for any sound of Jimmy running ahead. *There.* Had that been a branch snapping deep in the woods? She moved in the direction of the noise, tripping over unseen rocks and roots. One patch of darkness loomed blacker than the rest. She stepped closer. It seemed to be an opening through the trees. Praying for this to be the path that Jimmy had taken, she plunged ahead.

As she moved into the forest, her eyes slowly adjusted to the deeper darkness under the trees, aided by the occasional sliver of moonlight slicing through the canopy of branches above. This was definitely a path. She paused a moment, straining to hear any sound of pursuit. The dogs were still barking, but they didn't sound any closer.

The barking stopped. In the sudden silence, she heard the yip of a fox. She shuddered, remembering a saying of her *misoomish*, her grandfather. "Bad luck," he'd told her as a child. "You hear a fox bark in the night, that's bad luck." But then the dogs took up their call again, and she allowed herself a small thrill of hope. The barking was fainter now. The dogs, and presumably the men with them, were moving away from her. They hadn't found this path.

She was going to get away. The tension gripping her vanished, and her shaking legs gave way. She collapsed onto the soft cushion of pine needles that covered the ground, sweat soaking her t-shirt under her parka. She hugged her knees to her chest, shivering from the chill and the adrenaline still in her.

Now that the immediate danger was gone, another thought came to her. Just last week, a worker had died at the dam site. Animal attack, the cops had said. She swallowed. Because his body had been partially eaten.

Suddenly, huddled on the forest floor in the dark, she didn't feel quite as safe as she had a moment before. She wanted nothing more than to be home in her own bed, to hear her parents in the next room, talking or arguing, she didn't care which, just so long as she was out of this nightmare. With that image filling her heart, she stood and started along the path once more, still praying to catch Jimmy, to have him lead her out of these woods, to lead her home.

A brightness grew ahead. A few seconds later, she stepped into a clearing lit in cold luminescence by the half moon above and enclosed by high rock walls ahead and to her left. To her right, the clearing gave way to the pines again, the level ground sloping away sharply. She walked to the top of the slope, looking for a way down. Her heart fell.

Halfway down, the pines thinned and then disappeared completely where the forest had been cleared near the bottom. The slope ended at the road leading onto the top of the dam. Beyond the dam, the black surface of the lake rippled like some great beast shuddering itself awake in the night.

She'd run the wrong way, back toward the dam.

With a sudden sick feeling, she realized what she should have figured out earlier. The dogs would have followed a scent. They hadn't followed her, so they must have been on Jimmy's trail, which meant Jimmy had taken another path, not the one that had led her here.

She'd taken the wrong path.

She looked around the clearing, searching for some alternative to retracing her steps. The slope below led right back to the dam and the scene of the crime, so that route was out. The dark lake caught her attention again, recalling childhood memories of her grandfather's stories, the ones about the evil spirits that lived in deep water.

She turned her back on the lake and those memories. Enough. Time to go home. She considered the rock walls rising above her. The one facing the entrance to the path was almost sheer and rose too high for her even to think of trying to scale it. The wall facing the lake was less steep and offered some handholds for climbing.

It looked about twenty feet high. She examined its face for the best route, finally selecting a path that would bring her up beside a large boulder perched by itself at the top of the wall.

Or maybe it was a bush, since she saw something move on it, like branches shifting in the wind. Just then, a cloud scuttled across the night sky, swallowing the moon. As the clearing fell dark, she shivered at a sudden strange thought— that the shape had resembled something crouched there, and what she'd seen moving were actually long locks of hair.

Another gust brought a smell down to her, thick and heavy—the smell of mushrooms and rotting wood and wet moss. Bitter, and yet, at the same time, so sickly sweet she thought she would retch.

The cloud hiding the moon moved on. Pale moonlight shone down again, cold and cruel, and Mary finally saw what crouched above her, waiting.

Chapter 2

Deep Water

ED **TWO RIVERS** was dreaming. In his dream, he was no longer an old Ojibwe man with a bad back. He was a hell-diver duck, young and strong and full of life. The hell-diver had been his personal manitou since his vision quest when he was twelve. Fifty-five years ago. Dreams of the hell-diver had special meaning. He would learn something tonight.

He floated on a black lake at night, his webbed feet moving him easily over small swells. The moon shone full and bright and cold on the lake, but could not penetrate the water's dark surface, giving no hint of what lay beneath.

He dove, and darkness closed around him. The water was warm at first, warmer than the night air above had been. But a chill seeped through the soft down under his feathers as his feet drove him deeper. Deeper and closer. Closer to what lay below, to what lay waiting, had lain waiting for so long....

Ed woke, gasping for breath. He sat up, and as he did, pain stabbed his lower back and shot down his right leg. He groaned. The memory of youth and strength from the dream slipped away. He sighed. Back to reality. The bedside clock glared at him in red digits: 3:46 a.m.

Vera stirred beside him. "Ed?"

He grunted.

"You okay?" she mumbled.

No, he wasn't okay, but he wouldn't mention his dream. His wife was white and a Christian, but that wasn't why he didn't tell her. His vision dreams worried her. He'd been right too many times. "Damn back's killing me."

"Can you move? Want something for it?"

"I'm okay. Gonna get up for a while till it calms down."

Vera was snoring again by the time he managed to slip his legs over the side of the bed. He rose slowly, waited for the pain to subside, then pulled on his pants and went quietly into their small living room.

He and Vera lived above the general store they ran in Thunder Lake. The place was small, but big enough for them. Enough space for living and enough to be alone when they got on each other's nerves, which wasn't often.

He eased into the old armchair by the window overlooking the street below. Turning on the small television with the remote, he flipped channels, not watching what appeared, just wanting a flow of images to wash the dream from his mind. Finally, he clicked the TV off. Damn thing only got half the channels anyway.

Outside, the stoplight at the corner changed, throwing a patch of red on the room's faded wallpaper, like blood splashed on the wall.

Red, he thought. *Just red. Not blood. Damn dream, getting me all morbid.*

A dream of deep water.

He knew what that meant. He'd kept the old beliefs and practices. The priests at the residential school had tried to beat them out of him, but he'd been one of the lucky ones. He'd only spent four years in the school before his father spirited him away to live with his grandfather in the bush. And his grandfather had taught him the old ways.

He'd tried to pass those ways on to his son, but Charlie had never been interested. Charlie had never been forced into a residential school like Ed had, but to Ed, his son was still a victim. He'd lost his culture.

Charlie didn't see it that way. "What's that shit ever brought us?" Charlie had demanded recently, when he caught Ed and Mary discussing differences between Ojibwe and Cree shaking tent ceremonies. "Did it keep our land for us? Can it get us jobs? Why don't you conjure me up a new car?"

"Dad, I enjoy Grampa's stories," Mary replied.

Charlie glared at Mary. "And you, too. It was bad enough, him filling your head with all the stories when you were a kid. But you're going to university—"

"To study anthropology," Mary said. "And this relates to that. Shaman practices of the Ojibwe and other Anishinabe cultures share similarities with ancient rituals around the world."

"Ancient," Charlie had snorted, walking out of the room. "You got *that* right."

Ed shook his head as he sat in the darkness. Well, at least Mary still wanted to hear the old stories, hear him talk of the old ways, even if now it was just part of her studies of dead cultures. Dying, he corrected himself. Not dead yet. Just like him. Not quite dead yet.

Mary's face faded from his mind, morphing into the black lake of his dream. Having thoughts of his granddaughter alongside a vision of deep water sent a chill through him.

When he'd acquired the hell-diver as his personal manitou so many years ago, he thought the duck a particularly appropriate spirit guide. As a bird, it was one with the realm of the air. Spirits of the air were benevolent, more indulgent of the foibles of humans. But the hell-diver was also at home in the water, and the Ojibwe believed it acted as a messenger to the spirits of the underworld, malevolent beings who dwelled in the deep places of the world. Underground. Deep water.

No use having a spirit guide if it only picked up half the channels.

He knew what dreams of deep water meant. Something bad was coming, maybe already here. He tried to recall the dream. He had a feeling it had told him more than he remembered, which wasn't much, beyond a sense of foreboding.

Downstairs, somebody knocked on the door to the store. He jumped. Vera stirred in the bedroom. He stood, wincing at the pain in his back. With a feeling of apprehension, he started down the stairs. Didn't have to be a shaman to read this sign. A knock at four in the morning was never good news.

In the store, he shuffled past the new floor display of bathroom tissue. The only light came from the front windows. The thin curtain on the door window showed a silhouette wearing a familiar hat.

OPP. Ontario Provincial Police.

He stopped, putting a hand on a shelf to steady himself, knocking a tin of corn niblets to the floor. Was it Charlie? In an accident? Maybe just in another fight, and they locked him up until morning. But the cops wouldn't wake Ed for that.

The silhouette outside knocked again. He forced himself to move. What else could it be? Not Mary. She was a good kid. Never went to the bars. She'd be home safe in bed this time of night. Mary was okay. Charlie was okay.

Everybody's okay, he told himself as he unlocked the door.

A cold draft hit him. A female constable stood outside. White, stocky. Willie Burrell. Ed knew all the cops. It was a small town, and the store had been broken into twice. Plus all those times bailing Charlie out after some brawl. Behind her, another cop leaned on a cruiser. Frank Mueller. A real prick.

Willie's lips were pressed together into a tight line, as if afraid something might escape from behind them. She nodded. "Ed."

"Willie," Ed said, running a hand through his long gray hair. "What's up?"

"Afraid I have some bad news."

Don't ask, he thought. If he didn't ask, it hadn't happened. As soon as he asked, as soon as he heard, then it was real. At the curb, Mueller lit a cigarette. The sudden flame caught Ed's eye. Mueller flicked the match into a puddle. It hit the dirty water with a hiss, sending ripples across it that recalled the black lake of his dream.

He pulled his eyes back to Willie's face. "What's happened?"

"We've found a body. No ID, but a native girl, we think."

Native girl. Not Mary. No, not that. "Where?" he asked. It would be somewhere off the Rez, else the native police would be the ones at his door.

"Near the dam lake," Willie said. "Since you're a council elder, we're hoping you can identify her. Sorry."

The dam lake. Deep water. The thought came unbidden, and the coldness inside him grew. But he just nodded. "Gimme a minute."

Closing the door, he leaned against the wall. Native girl. Somewhere inside, he could feel something slipping away, some part of his life that wasn't coming back, as if it were sinking beneath the surface of that dark oily lake from his dream.

Leaving a note for Vera, he dressed, put on his coat, and stepped outside.

ED SAT IN the back of the cruiser, the cops in the front, Mueller driving. The dam site was about seven miles southeast of town, accessible by old logging roads and a drive of at least fifteen minutes.

They didn't talk much. Willie seemed shaken up, and Mueller never went out of his way to talk with any Ojibwe. The silence suited Ed at first, afraid to learn more of the victim, afraid it would sound like Mary.

But then the black forest flowing past the road started shifting into the dark lake in his dream, and he suddenly wanted something to take his mind off the vision. "How'd she die? This kid?" Not Mary, just some kid. Some poor other kid.

Willie paused before answering. "Animal attack by the looks of it."

"What do you mean? Bite marks on the body?"

Mueller's lip curled. *He's grinning,* Ed thought. *The asshole's grinning.* Willie looked back. "She was eaten, Ed."

He frowned. Animal encounters in the bush were common, but attacks were rare. Deaths even more so. "What did it look like? From the wounds. What kind of animal?"

Mueller shrugged. "What are we? The Discovery Channel? Something hungry. Not much left of the body."

Willie looked back at Ed again, but didn't say anything. A few minutes later, Mueller turned onto the dam road. About a mile in, he pulled over at the foot of a slope leading up to a forested ridge overlooking the dam and its lake.

"Thought the body was at the dam," Ed said as they got out.

Willie nodded up the slope. "On the ridge."

They started up the incline, Willie and Mueller leading the way with flashlights. Ed followed, wincing from the pain in his back whenever he missed his step in the dim moonlight.

"Who found the body?" he asked.

"Security guards from the dam," Willie said. "There'd been more vandalism, and they were chasing some suspects." Mueller snorted at the word "suspects." Willie continued. "Their dogs followed one trail but lost it. Whoever it was, they were heading back to the Rez. Then the guards turned the dogs loose again on another scent. Found the body in a clearing overlooking the dam."

They reached the top of the ridge, and Ed was glad to see that Mueller seemed as winded as he was. "Any chance the dogs killed her?"

The cops glanced at each other. Mueller's smirk disappeared. Willie shook her head. "The guards found the dogs huddled in a corner of the clearing as far from the body as they could get. Whining like they were afraid of it."

Ed frowned. "Probably could smell whatever attacked her."

Mueller snorted again. "These are Dobermans. Trained guard dogs. Not much those mothers are afraid of."

But they were afraid of something, Ed thought.

Willie led them to a path into the trees, marked off with yellow police tape. Ed looked at the tape. "You're gonna let a civilian into a crime scene?"

"The SOC officer cleared it with Forensic ID in the Soo," Willie said. "Our team's finished with the site. It's okay."

SOC. Scenes of Crime. Ed frowned. If the OPP Forensic Identification unit in Sault Ste. Marie had cleared access to the scene, then they'd already decided this was an accidental death.

Ducking under the tape, they started along the path, Ed behind the cops. The path was narrow, so conversation stopped until they reached a clearing. As they stepped out of the trees, he caught a whiff of mushrooms, sharp and acrid, mixed with something sickly sweet. A childhood memory tickled at the back of his mind, but then fled.

Four big torchlights sat on the ground in each corner of the clearing, their beams facing in. A man not in uniform knelt hunched over the body, while a uniformed cop shone a flashlight onto it. They blocked any view of the corpse's face, but the lower part of the torso was visible. Ed caught his breath.

All the clothing had been ripped off, and most of the flesh was missing from the limbs and pelvis, leaving bones shining white and red in the flashlight's beam. He turned away. Two other cops were completing a scan of the ground in the clearing. One was Bill Thornton, a staff sergeant and the senior OPP officer in Thunder Lake. He would be the SOC officer. Thornton said something to the other cop and then walked over to them.

Thornton shook Ed's hand. "Ed. Sorry about dragging you out here...." He kept talking, saying all the usual stuff. Ed nodded, not listening, trying not to look at the body.

The man kneeling beside the body stood up and started to walk toward them. He was balding and wore wire-rimmed glasses and a rumpled gray suit. Ben Capshaw, the local medical examiner. The corpse's face was visible now, but Ed didn't look at it, telling himself to focus on Capshaw, not the body. He didn't need to know yet.

Capshaw had a clear plastic bag in his hand. Something glinted in it, shiny and silver. Still avoiding the body, Ed's eyes ran to the brightness in the bag. It was a necklace, big silver loops with an oval pendant attached.

A sudden cry escaped him, and he took a step back as his legs almost gave way.

"Ed?" Willie said. "You okay?"

Ignoring her, he walked slowly to the body. To where his granddaughter, his beautiful granddaughter, lay dead.

Beautiful no more. He stared at the mutilated corpse, forcing himself to look at the face. Multiple parallel slashes that looked like claw marks had ripped most of the flesh away, but he could still recognize Mary. Just as he'd recognized the necklace he'd given her for her sixteenth birthday.

His tears came, and with them, a river of memories—holding Mary when she was born—her first birthday—playing the snow dart game with her— teaching her to hunt and fish—telling her stories in the hunting lodge on long winter nights—listening with her as the moon sang across a summer night sky—helping her review before her exams—watching her grow year by year into a beautiful young woman, smart and strong.

Wiping his eyes, he straightened and turned away from the thing at his feet. That wasn't Mary anymore. Mary was gone. She was in the Spirit World now. In the distance, the dark lake lay calm, reflecting the sinking half moon like an obsidian mirror. His dream of deep water intruded again. *Could've been the same time*, he thought. *I could've been having that dream when she was dying.*

No. His hands clenched into fists. No. Not dying. Being killed. Something killed her. Killed his granddaughter. And he was going to find out what it was.

But he let none of this show on his face as he walked back to the waiting cops. The Ojibwe way was silent fortitude in the face of hardship. But even if his emotions rarely showed, they were still there.

"Ed?" Willie asked.

"It's Mary," he said, his voice low but strong. Willie gave a little gasp. "It's my granddaughter." He stopped. No, not *it*. "She is my granddaughter." Or should he say, "She *was* my granddaughter?" What was correct here? He shook his head. *Get a grip.*

He pointed to the bag with the necklace. "That's hers. On that pendant, there's a blue heron. On the back, it says—" His words caught in his throat, and he had to look away before he could continue. "In Ojibwe, it says, 'Fly where your dreams take you.'"

"So she's *Charlie's* kid," Mueller said, as if that explained something.

"Jesus, I'm so sorry, Ed," Thornton said.

Ed knew he meant it. "Did it happen here?"

Capshaw nodded. "Yes, judging from the amount of blood where the, uh, the body was found. There's no blood anywhere else."

"When?"

"Probably not more than three hours ago," Capshaw replied. "The autopsy will confirm that, of course."

"So she helped torch the trucks at the dam site," Mueller muttered. "A trouble-maker like her old man."

Ed moved toward Mueller, but Thornton stepped between them. "Shut up, Mueller," Thornton said, his voice sharp.

Mueller glared at Thornton, but said nothing. Shooting a black look at Ed, he turned and stalked out of the clearing.

Thornton sighed. "Sorry, Ed. He's an asshole."

Ed didn't answer. He watched as Capshaw closed Mary's body bag, the sound of the zipper slicing into him like a knife.

"You want me to call Charlie and Elizabeth?" Thornton asked after a moment.

Elizabeth was Mary's mom. "I'll call them," Ed said quietly, still staring at the body bag. "What killed her?"

Thornton looked surprised. "Animal attack, for sure. Pretty obvious from the state of the, uh, well, you know...."

"What kind?"

Thornton shrugged. "Bear. Wolves, maybe."

"Find any tracks?"

"No, but this clearing's all rock. Capshaw'll be able to tell us from the bite marks and any hair he finds on the, uh...that he finds." Telling Ed again that he was sorry, Thornton left to talk to Capshaw.

Ed walked to where the clearing overlooked the dam and its captured lake. He shook his head. The dam had been bad news from the start, splitting the Ojibwe community. He and others had protested against the loss of their hunting territories, the impact on wildlife. More had argued that the money the provincial government was offering could buy much-needed social services on the Rez. Others, like Charlie, had just wanted the money that new jobs at the site would bring.

In the end, the money had won. Money always won.

He stared at the dark lake, remembering the priests teaching the story of Noah's Ark. That flood had been to cleanse the world of evil. *Guess it'd missed a few spots*, he thought. Seemed that white man floods destroyed what was good, not what was evil. The flooding here hadn't saved the animals in pairs—it'd killed them or driven them away.

Now his Mary was gone too.

Willie walked up beside him. She squeezed his arm. "Let me take you home, Ed."

He sighed and nodded. Turning to go, he glanced down the slope. He stopped. "Willie, give me your flashlight, will you?"

Willie handed the light to him, and he shone the beam over the ground. He'd been a hunter since he was a kid and a guide for years before he met Vera. He saw something. There. And there. "Something went down here. Not too long ago."

Willie squinted down the hill. "How can you tell?"

"Pine needles been kicked up. They're wet. Something turned them over recently." He started down the hill, grabbing tree trunks for balance with his free hand, avoiding areas that had been disturbed. He almost slipped twice, his back screaming each time.

Twenty feet down, he knelt beside an impression in the ground. The smell of mushrooms, acrid and sharp, stung his nostrils again. Again, something stirred in childhood memories but skittered away. The ground was softer here. He carefully brushed away dead needles and leaves from the impression. When he'd uncovered it all, he stood.

Willie came up beside him. "Find something?"

He pointed with the flashlight beam.

"Holy shit," she said.

It was a footprint. A barefoot, *human* footprint.

Chapter 3

The Shaman

IN A DARK FOREST GLADE, the shaman stared into a campfire, focusing on the vision dancing in the flames. A young woman lay dead, her body horribly mutilated. Police moved around her, looking but not seeing what was there. An old Ojibwe man stood over a footprint. *He sees*, the shaman thought. *He sees, but won't let himself believe.*

The shaman passed a hand before the flames. The vision faded.

The voices returned. The voices never left for long now. Neither did the hunger.

Comdowtah, the voices called in Ojibwe.

"That is not my name," the shaman replied, speaking to the air. "Comdowtah died long ago."

You carry his spirit. It is he who drew us to you. It is he that we see when we touch you. To us, you are Comdowtah.

The shaman now called Comdowtah shrugged. "So be it."

Beyond the fire, two shadows detached themselves from the blackness of the forest. They were huge and identical to each other, with the suggestion of something feline in their outlines. But Comdowtah knew these were not cats. These were something else. The shadows drew closer. Comdowtah suppressed a shiver.

You grow concerned.

"Another killing. Just a week after the first," the shaman said, eyes fixed on the two shadows, praying they did not come any closer.

A price you pay. It is necessary. You must feed the hunger you now carry.

"Ah yes, the hunger I now carry, as I now carry you. Like an infection."

We are an infection to you?

Comdowtah swallowed but did not answer.

The killings serve another purpose.

"What purpose?"

You must draw to you the Wolf and Boy.

"So you've said. But why?"

Do you want the power we promised?

"Do I have a choice anymore?"

The voices fell silent. The two shadows retreated to wherever they went. The fire died to embers, blood red on black. In the darkness, the vision of the dead girl returned.

"What have I done?" Comdowtah asked the darkness. But like the voices, the darkness did not reply.

WILLIE TOLD THORNTON about the print, and he called back the site team. He thanked Ed and told Willie and Mueller to take Ed home.

They were silent on the drive back. Then Ed finally spoke. "Mary didn't make that print."

Willie nodded. "Way too big. At least a size ten. Probably a guy."

"But it was recent," Ed said.

Mueller shrugged. "So there were two of them running from the guards. The guy just ran a bit faster."

Ed's anger rose again, but he didn't take the bait. "Running barefoot?"

"Maybe they were making out. The guards and the dogs followed the other trail, so Mary and her boyfriend were taking a break. Big bad wolf or something busts up the slumber party. The guy takes off and leaves her."

"So where are his shoes?"

"Grabbed 'em when he ran."

"Yeah, sure. First thing he'd think of. So where are the animal tracks?"

"The thing didn't follow him. Stayed behind to have dinner."

"Shut up, Frank," Willie snapped. Mueller shrugged, but he shut up.

Ed stared out the window. The sky was brightening over the trees in the east. "Something's not right. Bear would've covered the body with sticks, leaves. Wolves would've eaten some at the kill site, but then they'd have dragged the—" He swallowed. "Dragged the rest to their cache." Animals didn't waste food. And that's what Mary had been, how she'd ended her young life. As food. He caught a glimpse of the lake in the distance, and his dream returned.

"Cougar?" Willie offered.

Ed shook his head. "They cover their kills, too. Besides, there hasn't been a cougar around here for a good year." His thoughts took a sudden turn, remembering that last cougar.

"The guards said only two kids ran up the ridge," Willie said. "And the other kid took a different path, nowhere near where we found Mary. So she was alone."

"So who made that print?" Ed asked, as much to himself as anyone.

"Hey," Mueller said, chuckling. "Maybe it's like those stories you Indians have. You know, with people changin' into animals and animals into people."

Ed watched the dark trees flash past. He'd been thinking exactly the same thing.

THE COPS DROPPED ED back home just before 7 a.m. Vera was in the store, getting ready for the day. She looked up from restocking a shelf. He knew his face was as implacable as always, but it didn't matter. She straightened, dropping a box of bran flakes, suddenly pale. "What's happened?" she cried. Somehow, she always knew.

She broke down when he told her, and he held her in his arms as she sobbed. After a while, she stepped back, red-eyed. "Do Charlie and Elizabeth know yet?"

He shook his head. "Wanted to tell you first."

"Ed, you gotta go. They're going to be frantic already."

He hesitated. "There's something else." He told her about finding the human footprint.

"An animal did the killing, and a person left the scene?" Her jaw clenched. "My god, that sounds like a Heroka."

He nodded. "First thing I thought of."

"Leiddia's the only one of them around here now, isn't she?"

Now. Ed didn't miss that. "Only one I know of."

Vera was quiet for a moment. "No," she said finally. "No. Leiddia was Mary's friend. She'd never have hurt her."

Ed shook his head, trying to dislodge the memory of Mary's body. "I don't think so either. Besides, the footprint was way too big. Had to be a man."

She took a deep breath and wiped her eyes again. "You should go to Charlie and Elizabeth. I'll handle the store."

He nodded. "Gotta get something in the back." That was a lie, but he knew she wouldn't agree with what he planned. Going into their little office in the back storeroom, he sat at their computer and typed in an email address. A picture for the contact popped up. Dark, shaggy hair framing a lean face above a square jaw, a long straight nose splitting sharp cheekbones, and black eyes. He started typing his message.

"Jesus Christ. You can't be serious."

He turned. Vera stood in the doorway, hands on hips. Always a bad sign. She was staring at the screen. "*Gwyn Blaidd*? You're bringing *him* into this?"

He sat back, rubbing his face with both hands. In that moment, he felt a thousand years old. "The cops don't give a shit about this. Just another dead Indian. They'll bury Mary's file along with her. They're already calling it an animal attack. Her killer'll go free. Maybe kill again."

"We have a *Heroka* killing—"

"*May* have."

"—so you're going to invite *another* one of them to town?"

"Gwyn knows this town. And he knows Leiddia. If she *is* the killer—and I'm sure she isn't—then we'll need Gwyn to stop her. If the killer was another Heroka, we'll need Gwyn to find them. And to protect Leiddia."

"Protect her?"

"We're not the only ones who know that Leiddia is Heroka. Other elders know. Hell, Charlie and Elizabeth know. When news gets out about the footprint, somebody will suspect her, too. Maybe try to do something about it. And then, someone else *will* get hurt."

Vera broke down again. "Oh god, Ed. Our poor little Mary. Who could have done such a thing?"

Ed took her in his arms. *Who...or what?* That dark childhood memory from when he'd found the footprint flitted through his brain again, but slipped away. "Dunno. But we need Gwyn. Even if the cops wanted to, they couldn't handle this. They don't know what they're dealing with."

"Why would Gwyn help Leiddia? Things didn't end well between them, from what she told me."

"If I know him, he still cares for her. And he'll help me. He's a friend."

"I still don't like it," Vera said, her face set in hard lines. "Gwyn Blaidd attracts trouble. Always did."

"We already got trouble," he replied. He sat down and began typing his message again.

CHAPTER 4

THE WOLF

GWYN BLAIDD STEPPED OUT onto the broad promenade that ran the length of Cil y Blaidd, his sprawling wood and stone home that sat on a hidden wilderness lake in northern Ontario. Gelert, his huge hound and *pawakan* companion, followed him outside, whining at the distress he sensed in his master. Gwyn quieted the dog with a thought.

Leaning on the wooden railing, he stared down to where the midday sun shone bright and beautiful on the water below. Bright and beautiful. So different from the news he'd just received.

Mary dead? He couldn't believe it. He'd known her all her life, taught her to track and hunt, gone camping with her and Ed. It'd been two years since he'd seen her. Ed and Mary had been the only ones who came to say goodbye the day he'd left Thunder Lake. He remembered her as warm and caring, smart and confident, with a self-deprecating wit and quick smile. Ed had written not long ago that she was starting at U of T this fall.

Now she was dead. Just eighteen. He shook his head. Too short a life, even for a human. Killed in what the cops were calling an animal attack. But Ed suspected something quite different.

A Heroka killing? Leiddia was the only Heroka in that area—at least that he knew of. But she'd been one of Mary's closest friends. She could never have killed Mary. Hell, she could never kill anyone. Leiddia had a temper, for sure, but he could never imagine her killing someone.

Or eating them.

Leiddia. Two years together, and now two years apart. He tried to remember how she looked on the day they'd said goodbye, but her face kept morphing into Stelle's.

Which encapsulated perfectly what had been the problem in their relationship. He'd loved Leiddia. Maybe still did. But he had still loved Stelle, too.

Maybe still did.

When it ended between him and Leiddia, he'd told himself that they'd met too soon after Stelle had died. Leiddia had a simpler explanation—that he loved a dead woman more than he loved her. He wasn't sure she was wrong.

They had not parted friends. And now Ed was asking him to come back to save her.

He hadn't left Cil y Blaidd for those two years. He thought of Ed and Mary, of Leiddia, of all he'd left behind in Thunder Lake. He looked around. He'd built this place twenty years ago as his occasional retreat from civilization. But it had now become his permanent home. Or had his act of retreat become permanent?

He pushed that thought away. Ed had no right to ask him to come back. Heroka didn't kill innocent people like Mary. This couldn't be a Heroka killing. The police could handle it. And Leiddia had made it more than clear that she never wanted to see him again. She was a big girl. She was a Heroka. Predator class. She could take care of herself. She didn't need him. She didn't want him.

Turning his back on the lake, with Gelert trailing after him, he went back inside, into the main living area of his home, a large high-ceilinged room with oak floors, scatter rugs, and lots of couches and chairs. A stone fireplace flanked by bookcases filled one wall, and floor-to-ceiling windows overlooked the lake. A notebook computer attached to a satellite Internet link sat on a desk near the windows.

He sat down at the computer and sent Ed his reply. It was simple. It was short.

Sorry, but no.

Gelert raised his great head from where he lay beside Gwyn's chair and whined.

Gwyn glared down at him. "Shaddup. They don't need my help," he said. *And she wouldn't want it,* he thought, still trying to convince himself.

HE WAS STILL BROODING over his decision later that day when the sound of a plane brought him outside again. Staying out of sight, he searched the sky until he found it. The plane dropped lower, and he relaxed as he recognized its markings. It belonged to Michel Ducharmes, current head of the Circle of the Heroka and the only other person who knew the location of Cil y Blaidd.

He shook his head. Mitch was a friend, but he wouldn't have flown hundreds of miles for a social call. He would have a problem, one he'd want Gwyn to help solve. He thought about Ed's email. *Got enough problems right now, old friend.*

The plane did a circuit of the lake before landing, scanning for sunken logs that could rip a pontoon open. It pulled up to a dock hidden from above by arching willow branches, alongside Gwyn's own single-propeller de Havilland Turbo Beaver. A huge man, his hair and beard a mass of red curls, climbed onto the dock and began to tie up the plane. Mitch.

Gwyn straightened as a second person emerged from the plane. Much smaller, with a slim female figure and spiky black hair that did not ring any memory bells.

Swearing silently, he headed out of the house and down the path to the dock, Gelert loping behind him. Why would Mitch bring a stranger to Cil y Blaidd?

Mitch looked up as Gwyn stepped onto the dock. Gelert bounded forward to greet the big man, his tail wagging furiously. Mitch patted the dog, and then, with a nervous glance at the girl, he gave Gwyn a broad grin and stepped forward, arms out.

They embraced, and Gwyn stepped back. "You've brought a guest," he said, glaring at Mitch, then turning to the girl.

She looked somewhere mid-teens. She wore torn black jeans and an unzipped black hoodie over a wrinkled t-shirt proclaiming the band Metric. Now that he was closer, he could see that her spiked hair was dark blue, not black. Two silver rings pierced her right eyebrow, and she had a stud in her right nostril. A large gray rat perched on her left shoulder.

A familiar aura tinged her outline—the Mark of the Heroka, visible only to another Heroka. He focused on her aura, and the image of a brown otter superimposed itself on the girl for a heartbeat. Rodent clan, which he'd already assumed from the rat—her pawakan, no doubt.

The girl was smoking a cigarette and staring at her cell phone.

Mitch cleared his throat. "Gwyn, this is Cassandra Meadows. Goes by Caz. Caz, this is Gwyn Blaidd, an old friend."

Gwyn put out his hand to the girl, but she kept staring at her phone. "No signal," she said. "How...rustic."

Shooting Mitch another look, he dropped his hand and forced a smile. "Welcome to Cil y Blaidd."

The girl looked up at him then. She had big, gray-blue eyes framed by too much eyeliner. She took a drag on her cigarette. "Silly Blade? Weird name." The rat twitched its whiskers at him.

He took a breath. "*Seel ee Blah-heed.* It's Welsh. It means Lair of the Wolf."

"So why don't you just call it that? Or, you know…house?"

Mitch covered a grin with a hand. Gwyn bit back a retort. "Let me show you to the…house," he said.

Caz looked up at the sprawling structure perched on the rock face above them. "Wow. You can't even see that from the air."

"I like my privacy," he said, glaring at Mitch, who ignored him.

"Kinda creepy, you ask me," she said.

Nobody did, kid. At least they weren't staying.

He led the way up steps carved from the cliff face. Pines grew thick at the top, but a cleared path led into the trees and then followed the cliff edge.

Halfway along the path, Caz stopped, taking a step back and staring into the forest. "Uh, what are those?"

Two great stags emerged from the woods, their antlers barely missing trees on either side. Turning back to face the bush, the stags lowered their heads toward three gray shapes hovering behind them in the shadows.

"Looks like my totem feels I need protection from your troops," Mitch said with a grin.

Three large timber wolves stepped from the trees, keeping their distance from the stags. Gelert wagged his tail, but the wolves ignored him, focusing on the stags, Caz, and Mitch.

"That's Magula and some of his pack. They guard Cil y Blaidd for me," Gwyn explained.

"Wonderful. Predators," Caz muttered, slipping her rat into the pouch of her hoodie.

"Magula, take off. You should know Mitch by now," Gwyn said. The largest wolf stared at Gwyn for a breath, gave the newcomers a final appraisal, and then led the other two back into the forest. A moment later, the stags retreated as well.

Gwyn turned back to the trail, then stopped as he caught the sound of another plane. Staying hidden, he stepped to the edge of the trees and looked up at the sky. A familiar yellow seaplane with black markings was passing over the lake.

"Trouble?" Mitch asked.

Gwyn shook his head. "The Ministry of Natural Resources plane. Usually see it about once a month. It's early this time." *By at least a week*, he thought, then dismissed the incident as the plane disappeared up the lake.

They emerged from the forest path onto a graveled walkway leading to huge oaken doors set in the stone front of the house. Gwyn pushed open the doors and invited his guests inside.

Corridors ran off the entranceway into the two wings of the house. His bedroom lay in one wing, guest bedrooms and unused rooms in the other. A broad half-flight oak staircase led down into the main room.

Caz's gaze fell on Gwyn's computer on the desk. "Holy shit, technology. I don't believe it." She turned to Gwyn. "You got Internet?"

"Satellite link."

She moved toward the desk. "I'm gonna check my Facebook, okay?"

"No," Gwyn said, stepping in front of her. "Definitely *not* okay."

She glared up at him. "Why the fuck not?"

"Because I said so."

"God, what is your problem?" she said, taking a step back.

Before he could reply, Mitch cleared his throat. "Uh, Caz, why don't you go for a walk while Gwyn and I discuss business? Won't be long."

"A walk? Outside? With the wolves? Yeah, right," she said. "I don't suppose he's got TV?" When Gwyn just glared, she shrugged. "Figures. I'll wait on the dock." With that, she pulled out a pair of earbuds and headed to the door.

When she was gone, he turned to Mitch, but Mitch raised his hands before he could speak. "Okay, okay. Take it easy. I can explain."

"It had better be good. Want a drink?"

Mitch smiled. "About time. Scotch. Neat, please." Mitch settled his bulk into an oversized leather chair while Gwyn poured them both drinks. He handed a glass to Mitch and took a seat across from him. Mitch took a sip. "Nice. The Macallan? Eighteen year?"

"Twelve. Think I'd waste the good shit on you?"

"Cheap prick."

"So talk. Start with why you'd bring a stranger here. Especially her."

Mitch chuckled. "She'll grow on you over time."

"I'm not planning to give her the chance."

Mitch's smile faded. "Her parents are dead."

"Oh." *Shit*, he thought, wishing he could rewind his introduction to Caz. "Sorry. Recent?"

"Just after she was born. Two of the first ones we lost to the Tainchel. Older brother, too."

Gwyn frowned. Caz Meadows. *Meadows*. He knew that name. "Not Peter and Selma?"

Mitch nodded. "Jeremy, too."

"Their son. Yeah, I remember now. They did have a daughter. Younger than Jeremy," he said, thinking back. "Must have been hell for her."

He and Stelle had still been together at the time. Back then, he ran security for the Circle in the northeast, which had mostly amounted to ensuring the Heroka remained nothing more than creatures of legend. Shapeshifters. Werebeasts. Things from fairy tales. Things that no rational person would believe in.

Then came the Tainchel, a covert operation of the federal intelligence agency CSIS, formed, as they later learned, with the single goal of tracking down and capturing the Heroka. For scientific testing. Testing that the Heroka subjects generally didn't survive.

Tainchel. Old Scottish term: armed men advancing in a line through a forest to flush out and kill wolves.

The Tainchel developed specialized scanners from tests on early victims. Subtle differences in alpha wave patterns, infrared readings, and metabolic rates gave the Heroka away, even in crowded cities. Several Heroka, like Caz's family, disappeared before the Circle caught on.

But they had caught on. Eventually. And then things changed. Including between him and Estelle.

"So who raised her?" he asked, pushing away dark memories.

Mitch sighed. "It's more like who hasn't. She's had several foster homes, some with us, but mostly with humans who are sympathetic to us. She's... challenging."

"Gee, you think? So why—" He stopped as he felt contact with a wolf nearby. The mental touch had been brief, but long enough to know that the wolf was strange to the area, part of an intruder pack, not Magula's. He'd sensed alertness, even alarm, in the animal. He reached with his mind trying to reestablish contact, but with no success. He repeated the process with Magula and his pack, searching for any sense of danger from the guardians of Cil y Blaidd, but found no signs of concern there.

"Something wrong?"

He shook his head. If a new pack had wandered into Magula's territory, he had probably detected the intruders' fear of confrontation with the resident pack. "False alarm. So again, why is she here?"

"I'm her trustee. I arrange her foster care, and right now, she doesn't have any. So for now, I'm it."

"Her last foster parents kick her out?"

Mitch studied his drink. "They were killed."

Gwyn stared at him. "Explain, please."

"Cops called it a botched home invasion. Both her foster parents were shot. House was ransacked. Jewelry, cash, electronics taken."

"But...?"

"But the cops don't know the whole story."

"Which is?"

"Doorbell rings late at night. Four men force their way in. Demand to know where Caz is."

Gwyn swallowed as the old Tainchel chill ran down his spine. "And where was she?"

"Upstairs in her room. She hears all this and figures these guys are cops."

"Why?"

"She's got a record of petty felonies. And she'd done some shoplifting that day. Like I said, she's challenging. Anyway, she figures it's about that, so she slips out her window and takes off. Hard to stop one of the rodent clan at night. Comes back later to find her foster parents dead. She called me then."

"Shit," Gwyn said, shaking his head. "But if they weren't cops, who the hell were they? And why were they looking for her?"

"I have a theory."

"Yes?"

"I have a source inside CSIS," Mitch said. He looked at Gwyn. "He thinks someone's resurrected the Tainchel."

Gwyn swore. "Within CSIS again?"

Mitch shook his head. "My contact doesn't know, and he's pretty high up. They may have people there. Within the federal government, for sure."

"So you think this was a botched abduction of a Heroka."

Mitch nodded.

"Have you told Caz that theory?"

"No. She's feeling guilty enough about their deaths as it is. And with the Tainchel killing her parents…." He spread his hands.

Gwyn stared at Mitch. "That's why you're here, isn't it? You're trying to recruit me again, aren't you? Bring me back to fight the Tainchel."

Mitch shook his head. "Actually, old friend, I would expect no more success in bringing you out of seclusion this time than I've had in any of my attempts over the past two years."

Gwyn winced. "So why are you here?"

"I'm hoping to put your isolation to good use. If Caz has been targeted by the Tainchel, then I need somewhere safe to leave her until I can—"

"What?!"

"—until I can find a more permanent arrangement for her."

"You're kidding, right? You want me to play babysitter to that antisocial little—"

"Excuse me? *You* are calling *her* antisocial? She's not the one playing hermit."

Glaring at Mitch, Gwyn stood and walked to the window. "Don't start on that again. I—"

The pain from the first bullet dropped him to his knees. The next two shots came in quick succession.

"Gwyn! What's wrong?" Mitch ran to his side.

Though the wolves were miles away when it happened, Gwyn felt their deaths immediately. Felt each bullet shatter their bones and rip through their organs. Felt it as if he'd been shot himself. Felt them die. He slumped onto his side on the floor, weak and shaking, as he felt the life force of the wolves fade away, draining part of his own strength from him. Gelert appeared, whining and nuzzling his face, sensing his master's distress.

"Gwyn?" Mitch asked, kneeling beside him.

"Hunters," he managed to gasp. "Somebody's hunting wolves."

CHAPTER 5

THE BOY

IN THE SMALL OTTAWA APARTMENT where he lived with his mother, thirteen-year-old Zach Morgan tossed and turned in bed long after he heard his mom's door close and her mattress squeak. He felt for the clock on his night table and pressed the big button on top. The clock announced the time in a flat computer voice: "Twelve…twenty…three…ay…em."

Quincy, his black Labrador seeing-eye dog, whined and his tags jingled as he raised his head from where he lay beside the bed. "It's okay, Quince," Zach whispered. "Go to sleep." Quincy gave a soft "whuff" and lay back down.

Zach felt for his iPod in front of the clock. Putting his earbuds in, he thumbed it on, hoping music would help him drift off. He was going to be tired tomorrow, and he had a history quiz second period.

But he wanted to fall asleep for another reason. Sleep meant more than rest to him. Sleep meant dreaming, and dreaming was special for him.

Very special.

When he dreamed, he could *see*. See like a normal person. See things that he'd never seen before, not even in the five years of his life before he'd gone blind.

He'd mentioned that to his doctors once. They told him that wasn't possible. They told him anything he saw in his dreams could only be variations of the images from his memories from his five years of sight.

He hadn't argued with them. He'd known even then that adults didn't think kids were very smart, and that went double for blind kids. But *he* knew his dreams, something the doctors could never know. And he knew that in his dreams, he could see.

See things as they were in the real world.

He'd tested it once, way back when he was eight. He'd learned to control his dreams by then—make them turn out the way he wanted, play the parts he wanted to play, do the things he couldn't do in real life.

On his eighth birthday, Mom had given him a Lego set. She said it would help him learn to "see" objects by handling them, to recognize shapes by touch. Every toy Mom bought him was always about learning something, but this time, he didn't mind. He loved building things with the blocks.

When he opened the gift, Mom explained the blocks were different colors. Then she stopped talking, and he knew that she regretted mentioning something he couldn't see. Mom got like that, even though it never bothered him.

A few weeks later, before going to bed, he'd taken five blocks and stuck them together, one on top of each other. Nothing fancy. Nothing like the houses and bridges he'd learned to make by touch. Putting the stack of blocks into his jeans' pocket, he went to bed.

That night, he made himself dream that he was sitting on the floor in his bedroom just before bed, putting the blocks together just as he'd done before bed. In his dream, he stared at the result, following the colors of the blocks from top to bottom.

Black, black, red, black, green.

In his dream, he repeated the sequence over and over to himself, until he'd memorized it.

Black, black, red, black, green.

The next morning at breakfast, he'd pulled the stack of blocks from his pocket and put it on the table.

"Mom, can you tell me the colors of these blocks?"

She paused. "Why, Zach?"

He shrugged. "Just wondering." He knew she'd answer him, that she'd never say something like color didn't matter to a blind kid.

"Okay," she replied. "They're black and red and green."

"No, I mean in order."

"Uh, they go green, black, red, black, black."

He was disappointed at first, until he realized the reason for the difference. "Oh! That's from bottom to top, right?"

Mom didn't answer right away. When she did, her voice was real quiet, as if she were afraid. "Zach, honey, how did you know that?"

He'd known better than to tell the truth. He shrugged. "Just guessed. Was I wrong? Were they from top to bottom?"

"No, you were right. It just sounded like…." Her voice had trailed off. "Never mind."

He rolled over in bed. He knew Mom loved him, and that life had been hard for her, raising him on her own right from when he'd been born, then him losing his eyesight. But sometimes, he sensed that she was afraid too, afraid that something was wrong with him beyond his blindness.

That's why he'd never mentioned how he could see in his dreams. He had a feeling she wouldn't like him being any more different than he already was.

Finally feeling tired, he turned off his iPod and placed it back on the table, feeling for the space in front of his clock. He lay back in bed. Finally, he dropped off to sleep.

And began to dream.

In his dream, he stood beside a thick pine forest on the pebbled shore of a dark smooth lake at night. A half moon rested on top of the trees lining the far side of the lake, reflected in the oily water. He gasped as he looked up into a clear sky. He'd never seen so many stars or imagined that the sky could hold such a display. The moon and the stars cast a strange surreal light on the scene, blurring the edges of objects so that shapes flowed into each other.

A sound behind him made him turn. In the way that happens in dreams, he was no longer standing beside the black lake, but rather in a rocky clearing overlooking it. High rock walls enclosed the clearing on two sides, a dense forest on a third, funneling the moonlight to a small spotlight where he stood.

The sound that he'd heard came from something crouched on all fours in the shadows, its back to him. An animal? Hard to tell in the dark. The noises became clearer, and he realized the creature was eating something that lay before it.

That discovery brought a sudden sense of menace to the scene. Slowly, as quietly as he could, he began to back away from the huddled thing and its unseen meal. The creature wasn't aware of him yet, and he planned to keep it that way.

A root snagged his foot, and he fell, landing hard. Something sharp stabbed into his left palm, and he cried out. The thing's head snapped up. It spun around. It saw him. It stood up.

On two feet.

The thing was still in the shadows, but he could see its outline well enough to know this was no animal. It was at least seven feet tall and humanoid, with a large misshapen head and unnaturally long, thin arms and legs.

He couldn't make out its face, but he felt the thing's eyes on him. It took a step toward him. Its chest heaved, then its breath screamed out in a loud, eerie whistle, like the wail of a cold winter wind. He almost vomited as the smell of the thing reached him, reminding him of a dead and rotting bird that Quincy had once proudly brought home.

But what overwhelmed him was the *cold* that flowed from this creature.

The cold of a killing winter, the cold of deep water. A cold that froze him to the spot, even while every fiber of his being fought to flee or wake up.

He tried to scream but he couldn't even open his lips. Still in shadow, the thing drew closer. A spindly-fingered, clawed hand reached for him.

A canine howl cut the night. Snatching its hand back, the creature swung around. It sniffed the air, and then with another whistling breath, it dropped to all fours and skittered down the slope leading to the black lake.

Able to move again, Zach spun toward the direction of the howl. A shadow stepped from the forest. A dog. No, he thought, with a renewed fear. A wolf.

"Coyote, actually," a voice said in his head. A man's voice, and he imagined that if he could see the man's face, it would be grinning.

Zach jumped. "Who said that?" he shouted, whirling around but seeing no one. He turned to the coyote again, not wanting to put his back to this new danger.

The coyote sat on its haunches, head tilted to one side, staring at him. "You're a little slower than I expected."

Zach blinked. "Animals can't talk."

"We can't?" The coyote opened its muzzle and gave three quick coughs that sounded like laughter. "Well, then this won't do."

The coyote began to blur, its outline shimmering, expanding. New features formed within the now larger outline. A moment later, Zach stared at a man, down on all fours. He had brown skin and long straight black hair that fell past his shoulders. He was dressed in pants and a jacket made from a tan-colored animal skin. The jacket was fringed and decorated with beautiful designs in colored beads.

Still on his hands and knees, the man turned his head slowly to Zach, and then barked. Zach jumped. The man laughed and hopped to his feet, mischief dancing in his black eyes.

"Hey, little brother," the man said, a huge smile creasing his broad, flat face.

"I'm not your brother," Zach replied. "Who are you?"

"Me? You don't know who *I* am?" The man's eyes widened. He looked up to the sky and shook his head. "Man, this is *not* going to be easy. Okay. Fine. Step by step. My name is Wisakejack."

"Wee—what?"

The man looked hurt. "Wisakejack. Wee-SAW-kee-chack," the man sounded out. "Or Nanabush, if you prefer the Ojibwe to the Cree. Whites, they thought my people were saying 'Whiskey Jack' when they told my stories." He shook his head. "Just another drunk Indian to them. Wasn't enough they gave us the whiskey to start with—" He waved his hand. "Don't get me started. Wisakejack I am, little brother."

"I'm *not* your brother!"

"Kid, we're all brothers," Wisakejack said with an easy laugh. Then he frowned. "Well, okay, some of us are sisters." The grin returned. "But my point is that *everyone's* related. *Everything's connected.* You're gonna have to learn that, little brother." He laughed again. "But then, you're gonna have to learn a lot on this trip."

"Trip?" Zach said. "What trip?"

Wisakejack looked at the black surface of the lake below. "Not much time for learning, either." He shrugged. "Oh well, not like it's the *End of the World,*" he said, waving his hands. "No, wait...." He fixed Zach with eyes as black and deep as the lake itself. "Actually, it is." Grinning, Wisakejack walked toward him.

Zach screamed. And woke up.

He sat up in bed, panting and sweating. Quincy nuzzled his hand and whined. "It's okay, Quince," he whispered, stroking the dog's head. "Just a bad dream." Quincy gave a quiet "whuff," and Zach heard him settle again.

He lay back on his pillow, strangely comforted by returning to the darkness of his waking life. *Just a dream*, he thought, trying to convince himself.

His left palm was throbbing. He winced as he touched it with his other hand. His fingers came away sticky. He was bleeding from a cut. How had that happened?

A cold lump of fear grew in his gut as he remembered. Falling. Hurting his hand.

In his dream.

CHAPTER 6

THE MOTHER

THE NEXT MORNING, Kate Morgan pulled her rusting ten-year-old Honda Civic up in front of Zach's school, an old-fashioned two-story brownstone not far from their apartment in Ottawa. Parking in front with the school buses, a concession granted her by the principal because of Zach, she got out.

Before she could come around to help him, Zach was already out of the car, shrugging on his backpack. He opened the back door for Quincy, then stood holding his white cane in one hand and the other on the handle of Quincy's guide harness. His round face and dark glasses swiveled to find her, eerily accurate in estimating her position.

"Please don't kiss me goodbye," he said, as she leaned in to do just that.

She stopped mid-lean. "No. Of course not." She reached out to straighten his thick black hair.

"And don't fix my hair. I'm sure kids are looking."

She turned the hair reach into a shoulder squeeze instead, sighing. "Okay, that's a 'no' on the hair fixing. So have a good day. I'll pick you up tonight."

Zach grinned. "You too. See you tonight. Let's go, Quince."

Watching as boy and dog climbed the steps together, she tried to will away her daily fears. Zach had been in this school since kindergarten. Now in grade eight, he knew the school well and could get around easily and safely. Next year was high school. He was small for his age, and she didn't like to think about him learning his way around a strange and bigger school with much larger kids. At least he'd have Quincy. The dog would give his life for Zach.

But, of course, it was more than blindness and high school that worried her about her son.

She drove home, parked her car on the street, and got out.

"Miss Morgan?"

She turned. A tall man in a dark blue suit walked up to her. He had a square face and brown curly hair. Behind him, a black stretch limousine with tinted windows stood at the curb. *CSIS*, she thought. He might as well wear a sign. "Yes?"

"My name is Lessard. I'm with CSIS," he said. He produced a wallet containing identification for the Canadian Security Intelligence Service.

"I assumed. So am I."

Lessard nodded. "I'm aware of that, Ms. Morgan." His tone was polite, almost deferential, with a slight French-Canadian accent.

"What's this about?"

"I need you to come with me, ma'am."

She smiled at Lessard, keeping any sign of the sudden fear she felt from showing on her face—the fear that CSIS had discovered she'd lied in her application and interviews. The fear that they knew her secret—that they knew the truth about Zach.

But no. They couldn't. That fear was foolish. The hard part was behind her. It had taken her ten years, nearly a third of her life, but she'd found them. And *they* had recruited *her*. She was in. She had no reason to be afraid. This was something else. But what? "What's this about?"

"Mr. Jonas wants to meet you."

Now she fought to keep a smile from her face. Her mysterious boss was finally bringing her into his inner circle. This was what she'd been waiting for. For Zach. That was the most important thing. She was doing this for Zach.

She nodded. "Certainly, but how long will this take? I'll need to pick my son up from school. He's—" She stopped. Christ, she still had a hard time saying it. "He's blind."

"I'm aware of your situation, Ms. Morgan," Lessard replied. "I'll have you back in time for Zach." He opened the limo door for her.

Not missing the fact that he knew Zach's name, she got in. Lessard followed and sat across from her.

"Where are we going?" she asked.

"I'm sorry, but I can't tell you that," he replied, pressing a button on his armrest. The side windows darkened, and an opaque barrier rose between the driver's area and where they sat, blocking any forward view. She glanced behind her. The rear window had also opaqued.

"Seriously?"

Lessard smiled. "Our destination is top secret. And I'm afraid I'll have to ask you for your cell phone."

No GPS, either, she thought. Shrugging, she handed him her phone, trying to ignore the feeling she was being kidnapped. Lessard tapped on the driver's partition, and the car pulled away. She glanced casually at her watch, noting the time they left, and then settled back. As they drove, she mentally mapped their route, noting the stops and starts, the direction of turns, and counting off seconds after every turn to estimate the distance for each section of their route.

This is what it's like for Zach, she thought. Being blind. This was what his life was like. For her, the trip would end soon, and she would see the world outside again. But Zach had to navigate blind in that same world every minute of every day. The thought renewed her resolve. She would go through with this dangerous game she was playing. She would find the information she needed to help her son.

They drove for about thirty-five minutes, but if she had calculated correctly, their driver had doubled back several times. She was certain they'd remained in the downtown core and were no more than five miles northeast of Zach's school.

The car stopped. She heard something large and metal moving. *Door to a parking garage*, she thought. Sure enough, the car moved down an incline and then negotiated a number of slow, tight turns.

The car stopped. They exited the limo beside an elevator. As Lessard pressed the button, she took a quick look around. Not another car to be seen, but a self-serve "pay and display" parking machine stood nearby.

The elevator arrived. Lessard hit the top button for the twentieth floor. They rode the elevator in silence. When the doors opened, she followed him down a long carpeted corridor to a heavy, wood-paneled door. He knocked twice. She didn't hear any reply, but a moment later, Lessard opened the door and motioned her inside.

"I'll leave you here, Ms. Morgan," he said. "Mr. Jonas will join you shortly." The door closed behind her. She guessed Lessard would remain outside.

The room was a large office, twenty feet square, plushly carpeted with no windows, and smelling of coffee and old paper. A heavy wooden desk sat at the far end, an antique by its looks, cherry wood maybe, bare except for a computer screen and keyboard, a TV remote, a Bible, and a framed photograph of a young man in military fatigues. Baroque instrumental music wafted from unseen speakers. She recognized Corelli, but couldn't name the piece.

Floor-to-ceiling bookshelves, crammed with books, lined the wall to her right. The left wall contained a bank of twenty display screens, all currently blank.

Checking herself in a screen, she finger-combed her short brown hair and poked at an errant tuft of hair. She was still regretting her new cut, which made her round, short-nosed face look fuller than usual. Smoothing down her gray skirt and straightening the matching jacket she wore over a white blouse, she allowed herself a confident nod.

A noise made her turn. A wooden panel in the back wall swung inward—a hidden door. A gray-haired man entered.

He wore a camel jacket over dark brown slacks and an open-collared pale yellow shirt. He was tall and thin, with long legs and arms out of proportion with a short body. Approaching, he extended a bony hand to her. An image of a praying mantis unfolding its pincers came to her unbidden.

"Ms. Morgan, so pleased to finally meet you," he said, smiling. "I'm Simon Jonas."

She shook his hand. His grip was firm, his skin cold. He looked a fit sixty-something. "Mr. Jonas. I'm happy to finally meet my boss."

Jonas folded himself into a high-backed brown leather chair behind the desk, indicating a wooden chair in front for her. She sat.

He chuckled. "Boss? I don't often hear that. Not a very CSIS term. My official title is Unit Head, DCET." He pronounced DCET as one word, Dee-Set. Domestic Counter Eco-Terrorism, the CSIS unit that had recruited Kate. "Do you go by Katherine?"

"I prefer Kate."

"Kate, then." He tapped the keyboard and stared at the screen in front of him. "You graduated from Carlton fourteen years ago, majoring in IT and project management. Then, ten years ago, you made a career shift. Into law enforcement." He looked at her. "Not long after your son was born. An odd time for such a major life change, was it not?"

She swallowed, surprised by the direct question. Had he made the connection? Hiding her fears, she gave her prepared answer. "That was shortly after 9/11, sir. I'd been giving it a lot of thought. What kind of world would it be for my son? I decided I wanted to do something about it."

He nodded, then turned back to the screen. "A bachelors in Criminology, then a masters. Dean's list both times. You applied to CSIS two years ago, starting in systems and project admin, and were quickly promoted to an intelligence analyst. Assigned recently to DCET." He looked at her. "Assigned by my request, by the way."

"Thank you, sir," she said. She'd known, but kept that to herself.

"No need for thanks. You're smart, capable, and dedicated. Just what we need." Leaning back in his chair, he considered her. "Well, Kate, do you know why you are here today? Even if you don't know exactly where *here* is," he added with a chuckle.

"Actually, sir, I'd estimate we're within a block of Bank and Albert. I could narrow it down further, given time. I'd just need to identify a building with twenty stories, a two-level underground garage, a parking payment system by TechnoPark, and an elevator system by Otis that was last inspected eight months ago."

Something flickered across his face, and she regretted trying to impress him. Then it was gone, and his smile returned.

"Well, well. It would seem that my faith in your abilities was not unfounded. I trust you will keep that information to yourself." He continued not waiting for her reply. "Now, back to my original question. Do you know the reason for this interview? For an interview it is."

She hesitated. She knew why, but couldn't give that as an answer. "I hope there isn't a problem with my work," she said.

His eyes narrowed slightly. "Now, Kate, don't be disingenuous. You know there isn't." Steepling long fingers, he stared at her as if she were prey, reinforcing his mantis image.

She swallowed. Had they discovered her early inquiries? Learned that she'd been searching for Jonas and his very special unit for years? That she'd let them think *they* had recruited *her*?

Or worse. Had they found out about Zach?

His smile returned. "I should back up. Do you know why I requested your transfer to DCET?"

She let herself relax a bit. "I understood it was my earlier project management experience with large hydroelectric installations." Since eco-terrorists targeted such sites, she made a logical security analyst for such locations.

He nodded. "And your Cree heritage, Kate. Your analysis work on the James Bay sites allowed us to infiltrate the Quebec native group that had been disrupting operations there."

She just nodded. She wasn't proud of that. Her sympathies lay with her people, not the Quebec government, sympathies she'd hidden during the CSIS psychological assessments. But she'd left behind her Cree culture when she escaped the Rez at Waskaganish to study at Carlton. Betraying her people was just one more price she'd pay to protect her son. "Thank you, sir. I'm glad that I've justified your confidence."

"More than justified, Kate," he said, "which brings me to the reason for this meeting."

Keeping her face calm, she allowed herself a small thrill of hope. "Yes, sir?"

"First, what I am about to tell you is classified 'Top Secret' and must not be revealed under any circumstances."

"I understand, sir."

"Kate, I head another organization in addition to DCET, one that is covert and known only to a few key members of the government. It is a small but prestigious unit. And it is extremely...*selective*." He stared hard at her. "Based on your background and psychological profile, I believe that you would make an excellent addition to that unit."

Yes! "What is this special unit, sir?"

"It is called the *Tainchel*. An old Scottish term, once used to describe a group of hunters who would advance through a forest, a short distance apart, in order to flush out wolves." He paused. "And kill them."

"Wolves, sir?" she said, an old fear resurfacing.

He smiled again. She was beginning to dislike that smile.

"A metaphor, Kate. Although, in this case, one that is particularly apt considering the mandate of the Tainchel."

"Which is?"

Jonas studied her. Finally, he reached for the remote on his desk and stabbed it at the bank of monitors. The largest screen brightened.

"To protect our country," he replied, his eyes still on her, "from these."

As images began to flicker on the screen, she readied herself. She'd prepared for this moment, rehearsing how to feign surprise when and if Jonas elected to share the great secret that the Tainchel harbored. A secret that she knew already—only too well.

There are beasts among us, she thought.

CHAPTER 7

THE HUNTERS AND THE HUNTED

AS THE INITIAL SHOCK of the wolves' deaths wore off, Gwyn felt his strength slowly return, enough at least for him to struggle to his feet from where he'd fallen.

"Are you okay?" Mitch asked, helping him into a chair as Gelert whined and paced back and forth beside him.

He nodded, raising a hand to silence Mitch and calming Gelert with a thought.

Three of his brothers. Dead. Murdered. From the contact he'd received as they died, he knew that the dead wolves had been part of the intruder pack he'd briefly sensed before. He reached with his mind, hunting for any survivors.

There. One wolf. Just one? That made for an original pack of four, which was small. But they might have split from a larger pack that had been forced out of their territory. Although still alive, this wolf was hurt. Calming it as best he could, he reached deeper into its feral mind. He needed to find out where it was, where the shootings had occurred.

Controlling a wild wolf was far different from dealing with Gelert. Gelert was bonded to him as his pawakan, his Heroka totem companion, so tightly linked to him that the dog would react almost before he formed a thought. But with a strange wolf, he had to establish his own position as the alpha male. Wolves communicated mostly by scent, body posture, and touch, so he focused on projecting those sensory effects into the wolf's mind.

After a few moments, he could sense the wolf lowering its head, whining, tucking its tail between its legs, acknowledging Gwyn as its leader. Now in control, he pulled detailed images and scents from its mind.

Metal bars. Can't move. The wolf was in a cage on the ground. *Fear.* The smell of humans nearby. He had the wolf turn its head, grabbing more visuals.

He knew the spot, a rock-filled gulley cut by a small stream running down to the lake—and disturbingly close to Cil y Blaidd. Two men in hunting fatigues, rifles slung on their backs, stood over three dead wolves.

Searching with his mind, he found Magula. The alpha male had heard the shooting and was leading his pack to investigate. They were perhaps half a mile away from the shooting site. Gwyn sent a mental command. *Magula! Stop!* As the wolf halted the pack, he ordered Magula to hold his present position. He didn't want to risk any of his wolves being shot, but he wanted them close by in case he needed reinforcements when he confronted the hunters.

But right then, he needed them for another reason. Establishing links with the rest of the pack, he let their strength, their life force, the vitality of his totem flow into him, restoring the strength he'd lost from the death of the three wolves. Finally, feeling almost whole again, he stood.

"I know where they are."

"The hunters? How many?" Mitch asked.

"Just two. I'm going after them." He moved to the door with Gelert on his heels.

Mitch followed him. "You're going after armed hunters?"

"They killed my brothers. They're on my land."

"And if you find them, you plan to do exactly what?"

"Make a citizen's arrest." *After I beat the living crap out of them.* "Hunting wolves is illegal, plus they're trespassing." He stepped outside and started down the path into the woods, mentally plotting a route to the shooting site as he walked.

Mitch called after him. "Hang on! You're not going alone. I'll come with you. Just let me call Caz back up to the house, so at least I know she's safe inside."

Gwyn hesitated. He'd forgotten about the girl. "All right. I'll leave Gelert with her. She should have some protection." He sent that thought to Gelert. *And keep her away from the computer and my things*, he added. Gelert acknowledged his instructions with a "woof" and a tail wag.

AS HE MOVED through the trees, Mitch following, Gwyn continued to draw strength from his links with the pack and Gelert, trying to fill the void left inside him from the dead wolves. But an emptiness remained. He felt their absence from the web of life that all Heroka sensed, felt it as acutely as if their deaths had ripped a piece of his own flesh from him. He clenched his fists, his anger fighting with the pain of the loss.

"Gwyn," Mitch called from behind him.

"Yeah?"

"About Caz—"

"Seriously, did you really expect me to say yes?"

Mitch didn't reply right away. When he did, Gwyn could hear the fatigue in his voice. "Gwyn, I can't fight a war with the Tainchel and play father to a troubled teenager, too. One who's in danger already. If I had my choice, I'd focus on Caz and turn the Circle and the Tainchel problem over to someone else."

Someone like me, Gwyn thought, *is what you mean.*

"But there isn't anyone I can trust with that," Mitch said, then added, "at least, who's willing to do it." When Gwyn didn't take that bait, he continued. "That means I need a safe *temporary* home for Caz. No one knows where you live, and I can't think of anyone who'd do a better job of protecting her."

"Yeah, if I don't kill her myself."

"At least tell me you'll think about it."

Gwyn stopped. He'd taken a route that placed them directly downwind and a quarter mile from where the shootings had occurred. He sniffed the cool breeze. He could smell humans. Plus wolves.

"Okay, I'll think about it," he said. *Thinking, thinking…done. And the answer is still no.* "Right now, let's focus on this. I smell humans, so they're still here."

"They'll also still have guns."

"Kind of doubt they'll just shoot us."

"What are you planning exactly?"

"I'm planning to smile, give them a 'Wow! Are those wolves? Can I see them?' bit, and when I'm close enough, I'm going to knock their heads together."

"Somewhat gently, I hope. No killing, please."

"No killing." But even as he said it, he realized how much he wanted to kill those who'd killed his brothers. He suddenly felt older than this forest, older than his hundred and nine years. Though his strength had returned, he knew some of his vitality, the vitality of the Heroka as a race, had just been lost forever with these deaths. The Heroka had more than three times the life span of humans, but their strength was tied inexorably to their totem animals, animals that were dying as human hunger devoured their habitats. Hunger for land, for resources.

Hunger for blood.

Enough. Time for his own hunting. He sent a command to Magula to close in with the pack. They would cover the remaining distance in about ten minutes.

The forest thinned ahead, and the rocky ground began to slope up. A spring-fed stream higher up the incline had carved a shallow, boulder-strewn gulley down to the lake. As he and Mitch approached the end of the tree cover, he held up a hand to halt them.

About halfway up the gulley, two men in hunting fatigues, each with a scoped rifle slung on their backs, knelt beside three dead wolves. A small cage with a fourth wolf, still alive, stood behind them. A few paces away lay a dead white-tailed deer, a rope trailing from its neck to a metal stake driven into the ground. Looking up the slope, he could guess where the hunters had hidden, in the trees that lined the top above the gulley, providing clear shots at the deer left as bait.

He looked back to the hunters. Each held a large knife and was in the process of skinning the wolves. His anger rushed back, hot and strong. Killed for their pelts. He stepped from the cover of the trees and started up the slope toward the men, all thoughts of caution and waiting for Magula and his pack forgotten. Mitch tried to stop him with a hand on his shoulder, but he threw it off and kept going.

He was about fifty paces away from the hunters, Mitch trailing him, when one of the men looked up and saw them.

After, he would look back and know that he should have understood sooner. The lips on the man who had spotted them twitched, a twitch more like the start of a smile than the look of surprise that should have been there. The man said something to his companion, and he too looked up from his skinning to where the two Heroka approached.

But then the man glanced up to the cover of trees that lined the top of the gulley. Following the glance, Gwyn caught a flash of sunlight reflecting from something.

And he finally understood.

Turning on his heel, he yelled to Mitch. "Get down!"

Too late.

The first bullet caught Mitch in the chest, spinning him around. Gwyn launched himself at Mitch, hauling the big man to the ground behind a pair of boulders as a storm of bullets ripped the air and the ground around them.

The Tainchel had finally found him. And he'd walked right into their trap.

CHAPTER 8

THE TAINCHEL

KATE STARED AT THE MONITOR in Jonas's office. The video showed dark woods, the lighting surreal, obviously taken via a nightscope. The date displayed in the lower right was from seventeen years ago. Men in camouflage fatigues and holding rifles moved silently through the trees, the only sounds the soft breathing of the cameraman and the occasional snap of a branch underfoot.

Suddenly, a feral snarl filled the room, followed by a man's scream. The camera jerked, and she caught a glimpse of gray four-legged shapes leaping from the shadows. More screams and snarls. Then an even louder roar from right beside the camera.

The ground rushed up. The picture bounced, settled. The screen now showed a perspective from the camera lying sideways on a leaf-strewn forest floor. Then flashes of camouflage pants, boots, and….

And paws. Animal paws and legs.

The screen filled with a soldier falling to the ground, his throat ripped open, his face slashed and bloody. He stared at the camera with dead eyes, oblivious to the continued but diminishing screaming in the background.

The screen froze on that image. Shaken but unable to look away, she stared at the dead man.

"*Wherefore a lion out of the forest shall slay them, and a wolf of the evenings shall spoil them, a leopard shall watch over their cities,*" Jonas said quietly.

Tearing her eyes away, she looked at Jonas, who continued to stare at the screen. She glanced at the Bible on his desk, hoping he didn't expect her to cite the passage.

"*And every one that goeth out thence shall be torn in pieces,*" he finished. He smiled at her, an expression so incongruous with what she'd just witnessed that she had to suppress a shudder. "Isaiah 3," he added.

She swallowed but said nothing.

"What do you think you just witnessed, Kate?" he asked, his face unreadable.

She hesitated. "Some kind of animal attack on a squad of soldiers. I saw wolves—and at least one bear."

He nodded. "From tracks at the scene and the victims' autopsy reports, my predecessor estimated that twelve to fifteen timber wolves were present, along with four black bears and at least three cougars. We have to rely on that evidence—and this film fragment—since no one survived." Jonas stared at her, his jaw working. "Twenty agents dead. Including my own son." He glanced at the picture frame on his desk. "Ripped to pieces."

His son. *Hunting the Heroka because of his son. Just like me.* She pushed that thought away. "Were those men in the Tainchel?"

He nodded. "It had been formed the prior year."

"And no one survived?"

He shook his head. "Our men were armed solely with tranquilizer rifles. We weren't expecting an ambush. The goal had been to capture subjects, not kill them."

"Subjects?"

He stabbed the remote again. Another screen came to life, showing a naked man crouched in a cage six feet square. The man jerked and fell over, a small dart now protruding from his shoulder. His limbs twitched. He screamed.

He began to change.

The man's outline shimmered, became liquid, flowing, rippling. He started to glow. Soon, a silver aura hid him from view. The aura dimmed, disappeared.

She gasped.

Where the man had lain stood a full-grown timber wolf, its tail between its legs, whining.

She'd known, of course. Known? How many times had she tried to forget that night from fourteen years ago? But seeing the proof unfold again, even if only on film, was like reliving the visceral horror of those moments. At least she didn't need to manufacture a reaction for Jonas.

Jonas froze the film on the image of the wolf. He turned to Kate.

"It's a fake," she said, playing the game she'd rehearsed.

He shook his head. "The film is genuine, not the product of special effects." He leaned forward, pinning her with his dark eyes. "Ignore what your logical mind is saying, Kate—that what you just witnessed is quite impossible. Tell me instead simply what your eyes and ears told you."

She took a deep breath. "I just saw a man change into a wolf."

He nodded, as if knowing she needed that assurance. "They call themselves the Heroka. Her-row-kaw," he said, sounding out the name. "Winnebago Indian name for some type of spirit. Means 'those without horns.' We don't know the significance of that reference, if any."

Her own research hadn't discovered any significance either. "*They?*" she said, playing along, hoping he'd add to her own knowledge.

"The man you saw was not, unfortunately, an isolated freak, although they as a species may be a mutation. Certainly," he added, "an aberration of God's will."

She glanced at the Bible again. Or maybe it was something humans used to have, but lost. Maybe humans were the mutation. She caught herself. No. The Heroka *were* an aberration. "Species?" she said, feeling a thrill of hope for what that implied about the knowledge the Tainchel held.

He nodded. "We have DNA samples from captured Heroka. It isn't human DNA, Kate."

She fought to keep her face calm. She'd been right. The Tainchel had been researching Heroka DNA. They truly could have the answers she sought—if there *were* answers.

Jonas continued. "They exhibit other non-human traits. Superior strength and endurance, hyper-acute senses, and, as you saw in the first film, the ability to control their *totem* animals."

"Totem?"

"Each Heroka seems to be associated with one particular animal species, or rather, family. For example, a Heroka of the wolf totem can control not only wolves, but all canids."

Again, she didn't need to fake her surprise. "So they aren't all—werewolves?"

Jonas punched the remote again. Two more screens glowed to life. She watched the scenes play out. In one, an older man transformed into a bear. In another, a young woman became a cougar. Kate swallowed, fighting the fear of old memories.

Jonas continued. "We've identified five totems: canids, bears, cats, birds, and hoofed animals. It is conceivable, even likely, that there are others. And don't place too much emphasis on the 'were-' aspect of these creatures. Transformation to animal form is apparently rare, executed only under the direst circumstances."

"Then how did you manage what I saw?"

"From captured subjects, our biochemists synthesized a drug that recreates the chemical process that occurs in a Heroka when they shift."

"You mean you can *force* them to shift?"

Jonas nodded.

"And the Tainchel hunts and captures these creatures?"

"Yes. Once, as you saw in these films, we had several prisoners. Unfortunately, my predecessor was rather…extravagant in his testing."

"Testing?"

Jonas shrugged. "Testing drugs such as the one I mentioned. Testing their resistance to weapons, their ability to endure physical trauma. Regrettably, however, such tests often do not lend themselves to repetitions with the same subject. We no longer have any Heroka in custody."

She stared at the frozen images of captured Heroka, displayed on the screens on Jonas's wall like a hunter's gruesome trophies. They were all dead. *The Heroka aren't the only beasts among us.* She turned back to Jonas. "You said that the mandate of the Tainchel was to protect our country from these creatures. How are they a security threat?"

Jonas nodded, as if he'd been expecting the question. "We've accumulated evidence of their involvement with environmental extremists, including acts of sabotage at hydroelectric dams, logging camps, and mines. Our supporters within the government, therefore, classify the Heroka as a domestic terrorist group."

"Our supporters, sir?"

He settled back in his chair. "We are a covert operation. Even the head of CSIS is unaware of us. In my Tainchel capacity, I report unofficially to a very senior member of the government whom I'm not at liberty to identify. Officially, we don't exist."

Covert and illegal. What had she gotten herself into? But she simply nodded.

"Which brings us to the reason for our meeting today," he continued.

Her heart raced. Finally, she'd learn the role planned for her within the Tainchel. And then she'd be able to plan her own next step.

"I receive reports," Jonas said, "of any incident that could conceivably indicate Heroka activity—specifically acts of environmental activism, as well as animal attacks on humans."

He removed a manila folder from a drawer and slid it to her. "This report details two killings, a week apart, containing both those factors. Further, the second killing shows even stronger evidence of a Heroka involvement."

Killing? Why would a killing prompt Jonas to bring her into the Tainchel? She opened the folder.

"The police reports are attached," Jonas said. "I'll warn you that the photographs are rather graphic."

The cover memo was on DCET stationary. Someone had written a red "T" in the upper right corner—the flag, she guessed, for a Tainchel document. The memo detailed the killing of a young man last week and a teenage Ojibwe girl just last night, both near a controversial new hydroelectric project at Thunder Lake, the site of protestor activity on the nights of both killings.

Based on the teeth and claw wounds, along with the partially eaten state of the bodies, the local coroner had attributed both deaths to an animal attack. She frowned. Animal attacks were rare in that area, and deaths even rarer.

One section was highlighted. As she read it, a chill ran down her spine. Police had found barefoot human prints, not matching the victim's, near the second killing. Fighting down her old fears, she looked up. "You think a Heroka killed these people?"

Jonas nodded. "And if we can prove it, I can press my case that these monsters both exist and are a threat. I can then obtain an official mandate and budget for the Tainchel."

A sick feeling grew in her gut. "How does this concern me, sir?"

"I'm sending you to find my proof, Kate. To find the Heroka behind these killings and to capture them."

She felt her stomach fall away. This wasn't what she'd signed up for, either officially when she joined DCET or in her own secret agenda. Jonas was forcing her to confront a Heroka again.

"But I'm just an analyst, not a field operative."

He tapped the keyboard again. "You've received the standard field training. This report states that you're an excellent markswoman and have a second-degree black belt in aikido. Your martial arts instructor described you as 'ferocious.'"

Her father had taught her to hunt with a rifle at a young age, and after her encounter fourteen years ago, she'd taken up aikido. She never expected either of those skills to be justification for putting her into a situation she dearly wanted to avoid. "Sir, surely you have more experienced field agents—"

"Kate, because the Tainchel doesn't officially exist, I must struggle along, using funds and operatives diverted from actual DCET projects. Any Tainchel initiative must have a legitimate DCET cover. The sabotage activity at the dam provides that, and your background on such projects makes you the perfect choice."

She swallowed, grasping for a reason not to go. "My son—"

Jonas waved a hand. "Zach, of course, will accompany you. CSIS will provide a tutor so that his schooling won't suffer and to assist him as needed."

Despite all of her maneuvering to get into the Tainchel, she didn't think she could do this—confront her greatest fear. "Sir, I'm just not sure…." Her voice trailed off.

Jonas stared at her, his face hard, all trace of his prior charm gone. "Kate, this is an unprecedented opportunity for us. I hope that my decision to bring you into our fold will not prove a grave error."

Bring you into our fold. Like a sheep, she thought. *A sheep chasing wolves.* She swallowed. This was for Zach. She was doing this for him. And a murder investigation with Heroka suspects would provide a perfect cover to access the Tainchel's database on the Heroka. She took a deep breath. "No, sir. You haven't made a mistake. I'll do it."

He watched her, expressionless. He wanted more. So she pulled from the place inside her where she kept her deepest fear. "If these things exist, they're obviously inhuman, sir. More than that, they're an *infection.* Of our own species, masquerading as humans," she said, surprising herself at her own vehemence. But she knew where that came from. "I'm ready to help you find them."

Jonas's smile returned. "Excellent!" He leaned forward. "*And he had power to give life unto the image of the beast, that the image of the beast should both speak, and cause that as many as would not worship the image of the beast should be killed.*"

She swallowed, her throat suddenly dry. Jonas leaned back. "Revelations is speaking of the Devil, Kate. But Revelations also tells us that *there fell a noisome and grievous sore upon the men which had the mark of the beast and upon them which worshipped his image.*" He smiled. "Well, Kate, *we* are that noisome and grievous sore, and we *will* fall upon the beast."

Ohh—kay. She was now part of a noisome and grievous sore. She forced a nod. "Yes, sir."

Jonas got up to show her to the door. "Mr. Lessard will have the limo driver take you home. Lessard will brief you further when he picks you up in the morning. You leave tomorrow for Thunder Lake."

Tomorrow. She swallowed, but nodded again.

Jonas stopped, staring at the three screens still frozen on the caged Heroka, now all dead. "Imagine, Kate. You may soon be that close to a Heroka," he mused, shooting her a look from the corner of an eye.

She stared at the images. She didn't need to imagine. She'd been much closer than that to a Heroka.

JONAS STARED AT THE MONITOR in his office showing the limo driver leading Kate Morgan back through the Tainchel complex. A knock sounded. Lessard entered.

"She took the assignment," Jonas said.

"Does she suspect, sir?"

"Of course not. She wants what we have so badly, she thinks *she* found *us.*"

"I am still concerned, sir, that we risk losing the boy."

"They'll both be watched closely. The boy is key to this operation—he will act as bait, drawing any Heroka in the area to him."

"But today's operation could provide Heroka subjects, sir."

Jonas shook his head. "Today's operation has a much different purpose," he replied, glancing at the photograph on his desk. "Call me from the airport tomorrow morning." Lessard nodded and left.

On the monitor, Jonas watched Kate Morgan step into the elevator to the garage. He'd suppressed his disgust for her during their meeting, but now it rose in him again. "*And if a woman approach unto any beast, and lie down thereto,*" he said quietly, "*thou shalt kill the woman, and the beast.*"

The elevator doors closed on Kate. Jonas punched a button on the remote, and the monitor went dead.

CHAPTER 9

THE HUNGER THAT WALKS

GWYN SNATCHED A LOOK over the rock he huddled behind with Mitch. Two shots screamed off the boulder inches from his head. He ducked down again, but he'd seen enough.

The shots had come from the cover of the trees at the top of the slope where he'd seen the flash of light. Below that, the two supposed hunters, their rifles now trained on his and Mitch's hiding spot, were slowly descending the slope of the gulley toward them, one moving to the left, one to the right, leaving a clear line of site for the men hiding in the cover of the trees. They obviously knew what Heroka were capable of and were taking no chances. The shooters in the trees would keep them pinned down until the hunters had clear shots to finish the job.

The two hunters were about forty paces away still. That meant Gwyn had a few precious seconds. Mitch lay beside him on his back, his chest covered in blood, his breath coming in great gasps. "Gwyn…," he wheezed, coughing out a red foam.

"Don't talk," Gwyn said. He ripped open Mitch's shirt. Blood gushed in rhythmic spurts from a hole on the right side of his chest. He pressed down on the wound. At least they'd missed the heart, but even Mitch's Heroka metabolism wouldn't save him unless Gwyn could get him to a hospital soon. First, they needed to survive the next few moments.

He felt Gelert in his mind. Sensing Gwyn's danger, the dog wanted to come to him. He ordered his pawakan to stay where he was and to keep Caz with him. He broke the link and reached for Magula.

Contact was immediate. The scent of humans came sharp and strong from the wolf's mind. The pack was close by. An image from Magula showed that they were at the top of the gulley in the trees on the opposite side of the stream. He heard the crunch of gravel as the two hunters approached. He'd run out of time.

He sent Magula the command, the command that would send his brothers to their deaths to save him and Mitch.

Attack!

A chorus of howls rose immediately from the trees above. The firing stopped, and Gwyn chanced another look over their protecting cover. The hunters, their backs now turned to him, were raising their rifles, trying to draw a bead on three wolves bounding down the slope toward them. Both men fired. Both missed. The wolves were on them.

At the top of the slope, more lupine shadows raced through the trees. Automatic weapon fire followed. A moment later, screams erupted from the trees mixed with feral snarls. At least some of the wolves had made it through the bullets.

Both hunters were dead, and the three wolves were tearing at their bodies. Gwyn sent them to join the rest of the pack attacking the shooters at the top of the gulley. He rose to follow them, but ducked back down when a volley of shots narrowly missed him. More shots found two of the wolves on the slopes, and they fell. The third made it to the top and into the trees, but the firing continued.

Enough. His wolf brothers were dying for him, and he didn't expect that they'd last much longer. He had one chance left. In his wolf form, he was stronger and faster, able to endure injuries that would kill him as a man.

And the wolf was a natural killer.

Closing his eyes, he reached for the place inside him where he lived as a wolf, to begin his shift.

THE VOICES WOKE the shaman now called Comdowtah from a fitful sleep.

Awake! Awake!

For a moment on waking, Comdowtah had the sensation, not of staring ahead into the blackness of the room, but of falling into the inky depths of a bottomless lake.

Awake! There is danger!

Throwing off that feeling of dread, Comdowtah sat up, alert and looking around. "Where?"

Not here. Not to you. To us. To our plans.

"How?"

They hunt the Wolf. Men with guns.

"So what's the problem? He's your enemy."

He must meet the end we choose. At the time we choose. In the place we choose. You must draw to you the Wolf and Boy.

Comdowtah sighed. "So you keep telling me. What must I do?"

Protect the Wolf.

"How?"

Send the Hunger That Walks.

The winter that lived now inside Comdowtah stirred into an icy river rushing through veins and limbs, chilling the shaman's heart into a frozen lump. "No! No more killing."

It is part of you now. Each day the Hunger grows. Soon it must feed again. Why not tonight?

Comdowtah slumped back onto the bed, defeated. "Show me."

Here. Choose one. Their hearts are already empty, ready to be filled.

A vision filled Comdowtah's mind. A dark forest beside a dark lake, but not the one that haunted the shaman's dreams. Gunshots. Men hiding in those woods. Men with guns. Men with hate, hate that sat like an emptiness inside them, a black hole waiting to be filled.

Now!

With a sadness as deep as that dark lake, the shaman chose one of the gunmen and reached for him.

STILL CONCENTRATING on his shift to wolf form, Gwyn stopped. Something felt…different.

He opened his eyes. He blinked. He stood up, still in human form.

He had not changed, but the world around him had. He still stood in a small gulley within a forest beside a lake. Yet everything was different.

Night had fallen here, and the air was chill. This lake was darker and as still as a corpse. The trees were taller, the woods thicker. And along the shore of the lake, where Cil y Blaidd should stand, rose nothing but a rocky slope.

He shivered, but not from the cold. His wolf soul sensed something primal about this place. Something old—*very* old—and yet, at the same time, something new, virgin. And quiet, as if this world had just taken its first breath and was holding it in, waiting for just the right moment to exhale, to start the beginning of time itself. Above, the moon was full. Last night, at Cil y Blaidd, it had been a waxing half moon. Somehow, he knew that here, in this place, the moon was always full.

Grandson.

The word rang in his mind, like an echo from a distant past. He spun around.

The largest wolf he'd ever seen stood before him, its fur shining in the moonlight like polished silver, giving the beast an aura that was almost blinding against the surrounding darkness.

Grandson. The wolf was speaking to him. In words. A wolf using words.

He felt an almost overpowering urge to drop to his knees, to prostrate himself before this vision. *Get a grip. It's just another wolf. I'm the alpha male here.* "As far as I know, pooch, I'm not your grandson." He reached out with his mind to control the animal.

The wolf brushed his mental grasp away, as a parent might stop a child reaching for something dangerous. *Then you know little, grandson. We are related. All things are related. Everything is connected. Your kind knew that once. You knew that once.*

Gwyn swallowed. "Who are you?"

I am Mahigan. And you are my grandson. All of the wolf totem are my grandchildren.

Not knowing how to answer that, he turned his thoughts back to the danger he'd left behind. "Okay, gramps, then how about helping me out? Some bad guys are killing my brothers—your grandchildren—and are trying to kill a friend. And me."

I know. Those men die as we speak.

He felt a surge of hope. "Is that your doing?"

It is not. They die at the hands of something else. Something I have fought since the beginning. Something that all life must fight to survive.

"Mitch—my friend—he's dying."

Sadness flowed from Mahigan. *He is already lost to you. Even to me. Even to Moswa, who rules his totem.*

"No!" he screamed at the wolf. He whirled around, searching for something familiar, for a way back to the real world. "Let me go. I can save him. I can save my brothers."

You cannot fight the thing that kills the men who hunt you. Not yet. You would die.

"I'll take that chance. If I die, I die. I've lived a long life. I'm willing to risk it for the life of my friend, the lives of my brothers."

Another wave of regret, but tinged with the pride of a parent for a child. *No, grandson.*

Understanding came to him then, and with it, anger. "You're keeping me here? You're keeping me safe while my friends die?" With a roar of rage, he leapt at the silver wolf.

The next moment, he lay on the ground, the great jaws of the strange wolf around his throat, a huge paw on his chest holding him down.

Forgive me, grandson. You are needed for a different purpose. The fate of your world depends on you.

And there the wolf held him, helpless in his rage, unable to move, unable to save Mitch, unable to save his brothers.

CHAPTER 10

BEGINNINGS

THAT NIGHT OVER DINNER in their small apartment, Kate told Zach, omitting the Tainchel aspect, that he'd be coming with her to Thunder Lake. His reaction was the opposite of her own.

"This is great!" he cried.

"Yeah," she said, forcing happiness into her voice. "Great."

"Maybe I'll meet some Ojibwe kids. I could learn more about our culture."

Our culture? She was full Cree and didn't even think of it as her culture anymore. "You're part Cree, not Ojibwe."

"Yeah, but some stuff's the same, right? Like the stories?"

Like the poverty and the way whites treat us, she thought. But she just nodded. "Yep. Language, too. Anthropologists lump the Cree, Ojibwe, Blackfoot, Micmac together as the Algonquian people, because our languages are so similar. But we never call ourselves that." She stopped. We? Where had that come from? "Where I grew up, we called ourselves the *Eeyouch*. The Ojibwe, the Odawa, the Algonquin—they all call themselves the *Anishinabe*. Both words mean 'The People.'"

He peppered her with more questions about the trip. She hadn't seen him this excited since the day they'd bought Quincy. He wolfed down the rest of his dinner. "I'm going to pack."

"Dishes first."

Later, lying in bed with Zach asleep in the next room, she reflected on her day. At least Zach was happy about the trip. Despite his blindness, he embraced change better than she did. But she was right to be afraid. She'd lied her way into a shadowy, covert government agency, and now was trying to capture some inhuman, murderous creature that was probably a Heroka. And bringing

Zach with her. And she didn't relish being thrown back into a First Nations community. She'd left that behind in Waskaganish when she'd escaped the Rez on a university scholarship.

But today, in Jonas's office, she had realized there was more to her fear than these reasons.

An infection.

She'd told Jonas the Heroka were an *infection*. And though she'd been acting for his benefit, she had meant it when she'd said it. Fervently, passionately.

Well, she *had* been infected, hadn't she? She'd loved and trusted Zach's father—and he'd put something inhuman in her.

So what did that make Zach? Did she think of *him* as an infection?

No! She loved her son with all her heart. She was doing all of this for him.

Liar. Yes, she loved him, but part of her also feared him. Feared what he might be, what he might become.

She was afraid of her own son. How messed up was that?

ZACH WAS DREAMING. Or thought he was.

Normally, he knew he was dreaming if he could see. At that moment, he could detect light and shadow around him, but a thick gray mist shrouded everything. He was also floating, unable to feel anything solid beneath him.

"Let me tell you a story, little brother," a voice said.

Zach's heart jumped. He caught a glimpse of a figure beside him, but when he turned toward it, he just kept turning, round and round. A hand stopped him spinning. Wisakejack grinned at him.

"Moving's a little tricky in this place," Wisakejack said, then gave Zach another spin.

"Cut it out!" Zach cried, grabbing hold of Wisakejack's fringed jacket to stop spinning. Then he remembered his fear from last night's dream, and he pushed himself away from the man. This sent him flying backward through the grayness. Wisakejack grew smaller and smaller, finally disappearing in distance and mist.

Zach bumped into something soft. He turned and found himself staring up into Wisakejack's face again. "You don't trust me, do you?" Wisakejack said.

"No," Zach said. "I mean, yes. I mean—"

"And you shouldn't," Wisakejack said. "You should always be very careful about spirits you meet in dream. And I probably scared you last night with that 'end of the world' stuff."

"So the world *isn't* going to end?"

"Oh no, that's still a definite possibility. That's why I'm here."

Zach swallowed, his fear returning.

"Look," Wisakejack said, "I *did* save you last night, right? Why don't you cut me some slack until I can explain some things? Deal?"

Zach sighed. "Okay. Deal." He looked around the grayness. "Where are we?"

"Nowhere."

"That makes no sense."

"I get that a lot. But in this case, it's the only answer that *does* make sense. This is what *was* before *anything* was. You see, the question you should ask is '*When* are we?' We're before the beginning. Before the world existed. So, since there's not anywhere for us to be yet, we must be nowhere."

Zach groaned. "I want to wake up."

"First, let me tell you a story—"

"Stop!" Zach cried again. "You said that this was about the end of the world. That I played a part, that I had a lot to learn. Instead of telling me stories, why don't you teach me what I need to know?"

Wisakejack scratched his head. "But I *am* teaching you. The People use stories to teach their children. At least, they used to."

"I'm not a child."

Wisakejack ignored him. "The People didn't have schools. Didn't need them. From fall to spring, each family was in their hunting territory, alone with each other. Storytelling in the family hunting lodge was entertainment on those long nights, a way to forget that hunger was always ready to take them, if a hunt went bad, if the animals grew scarce. Parents used stories to teach their kids the ways of the People, their values, their beliefs."

Zach looked hard at Wisakejack. "Your stories—will they be *true?*"

Wisakejack shrugged. "A story is true if its *meaning* is true. That's all that matters—for you to learn the true meaning of the world."

"The world of the Ojibwe? Or the Cree? Or the whites?"

Wisakejack smiled sadly. "There's only *one* world, little brother. And we *all* live in it. Everything's connected."

Zach sighed. "Alright, I give up. Tell me a story."

"Been trying to, but you keep interrupting." Wisakejack frowned. "I kinda gotta break the rules. Only supposed to tell the old stories, especially ones about the great spirits, on long winter nights, when those spirits are far away and can't hear. Else, well, some spirit might come calling."

"I get the feeling that breaking rules isn't a problem for you."

Wisakejack grinned. "You're learning already. Besides, winter's a lot closer than people realize this time around. We're running out of time, so I *gotta* tell you the stories now."

"About the end of the world that's coming?"

"Nah. About the *beginning* of the world. How're you gonna stop the world ending if you don't know how it began? Now, you gonna shut up?"

Zach sighed and nodded.

"In the beginning," Wisakejack began, "Kitche Manitou, the Great Spirit of the People, dreamed of this world. Kitche Manitou knew that dreams are important, even for him, so he meditated on his dream and realized that he had to bring what he had dreamed into being.

"So, out of nothing—the nothing that we're floating in right now—he made four elements—rock, water, fire, and wind. Into each, he breathed the breath of life, giving each its own spirit."

Zach suddenly felt solid ground under his feet. Rain wet his face, and a breeze moved his hair. He felt the heat of flames and smelled smoke. He still could see nothing but mist.

"From these four elements," Wisakejack said, "he created the four things that form the physical world: the Sun, stars, Moon, and Earth."

Zach gasped. The gray mist was gone. A red sun sank over a broad bare plain of gray rock cut by a winding river, while a full moon peeked yellow-white over a tall, barren mountain under a canopy of stars in a darkening sky.

"Then Kitche Manitou made the plant beings, in four kinds: flowers, grasses, trees, vegetables."

From the bare expanse of rock, a forest of huge trees and undergrowth suddenly rose. Zach sensed something primal about this place. Something old—very, very old—and yet, at the same time, something still new.

"And to the plants, he gave four spirits—life, growth, healing, and beauty."

"He liked to do things in fours, didn't he?" Zach said, looking around in wonder.

Wisakejack grinned. "See? You *are* learning. Next he created animals, each with special powers—two-legged, four-legged, winged, and swimmers—yep, four again."

Zach heard chirping and looked up to see a blue jay on a tree branch. When he looked back down, the coyote from his first dream sat beside him.

"Wisakejack?"

The coyote's outline shimmered, and Wisakejack took its place. He stood up, brushing himself off. "Last, Kitche Manitou made the People. Humans." He raised a finger. "*Last*—not first. That's your most important lesson tonight. The plants came *after* the physical world, because they needed the earth, air, rain, and sun to live. The animals came *after* the plants, because the meat-eaters needed the plant-eaters, and the plant-eaters, well, they needed the plants."

"And people came last," Zach said slowly, "because we depend on everything—sun, water, earth, air, plants, and animals."

Wisakejack grinned. "Yep. None of the other orders of life needs humans to survive, but people depend on *everything*. You're the *weakest* of the four orders—something the white man has never figured out. But Kitche Manitou wasn't finished. Because the People were the weakest of his creations, he gave them the greatest of all his gifts—the power to *dream*." He looked at Zach hard, his grin gone. "You believe that, kid? That dreaming is a power?"

Zach considered this. "When *I* dream, I can see."

Wisakejack nodded. "We just gotta get you to see the *right* things, dream the *right* dreams."

The fear from his first dream returned. "This isn't going to be easy, is it?"

Wisakejack's face was grave. "Like I said, little brother—you *are* learning."

CHAPTER 11

ENDINGS

THE PRESSURE ON GWYN'S CHEST and throat suddenly vanished. He opened his eyes. The silver wolf, Mahigan, was gone. The strange, primal dark forest was gone. Sunlight lit the late afternoon sky above him again. Pushing himself up, he looked around.

He was back in the gulley of the ambush, where an ominous silence had fallen. No gunfire. No cries or curses. No howl or snarl of a wolf. Nothing. He looked up the slope to the trees from which the ambushing fire had come, but he could detect no sign of movement, of either humans or wolves.

Mitch still lay beside him, his head now lolled awkwardly to one side, his great chest not moving. Kneeling beside his friend, he felt for a pulse, then slumped to the ground, hanging his head.

The Bull was dead.

The rage he'd felt being held by the silver wolf returned, hot and hard. Leaping to his feet, he charged up the gulley, past the two dead hunters, past the two dead wolves and the caged wolf. As he neared the top, he slowed, caution overcoming anger. But the forest above him remained silent and still. Cresting the top of the slope, he stepped into the copse of trees where the ambushers had hidden.

The smell was the first thing to hit him. A strange smell of mushrooms, fungus, rotting wood. A stench of decay and corruption, so nauseating that he had to fight not to retch.

The dead lay all around. Dead men. Dead wolves. He counted three of his gray brothers, but none was Magula. That meant Magula and five of his pack had escaped. But where were they? Why had they fled?

The dead humans outnumbered the wolves, ten corpses in all. But the state of those corpses seized his attention more than their number. The men had all been dressed in camouflage fatigues, fatigues that were now shredded on each corpse exposing the flesh beneath.

Or what flesh remained. He'd seen enough predator kills to recognize half-eaten bodies. He'd instilled a strong taboo in his pack against consuming human flesh. But what else could have done it? Then he saw another Tainchel body, a body that differed extremely in its condition from the others. He moved closer.

The strange smell was strongest around that body. The man lay completely naked, but his flesh showed none of the signs of being eaten that the other bodies exhibited. But neither was his flesh unmarked. Bullet holes riddled his corpse. Gwyn stopped counting at thirty, most of which would have been instantly fatal. But the most disturbing aspect was the blood staining the man's lips and the lower part of his face. Something hung from his partially open mouth.

Extracting the object with the end of a stick, he held it up for a closer look, to verify what he suspected. It was a strip of skin, flesh still clinging to it. He dropped it to the ground. Inspecting the man's hands, he found more blood along with bits of skin hanging from torn fingernails.

He sat back on his haunches, surveying the gruesome scene, trying to decipher what had happened here. The only guns belonged to the Tainchel, so the Tainchel gunmen had fired on this man, presumably their own comrade and presumably because he'd attacked them.

Attacked them. Killed them. Eaten them. Despite being riddled with bullets.

Another thought occurred, an even more disturbing one. A Heroka in animal form is very hard to kill. A shift shreds whatever clothes they are wearing. If killed in animal form, they return to human form on death. Had this bullet-riddled man been a Heroka? Had he killed these men in his animal form, being shot in the process multiple times, and then succumbed to his wounds?

He shook his head. A Heroka in the Tainchel? Impossible. Besides, not even a Heroka could take the amount of damage this corpse showed and still live, let alone be able to kill this many men. He swallowed. And eat them. But then what had happened here? He needed a witness. Then he remembered he had several.

He searched for Magula's presence. It took several tries, but he found him—and was immediately thrown from the wolf's mind, expelled by as pure a terror as he'd ever sensed in an animal. The big male and five of the pack were still alive. And still running from whatever they'd encountered here when they'd attacked the Tainchel.

He touched Magula's mind again, soothing the wolf and calling for him to stop. Reluctantly, the wolf halted the pack and let him stay in its mind. He dove into Magula's recent sensory memories, feeling what the wolf had felt during the attack.

The first memory he found was of cold. Bone-chilling, numbing cold, as if winter itself had shoved an invisible hand into the wolf's chest and squeezed his wild heart.

And then the smell hit him. The same nauseating smell of mushrooms, fungus, and rotting wood. Of decay and corruption.

Then another smell. Blood. The blood of the Tainchel.

Finally, the flash of a visual memory. Something big. Long dark hair or fur. Sharp teeth. Something standing on two legs.

The wolf's memories ended. At that point, Magula and the remaining wolves had turned and run, fleeing in terror from….

From what? What had the wolves encountered? He'd known Magula from a pup and had chosen him to lead the pack that protected Cil y Blaidd for a reason. The wolf had never run from anything. The thing had not been human, but from Magula's brief glimpse, neither did it resemble any animal Gwyn knew. His Heroka theory seemed even less likely. So what was it?

He stood. That answer would have to wait. The Tainchel had found him. When this group didn't report in, the Tainchel might send more gunmen. He had to get out of here. But first, he'd give his friend and his wolf brothers a proper burial. The Tainchel could rot where they died.

There was one more thing to do. Walking back down the gulley, he sat beside Mitch's body. "Well, old friend," he said quietly, "looks like you're going to get your wish." Opening a contact with Gelert, he told his pawakan to bring Caz to him.

ABOUT FIFTEEN MINUTES later, Gelert trotted out of the trees into the gulley, Caz trailing behind him.

"Your stupid dog practically dragged me—" she began, then froze, like a rabbit confronting a wolf. She looked at the dead hunters on the slope, then at Mitch's still form. Both hands came up to cover her mouth, and she began to shake her head back and forth, back and forth. "No. No. Not again. No."

Not again. He swallowed. Her parents and her brother when she was a child. Her foster parents recently. Now Mitch. He walked up to her. "Caz," he said gently, "I'm sorry. It was a trap. I think it was the Tainchel—"

Ignoring him, she ran to Mitch's body and began shaking him. "No, no, no. No, damn you! Get up, get up, get up. Goddam you, get up!" She was screaming by the end, beating on Mitch's bloody chest with both her hands.

Running to her, he grabbed both of her arms and pulled her up. "Stop it! He's—"

She shoved him away with a fierce strength. "WHERE WERE YOU?!" she screamed at him. "He trusted you! You were supposed to be his friend." She backed away, shaking her head. "Oh god, oh god, oh god."

He started toward her, but Gelert grabbed his pant leg in his teeth, holding him back. He sighed and put a hand on the great hound's shoulder. "Yeah, maybe you're right," he muttered.

Besides, what was he going to say to her? Mitch *had* trusted him. And now his friend was dead because of him.

He should have figured it out earlier. The fake MNR plane arriving off schedule and right after Mitch landed. The brief alarm from the strange wolf he'd sensed but ignored. The shooting of wolves so close to his hidden home.

The Tainchel had planned it well. They'd followed Mitch's plane somehow, bringing along the wolves and the dead deer to stage the shooting scene. Killing three of the wolves had seized his attention. They'd left the fourth wolf alive so that he'd use it to locate them. So that he would rush right into their ambush. They'd played him. He felt a chill at what this operation showed about the Tainchel's knowledge of the Heroka. And of him.

"I'm sorry," Caz said.

He looked up, thinking she was addressing him. But she was sitting on the ground, staring at Mitch. "I got you killed. Just like my foster parents. It's my fault."

He thought about that. Had the Tainchel been after Caz, not him? Using wolves as bait pointed to him as their target, but either Caz or Mitch had led them here. Now, however, was not the time to have that discussion.

He stood up. He had a funeral to prepare.

By the time he'd finished readying Mitch for his final journey, the sun had set and a half moon hung remorseless over the trees, oblivious to the death scene below. Before him, Mitch lay on a huge funeral bier built from dead branches. The big man had been too heavy to move very far, so Gwyn had built the bier beside him. The dead wolves lay around Mitch on the bier.

Gelert stood by Gwyn's side, whining, sensing his master's pain. On the hound's other side sat Magula along with the survivors of his pack and the wolf the Tainchel had caged.

Caz stood on the opposite side of the bier, as far from him as she could get but still be near Mitch. Eventually, she had joined him in the preparations, but she still refused to look at him or talk to him. The anger had died from her face, replaced by an emptiness of expression that bothered him more than her anger had.

She pulled out her lighter to start the fire, but he shook his head. "No. Not yet."

"He's not coming back," she said, her voice a dead thing. "He's not coming back, and I want this over."

"Wait."

"For what?"

A twig snapped in the trees behind them. "For this," he said.

A great bull moose was the first to appear, stepping from the shadow of the forest with a grace belying its size. Two great white-tailed deer bucks followed, perhaps the two that had greeted Mitch on his arrival. Then a doe and her fawn. Another moose, a cow this time, with a spindly-legged calf. Another doe.

Still they came. Came to pay their last respects to their fallen brother. Each would approach the bier, touch their nose or antlers to his chest, then lay a branch on top of him and slowly turn away, to stand heads lowered in a semi-circle around the bier. This continued until Mitch lay cloaked in a covering of the forest.

Gwyn watched them silently. He'd seen too many of these ceremonies in his long life, lost too many people he loved. Mitch had died because of him. Because of his recklessness, his anger. It should have been him in Mitch's place. His anger at the silver wolf returned. "Want to say anything?" he asked.

Caz swallowed. She shrugged. "He was good to me. I liked him."

He stared at the body of his friend. "You were a good man. A good leader. A good and loyal friend. And I failed you. You came seeking my help, and I refused you." He lowered his head and swallowed. "I just want you to know that...that I've changed my mind."

Caz looked at him, but said nothing. She flicked her lighter and tossed it into the bier.

The dry wood caught quickly. As the fire rose to consume the bodies, Magula and the wolves raised their heads and howled. Gelert joined them.

The fire died. The smoke died. It was over. Mitch was gone. The assembled animals turned and, one by one, disappeared into the trees while he and Caz stood staring at the smoldering ashes. Finally, he spoke. "You okay?"

"Oh, yeah. Sure. Great," she said, cradling her rat to her chest.

He sighed. "Caz, I'm sorry, but we have to fly out of here as soon as it's light."

"What's the rush?" she said, her voice a monotone.

"The Tainchel know we're here. I figure the only reason they haven't sent more troops is that they don't have many to start with if they're an unsanctioned operation. I counted twelve bodies. This probably dealt them a pretty severe blow."

"Not near severe enough," she muttered. "Fine. Drop me back in Ottawa."

"You're coming with me."

"No," she said, crossing her arms and glaring at him. "I'm not."

"It's what Mitch wanted."

"What?!"

He'd been afraid of this. Mitch hadn't explained to Caz the purpose of their visit here. Great. "He wanted you to stay with me. For your protection."

"Yeah, because you're such a great protector, aren't you?"

He fought back a retort. "I'm flying to Thunder Lake, and you're coming with me."

"Again, no. I'm not."

"Then you can stay here and face the Tainchel alone. They seem pretty interested in finding you."

She paled, and he felt bad, but he couldn't leave her behind. She turned to stare at the still smoldering bier. "Where the fuck is Thunder Lake?"

"East end of Lake Superior."

"Why there?"

"I used to live there. I have friends there." *And enemies.* But he didn't say that. "One of those friends has asked for my help. His granddaughter's been killed."

"Great. More dead people. Y'ever think it might be you?"

Sometimes, he thought. He related the information in Ed's email, including the signs of a possible Heroka involvement. He didn't mention Leiddia. "And something else occurred to me. The Tainchel used to track any incidents involving animal attacks, especially any connected to environmental activist targets, since those could be signs of Heroka presence in the area. Mary's killing has both of those."

"You really think a Heroka killed her?"

Leiddia's face floated in front of him. "No, but the Tainchel will. I think we'll find the Tainchel there very soon."

"You have funny ideas about keeping me safe."

"Caz, they're after you. I'm sorry, but they are. No matter where you go, you have that. At least, with me, you have my protection, even if you don't value that very much. And you'll have Gelert to protect you, too."

"Gelert? Is that him?" she asked, nodding at the hound. Gelert wagged his tail.

"Yes."

"Weird name."

"Now how did I know you'd say that? He's a wolfhound, named after the legendary hound of Prince Llewellyn of Wales."

"You have a pawakan that was bred to hunt your totem?"

"I like the irony. So, are you coming?"

She stared out over the lake, not answering.

"Caz," he asked quietly, "where else can you go?"

She continued to stare at the lake. "Rizzo," she said finally.

"What?"

She held up her rat. "His name is Rizzo. Yeah. Okay. I'll come. Why not?"

He relaxed and nodded. He began to cover the remains of Mitch and the wolves with rocks. After a moment, she joined him. When they finished, they stood for a silent moment before the pile of stones, and then turned away.

"Rizzo," he said, as they walked back to Cil y Blaidd. "That's funny. I like that."

"I can't tell you how thrilled that makes him."

Oh, yeah, he thought, *this is going to work out just fine.*

CHAPTER 12

LEAVING HOME

THE NEXT MORNING, Kate was all ready, with Quincy walked and their bags sitting by the door by six-thirty, waiting for Lessard to arrive. She'd been up since five, tired of laying awake in bed worrying about the trip. Advised not to dress as if she were from a big city, she'd gone with jeans, hiking shoes, and a white cotton sweatshirt.

Zach seemed more subdued than last night, but she just put it down to his being as tired as she was. Lessard arrived precisely at seven with a stretch limo. Grabbing their parkas, she led Zach and Quincy to the car.

At the airport, Lessard brought them quickly past security and into a private airline club lounge, thickly carpeted and furnished with dark leather armchairs and sofas. They seemed to have the lounge all to themselves. The only other occupant was a small thin man, balding with sharp features and big round glasses that made him look like an owl. Lessard introduced him as Colin Macready. "Colin will be Zach's tutor in Thunder Lake."

"Pleased to meet you, Zach," Macready said, waiting for Zach to hold out his hand before giving it a vigorous shake. He turned to her. "And you, too, Ms. Morgan."

"Kate, please," she replied, giving Macready credit for introducing himself first to Zach, his student.

Macready handed her an envelope. "This is my résumé, with references, including many in the MNR."

The reference to the provincial Ministry of Natural Resources puzzled her, until she remembered her cover, working on the hydroelectric project.

"Colin, why don't you and Zach get acquainted, while I finish briefing Kate?" Lessard said. While Macready helped Zach into a chair, Lessard led Kate to a low table out of earshot in a far corner on which a notebook computer sat beside a small metal case and a smaller plastic case.

"Macready comes highly recommended," he said, sitting across from her, "but if you aren't satisfied, contact us."

She finished reading Macready's résumé. "He seems excellent. But how *do* I contact you once I'm there?"

He turned on the notebook. "With this. It has a secure satellite communication link. You can connect anywhere." He told her the password and showed her how to establish an encrypted connection into the CSIS network.

Then he clicked on a video icon. Simon Jonas appeared on the screen. "Good morning, Kate," Jonas said, his voice sounding tinny from the small speaker. "We will communicate in this manner during your assignment. Now, I need to review some other devices you will be using. Mr. Lessard, please."

Lessard handed her what looked to be a cell phone and its charger.

Jonas continued. "As Jesus said in Matthew 10, *Behold, I send you forth as sheep in the midst of wolves. Be ye therefore wise as serpents, and harmless as doves.* Well, this should help you with the wisdom part."

She inspected the phone. "I don't understand, sir."

"Heroka," Jonas said, "display unusual alpha-wave brain patterns. You are holding an alpha-wave scanner that operates in the range of eight to fourteen megahertz. It resembles a phone so that you may scan suspects without being conspicuous. Leave it on and carry it at all times. If it detects their alpha-wave signature, it will ring like a real phone. Just pretend to answer it. The display will show the subject's position relative to you."

A sudden thought seized her. What if Zach had the alpha-wave pattern of a Heroka? She glanced at Zach sitting across the lounge, about fifty feet away. "What's its range, sir?"

"You'll need to be within about ten paces of a subject. Mr. Lessard, next, please."

She slipped the scanner into her purse, turning it off as she did so. She'd test it around Zach later when they were alone.

Lessard opened the small metal case. Her stomach tumbled. Inside, imbedded in a foam rubber placeholder, lay a pistol. The smaller plastic case held nine darts, three black, three red, and three green.

"Despite my earlier reference to the gospel," Jonas said, "You must only *appear* as harmless as a dove. You will need these should you succeed in locating a Heroka."

Lessard removed a black dart. "Black for black-out, as in unconscious. Heavy-duty tranquilizer. Fast acting. Hit your target anywhere, but the chest or neck works quickest." He demonstrated loading a dart, and had her repeat the action.

"And the other colors?"

"The red darts," Jonas explained, "contain the drug used in that man-to-wolf film clip you saw. Red for danger. They force a Heroka to shift to their totem animal form."

"Why would I ever want to do that?" she asked, suppressing an old fear.

Jonas smiled his mantis smile from the screen. "Assuming you successfully capture a Heroka, you may need to demonstrate its true nature to convince local authorities to detain the creature. Just ensure it's behind bars when you use the red dart."

She imagined that conversation. *Hey, Mr. Police Officer? Want to see a neat trick?* "And the green darts?"

"Green for safety," Lessard said. "They force a shifted Heroka to return to human form, and most importantly, prevent any shift to animal form for up to twenty-four hours." Unloading the gun, he returned it and the darts to the case.

"If all goes well," Jonas continued, "the sequence in which we demonstrated these devices should parallel your mission. Identify a subject with the scanner, trank it for capture, demonstrate its nature if necessary, and then, most importantly, prevent it from assuming its animal form."

She swallowed. "Yes, sir."

"Check in every evening, Kate," Jonas said. "If I don't appear, leave a video update. Good luck." The screen went blank.

Lessard checked his watch. "Time to go, Ms. Morgan."

A lump of fear was growing in her stomach, as cold and heavy as the gun she'd held in her hand. What had she gotten herself into? What had she gotten Zach into?

AFTER DROPPING HIS LINK with Kate, Simon Jonas looked up as a knock sounded on his office door. Dupuis, the limo driver for Lessard and Kate Morgan the day before, entered.

Dupuis cleared his throat. "Sir, we've lost contact with the wet ops team going after Blaidd."

Jonas hands clenched involuntarily. "What do you mean?"

"They've missed their last two check-ins. We can't raise any of them. And a fly-over by the pickup plane showed no biometric readings for the men or the targets."

"A dozen armed men? Dead?"

Dupuis just nodded, looking grim.

"And Blaidd?"

"The pilot landed. Blaidd's plane is gone."

Feeling weak, Jonas slumped back in his chair. After a moment, he reached for the picture frame in front of him. "I'm sorry," he whispered to the young man in the photograph.

Dupuis shifted nervously. Jonas looked up, remembering he wasn't alone. "Get out," he snapped. "Update me as soon as you have more news."

Dupuis left. Jonas sat for a while, holding the picture before him. He touched a finger to the young man's face. "*And they worshipped the Beast,*" he whispered, "*saying, 'Who is like unto the Beast? Who is able to make war with him?'*"

He carefully replaced the photograph, adjusting its position on his desk with an almost tender care. "I am," he said quietly to the empty room, his voice calm and strangely gentle. "I will make war with the Beast."

KATE CHECKED HER WATCH as the Greyhound bus rolled along tree-lined Highway 101 toward Thunder Lake. Five-thirty in the evening. Still another two hours before they arrived.

With no direct flights to Thunder Lake, they'd flown from Ottawa to Toronto and connected to Timmins, where they picked up the bus. CSIS could have flown them directly to Thunder Lake by helicopter, but Jonas didn't want Kate to appear to be anything more than a normal MNR employee arriving from out of town.

She groaned, stretching stiff muscles. Well, she certainly didn't feel as if she were getting any special treatment. They'd taken seats at the back so Quincy wouldn't get in the way as passengers got on and off at each stop. In the seat across the aisle from her, Zach sat slumped against the window asleep. Quincy lay sleeping in the aisle beside him. Macready sat in the row ahead, reading a book.

Before Macready had joined them on the bus, she'd tested the scanner to see if Zach would trigger it. To her relief, nothing happened. Zach's heritage would remain her secret, safely hidden from Jonas and his Tainchel.

Zach's *Heroka* heritage. What about his Cree heritage? *Her* heritage? This trip was already bringing back too many memories. Just looking out the window reminded her of the home she'd left behind. The sky was a deeper blue here, and what flashed by were trees, not buildings. Even the trees were different. Here the startling yellow of tamarack pines and the white of birch trunks broke the late October parade of evergreens and brown leafless deciduous trees.

The birches grew on the edges of the bush where the trees had been cut back from the highway. She remembered her grandfather teaching her how birches were always the first to grow back in a cleared area. She hadn't thought of her grandfather for years.

She slumped back in her seat. What was she doing? She'd spent years running away from both her roots and the Heroka. Now every passing mile brought her closer to both.

But closer to her goal as well.

Jonas had confirmed that the Tainchel possessed DNA data on the Heroka. Now that she was inside, she would find that information. She would find answers to her questions about her son. What did Zach's Heroka blood mean? Was he human or Heroka? Would he become one of those monsters? Could she prevent it? How? She swallowed, looking at where he sat across from her.

Or was he already one of them?

ZACH WASN'T SURE when the swaying of the bus and his lack of sleep the night before had combined to send him into slumber, but he knew he was now dreaming.

In his dream, he sat in a tall teepee. A small fire burned in the center of its dirt floor, its smoke curling to the opening in the top. Around the fire walked a circle of black ducks, mallards, and Canada geese. No, not walking. They were…dancing. With their eyes closed.

On the far side of the teepee, Wisakejack crept slowly closer to the birds, the flames glinting off a knife he held. "That's it, my brothers!" he sang. "Do the 'eyes closed' dance! Soon we'll have all the food we need for the winter." He reached for the nearest bird.

"What are you doing?" Zach cried.

At that sound, the birds opened their eyes. Seeing Wisakejack with his knife, they began running around the teepee, flapping and squawking. Wisakejack lunged at one bird after another, but finally all escaped through the tent flap, leaving him empty-handed. Getting up, he dusted himself off, glaring at Zach.

"Well, you were going to kill them," Zach said.

Slipping his knife into his belt, Wisakejack shrugged. "I was hungry."

"So you were going to slaughter some innocent birds?"

"Innocence has nothing to do with life or death, kid. Hunger does. Hunger is a powerful force. For my people—*our* people—hunger was a constant companion. If a winter was bad, if a hunt went bad, if the animals didn't offer themselves—we died. How do you think we survived? Ran down to the local McDonalds?"

"Why would an animal offer itself to be killed?"

"Because everything's connected. All life shares a common spirit. Remember the four orders of the world? Humans depend on everything. You're the weakest. The animal spirits know that. When a hunter has a true need, they offer up one of their grandchildren to him."

"True need?"

"If the hunter's not just being greedy, killing more animals than his family needs. And if an animal is offered, the hunter must treat them with respect."

"How do you do that?"

"Ah, well, let's say you're hunting a…a bear. Yeah, a bear." Wisakejack licked his lips. "Ooh! Bear steaks!"

"Wisakejack."

"Right. Sorry—still hungry. Anyway, the hunter, he first explains to the bear why he must die. If the hunter does this with reverence, the bear will die without a big struggle."

"That's it?"

Wisakejack shook his head. "When you're eating, you put part of the bear into the fire with some tobacco, to thank the spirits. And you use every part of him. You hang and smoke the meat. Or boil some into soup. And you treat his bones with respect, too—hang them from a tree so other animals can't violate them."

"Sounds like there was a lot to being a hunter."

Wisakejack nodded. "The most valued person in our society."

"So I guess you didn't rank very high."

"Ha! Good one, little brother." Wisakejack grinned and picked up a stray feather, twirling it between his fingers. "I'll get 'em next time." He sat down. "Now—"

Zach sighed. "—you're going to tell me a story."

Wisakejack grinned again. "You are definitely learning."

"What's this one about?"

"Last night, I told you how the world began. Tonight, I'll tell you how it ended."

"Um, in case you hadn't noticed, the world's still here."

"Different world. The world you're in now was recreated after the flood."

"The flood in the Bible?"

Wisakejack shook his head. "Different flood. Or at least, a different story."

"So why do I need to know this?"

Wisakejack's normal smile faded. "Because—unless we can stop it—it's going to happen again."

CHAPTER 13

GOING HOME

GWYN HAD BEEN FLYING for about an hour since sunrise, with Gelert curled on the back seat, and Caz staring out the side window, Rizzo on her lap. With a refueling stop, he expected to get to Thunder Lake by early afternoon. He'd emailed Ed to pick them up at a small lake just east of town. He hoped Ed could put them up in his back storeroom, else they'd stay at one of the town's two motels. Worst case, they'd camp by the plane, although he didn't relish having that conversation with Caz.

He'd packed his computer and data backups, leaving nothing behind that could lead the Tainchel to him, his friends, or any other Heroka. Before leaving, he'd gone over Mitch's plane inside and out, but found no trace of a tracking device, which didn't concern him that much, since that plane would remain at Cil y Blaidd. The same did not apply to Caz's backpack and its contents. That discussion had not improved their relationship.

"You want to go through my underwear?" she had said. "What kind of creep are you?"

"You can either let me go through your backpack, or you can leave everything here, and we'll buy you new stuff in Thunder Lake. I'd prefer that, actually."

"God, what is your problem with me?"

"Caz, someone led the Tainchel here. I'm sorry, but it was either you or Mitch, and I couldn't find anything on his plane."

She had paled at that. After a hesitation, she shoved the backpack at him, then stood with crossed arms as he went through it. He found nothing, but they transferred her things to an old duffel bag of his, and left the backpack behind, just in case.

The cell phone had been the next battle. The SIM card had no manufacture markings and he was loathe to bring anything designed to be tracked to start with. He tossed it into the lake. She had sworn colorfully at him and stormed away.

She hadn't spoken to him since, and given their past conversations, he was fine with silence, concentrating instead on flying as the trees flowed by beneath them in the sharp morning sunshine.

"Why are they after me?" Caz asked suddenly.

He looked at her, but she was staring out the window. "I don't know, but the Tainchel—if it is them—used to hunt us, to capture us for tests. I'm guessing you triggered one of their scanners somewhere, and they targeted you."

"So I got my foster parents killed," she said. He swallowed but didn't answer, not knowing what to say. "What kind of tests?"

"Nothing you want to be part of. How we work, how we shift, how much damage we can take. Testing drugs on us. Improving their scanners."

She stroked Rizzo where he lay in her arms. "So we're like lab rats to them."

"Yeah." *And that's never good news for the rat.*

"Didn't seem like they were trying to capture us back there. I mean, coming in all *Die Hard* like that."

"They weren't after you. And no, they weren't out to capture. They came to kill."

"Why'd they want to kill Mitch?"

He sighed. This would not end well. But she deserved the truth. She was blaming herself for Mitch's death. "Not Mitch."

She finally looked at him. "You. They wanted you. But Mitch died instead."

He wanted to deny the accusation, to deny the guilt ripping him up inside. But she was right. He nodded.

She fell silent again. "For the Ambush, right?" she said finally.

He heard the capitalization she put on the word. The deadly battle with the Tainchel was the stuff of legends for young Heroka. "Yeah. I think so."

She stared out the window at the forest passing beneath them. "You led it, didn't you? What happened?"

Most Heroka knew better than to raise that subject with him. But given what the Tainchel had done to her young life, he owed her a reply.

"Once we finally realized we were being hunted, we set a trap. I leaked word about a gathering of Heroka planned for an isolated spot. About twenty Tainchel walked into the ambush. They were still focusing on capturing subjects, so they only had trank rifles. They didn't walk out. We were all predator totems. Wolves, bears, the big cats, birds of prey. We didn't take prisoners."

"You killed them all? Twenty people?"

His felt his old guilt rise. "We were fighting for our lives."

She looked at him. "S'okay. Chill. They killed my parents and my brother. They killed my foster parents. Now they've killed Mitch." Her voice was a dead, flat thing. "I'm happy you killed them." She turned back to the window. "Wish I could've helped."

He looked at her. *So much hurt, so much hate. Was I like that back then? Am I still like that?*

She slumped down in her seat. "I'm grabbing some z's. Wake me when we get there. Or if we're going to crash." She was snoring in seconds, leaving him alone with resurrected memories, all of them painful.

The ambush had ended the Tainchel and the danger to the Heroka. After, he'd contacted Justice and CSIS, sending a list of the remaining Tainchel agents they'd identified, present locations, recent activities, and a note saying, "We know who you are. We know where you are. We will kill to protect ourselves. Back off." They backed off. CSIS disbanded the Tainchel, and an uneasy truce began.

The truce lasted. He and Stelle didn't. She argued against the ambush, the killings. He argued that the Heroka were fighting for their very existence.

In the end, they'd just argued.

They split. He always told himself that they'd get back together one day. Then she was dead, and that day was never going to come, leaving him with memories, regrets, and his love for a dead woman. A love that had destroyed him and Leiddia.

Gelert nuzzled him from behind. He touched the dog's mind and sensed only excitement over this unexpected trip after two years of seclusion, a feeling of anticipation of a coming adventure—the doggie equivalent of "change is good."

"Wish I could agree with you, buddy," he muttered. What he felt was foreboding, not anticipation. In the past day, he had lost two friends in Mary and Mitch, and five wolf brothers, learned that an old girlfriend was a murder suspect, become responsible for a troubled teenager who despised him, had an old enemy resurrected, narrowly missed being killed, and had been forced to abandon his home. Change sucked.

And he'd had an encounter with an apparent spirit. He thought again of the words of the silver wolf. *You are meant for another purpose.*

Dream on, Fluffy, he thought, as the trees flowed by beneath the plane. *Nobody's pulling my strings.*

COMDOWTAH PAUSED BETWEEN mouthfuls of dinner. The voices were speaking. They never left anymore. They were always there, whispering in some dark corner, too low to hear but too loud to ignore.

This time, a feeling of triumphant joy accompanied their words.

They are coming! the voices cried. *The Wolf and the Boy draw near.*

"When?" Comdowtah asked, not wanting to know.

Tonight! It begins tonight!

Comdowtah swore silently. The beginning…of the end.

CHAPTER 14

MARY REPRISED

MARY TWO RIVERS leaned against a jack pine that was larger and taller than any jack pine had a right to be. She'd been walking through this dark forest since last night, haunted by a feeling in her heart that she was supposed to be doing something, supposed to be going somewhere. But she still had no idea what or where that might be, and she needed to rest.

Above her, the biggest, fullest moon she'd ever seen shone down through treetops rising taller than the buildings in Toronto she'd gawked at when she'd visited the U of T after being accepted.

Won't be going there, she thought. *Won't be doing a lot of things.*

Like living.

Two things had become unpleasantly clear to her.

First, she'd figured out she was dead, which had severely pissed her off. It had taken her longer to come to that conclusion than perhaps it should have. Standing unseen, unheard, unnoticed while a coroner zipped up a body bag with *her* body inside really should have clued her in right away. But since this was the first time she'd ever died, she decided to cut herself some slack.

Harder had been watching her grandfather, seeing his grief when he recognized her body. She'd tried to call to him, to hug him, to tell him that she was still there, but he couldn't hear her, couldn't feel her touch, didn't know she was there beside him.

And then she wasn't. There, that is. One moment, she'd been staring miserably at the scene of her grisly death. An eye blink later, she was in this strange, huge, dark forest.

That was when she'd discovered the second thing.

She could still smell it around her, the way she'd smelled it in that rocky clearing where she'd died. Mushrooms, fungus, rotting wood. The sickly sweet smell of corruption and death.

The creature that had killed her had come from this very place. Wherever this place was.

Exhausted, she stood again and began to push deeper into the forest, following the strange pull in her heart, wondering if it was possible to die twice in one night.

PART II:

SPIRIT DREAMS

"We know what the animals do, what are the needs of the beavers, the bear, the salmon, and other creatures, because long ago men married them and acquired this knowledge from their animal wives. Today the priests say we lie, but we know better."

—*Diamond Jenness*

CHAPTER 15

THINKING LIKE A PREDATOR

WHEN **G**WYN **PULLED THEIR PLANE** up to a rickety looking wooden dock on Deer Lake under a mid-afternoon sun, Ed was waiting, leaning against the same battered Ford pickup that Gwyn remembered and still looking as weathered and indestructible as the rocks he stood on. His long gray hair was in a ponytail, and he wore a plaid shirt, jeans, and a deerskin jacket with a thunderbird design in beadwork.

Gelert jumped out of the plane and bounded up to Ed. Ed took Gelert's head in both hands, rubbing him behind his ears. "Hello, you great beast, you." He and Gwyn embraced each other.

"Ed, I'm so sorry about Mary," Gwyn said, wanting to say more but not finding the words.

Ed nodded. "Thank you, Gray Legs. She knew you were her friend." He eyed Caz where she still stood beside the plane.

"Ed, this is Cassandra Meadows—"

"Oh, god. *Caz*, not Cassandra," she interrupted.

"She's…I'm kind of looking after her for a while," he said, not knowing where to start to explain how she came to be there.

"Looking after me? What am I? Seven?"

Ed looked as if he were fighting back a grin. He walked up to Caz and shook her hand. "Welcome to Thunder Lake. You Heroka, too?"

Caz just nodded. Rizzo poked his nose out of the pocket of her hoodie.

Ed shot a grin at Gwyn. "Two Heroka and a rat. Vera's gonna love this. C'mon." Grabbing one of their bags, he walked back to his truck.

Gwyn unloaded the other bags from the plane, tossing Caz her duffel.

"Who's Vera?" she asked.

He grimaced. "Ed's wife. She knows I'm Heroka. Not my biggest fan."

"Like you have so many. Why'd he call you 'Gray Legs'?"

"Running joke between us. Ojibwe legend says that calling a wolf by its name might attract it. So they used other names—Golden Tooth, Silent One, Gray Legs."

"I could suggest some for you."

"Can we at least try to get along?"

They threw their bags into the truck bed, and Gelert jumped in after them, sniffing at a cooler. Ed opened it. "I made some sandwiches. Figured you'd be hungry. Ham or turkey? Hope you're not vegetarian, Caz."

"Rodents eat anything," she said. "Turkey, please."

Sure, with Ed, she's polite, Gwyn thought, taking a ham. "Thanks. I figured we'd eat in town."

Ed opened a package of cold cuts for Gelert, who devoured them in two bites. "I want to take you up to where—" His pause was just enough to notice. "—where Mary was killed. Before we lose the light today. Hasn't rained since, but it might rain overnight, and I don't want anything to be washed away. I'm hoping those Heroka senses of yours will find something the cops missed."

Gwyn nodded. "I might be able to pick up a scent. Can't promise anything, but if it was an animal, I'll know which kind."

Ed looked at him. "And if it wasn't?"

He knew what Ed was asking. If it hadn't been an animal, then the suspicion would swing heavily toward a Heroka killing. And toward Leiddia. "I'll be able to tell if her scent was there, too," he said quietly, remembering that scent, remembering all of her scents. Her breath as she lay beside him at night, her hair in the morning, her skin when the sun warmed it. Remembering the woman he'd loved, maybe still did.

"Whose scent?" Caz asked, between mouthfuls.

"A local Heroka named Leiddia Barker. We used to be…close."

"How close?" she asked.

Ignoring her, he turned to Ed. "Has there been any talk?"

"Just some muttering around town so far, from a few who know she's Heroka."

"I'll be straight with you," Gwyn said. "If I don't find her scent there, I'll be trying to prove she's innocent, not guilty."

"So I'm guessing *close* close," Caz muttered.

"Works for me," Ed said. He shook his head. "Can't believe she could've done this. Not to Mary. Not to anyone."

"Neither can I. Your email mentioned an earlier killing, before Mary," Gwyn said, wanting to change the subject from Leiddia.

Ed nodded. "Kid named Rick Calhoun. Killed working on top of the dam at night a week ago. Can't get you into where he died. Probably been too long anyway, and it's rained since he was killed. Cops gave the same story—some sort of animal attack. You ask me, it's the main reason they're saying an animal killed Mary, too. One easy answer to explain two killings. Even if they can't identify the animal. Even if we've never had two fatal animal attacks in a year, let alone a week apart."

They finished eating. "Let's go," Ed said, climbing into the truck. Caz got in the other side. Gwyn started to get in as well, but stopped. Turning to the surrounding forest, he closed his eyes and reached out with his mind. Nothing. Gelert whined from the back of the truck.

"Gwyn?" Ed called.

He opened his eyes. "There used to be a wolf pack here. I can't sense them. I can't sense any of my totem. Wolf, coyote, fox. Nothing." He turned to Caz. "What about you?"

Leaning out the window, Caz closed her eyes. A few moments later, she opened them and shrugged. "Nothing. I don't have much of a range yet, though."

Ed looked grim. "The flooding for the dam wiped out a lot of territories. All the guides say the same thing—nothing left to hunt."

Gwyn shook his head. Something was wrong here, something more than flooded land. "Guess that's it," he said, keeping his thoughts to himself. Giving the woods another look, he got into the truck.

ON THE DRIVE to where Mary had died, he told Ed of the Tainchel attack and Mitch's death, and how Caz came to be with him. He omitted his encounter with Mahigan, the wolf spirit, as well as the part about the partially eaten bodies, the strange smell, and the bullet-ridden naked corpse. He hadn't told Caz about any of that and wasn't ready to get into it now. It was all too strange, and he didn't see how it could possibly relate to Mary's death here. Besides, he didn't want Ed thinking he was losing his mind.

Ed was silent through the story, but when he stopped the truck at the base of a slope below a forested ridge, he turned to Caz. "I have lost a granddaughter. You have lost your foster parents and a friend." He put out his hand. "We are family in our loss." Caz swallowed and shook Ed's hand. Ed got out of the truck, closing the door behind him.

Caz wiped at her eyes, trying to cover it by running a hand through her hair. "He's okay," she said quietly.

Gwyn nodded. "He's a friend. I don't call many people that."

"Again, you ever think maybe it's you?"

Again, sometimes. He got out of the truck and walked to where Ed stared up the slope. Gelert trailing him. "Sure you want to do this?"

Ed nodded. "You won't find anything if you can't find the spot. And you won't find the spot without me." Without another word, he started up the hill. Gwyn followed, Caz and Gelert behind him.

Ed fell silent again as he led them along a winding path through thick bush. Gwyn respected that silence, knowing how hard this must be for him, returning to where Mary had died. He stopped Ed several times as they went, dropping down to sniff the path, but he couldn't pick up anything unusual beyond forest smells and traces of humans. He filed the human scents away. One of them might be the killer. Thankfully, none of the smells so far belonged to Leiddia.

They stepped into a small clearing enclosed by a rock wall ahead and to the left. To the right, the ground sloped away sharply, the pines trees thinning as they ran down to the dam and its captured lake.

He sniffed the air. He could smell it. The ground here was rocky, so he could still see it too.

Blood. Dried now, but blood. He swallowed. Mary's blood. She'd died right there. He walked over to it, while Ed stayed well back, Caz and Gelert beside him.

He knelt down, sniffing, isolating as many smells as he could, matching each one to the scents he'd detected on the path. They all matched—except one.

Something else had been here. And to his surprise, he'd smelled it before—but not here. The smell of mushrooms, fungus, and rotting wood. Of decay and corruption. The same strange scent from Cil y Blaidd where the Tainchel had died.

He stood up, scarcely believing his own senses. How could that be possible? What connection could Mary's death here have to the Tainchel attack on his home?

"Show me the footprint," he said, still pondering his discovery.

The print Ed had found was now very faint, but Gwyn could make it out. He knelt and sniffed again, finding the same strange scent here, too. But to his relief, one smell was missing from the entire scene. He stood up. "It wasn't Leiddia. She wasn't here." Ed just nodded, but his shoulders relaxed a bit. Gelert wagged his tail.

"Animal?" Ed asked.

He shook his head. "No scent that I recognized." He climbed back to the top of the slope.

Ed looked at him. "Not an animal and not Leiddia. So what was it?"

Instead of answering, he walked back to where Mary's blood still stained the ground. He looked up at the rock walls. The one facing the path was too high. But the other one, the lower one....

"Gray Legs, what are you doing?"

"Thinking like a predator. Whatever killed Mary was here, waiting for her."

"Why couldn't it have tracked her along the path?" Ed asked.

"Because on the path, I didn't smell what I smell here."

"What kind of smell?"

"Sweet like rotting wood, bitter like mushrooms, bad like something dead. Remind you of anything?"

Ed's mouth twitched, but he just shook his head, his face as unreadable as always.

Gwyn sniffed the cool air dropping off the rock face. The same smell again. Picking out a route, he began to climb, pulling himself from one handhold and toehold to the next until he hauled himself over the top.

Crouching on all fours, he sniffed the ground. The smell was almost overpowering here. A small pile of gray-green lumps lay on a flat rock near the edge. He picked one up and sniffed it. Some kind of moss, mixed with saliva and the same strange smell. Scooping up the lumps, he put them in a pocket of his leather jacket.

He tracked the scent away from the edge. The ground turned from rock to sun-baked dirt and then to softer earth under the cover of coarse grasses. Something had trampled down the grasses in one spot. He brushed away leaves and pine needles from the spot, revealing a small indentation in the soil, made by something tapering to a point. Someone using a walking stick, maybe.

The only other mark was more than a foot away, an oval depression the size of his palm. The two marks together didn't resemble any animal print he recognized. Besides, that would imply a foot almost eighteen inches long. He sniffed. Both marks held the same strange scent.

Farther into the trees, pine needles softly carpeted the ground, and he found no sign of further marks or any other smell rising above the ubiquitous scent of pine. Walking back to the top of the rock face, he stared into the clearing below.

"Find anything?" Ed called.

Not answering, he crouched down. The modern human slipped into the dark forests of his mind, and something more primitive emerged. Something feral, something hungry.

The hunter. The predator.

It crouched here that night, a half moon above, chill air on its skin, the scent of its prey in its nostrils. Prey that stood below. A young woman. Mary. All it took was one leap.

He leapt.

Ed jumped back swearing as Gwyn landed beside him. "Scared the shit out of me. What was that about?"

Standing, Gwyn looked up at the wall. "It was up there. Waiting for Mary."

Caz swallowed, and Gelert growled. Ed looked up, his hands balling into fists. "What was it?"

Gwyn shook his head.

"But you found something?"

"Same smell, only stronger. And some strange prints." He described the marks he'd found. Again, something flickered across Ed's face. Gwyn reached into his pocket. "I found these too. It's chewed moss."

Ed took one of the lumps. He sniffed it. His jaw clenched, but he said nothing.

"There's something else," Gwyn said. He had to tell Ed, now that it could be connected to Mary's death. "I've encountered this smell before." He related what he'd found at Cil y Blaidd where the Tainchel had been killed, but still omitting his encounter with Mahigan. That was still too strange and, somehow, too personal.

"The guy *ate* people? Eww, gross," Caz said, making a face. "But how? If he'd been shot so many times? And what has that to do with, you know...?" She waved at the patch of blood.

"I don't understand either, but whatever the connection, it's more proof that Leiddia's innocent." He turned to Ed again. "Ed? You ready to tell me what you're thinking? Because I know you recognized what I was describing."

Ed said nothing. Instead, he walked back to the top of the slope to stare at the lake below. Gwyn sighed and came to stand beside him. A chill morning wind was in their faces, whipping up the water. Waves pawed the stony shore, like some beast scrambling to escape the lake. He knew better than to push Ed to talk before he was ready. He just shook his head. "All that land flooded."

"Thing's not even operational yet," Ed said, nodding at the brooding mass of the dam. "Part of where they flooded was an ancient burial ground. The band council managed to get a court order blocking them from deepening the lake any further. Won't stand up, just slow them down." He sighed. "Charlie's pissed with me over that. He got a job in the maintenance crew, but it won't start until the site's producing power."

Gwyn stared at the lake, struck again by what his Heroka senses told him. This whole area felt different, profoundly changed from when he'd lived here. It felt empty. "I still can't sense any of my totem."

"Me neither," Caz said, coming to stand beside them.

"And I don't think it's just our totems. I don't even hear a bird. It's as if all the animals have disappeared."

Ed nodded at the lake below. "That thing destroyed migration routes, grazing paths, hunting territories."

"But there should still be *something* left here," Caz said.

"There is," Gwyn said. "Something killed Mary." He turned his back on the water. "So are you ready yet to tell me what you think it is?"

Ed turned back to stare at the bloodstained ground. He didn't say anything for several breaths. When he spoke, it was just one word. "*Windigo.*"

"Windy what?" Caz asked.

"You've got to be kidding," Gwyn said.

Ed shook his head, then with a final look at where Mary had died, he turned and disappeared along the path.

"What just happened?" Caz asked.

Gwyn shook his head. "Go ask Ed."

"Asshole," she muttered, and stalked off after Ed.

He started to follow them. Suddenly, the hairs on the back of his neck stood up. He spun around. Gelert growled again.

Nothing.

The feeling had been unmistakable—the sense of being watched. He listened and sniffed as he scanned the area. The only thing moving was the lake, its waves scratching at the pebbled shore below. With a last uneasy look around, he turned and left the clearing, Gelert beside him.

CHAPTER 16

COPS AND COUGARS

KATE CHECKED HER WATCH as the bus pulled into Thunder Lake. Seven forty-five at night and, being this much further north, dark already. Groaning, she rubbed her eyes, groggy from dozing off at the end of the four-hour ride.

Zach stirred. Almost simultaneously, Quincy woke, and she wondered not for the first time about the link the two seemed to share. The dog waited for a pat from Zach, then moved forward in the aisle to let him stand. Macready handled their carry-on bags as Kate helped Zach into his parka and off the bus.

She shivered as she stepped down. Colder here too. While the driver unloaded their suitcases from under the bus, she looked around the street. Thunder Lake was too small for a bus terminal, so they'd stopped in front of a one-storey orange-bricked building that declared itself the city hall and library. The rest of the street was a mix of small houses with white siding and some commercial buildings, including a garage, a bar, and an outfitter, all of it reminding her far too much of her hometown.

In the parking lot behind the building, they found a red Toyota Camry, the MNR car that Lessard said would be waiting for them. They drove five blocks to their small motel, a white, L-shaped two-storey building on a dead-end sitting beside the Thunder River, the dark sluggish waterway that cut a winding course through town. The motel had eight rooms per floor, all with bright blue doors facing the parking lot. Kate and Zach had adjoining rooms on the first floor, Macready on the second. A diner called The Outfitter sat across the road.

After getting Zach settled in and asking Macready to take him to the diner for some supper, she drove to the OPP station. Lessard had informed the senior officer there of her coming arrival, confirming her authority in investigating the two deaths. To give her a cover story for visiting the police, perhaps more than once during her stay, the MNR had instituted a new policy at the request of CSIS. Citing the recent deaths and activist attacks, the Ministry now required all new project staff to check in with the OPP on arrival in town for a criminal background check.

The OPP building was on the main highway a half mile out of town, a red-bricked two storey with an attached garage for the cruisers. A uniformed female officer, stocky and white, sat at a desk behind the counter. Kate identified herself as a new employee on the dam project and asked for Staff Sergeant Bill Thornton, the senior officer.

The female officer introduced herself as Constable Burrell. "But you can call me Willie," she said, as she led Kate past desks covered with file folders and coffee cups to a frosted glass door at the back. She tapped twice, then stuck her head inside. "Kate Morgan, sir. She just joined the dam project." Willie motioned Kate in, closing the door behind as she left.

Thornton was big and barrel-chested with a waist that had caught up to his chest. He had sandy, crew cut hair above big ears and a weathered, reddish face. He stuck out a huge hand that swallowed Kate's, and then motioned her to a rickety-looking swivel chair.

Leaning dangerously far back in his own chair, he sized her up. "Been here for seventeen years and never had so much as a call from CSIS. Now, the feds want to do our job for us?"

Welcome to the team, she thought. "I realize—"

"I could understand," he interrupted, "if this was about the vandalism at the dam. Been asking for help on that for months—and getting nothing. Then we have a couple of animal attacks, and you folks are all over us."

She forced a smile. "Sergeant, we believe the incidents at the dam and the killings are related. I can't give you details yet, but CSIS views this as a national security issue."

His eyes narrowed.

"And one of its highest priorities," she added, which was true as far as the Tainchel was concerned.

He considered this, then sat forward. "All right. So how can I help you?"

At least she had his attention now. "We requested DNA samples from the two victims."

He nodded. "Mary—Mary Two Rivers, the second victim—she was still in the morgue...." He sighed, shaking his head. "So Dr. Capshaw, our coroner, was able to prepare her samples as requested: swabs from the wounds for saliva testing, along with any foreign hairs, preferably with roots intact, found on the body or clothes. A CSIS chopper picked up those samples today."

Jonas had told her the CSIS lab could turn around the results from a polymerase chain reaction DNA test in under forty-eight hours. Pulling out her tablet, she made a note to expect the results the day after tomorrow. "Good. And the first victim? The one found at the dam itself?"

"Rick Calhoun." He looked out his window, and shook his head again. "I play hockey with his dad. Anyway, we buried Rick a week ago. Capshaw says the embalming and body preparation would've destroyed any chance of getting a sample from the body, even if we exhumed it."

Shit. Jonas wouldn't like that.

"However, Capshaw kept Rick's clothes, at least what was left of them. Bagged them and sent them to the OPP forensics centre in Wawa last week. He says your lab might be able to recover some hairs from them. Your Mr. Lessard said he'd have them picked up tomorrow."

She made another note to expect the DNA test results from Rick Calhoun's killing the day after Mary Two Rivers's results.

"Anything else you need?" he asked.

A job without dead bodies? "How common are animal attacks around here?"

"Not very. Maybe one every two years. And rarely fatal. Last incident was over a year ago. That animal belonged to a local lady named Leiddia Barker."

"Her dog?"

He ran his hand through his hair. "Cougar."

She blinked. "Cougar? She has a pet cougar?"

"Had. Thing died a while back, so you can cross Leiddia off your list."

Or add her to the top of my possible Heroka list, she thought. *A pet cougar?*

Thorton's eyes narrowed. "So…what? CSIS thinks these protestors are bringing in wild animals to attack the dam workers?"

She could work with that. She nodded. "It's one of the scenarios we're investigating, since it's happened at other protest sites." Which was true, if you believed Jonas's tales of the Heroka and counted human shapeshifters as animals. "So tell me about this Leiddia Barker."

Thornton shrugged. "She lives in a cabin her mom left to her when she passed away, north of town near the new dam site."

"Have there been any other incidents with her?"

"Nothing recent. Like I said, the cougar died over a year ago."

"Nothing recent? Meaning…?"

"She was involved in some early protests against the dam, but…." He shifted in his chair. "No. Not really."

"But there's been something?"

He waved a hand. "Local superstition, Indian legends, that sort of stuff. Let me assure you, Leiddia Barker has nothing to do with these deaths."

A knock sounded on Thornton's door. Willie Burrell poked her head in, her round face drawn in tight lines. "Sir, there's a mob moving up Assiniboine Road."

Thornton scowled at her. "Mob? Another protest?"

Willie shook her head. "Looks like they're headed for Leiddia Barker's place."

Thornton shot Kate a look, as if this were somehow her fault. "Willie, stay here and cover the desk. Radio Mueller to get up to Leiddia's place pronto. I'll meet him there."

Willie left. Thornton grabbed his hat and jacket from behind his door. "I'd suggest you get back to your motel, Ms. Morgan."

"Is this related to the killings, Sergeant?"

He stormed out without answering. She walked to the front where Willie had just finished talking on the police radio. "Uh, Sergeant Thornton hadn't finished with me," she lied. "Okay if I wait here till he comes back?"

"Sure," Willie said. "I could use some company."

Kate pulled up a chair. "Wow! A mob!"

Willie shook her head. "Hope you're not getting a bad impression of our town. Things aren't usually like this. Bar fights, sure, D&D's, B&E's...but not mobs and killings and...." Her voice trailed off.

And people being eaten. "Killings?" Kate said, playing dumb. "Is it not safe here?"

"No, no," Willie said quickly. "Just a couple of animal attacks. Very unusual...." She went on to explain the two deaths, and Kate pretended she was hearing it all for the first time.

"Thanks for the warning. I'll make sure I don't go wandering around in the bush. So what do you think this mob wants with this poor woman? This...."

"Leiddia Barker." Willie considered her, as if deciding whether to trust this newcomer. Kate sat patiently, trying to look innocent. "You have to understand, Ms. Morgan—"

"Call me Kate."

"Kate, you have to understand that folks around here hold to some beliefs you might find...unusual, coming from a big city."

"I'm Cree," Kate said, surprised at how quickly she volunteered that.

"Well, then, you might understand better than most. Your people and the Ojibwe have lots of legends of animal spirits and such. Still some practicing shamans around here, too. My point is that what somebody might call superstition might be part of somebody else's belief system, Ojibwe and white."

Kate nodded. "Sure, but how does this relate to Leiddia Barker?"

"Sarge tell you about the cougar?"

"That she kept one as a pet?"

Willie shook her head. "Didn't keep it, so to speak, but it was always around her cabin, or at least never far away. Well, some people believed Leiddia could control that animal. Make it do things she wanted."

Excitement battled with an old fear inside Kate. Excitement won, beating away an urge to return to the motel and the escape of sleep. She pulled her chair closer. "I used to love stories about that kind of stuff. Tell me more."

AFTER DINNER at The Outfitter, Colin Macready accompanied Zach as he walked Quincy for the night. Back at the motel, he checked that Zach could get ready for bed himself, then said goodnight and returned to his own room.

Opening his notebook computer, he established a secure link and submitted a brief video report to Simon Jonas. "Ten-fifteen p.m. Have arrived in town. Trip uneventful. Boy's down for the night. Mother's checking in with the OPP. Next update tomorrow evening."

Shutting down the computer, he flopped on the bed and began mindlessly flipping channels, thinking about Zach Morgan.

To Jonas, the kid was an abomination in the eyes of God. Macready went along with Jonas's Bible thumping because he knew better than to let on that he didn't give a shit about religion one way or the other. He actually shared Jonas's distaste for the little half-breed, but for a different reason.

He just didn't like freaks.

AFTER MR. MACREADY left him, Zach did circuits of his room until he was completely familiar with its layout. Then he got ready for bed, made sure Quincy was set for the night, and got under the covers. He closed his eyes.

And began to dream.

In his dream, Zach now sat with Wisakejack outside the teepee under a canopy of stars blazing in a night sky. "So what about this flood that destroyed the world?" Zach asked.

Wisakejack was smoking a long pipe and letting out puffs of smoke that formed themselves into the shapes of different animals. "The flood. Right. Well, it happened not long after I got tricked by this shaman and kidnapped to be his student, which translated into doing all the crap jobs around his lodge." Wisakejack slapped his knee. "Man, the stories I could tell about—" He stopped as

Zach glared. "Uh, none of which are really relevant to your current problem—although his bones *are* buried around here somewhere. Anyway, I eventually escape, because I was way smarter than the shaman—"

"Then how'd he catch you in the first place?"

"Shaddup. Anyway, I get home to find that my brother had changed himself into a wolf."

"Why'd he do that?"

Wisakejack scratched his head. "You know, I never asked him. Guess it seemed like a good idea at the time. Anyway, I'm happy to find my brother again, even a four-legged version, but then the woodpecker tells me the news."

"Woodpecker?"

"The one that found my brother. Stop interrupting. The woodpecker tells me that the *Misipisiwas* are not happy with my bro."

"The Missy who's?"

"The Great Water Lynxes," Wisakejack said. "They live in deep water and rule the deep places of the world. They're the head honchos of a bunch of spirits who aren't too fond of humankind. They look like they have tufted ears like lynxes, but those are really horns. Most spirits of the deep places have horns. So they aren't really lynxes. Not cats at all. But early humans who had the bad luck to meet them, but the good luck to escape, thought they were some kind of water lynx, and the name sort of stuck."

"So why were they unhappy with your brother?"

"Well, you see, he's new to being a wolf and doesn't know how to act. He's killed way too much game. Got greedy, like humans sometimes do, and the Lynxes especially aren't fond of greedy creatures. Now I know the Lynxes and their tricks. I warn my brother to stay away from deep water, and to never try to jump over a stream, no matter how narrow it seems." Wisakejack shook his head. "Of course, if he'd listened, I wouldn't be telling you this story. One day, my brother's chasing a moose and jumps over a narrow stream. Problem is, the stream only *looks* narrow. He falls in and sinks down to *Saputawan*, the underwater lair of the Lynxes...." Wisakejack paused, his jaw muscles working, "where they kill him."

Zach swallowed. "I'm sorry."

Wisakejack shrugged. "Long time ago," he said quietly, but his jaw kept working.

"What did you do?"

Wisakejack stared into the fire, all traces of his usual mirth gone. "The Lynxes, they'd dance each night on the beach beside the lake that hid Saputawan, tossing my brother's fur back and forth, like it was a game. So one night, I creep close and shoot them with my arrows. But I only wound them, and they slip into the water and back down to their lair. I wait. Soon, *Ayekis* appears, the frog spirit and a shaman of strong medicine. He's going down to heal the Lynxes and stop the flood."

"Uh, what flood?"

"The Lynxes rule the deep places, including the seas. Legend was that if they died, the waters would pour out from all the deep places in the spirit world and flood the Earth."

"You knew that? And you still tried to kill them?"

"Hey, it was just a legend, right? Besides, they'd killed my brother. Wouldn't you want me to avenge you, little brother?"

"Not if it meant killing everyone in the world!"

Wisakejack shrugged. "We have different codes of honor, I can see that. Anyway, so I kill the frog, put on his skin, enter Saputawan in disguise, and kill the Lynxes, and send them back to the Spirit World. Brother avenged."

Different codes of honor, for sure, Zach thought. "And the flood?"

"Uh, yeah. That flood legend? Turns out it was less legend and more flood. Yep, lots of water. World drowned, including the first humans and most of the animals too."

Zach swallowed. "You destroyed the world?"

"Personally, I blame the Lynxes. But hey, I recreated everything—the earth, people, plants, animals. So, you know, no big."

"*You* recreated the world? Like, you're *God*?"

Wisakejack shook his head. "No, no, no. Nothing like that. I just worked with what Kitche Manitou gave me and what was at hand. But that's another story for another time. Hopefully, I won't have to do that again."

"Hopefully?"

"That's why I told you this story. That's what you have to help me prevent. Another flood." He looked hard at Zach. "End of the world. Again."

CHAPTER *17*

THE CAT

GWYN STARED AT THE PASSING FOREST darkening in the failing light as Ed negotiated the truck along the twisting logging road toward town. No one had spoken since they'd left the scene of Mary's death. Caz, sitting between them, finally broke the silence. "So what's a *windigo*?"

Gwyn snorted. "A story to scare kids."

"A windigo," Ed said, ignoring him, "is a person infected by the immortal Windigo spirit."

"Which is…bad?"

"They change into a flesh-eating monster," Gwyn said.

"They shapeshift, you mean?" Caz asked. "And *you* are having trouble believing that? You, who can change into a carnivorous beast?"

"It's not the same thing," he said. "The Heroka exist. We're not some myth."

"The Windigo spirit is the spirit of hunger," Ed said, "a hunger born of greed and gluttony. It is the spirit my people have always feared more than any other."

"How can you get, uh, *infected* with a spirit?" Caz asked.

"A greedy person can attract the Windigo spirit. My *misoomish*—my grandfather—told us tales of the Windigo as children, how it hunted our people each winter, when families were alone in their hunting territories, when food was scarce and starvation as close as one bad hunt. If a person was greedy, ate too much of the food, they would attract the Windigo spirit—and become a windigo."

"And again, this is bad how?"

"They'd kill and eat their own family," Gwyn said. Caz paled. "Yeah, I know the stories. Just a way to teach kids the importance of the hunt and family and sharing."

Ed said nothing. Caz shivered. "So what makes you think this is a windigo, anyway?" she asked Ed.

"Because of what Gray Legs found where Mary was killed. The tracks, the smell, the moss. A windigo's feet are twice the length of a man's, with pointed heels and one huge toe. It smells of rotting wood, mushrooms, and corruption. And when a windigo can't find human flesh, it will chew moss."

Caz looked at Gwyn. "You found that same smell where the Tainchel were killed? Did you find those other signs as well?"

Gwyn shook his head. "No, but I wasn't looking for anything else. I wanted to bury Mitch and get out of there as soon as we could."

They all fell silent again. He shook his head. Whatever killed Mary, it was something real, not a supernatural creature. But then he remembered the fear of the wolf pack of Cil y Blaidd. They hadn't been running from some common animal. But what had they encountered?

And then there were the strange warnings of Mahigan, the silver wolf. *They die at the hands of something else*, Mahigan had said of the Tainchel. *Something I have fought since the beginning. Something that all life must fight to survive.*

Something. Big help. He shook his head again. Windigo spirits. Wolf spirits. He didn't believe any of it.

They pulled up in front of Ed's store. "Come on," Ed said to Gwyn with a grin, their disagreement forgotten. "Vera's dying to see you again." He went into the store.

"Don't let Vera see Rizzo," Gwyn said to Caz as they followed him inside.

Vera was serving a customer. When she saw Gwyn, her smile disappeared. She gave him a grim-faced nod, stared hard at Caz, and then glared at Ed.

Ed shrugged and led Gwyn and Caz into the back room. He cleared some invoices from a wooden table. "Grab a chair."

They sat, and Ed looked at Gwyn. "So you don't buy my windigo theory." He held up a hand before Gwyn could reply. "That's okay. Didn't expect you would. That's why I didn't say anything at first. But you found no scent of either Leiddia or any animal. So what does that leave?"

Not a windigo. "With the footprint you found, I'd say we're still looking for a shapeshifter. A Heroka."

"With a serious dietary problem," Caz muttered.

"So how do we start looking?" Ed asked.

The door from the store opened. Vera came in. She shot Ed a dark look, then turned to Gwyn, her lips a thin line. "Gwyn."

"Vera."

She looked at Caz. "One of your kind?" Gwyn nodded. Shaking her head, she turned to Ed. "Where are they staying?"

"Storeroom," Ed replied, meeting her glare and holding it.

"Or maybe a motel...?" Caz offered.

Vera looked at Gwyn again. Her lip quivered. "You going to find who killed our Mary?" she asked, her voice barely a whisper.

Gwyn felt Ed's eyes on him. He nodded. "I'll find them, Vera."

Vera stared hard at him for a few more seconds, and then turned to Ed. "They use the *back* door." She left, closing the door behind her.

Caz shifted in her chair. "Jeez...."

"She grows on you," Ed said, grinning at Caz. He turned to Gwyn. "So how do we find your mystery Heroka?"

"I'll scout around town, looking for anyone with the Mark."

"I can help. We can cover twice as much territory," Caz said.

"Not by yourself. You'll come with me."

"Always wondered what that looks like to your kind. The Mark," Ed said.

"Why can't I go around on my own?" Caz asked.

He ignored her. "It's like a superimposed image that we can see on each other, if we focus in a way—" He shrugged. "—in a way we just know how to do."

"What kind of image?"

"Depends," Gwyn replied. "Alphas—adult Heroka—show their totem animal. For Caz, I see a dark brown otter. For me, she sees a timber wolf, big, black—"

"Mangy, bossy, grouchy...."

"For whelps—pre-teen Heroka who haven't done their spirit quest to learn their totem animal—their Mark will cycle through animals in their totem *species*. So when I was young—"

"Ever so long ago," Caz muttered.

"—I could've shown any canid. Dog, wolf, coyote."

Ed looked thoughtful. "It's like you show your spirit guide."

"One more wrinkle: Sleepers. Half-human, half-Heroka. They'll never become a full Heroka unless one of us wakes them. They show just a green aura around them. No hint of any animal."

"So that's what you saw on Leiddia, when you first met her," Ed said.

Gwyn nodded, remembering that young, pretty woman he'd first met right here in Ed's store.

"Wait. This Leiddia was a Sleeper?" Caz asked.

Gwyn sighed. "Yes. I woke her. Five years ago."

"Always wondered how you did that," Ed said.

The phone rang in the next room. Gwyn heard Vera answer it. "Not something we generally talk about," he said.

Ed just nodded. He respected people's privacy. Caz did not. "An exchange of bodily fluids is involved," she said, grinning. "And I can just bet which fluids you two used."

Gwyn glared at her, but she just winked at Ed, who smiled. "Maybe Leiddia's noticed someone with the Mark herself," Ed suggested.

He'd wondered that himself. "I'll ask her when I see her."

"I can take you up there tonight," Ed said.

Gwyn hesitated. He wasn't ready for that reunion yet. "In the morning."

"Afraid?" Caz asked with a small smile.

"No," he lied. "I've been awake since yesterday morning. I'm beat and—"

The door flew open, and Vera rushed in. "Ed! That was Elizabeth. She said there's a mob on their way to Leiddia's. Somebody heard about the footprint. They think she killed Mary."

Gwyn swore. He jumped up. "Ed, can you drive us?"

Ed stood, grabbing his coat. "How'd Elizabeth hear about the mob?"

Vera swallowed. "Charlie's leading them."

Ed stopped, his jaw muscles working. "Call Thornton. Tell him to get a cruiser up there. Fast." Without another word, he headed out the door.

"Guess you're seeing your old squeeze tonight after all," Caz said grinning, as they followed Ed to his truck.

The drive to Leiddia's cabin brought back too many memories for Gwyn. The last time he'd been on this road, he'd been going the other away. Leaving Thunder Lake. Leaving Leiddia.

"So I'm guessing this Leiddia is a predator totem, what with her being a suspect," Caz said as Ed gunned the truck up a hill on the bumpy road.

Gwyn clenched his jaw. "Cat. She shifts to a black leopard."

"Oh, great," she said, stroking Rizzo protectively. "Mitch told me that you have to petition the Circle to wake a Sleeper."

He swore silently. "I didn't petition. I just did it."

"Shit. And you dump on *me* for blowing off rules?"

He was getting tired of defending his past. Or was he feeling guilty? "Her stepfather was beating up her mom. She was living with them. I figured she and her mom needed some protection."

"Why the petition step?" Ed asked.

Caz shrugged. "So the Heroka head honchos can make sure that the candidate isn't some sort of homicidal…." Her voice trailed off. Ed shot Gwyn a look.

"She's a good person," Gwyn said, knowing he was right.

"Yeah? How well did you know her?" Caz asked.

"We lived together for nearly two years."

"So why the split?" she asked.

Because she thought I loved a dead woman more than I loved her. "That's personal." But he *had* loved Leiddia. Intensely and deeply. And now?

Ed turned the truck onto a rutted path, which seemed more intended for walking than driving. "Leiddia was Mary's friend. I never thought she did this either. That's why I sent for you. To protect her if something happened." He wrestled the truck around a curve and into a clearing in front of a wooden cabin.

"Something like this, I'm guessing," Caz said.

A mob of maybe two dozen people stood facing the cabin, about twenty feet back. They were a mix of Ojibwe and whites, mostly male. Some carried electric lanterns, some lit torches. Several had rifles. Ed stopped the truck at the edge of the clearing.

"What? No pitchforks?" Caz said. "What self-respecting mob brings torches and forgets pitchforks?"

On the cabin's porch stood a tall, slim woman, dressed in a black parka open over a dark blue top and tight jeans. Long black hair hung to her waist, framing a triangle of a face, with a small chin and sharp features except for a full mouth. She stood with her hands on her hips, unarmed, facing the mob. A large black cat peered from behind her legs.

"That her?" Caz asked. "Man, your ex is a hottie."

Gwyn ran his eyes over the face and the body that he had known so well. He swallowed, taken by surprise by the intensity of the sudden ache in his chest.

Caz nodded at the crowd. "They brought dogs."

Gwyn shook his head. "I'm not using the dogs against these people. They think Leiddia was behind a deadly animal attack. Maybe two."

"Right. Not our best PR move."

Gwyn sent a command to Gelert to stay in the back of the truck, and another to calm the dogs in the mob that were already reacting to his presence. He and Ed got out, Caz behind them. Some of the mob at the back had noticed them. The shouting died, replaced by a low murmur that spread as they approached. The crowd parted before them, and as they passed through, Gwyn recognized many of the faces and heard his name whispered.

When they reached the front of the mob, a man who looked like a younger version of Ed stepped forward to block their way. Charlie.

"I'll handle this," Ed said in a low voice to Gwyn and Caz.

Charlie glowered at Gwyn, then turned to Ed. "You brought *him* to town? Another one of *them*?"

"Does *anyone* like you here?" Caz whispered, looking around nervously.

Charlie jabbed a finger at Leiddia, who still stood calmly on her porch. "She killed Mary! She killed my daughter!"

The muttering grew. Somebody shouted "Killer!" Or maybe it was "Kill her!" Gwyn looked at the faces around them. This could get ugly very quickly. He touched the minds of the dogs in the crowd. Despite what he'd told Caz, he would protect themselves if necessary. In the back of the truck, Gelert stood up, instantly aware of his master's needs.

Charlie stepped closer to Ed. "She killed your granddaughter!" he shouted, poking Ed in his chest.

Ed's face was unreadable. He said nothing. He spread his gaze over the mob, and his eyes seemed to spread silence over them as well. The shouting died to nothing. Ed turned back to Charlie. "Step aside," he said, just loud enough for everyone to hear him.

Charlie's hands balled into fists, but then his eyes darted over the crowd. They were all watching him, waiting. Ed was a council elder and respected in town. And respect for parents and elders was core in Ojibwe culture. Charlie glared at Gwyn—then stepped aside.

Ed climbed the cabin steps to stand beside Leiddia on the porch, facing the crowd. Leiddia folded her arms as Gwyn came to stand on her other side, Caz beside him. She wasn't smiling. She threw him a cold look, then turned back to the mob. "Hello, Dog," she said.

"Cat," he replied, trying to ignore how good she smelled.

"Don't need your help."

"Because you're handling this *so* well yourself," he replied.

"Glad you two've stayed friends," Caz muttered. "Not a lot of couples can do that."

Ed stepped forward. The muttering that had begun to build again in the crowd died. "My *nigozis*—my son—is right," he said in a loud, strong voice.

"Oh yeah, I am *so* glad you guys showed up," Leiddia said quietly, eyeing the crowd and looking worried for the first time.

"Still not too late for the dogs," Caz whispered.

"Let him speak," Gwyn growled, hoping Ed knew what he was doing.

"Charlie is right—about *one* thing," Ed continued. "Mary was my granddaughter." Silence fell on the crowd. "But he is wrong about this woman." He put his hand on Leiddia's shoulder. "And he is wrong to do this. You are all wrong to do this. This is not our way." He swept his eyes over the crowd. "You *know* what Mary meant to me. Do you think I would stand here beside Leiddia if I thought she did this thing?"

Many in the crowd exchanged glances, shaking their heads. Ed pointed at a young Ojibwe man in the crowd. "Jimmy, you think I'd stand beside Mary's killer?"

Jimmy shook his head and looked down. Ed pointed at a big white man holding a rifle. "Lars? Do you?" Lars looked sheepish and lowered the gun.

Ed scanned the crowd. "Anybody?" Most of the crowd shook their heads. Others just stared at the ground. Ed nodded. "Then go home. Go home to your families. Go home to bed."

But Charlie stepped forward again. "Then who killed Mary, if she didn't? Tell me that, old man."

"Not our place to say," Ed said. "Police will handle that."

Charlie laughed. "The cops? The same ones who forced us off our lands at gun point so the government could flood them? Those the ones?" He walked toward Ed. Gwyn braced himself for a fight, but something went out of Charlie just then. His shoulders slumped. He looked up again at Ed, his eyes glistening. "Those the ones who're going to tell me, pop? Tell me who killed my little girl?"

The muscles played along Ed's jaw. He stepped off the porch and reached for his son. But Charlie just shook him off. Turning, he stalked away. Leiddia took a deep breath and let it out, and then walked down the steps to give Ed a big hug.

"You may not have many friends, Gwyn," Caz said, nodding at Ed, "but the ones you do have are very cool." Suddenly, she bent an ear towards the road. "Car coming."

Gwyn nodded. "Two of them."

"Cruisers," Leiddia added.

A minute later, two OPP cruisers, white with a blue stripe, pulled into the clearing, their lights flashing. Most in the crowd, with a few glances back at the cabin, were already heading to their trucks and cars. Bill Thornton climbed out of the first cruiser. Putting on his hat, he walked to the cabin, eyeing the scattering mob. He stopped in front of the cabin, touching the brim of his hat. "Leiddia. Ed."

"Evening, Bill," Leiddia said, leaning casually against a porch post. Ed just nodded.

The cop eyed Caz, then locked on Gwyn. "Blaidd."

"Bill," Gwyn replied.

Thornton eyed Gwyn a moment longer, then turned to Leiddia. "Trouble?"

Leiddia shrugged. "Nah. Just an impromptu town hall meeting."

"Uh huh," Thornton said, looking to where the other cop was herding the stragglers out of the clearing. "Think it might reconvene?"

Leiddia shrugged.

"Maybe you'd be safer spending a night with us," Thornton said.

The other cop joined Thornton. Gwyn recognized him. Frank Mueller. A real prick. Mueller saw him and swore. "Fuck. Gwyn Blaidd?"

"Like I said, does *anyone* like you?" Caz whispered.

"You arresting me, Bill?" Leiddia asked.

Thornton shook his head. "Protective custody. For your own safety."

"I feel pretty safe right here," she said. Whether it was conscious or not, Gwyn couldn't tell, but she moved closer to him.

Thornton sighed. "Then I guess I'm arresting you. On suspicion of involvement in the deaths of Richard Calhoun and Mary Two Rivers."

Leiddia looked at him wide-eyed. "You're shitting me, right?"

"On what grounds?" Gwyn asked.

"Stay out of this, Blaidd," Thornton snapped.

"On what *grounds*, Bill?" Leiddia yelled.

"Both involved an animal attack—"

"Oh, really? You know that for sure?"

"And there were those incidents with that cougar you kept around here—"

"Didn't keep him. And you know he's dead."

Gwyn looked at her. Painter was dead? He'd helped her find her cougar pawakan after awakening her to being Heroka. She'd been as inseparable from the beast as he was with Gelert. He remembered the death of his first pawakan, remembered the emptiness that every Heroka felt at the loss of a pawakan.

And he hadn't been here to help her through it. He hadn't even known.

Thornton sighed. He took off his hat and ran his hand through his hair. "Don't make this harder than it has to be, Leiddia."

She glared at him, and then shook her head and threw up her hands. "Fine. Fuck it. Fine." She pulled some keys from her pocket and handed them to Ed. "Lock up, will ya?" Then she stomped off the porch and toward the cruiser. On the porch, the black cat mewled, watching her go. At the cruiser, Mueller reached for his handcuffs.

"You try to put those on me, you little prick," she said, "and you'll have even fewer balls than you do now."

"I begin to understand what you two saw in each other," Caz said.

Mueller paled and looked at Thornton, who shook his head. Glaring at her, Mueller opened the back door of the cruiser.

Gwyn jumped off the porch and caught up with Leiddia. "Cat—"

She spun around. "What?" she snapped.

He swallowed. "I just wanted to say—that I'm here for you...." He trailed off.

She stared at him open-mouthed, then looked away, shaking her head. "You're *here* for me?" She stepped up to him. "You walked out on me, Blaidd. *You*—left—*me*. Three years ago. Not a word since. And now, you're *here* for me?" She looked at him. There were tears in her eyes. "I *loved* you, Gwyn. And you left me."

"Cat," he said, reaching for her.

She backed away, shaking her head. "Fuck you, Blaidd." She got into the cruiser. Mueller closed the door on her, grinning at him.

Gwyn watched the cruiser disappear behind the trees, realizing in that moment what he'd known but had denied for these past two years—that he was still in love with Leiddia Barker.

CHAPTER *18*

MOTHERS AND FATHERS

SITTING IN A METAL CHAIR in the cramped waiting area of the OPP station, Kate picked up the same magazine she'd just read for the second time, then threw it down again. She checked her watch. Almost one a.m. She groaned. The day from hell continued.

After calling Macready to make sure Zach was safely in bed, she had decided to move to the official waiting area at the station until Thornton returned, to keep with her cover. Her talk with Willie Burrell had convinced her that Leiddia Barker either was a Heroka or knew someone who was. Or was very good at training animals.

Large, wild, dangerous animals.

Two cars pulled up outside. A few moments later, the door opened. Thornton entered, followed by a tall, young, black-haired woman. She wasn't handcuffed, but she didn't look like she wanted to be there, either. She looked frightened.

Was this Leiddia Barker? Kate looked the woman over in a self-conscious appraisal. She was a good half-foot taller than Kate's five foot two, with long, shiny, black hair to Kate's cropped and frizzy. Late twenties to Kate's thirty-four. A fashion model's face to Kate's pug-nosed, round, flat features. Long legs to short. Slim hips and trim waist to her chunkiness. And big tits.

She didn't know if this woman was Heroka, but she already didn't like her.

Thornton stopped when he saw Kate. "You still here?"

"Sergeant, I still need that security clearance form signed so I can report to work tomorrow at the dam. You were about to do that when you rushed out." She hoped Thornton was sharp enough not blow her cover in front of this woman.

His eyes narrowed, then he nodded. "Right. Forgot. I'll get it from my office." He turned to Willie. "Willie, process Leiddia and get her settled into a cell. She's staying with us for a bit. Mueller'll do the paperwork." Willie's eyebrows shot up but she nodded.

Kate swallowed. So this *was* Leiddia Barker.

Leiddia was staring at Kate. "I think it's for you."

"What?" Kate said, confused.

"Come on, Leiddia," Willie said, flipping up the counter. "I'll take you to the back."

"Your purse," Leiddia said, still looking frightened. "It's ringing."

Kate's heart jumped. The scanner. Her purse sat on the floor beside where she'd been sitting. She couldn't hear a sound until she opened it. Even then, the ringing wasn't that loud.

She fished out the phone-scanner. No more wondering. She'd found a Heroka. She looked at Leiddia and forced a smile. "Thanks! You have very good ears."

Leiddia considered Kate. "Runs in the family." Her frightened look had disappeared, replaced by an expression Kate couldn't read. "You gonna answer it?"

Kate still held the ringing phone. She punched a button to silence it and shrugged. "It can wait. Yay for voice mail."

Willie escorted Leiddia to the door to the cell area at the rear. Leiddia stopped and looked back at Kate. "Some people just have no consideration," she said, her face still unreadable.

"Excuse me?" Kate asked.

"Kind of late to call someone, isn't it?" Leiddia went through the door, followed by Willie, and Kate watched her all the way.

Thornton came out of his office, his coat on. He handed her the security form. "Here you go."

"How long are you keeping her?"

Thornton sighed, running a big hand over his face. "Ms. Morgan, it's very late, and I've had a long day." He turned away.

She stepped in front of him. "So have I," she snapped. Thornton stopped, his eyes widening. "How long are you keeping her?" she repeated.

Thornton folded his arms. "Until she wants out."

"What? She's not under arrest?"

"Protective custody. And unless your DNA tests indicate a cougar attack, I have nothing to hold her on. Even then, it'd be a stretch. I brought her in because of that mob. She says she's not afraid, but you ask me, she came along mostly for the same reason."

For a moment, her impression of Leiddia Barker as dangerous quarry wavered. What was it like to have a mob after you? She knew what it was like being a single woman, alone, unprotected, no one to lean on....

She shook her head. Get a grip, Morgan. Leiddia Barker was a Heroka. A monster walking among us. An infection. There was *nothing* that they shared.

"You are going to hold her until I tell you different," she said. "And you're going to get a DNA sample from her for pickup by CSIS by noon tomorrow."

Thornton scowled. "Just who do you think—"

"I think," Kate said, cutting him off, "that I'm the lady who is going to get your ass shipped to the most dead-end posting the OPP has if you don't do exactly what your country's security service is telling you to do."

Thornton's jaw worked, and his eyes narrowed to slits, but he gave her a curt nod. "All right. But legally, she can refuse to provide a DNA sample."

She opened the door. "I don't care how you get it—just get it. And I need it by noon."

She got into her car and leaned her head back. Was it over already? She could tell Jonas tonight that she already had a Heroka in custody. Maybe she and Zach could go home.

The frightened face of Leiddia Barker suddenly rose in her mind. What would Jonas do with the woman? Leiddia's face faded from her thoughts, replaced by images from Tainchel videos of captured Heroka, caged like animals, all of them now dead.

She swallowed. She knew exactly what Jonas would do. She and Zach could go home. Leiddia Barker never would.

BACK AT THE MOTEL, Kate stood beside Zach's bed, watching her sleeping son.

She hadn't sent her report to Jonas yet. She'd needed to see Zach first, a need that was more than just normal maternal concern. She wanted to remind herself why she was about to illegally condemn a young woman to a life of captivity.

Or worse.

She watched Zach as he slept. So peaceful. So innocent. Such a beautiful boy. Could that face be hiding a beast, something inhuman?

She swallowed. The truth was that she no longer knew what she believed about what he might become. She needed answers, and the Tainchel databases held those answers. That meant she had to complete what she had come here to do.

Bending over Zach's sleeping form, she kissed him gently. Then she closed his door softly behind her and went to send her report on Leiddia Barker.

IN HIS DREAM, Zach still sat outside the teepee across from Wisakejack. A small fire now burned in front of them. Zach didn't remember when that appeared, but its flames did nothing to dispel the chill that had settled on him. "How can *I* help stop the end of the world? I'm just a kid! And a blind kid, too."

"Magic."

Zach sat forward, his fears forgotten. "You're going to teach me magic?"

"Yep. But first, let me tell you a story."

Zach groaned, but said nothing.

"My father," Wisakejack said, "was Tawaham. My mother was Chichipistikwan." He shook his head. "One day, Mom and Dad kinda had a falling out."

"You mean they split up?"

"Well, Dad split Mom up. Cut her head off."

Zach stared at Wisakejack. "I don't like this story."

"Hey, you're just listening to it, little brother. Try living it. You see, Dad's a hunter, so he's away a lot. Mom gets, uh, lonely, so she finds a boyfriend. A snake."

"You mean a bad person?"

"No, I mean a snake."

"Is this one of those Freudian dreams?"

"The snake's a shaman and puts Mom under a spell. But Dad gets suspicious. He follows her one day, finds her with the snake, and kills it. Then he and Mom have this big fight."

"And he cuts off her head?"

"Oops. Getting ahead of myself. No, *first* he cuts off her head, *then* they have the big fight."

Zach groaned. "Can I wake up now, please?"

"So Dad fights Mom, minus her head. He spins her around and around, faster and faster, until they rise to the heavens." Wisakejack pointed to the night sky. "Where they still are to this day. Dad's the North Star, and Mom's the Big Dipper."

"Which spins around the North Star," Zach said. "I get it."

"Story's not over. Remember my little brother? Well, this is way before he changed into a wolf. We're still just kids." Wisakejack looked at him. "*Just like you.* So now I had to help us both escape."

"From what?"

"From Mom's head," Wisakejack said. "Stop pinching yourself. You're not waking up until I'm finished. So fortunately, Dad had given me a powerful medicine bundle. In it, I find a bone awl, a fire-flint, a stone to strike the flint, and a piece of birch bark to catch the spark. So, we're running away from Mom's head—"

"How can a *head* chase you?"

Wisakejack blinked. "By rolling, of course. Thought that would've been obvious. So, anyway, we're running, Mom's rolling, and I toss the awl behind us. Up sprouts a forest of thorn bushes. But Mom just rolls right through them. Next, I toss the birch bark, and a wall of fire appears. But she just rolls through that, too. I toss the stone, and it forms mountains—"

Zach sighed. "But she just rolled right over them."

"Yep. We primal spirits are pretty tough. Mind you, she's not looking too good by now."

"Starting with the lack of a body."

"But she's still coming. So I throw the flint, but I stumble—"

"Hard to believe."

"Quiet. I stumble, and the flint lands in *front* of my brother and me, not behind us. Whoosh! Suddenly, a raging river is blocking our way. We're trapped!"

"So what did you do?" Zach asked, despite himself.

"Ha! You're hooked, right? I call Grandfather Gull and ask him to please carry me and my brother across the river on his back."

"That must have been one big gull."

"Primal spirit, remember? Anyway, because we're in need and have always treated his kind with respect—remember that?—Grandfather Gull carries us across the river."

"But your mother just rolls through the river, right?"

"What? You nuts?" Wisakejack shook his head. "She'd drown. Can't breathe underwater. And a head can't swim."

"But she didn't have a body to breathe with anyway—oh god, forget it. Just tell me what happened."

"Mom has her own connections in the spirit world. She convinces a river serpent to carry her across. But remember what I said about the beings who dwell in the deep places, in deep water especially? There's a problem with trusting them. You can't. Trust them, that is. The serpent dumps Mom in the drink halfway across." Wisakejack sighed. "And that's the last we saw of her." Wisakejack settled back and grinned at Zach.

"That's it?"

Wisakejack shrugged. "Well, I was kidnapped by that shaman shortly after that, but that's another story."

"Which you will no doubt tell me," Zach cried, jumping up, "whether I want to hear it or not. You said your stories would *teach* me. What could I possibly need to know in that story?"

"Aside from how cool and heroic I was?" Wisakejack asked. Zach glared at him. "Okay, so you don't see *any* parallels in that story to your own life?"

"Are you insane? Yes! Yes, you are. That story has *nothing* to do with *my* life."

"Oh," Wisakejack said, nodding slowly. "So, *your* parents are still together, then."

Zach swallowed, suddenly unsure. "No," he said quietly. "They broke up, before I was born. Don't know who left who, really." He glared at Wisakejack. "But whoever my dad is, he didn't cut off Mom's head."

"But I bet he broke her up pretty bad when he left. Bet she felt like she was split in two—her head telling her one thing, her heart another."

"She never talks about it, but yeah, I know it did," Zach admitted. "Ok, I get it. It's a metaphor. But your mother tried to hurt you. What's *that* got to do with me?"

Wisakejack shrugged. "I think my mom just got it into her head—which was all she had left for anything to get into—that she was *afraid* of me and my brother." He looked at Zach, any trace of his normal joking expression gone. "You think maybe your mother's afraid of *you*, Zach?"

Zach suddenly wanted to wake up, but as much as he tried, he couldn't. "My mom loves me," he whispered.

Wisakejack nodded. "Oh, my mom still *loved* us, even when she was chasing us. But I think she was *afraid* of the power she knew we had. Afraid of what we might become." He looked at Zach. "Maybe your mom's afraid of some power *you* have. Afraid of what *you* might become."

Zach wanted to cry. "I don't have any power."

Wisakejack's grin returned. "Oh, you've got power, kid. You've got magic. You just haven't found it yet."

"So why don't you just *tell* me?" Zach yelled.

Wisakejack shook his head, serious again. "Doesn't work that way. Magic's something you have to find inside yourself. I'm just trying to lead you to it the only way I know how, and trying to teach you as you're travelling that path. Because once you find the magic, you gotta know how to use it. Magic's *dangerous*, kid."

Zach kicked a stone into the fire. "This is stupid. You're stupid. These stories are stupid. *That* was supposed to be about *me*? I don't have a wolf for a brother. I don't even have a brother. And my dad—whoever he is—isn't some magical hunter."

"Yeah?" Wisakejack replied. "Well, I see a wolf in your future, little brother. And, tell me—what *do* you know about your father?"

Zach swallowed, bowing his head to hide his tears. "Nothing. Mom never talks about him."

Wisakejack scratched his chin. "Hmm. I wonder why?"

Zach looked up at the North Star and Big Dipper. He'd always wondered the same thing.

CHAPTER 19

MEMORIES AND MONSTERS

HAVING SPENT THE REST of his day dealing with the botched ambush on Gwyn Blaidd, Simon Jonas was exhausted when he pulled into the driveway of his home in the Glebe in Ottawa. When he walked in, Florence, his wife's nurse, came downstairs.

"You're late, Mr. Jonas," she said, but she sounded worried, not angry. Florence was a plump, matronly RN whom he'd hired away from an Ottawa hospital.

"I am so sorry, Flo," he said, throwing his overcoat onto a chair.

"That's all right. I made myself some dinner." She shook her head, looking at him. "You work so hard, Mr. Jonas. Then you come home to more stress."

He glanced upstairs. "How was she today?"

"Oh, you know, sir. She has good days and bad days." She put on her coat, and then gave him a little smile. "This was a bad one, I'm afraid."

"Was she asking about Daniel again?"

Florence nodded, her hands twisting the strap of her purse. "I just didn't have the heart to tell her again. It's just too hard on her." She sighed. "And on me, to say the whole truth. I'm sorry to leave that for you."

He squeezed her shoulder. "It's all right. She'd have forgotten by now anyway. I'd just have to tell her again. This saves both of you some pain." He opened the door. "Your husband's waiting. Off you go. I'll see you in the morning."

Florence touched his arm as she stepped outside. "I'm sure tomorrow will be a better day for her, sir."

He closed the door behind her. A frail female voice called from upstairs. "Simon? Is that you?"

No, he thought. *Tomorrow will not be a better day. Each day will be a little worse, until....* He left the thought unfinished. "Yes, Patty," he called. "It's me."

"Is Daniel with you?"

His guts clenched. He forced himself to take a deep breath and let it out. He went upstairs and into his wife's room.

She sat in her favorite armchair by the window. A CD was playing softly. "Big Hits from the Sixties." Familiar songs. Songs she still remembered. Songs from the part of her memory that hadn't slipped away yet.

Florence had left all the lamps on, and a warm comforting glow lit the room. Framed photos covered the dresser and tables. Photos of Patricia and himself with friends from many years ago. Photos of their wedding day.

Photos of Daniel.

He wondered again if he should hide those, if having them out where Patty could see them didn't make things worse, rather than better. But anytime he picked up a picture of Daniel, ready to bury it in a drawer, he would put it down again.

If they couldn't have their son, they would still have their memories of him. He would not hide Daniel away. He would bear the pain.

He walked over to Patricia and kissed her. Flo had changed her into her nightgown, and she was ready for bed. She looked so thin. He'd forgotten to ask Flo how much she'd eaten today.

Patty smiled, and then looked behind him. "Where's Daniel? He should be home from school by now. Is he over at Larry's?"

He pulled up an ottoman and sat down beside her, taking her hands in his. He wanted to tell her yes. But then she would want to call Larry's mother, and Larry's family had moved away many years ago. He still remembered how heartbroken Daniel had been that day.

It didn't matter. He'd tried everything. Nothing worked. She always asked, every day, wanting to know where Daniel was, wanting to talk to him, wanting just to know that her boy was safe. She kept asking—until he told her the truth. Every day.

She raised a trembling hand to her face. "Simon, I feel so confused all the time."

"My love, you're sick," he said quietly. "You have Alzheimer's. You have trouble making new memories. You forget things."

"Oh. I see." Shaking her head, she looked around again. "Where's Daniel?"

He wanted to yell at her. He wanted to tell her to stop asking, to stop being stupid, to remember what had happened to Daniel. To remember what they'd gone through. To stop making them both go through it again every day.

Every day.

But he swallowed his anger with her as he always did. He squeezed her hands and spoke softly. "Honey, Daniel isn't in school with Larry anymore. Daniel grew up and went to University. Then he got a job, working for our government, for his country."

She nodded slowly. "I remember. We were so proud of him." She smiled at him. "*You* got him that job, didn't you?"

His jaw clenched. He *had* gotten Daniel the job with CSIS. *He* had gotten Daniel into it. *That* she remembered.

"Is he at work still?" she asked.

"No, my love." He looked at her, tears in his eyes. It didn't matter how many times he told her, it never got any easier. "Danny's dead. He died eighteen years ago. He gave his life for his country."

Her hands went up to her face. They were trembling. "Oh!" she whispered. "Oh, no! Oh, Simon." She started to cry. Taking her in his arms, he held her as she sobbed into his shoulder. "Oh, Simon. Our little baby."

He held her as she cried, held her as he always did until she finally stopped. Then he helped her into bed and turned off the lights. He sat by her bedside until she fell asleep, until her breathing was deep and slow and peaceful, well after midnight.

He left her then, going downstairs to his study. Clicking on his computer, he slumped back in the big leather chair and buried his face in his hands.

How much more of this could he take? How long could he take care of her?

But as bad as this life was, it would be worse when she was gone. What would he have left then? Nothing. He bent his head and wept. He should have Daniel. He should have his son. A man should not outlive his son.

No.

A man's son should not be taken from him. Murdered. By monsters.

His computer beeped. He looked up. Two video messages were waiting. He listened to Macready's brief update first, and then clicked the next message.

Kate Morgan's face appeared. As she began to relate the history of Leiddia Barker, he sat up in his chair. When she described the woman's arrest and the ringing of the scanner, he began to tremble. He had to stand up and take several deep breaths before his shaking subsided. Sitting down again, he replayed Kate's message and then sat back.

He'd done it. He'd found a Heroka.

Now, how to proceed? He was tempted to send a team immediately to bring this woman back to his covert Tainchel base. But too many people would know that the OPP had arrested Leiddia Barker and then handed her over to CSIS. He had no legal basis for keeping her in custody, no proof that she had committed any crime.

But if her DNA linked her to the killings, then he could present his entire case. Prove that the Heroka existed. That they were killers. A threat to society. He nodded to himself. He'd wait for Leiddia Barker's DNA samples.

This Barker woman would know others of her kind. She would tell him who they were, where they were. He would make her tell him. And then....

"*For that which befalleth the sons of men befalleth beasts,*" he whispered. "*Even one thing befalleth them: as the one dieth, so dieth the other.*"

CHAPTER *20*

CAT AND DOG

THE NEXT MORNING, Gwyn stood with Caz and Ed beside Ed's truck outside the store. Ed had a street map of Thunder Lake spread open on the hood and was suggesting spots in town where people congregated. Gwyn had finally agreed that he and Caz could split up to look for anyone with the Mark, provided she let Ed and Gelert accompany her. She hadn't objected to teaming up with Ed, but Gelert was another story.

"I have to take him, too?" she'd replied, eyeing Gelert warily. The huge hound looked up at her, wagging his tail. "Because of my totem's natural affinity with large predators?"

"Because you're *looking* for a predator—a Heroka who may be a killer." He didn't want to scare her, but she needed to understand the danger. He still wasn't sure he was doing the right thing, but this would let them cover more ground faster. Besides, if the Tainchel attack at Cil y Blaidd had been targeting him, not Caz or Mitch, then she might be safer away from him than around him.

Caz shrugged. "If we find someone with the Mark, we'll just follow them. All discreet like."

He sighed. "If you can see the Mark on someone, then they can see your Mark, too. And if a Heroka *is* in hiding here, they'll want to protect their secret. And remember, the Tainchel may be here looking for Heroka, too, and they'll have scanners."

Caz's jaw clenched, and he guessed she was thinking of all the people in her life she'd lost to the Tainchel. She looked at Gelert. "So he'll protect us?"

"No," Ed said, with a grin. "He'll follow whoever attacks us. Wouldn't want to lose them after all our hard work."

Caz laughed and punched him in the arm, suddenly relaxed again. She and Ed seemed to genuinely like each other. *She's almost Mary's age*, he thought. *Probably does Ed good to have her around. Especially today.* Mary's burial ceremony was that night.

And Caz needed a father figure. *Which sure as hell isn't me*, he thought. All of their conversations continued to be laced with tension.

Ed folded the map. "So we'll take this side of the river, and you the other?"

Gwyn nodded. "Drop me at the cop shop first."

Ed raised an eyebrow. "Leiddia wasn't too thrilled to see you last night."

"I still need to see her."

"Oh yeah," Caz said. "You're totally over her."

He glared at her. "Someone should ask her what she knows."

Caz just smirked. "But you couldn't smell her at the scene," Ed said.

"She didn't do it, but this still looks like a Heroka killing. She might know of another Heroka in the area." *Besides*, he admitted to himself, *I want to see her.*

They drove to the OPP station. Gwyn got out. Ed leaned over to call out the window. "We'll scout the town until four o'clock. Then I'm at the community center. Doing a storytelling class after school for the Ojibwe kids. Trying to keep the old ways alive. Losing battle, but…." He shrugged. "Meet us back at the store about five-thirty, and we'll head over…." He left the sentence unfinished.

Head over. To the cemetery. Gwyn just nodded. Caz flipped him a wave, and they drove away.

Inside the station, he was happy to see that Willie Burrell was the cop on duty, and not Frank Mueller. Willie had been one of the few cops who hadn't always treated him like a criminal. She smiled as she came to the counter. "Hi, Gwyn. Sarge told me you were back in town."

"Hi, Willie. I'd like to see Leiddia if I could." *And if she wants to see me.*

Willie nodded. "She said that you might drop by."

"She say anything else?"

She smiled again. "Nothing I'll repeat. But, yeah, you can see her. C'mon." She flipped up a section of the counter.

A metal door in the back of the station opened into a room with a concrete floor and two barred cells. Each cell was about six by five feet, with a sleep shelf, a stainless steel sink, and a toilet. A camera, mounted high in the wall beside a barred window, faced the cells.

The first cell was empty. In the second cell, Leiddia sat on the bunk, one leg up, leaning against the wall, wearing the same dark blue top and jeans from last night. When she saw Gwyn, she stood and walked to the bars, arms folded, eyes locked on him. "Willie, could we have some privacy, please?"

Willie grimaced. "Can't leave you alone. Sorry. Rules." She stepped back through the open door to stand as far away as she could while still keeping Leiddia in view. "But I have really lousy hearing, so if you talk quiet...."

Gwyn walked up to the bars. Leiddia glared at him. He swallowed. Seeing her, smelling her, being this close to her again brought it all back, the memories of their two short and intense years together. There'd never been a middle ground with them—it seemed they'd spent two years either making love or fighting like cats and dogs. But he had loved her through it all. And now?

"Can you hear me?" he asked, dropping his voice to a bare whisper, audible only to Heroka ears.

"Hear you just fine," she said, managing to imbue even a whisper with anger. "So? Ask me. That's what you came for, isn't it?"

He shook his head. "No, it isn't. I know you didn't kill Mary. You could never do that."

Something softened in her posture. She slumped a little. "Thank you," she said. She shook her head. "Oh, Gwyn, we were friends. Poor Mary...."

He put his hand over hers where it rested on the bars. She didn't pull away. They stood there, silent. After a few moments, she looked at him. "So? Now what?"

Was she referring to Mary's death? Or to him and her? He took the easy way out. He told her about what he'd found where Mary had died, along with Ed's windigo theory. That led to the story of the Tainchel attack at Cil y Blaidd. Again, he omitted his encounter with the wolf spirit, Mahigan.

"I'm sorry," she said when he finished. "I never met Mitch, but I know you two were close." She shook her head. "God, the Tainchel are back? This keeps getting worse. And somebody eating all those bodies? Besides being horribly gruesome, it doesn't make sense. How could your Tainchel attack be connected to the killings here?"

"It could if a Heroka was involved in both sets of killings. Do you know of any Heroka in this area?"

She shook her head. "But I suppose there could be. I don't get into town much. Still doesn't seem likely that I'd never have noticed them, though."

"We're going to look around town for someone with the Mark—"

"We? Oh, right. You and your new ward." She grinned. "Or is she more than that?"

"What!? Gods, no. She's a kid. I'm just trying to keep her safe. And not kill her myself."

She laughed, and it felt good to hear that sound again. "I'll bet. You never struck me as the fatherly type."

He smiled. "I'm learning I'm not." He shook his head, wanting to change the subject. "If we don't find anyone with the Mark, I'm not sure what that leaves us."

She shrugged. "Windigo?"

He groaned. "Not you, too."

"Doesn't have to be Ed's spirit thingy. Windigo psychosis is real, with actual diagnosed cases in the 1800s. Cree hunters eating their families in a bad winter."

"One, this isn't the 1800s. Two, how the hell do you know that stuff?"

Her sadness returned. "Mary. She was going into cultural anthropology at U of T. She used to talk to me about what she learned from Ed or Walter or the other elders."

"Walter Keejek?" Walter was one of Ed's closest friends. "I guess he'll be at Mary's funeral tonight. I'll ask him what he thinks of Ed's windigo theory."

She frowned. "I doubt Walter will be there. He and Ed had a huge fight a while back."

"What about?"

"Don't really know. Something about what Walter was teaching Mary. But yeah, if anyone knows more about windigo lore than Ed, it would be Walter." She shook her head. "Mary's funeral, and I can't even go. But, then I wouldn't be welcome either, beyond Ed."

They both fell silent, until she looked at him again. "So? What about *us*?"

And there it was. What could he say? He swallowed. An apology seemed like a good start. "I'm sorry I left. I woke you as a Heroka. I should have stayed. But things weren't good between us, there at the end."

She nodded. "Yeah. I was a bitch to live with after I changed. I just couldn't deal, you know, with all that wildness in me all the time. I didn't know how to handle it."

She looked back at him, some of the hardness returning to her face. "But you *made* me Heroka, Gwyn. You should've stayed to teach me *how* to be one."

"I stayed for two years, remember?"

The temper he knew so well leapt into her eyes for a second. "Yeah? Well, you forgot to teach me a few things. Like what happens when your pawakan dies."

He swallowed. "I'm sorry about Painter. What happened?"

"Fucking hunter up from Toronto shot him. Bastard left town before I found him. Lucky for him."

"I'm sorry. I know how hard it is to lose your pawakan."

She stared out the small window set high in the cell wall. "Hard, the man says." She laughed, a sound with no joy. "There's this place, inside my head—" She touched her temples with her fingers. "—where I linked with Painter."

Gwyn nodded. All Heroka described their connection to their pawakan in a similar way.

"A piece of your pawakan lives inside you," he said. "Becomes a part of you."

"Yeah, but when he died, it was like someone cut me open and ripped that part out, ripped out something I never knew I'd had until it was gone. Like I had this hole inside me. Like I was empty."

He swallowed, recalling his own feelings earlier of the emptiness inside him that the murdered wolves at Cil y Blaidd had brought.

She turned back to him. "You weren't here to tell me what was happening to me, why I was feeling like that. You weren't here to tell me what to do. You could've helped me." She glared at him, but the anger was gone. She just shook her head. "You should've been here."

He sighed. "I wish I had been."

They both fell silent, but she squeezed his hand. From the doorway, Willie cleared her throat.

"I'd better go," he said.

"I love you," she said.

He looked up, surprised. He swallowed. "I love you, too," he said, knowing it was true.

She leaned a little closer to the bars. They kissed. She broke it off first, then looked at him with a sad smile. "Am I still going to have to share you with a dead woman?"

He thought about Stelle. He thought about Leiddia. He shook his head. "No. No, you won't."

She smiled. "Yeah. Right." She sighed. "Get me out of here, Dog, and we'll see where things go."

He walked to the door. Willie gave him a little smile.

"Hey!" Leiddia called.

He turned back.

She was grinning. "Glad you're here."

He grinned back and left. Outside, he stood on the steps of the police station for a moment, remembering the taste of her lips.

Could they really restart a life together? *Sure*, he thought. *All I have to do is clear her of a murder charge and find Mary's real killer, while I evade the Tainchel and play daddy to a messed-up teenager who hates my guts.*

Still, he was smiling as he walked back into town.

CHAPTER *21*

THE LADY AND THE LAKE

KATE TURNED HER CAR onto a dirt road marked "Powerhouse" and followed it through thick bush until she reached a metal gate in a tall chain link fence. Beyond lay a graveled parking lot with several cars parked beside four white trailers. Behind the trailers squatted the dam's powerhouse, a six-hundred-foot-long, fifty-foot-deep, and forty-foot-high gray box, dwarfed by the looming white concrete slope of the dam wall rising into the sky behind it.

The guard at the gate validated her credentials, then directed her to the farthest trailer. She parked, grabbed her briefcase, and got out. Climbing the steps to the trailer door, she shrugged off her parka, smoothed her gray pantsuit, and stepped inside.

Five people sitting around a table covered in coffee cups and paper looked up as she entered. A small balding man with a droopy mustache peered at her over big black glasses. "Can I help you?"

"Good morning. I'm Kate Morgan, the new project manager for the production process deployment."

The balding man reached across the table to shake hands. "Oh, hi, Kate. I'm Mike Vickers, the project director." Vickers introduced the others, each managing a different aspect of the project. "Grab a seat. This is our weekly status meeting. We're almost done." With that, he returned to the discussion she'd interrupted.

She half listened as each team lead gave their report. Aside from the table, the trailer held six metal desks. One was bare save for a computer, and she assumed that was hers.

Her day had started with an email from Jonas, confirming that the DNA samples from Mary Two Rivers' corpse had arrived yesterday. Results would be ready tomorrow. Rick Calhoun's clothes and Leiddia Barker's DNA sample would arrive later today. Those results would be ready the day after tomorrow.

According to Thornton, Leiddia Barker had provided her sample willingly, which seemed to argue against her guilt. Was she handing an innocent woman over to the Tainchel? She pushed that thought away, repeating what had become her mantra—this was for Zach. Tonight, she'd search Tainchel databases for clues to Zach's future as a half-blooded Heroka.

Vickers wrapped up. "Okay, folks, get your updates in." He stood up. "Kate, I'll take you around the site later today. In the meantime, Carrie here will get you onto the project library system so you can get caught up." With that, he left.

She spent the morning reading key project documents. Not realizing she had to bring her lunch, her stomach was protesting loudly when Vickers poked his head in around one o'clock. "Ready for your grand tour?" he asked, grinning.

Grabbing her parka, she followed him outside. "We'll start with the powerhouse," he said. Walking to the large entrance doors, Vickers swiped his pass card to let them in.

From her previous hydro projects, she knew that most of a powerhouse lay below ground. The ground floor was one cavernous room, rising the full forty feet of the powerhouse. Five metal domes twice her height and forty feet in diameter, stretched in a line down the powerhouse, covering the generators below. Above, the huge crane used to lift the generator-turbine pairs during maintenance hung from ceiling tracks running the length of the building.

"The generators and turbines are in," Vickers said, "but we won't be operational until we clear up this land rights issues with the Ojibwe. Once we're up, this site will generate—"

"Five hundred kilowatts at peak production," she interrupted, "assuming all five pairs are operating, a head of thirty meters, and an inflow of three cubic meters per second."

Vickers nodded. "You've done your homework. Excellent." He led her down a set of metal stairs to the generator level, where five huge metal cylinders, the enclosures for the generators, rose twenty feet from floor to ceiling, almost completely filling the room.

They descended another set of stairs. If the generator level had seemed cramped, this one, a third the width and half the height, was almost claustrophobic. Huge steel shafts rose from the gate mechanism at the top of each turbine, disappearing into the ceiling where they connected to the rotors in the generators above.

"What do you remember about our turbines?" Vickers asked.

She thought for a moment. "You have a medium head site here, so the higher efficiency Pelton-type runners weren't an option, leaving a choice of Francis or propeller runners. They went with propellers since they're less prone to cavitation." She looked at him.

He grinned again. "Yep. Maybe you can start giving these tours." He started back up the stairs.

She began to follow but stopped. She'd been down this far in a powerhouse before, but never in one not yet operational. The difference here was the silence. No roar of water rushing through the penstock. No thrum of whirling turbines throbbing up your legs like the beat from a great subterranean drum. No whine of rotors spinning magnets bigger than she was inside the generators above.

But it seemed a strange silence—one filled not so much with the *absence* of sound but rather the *expectation* of it, as if the lake lying above was a giant creature slowly drawing in a great watery breath and waiting for just the right moment to let it out.

Waiting, waiting….

She shivered, suddenly picturing the enormous weight of water above her held back by the dam. The walls seemed to close in then, and she felt suddenly vulnerable, as if this dam could not possibly contain the captured beast that was the lake, as if all that water was about to smash through these walls, crushing her like a bug in this dark little room. Climbing the stairs quickly, she caught up to Vickers. As they reached the ground floor again, the panic she'd felt underground receded in the open spaces of that level.

"Control room next," he said, leading her up more stairs to a raised room with glass walls. A large instrument panel dominated the control room, running its entire length. Vickers watched her look over the panel. "Want to take a crack at it?"

She pointed to a set of gauges. "Those monitor the generators and power output. They're showing zero, because…," she said, indicating a set of switches, "…the gates on the main dam are closed, since you're not ready to produce power yet. But you need to regulate the level of the lake." She pointed to another set of switches. "So the control gates for the spillway are open and set, I'd guess, to match the lake's inflow."

"Perfect again," Vickers said. "We'll drive up to the top of the dam now."

Vickers' car was a beat-up Chevy with about as much of its original paint as Vickers had hair. As the road to the top of the dam climbed, she caught glimpses through the trees of the powerhouse and trailers falling further and further below them. After about a mile, the road emerged from the forest, providing a view of the dam and its captured lake.

Seen beside the water that it held back, the dam appeared almost fragile, inadequate for its assigned task. The lake wasn't large and was well below its operational level, but its silent darkness seemed to hint of a depth and mass of water beyond the norm. A memory of her fear from the turbine room returned, then was gone.

The road straightened and ran onto the top of the dam. On their right, the dam wall sloped down to the powerhouse below. On their left, the lake rippled blackly.

"Oh, crap," Vickers said. "Not again."

A chain link fence and gate stretched across the road, blocking access to the top of the dam. On this side, about a dozen people stood shouting at a guard behind the gate. Another guard sat on a stool beside a small Quonset hut, watching with bored detachment. Four men in the crowd were carrying a huge rolled-up piece of canvas on their shoulders. Vickers gave his horn a short honk, and the group turned to face the newcomers.

"Protestors?" Kate asked.

Vickers nodded. "You'll get used to it. Unfortunately."

Most in the crowd were Anishinabe and male, but she saw a couple of whites and three women. Vickers slowed the car to a crawl. Several protestors gave way, but three men in front of the gate didn't budge, instead just folded their arms and stared at Vickers.

Vickers stopped his car. Rolling down the window, he called to the nearest protestor. "C'mon, Joe. Do I have to call Thornton and have him send a cruiser up? Again?"

The man called Joe walked over and peered into the car. He looked Ojibwe, maybe about forty. His gaze fell on her. "Anishinabe?" he asked.

"Cree," she answered.

"So you with *them*?" he asked, nodding at Vickers.

Them, she thought. Us and them. Sides had been chosen here, and she couldn't help feeling that she was on the wrong one. She nodded again. "Project manager."

Joe didn't reply, just stared at her, and in that gaze she felt a sudden memory. Her *nokoomis*, her grandmother, had looked at her that way on the day she'd left home for university. Looked at her as if she had betrayed her. Betrayed her people.

"Joe Makademik," the man said, extending his hand past Vickers' face.

She shook it. "Kate Morgan."

"C'mon, Joe," Vickers said. "Don't you have something better to do?"

Joe shrugged. "Like a job? Not much demand for a hunting guide anymore, since your dam flooded all the animals out."

"Still jobs on the dam," Vickers said.

"Sure. How about yours? Can't be that hard if they got you doing it, Mike," Joe replied. The rest of the protestors laughed, and Vickers reddened.

Asshole, Kate thought. "His job is more than you could handle," she shot back. "Now are you going to get out of our way or do we call the police?"

The laughter died, and she heard some cursing. The protestors looked at Joe, who seemed to be their leader. He stared at her, then shrugged and turned away. Grumbling amongst themselves and shooting looks at the car, the rest followed him back to their vehicles.

"Nice meeting you. Enjoy your new job," Joe called to her, putting just enough emphasis on "job" to make his point.

The guards opened the gate. Vickers drove through. "Thanks," he said, still looking embarrassed.

"No problem. What were they trying to do anyway?"

"Hang a banner on the dam wall, probably. That's why we have guards now. It's killing my budget."

The dam road and the dam ended far ahead at a sheer rock face on the opposite side of the valley. Vickers drove halfway across the dam, stopping beside a concrete observation platform about fifty feet long and extending twenty feet out over the lake. They walked to the edge of the platform where a wall about waist height stood between them and a drop of maybe thirty feet to the black water below.

Vickers nodded at the lake. "We've flooded nearly two-hundred and fifty acres. Lake's over a hundred feet deep now." He sighed. "And yeah, that flooding was not popular. Dislodged people from their homes. Wiped out hunting territories. And, apparently, screwed up the local wildlife, at least in the short term. The animals will recover, find new migration routes…you know." He shrugged. "I mean, yeah, the dam's brought changes, but it's brought jobs and money, too. Change is part of progress, right? What do they have against progress?" he asked, sounding as if he were trying to convince himself, not her.

She peered down into water so dark she could see no more than three feet deep. Shivering at the thought of slipping over the edge and into those murky depths, she straightened. She'd never learned how to swim. "I heard a worker was killed up here."

Vickers nodded. "Rick Calhoun. He was checking the sluice gate installation. They found him—or what was left of him—just over there." He pointed at a dark rusty blotch on the pavement about twenty feet away.

"Are those blood stains?"

"Yeah."

"I understand he was killed by a wild animal."

Vickers nodded. "That's what the cops said. Only thing that makes sense."

She stared back along the road. *Long way from the cover of trees for any animal. And behind the security gate, too.*

Shouting erupted again from the protestors at the gate. "Dammit!" Vickers said. "Where's that cruiser? Sorry, Kate. Wait here. I'll just be a minute." Getting in his car, he drove back to the gate.

Leaning on the wall, she gazed out over the lake. What did the Ojibwe have against progress? Lose your land. Lose your way of life. In return, get a handful of temporary jobs at minimum wage and promises for social programs that never come.

Some people were just never satisfied.

So why didn't they leave? Get an education. Get a career.

Get out. Like she had.

Because, she admitted to herself for the first time since she'd left home, maybe they loved their way of life. Maybe they loved their land. Maybe they wanted no part of any progress that destroyed that life and that land.

She stared down into the dark water, thinking back to her childhood, remembering long canoe trips with her father, how she had loved to lean over the side and stare into the water as her father's smooth strokes propelled them over the glassy surface, water so clear she could see deep into it, see fish flash by, see....

She blinked, her thoughts rising up out of the deep water, a sudden fear rising with them. Something had changed. Something was wrong. She looked around.

She was alone. The lake still lay before her, but it seemed even darker, almost black. The valley and its surrounding forest remained, but this forest was taller, thicker, more...primal.

The dam road was gone. The dam itself was gone. She stood atop a huge ridge, an enormous spine of land spanning a strange valley, holding back the black lake on one side and dropping off sharply on the opposite.

Fighting a rising panic, she looked back to the lake. Suddenly, she sensed something else, something hidden below in those dark depths. *Two* somethings.

Two somethings that were calling to her.

And despite the screaming protests from her mind, her legs were answering that call. Step by step, she was moving helplessly closer to the cliff edge above the water. As she reached the very brink, the dark lake changed again. She stared down now into, not a body of water, but a black abyss. And the things that hid in its depths called to her.

You are no longer needed in this.

She felt another tug at her legs, an urge to take one more step, to plunge into the abyss below, to escape from this world, from this life.

From Zach.

Images of Zach left alone, with no one to protect him flooded her. Fear for her son fought the voices in her head, a fear that turned to the fury of a mother defending her child.

"NO!" she screamed, wrenching back control of her body, twisting away from the edge. She fell, but she fell backward. The impact of the ground forced the breath from her. Pain shot through her shoulder. Her head cracked against something hard and unforgiving.

As consciousness slipped away, the words rang in her head again. *You are no longer needed in this.*

SOMEONE WAS YELLING her name. Her eyes blinked open.

Vickers' worried face, framed by blue sky, filled her vision. "Kate, are you all right?"

She was lying on her back. Her left shoulder throbbed. She felt like she'd been dropped on her head. Groaning, she pushed herself up to sitting, with help from Vickers.

"What happened?" she mumbled.

"That's my question," Vickers said. "I'm driving back, and I see you lying on the road."

"Must've fainted," she offered. Vickers looked at her doubtfully, and she grasped for a better explanation. She certainly wasn't going to tell him the truth. She wasn't even sure she believed it. "I'm really tired, you know, from the trip up here. And I didn't have lunch."

Vickers nodded, looking relieved. "Yeah, that'll do it. Look, why don't you take the rest of today off and get some sleep? Start fresh tomorrow."

She gratefully agreed, and he drove her back. After he'd gone back inside the project trailer, she leaned against her car, gazing up at the dam towering huge and ominous above her. Her head still throbbed, and she was having trouble reconstructing what had happened to her up there. A hallucination? A waking dream? Or just what she'd told Vickers?

Sure, that was it. She'd fainted from lack of sleep and food, hit her head, and blacked out. She'd just been dreaming while unconscious. The lake hadn't really disappeared, hadn't become a black abyss. Strange voices hadn't tried to draw her to her death.

Words whispered in the air behind her. *You are no longer needed in this.* She spun around.

Nothing was there. Feeling dizzy again, she leaned on her car to steady herself. Bump on the head. There weren't any voices. She was just disoriented.

Liar. She knew what she'd heard.

The dam loomed above her, making her feel tiny and fragile. A strange thought came to her—that if she were on the opposite side, she'd be near the bottom of the dark lake, from where her strange voices had seemed to come. She shivered. Turning her back on the dam, she got into the car.

You are no longer needed in this, the voices had said.

We'll see about that, she thought, trying to convince herself that she meant it.

CHAPTER 22

THE TRICKSTER

IN ZACH'S MOTEL ROOM, Colin Macready closed the history textbook that he'd been reviewing with Zach. "Very good, Zach. You know this unit quite well."

"Thanks, Colin," Zach replied, rubbing his temples. "Could we take a break? I'm kind of tired."

Macready considered the boy. He needed to monitor Zach's health as well as his whereabouts. Jonas would blame him if the kid got as much as a cold on this trip. "Not sleeping well?"

The boy just shrugged. "No. Yeah. Bad dreams."

Macready made a mental note to add that to his next report. "Tell you what. Let's call it a day. Quincy needs a walk, anyway." Hearing his name, the dog raised his head, tail wagging. "And I heard about something that might interest you."

"What's that?"

"You want to learn more about your Cree heritage, right? Apparently, the community center here holds an Ojibwe storytelling class every weekday at four o'clock. Lots of similarities between Ojibwe and Cree stories. We can just make it if we leave now."

"Colin, that's great!" Zach cried, grabbing his white cane beside the chair. "I'll get my coat." The boy got up, smoothly maneuvering his way to the closet.

Macready shrugged on his own jacket. He didn't give a shit about the kid's interests and would have much preferred taking a break from the little abomination. But Jonas had ordered him to locate any Heroka in town, and he couldn't do that sitting here, nor could he leave Zach alone without arousing Kate Morgan's suspicions. The community center would let him scan large numbers of people while keeping Zach close.

"Thanks, Colin," Zach said, his face beaming, as they stepped outside. "I really appreciate this."

Macready checked that his phone-scanner was on, then patted Zach on his shoulder. "No problem. Anything for my favorite student."

JUST BEFORE FOUR that afternoon, Ed left Caz with Gelert at the store and headed over to the community center for his daily storytelling class. He'd started the class three months ago, and he now usually had at least fifteen kids show up. He needed this class, to give him some hope, even more since Mary's death. Hope that his culture was not going to die with his generation. Many of these kids had never heard these stories, because their parents had never heard them, because the government had forced those parents into church-run residential schools that hadn't allowed these stories.

He shook his head. Stories were how kids were supposed to learn.

Most of the kids at his classes ranged from six to twelve, but lately some Ojibwe teenagers had started hanging by the door. They mostly talked and laughed amongst themselves, laughing, he guessed, at the old fool telling old stories, stories of a dying culture, a dying way of life.

But lately, some of them had been listening, too. Maybe there was hope.

When he reached the community center, an Ojibwe boy, about eighteen, was lying outside the door slumped against a wall, an empty mickey of rye beside him. Ed sighed. Or maybe he *was* just an old fool. He shook the kid awake, gave him hell, and sent him home. He went inside.

The center let him use the main meeting room, plus a closet to store his books. All of the books were by Ojibwe or Cree authors, some in English, some in the native syllabary. Hauling the boxes to the table at the front, his back screaming with every step, he started pulling out books, laying them out on the table for the kids to look at or borrow.

He never read to the kids from the books. Storytelling was an oral tradition, not a written one. Reading the stories didn't let him change them, adding something each time around to give a slightly different meaning to the story from the last time he told it.

Besides, he liked his versions better.

The chatter in the room had grown. Looking up, he did a quick head count. Twenty-one kids. First time he'd ever broken twenty. Yeah, maybe there was hope.

A boy, maybe twelve or thirteen, appeared in the doorway. Dark glasses, white cane, and a beautiful black Lab for a seeing-eye dog. This was definitely the day for firsts. He grinned to himself. Another benefit of oral storytelling—it worked for blind kids too.

Bonnie Makademik walked over to the boy. She was a good kid. She'd make him feel welcome. Sure enough, a few seconds later, Bonnie took his arm and led him to the storytelling circle. Too bad the boy couldn't see how cute Bonnie was. About his age too.

Time to start. Pulling out a book on the star of today's story, he stood it up on the table so the kids could see its title: *Nanabush—The Trickster.*

ZACH STOOD JUST INSIDE a doorway to a room. From the voices he heard, the room had at least a dozen noisy kids in it, some younger than him, some older. From the echoes, it was a big room, school gymnasium size, with a high ceiling and no drapes or carpet. Colin had left him and would pick him up after the storytelling.

The kid's voices were now concentrated in one area. Giving Quincy's handle a gentle tug, he started to move in that direction.

"Hi!" said a girl's voice to his right.

He stopped, turning toward her voice and holding out his hand. "Hi. I'm Zach."

A soft, warm hand took his and gave it a gentle squeeze. "I'm Bonnie. Are you here for the storytelling?"

He could tell from the direction of her voice that Bonnie was taller than he was. But girls grew earlier, right? And she sounded about his age. "Yeah. Where do I go?"

"I'll show you," Bonnie said, slipping her arm through his. She smelled of soap and freshly washed skin. He liked it. "Ed—Mr. Two Rivers—he's the storyteller. He's really great," Bonnie said. "You have good timing. He's just about to start."

With her smell in his nostrils and her body warm beside him, at least one part of him was agreeing with Bonnie about his timing being good.

SETTLING DOWN CROSS-LEGGED on the floor, Ed looked around the circle of kids. The blind boy sat beside Bonnie, his dog lying behind him. Time to get started. "Boozhoo!" he said, greeting the circle.

"Aanii, Misoomish!" the kids replied.

"We have some new faces today," Ed said. "A special welcome to you. And, I see one face I don't know. Perhaps our young friend with the beautiful dog could introduce himself." Seeing the boy closer, Ed wondered if he didn't have some Anishinabe blood.

The blind boy straightened up. He swallowed. "My name is Zach Morgan. I'm from Ottawa. I'm here with my mom. She's working on the hydroelectric project."

Some kids started whispering. Tommy Auginash, one of the older boys hanging by the door, stepped forward. "That dam flooded my dad's trap line," Tommy called in a loud voice. "He can't trap no more. But your mom, she can come here and take a job they won't give him? That what you saying, white boy?"

The younger kids became very quiet, glancing between Ed, Zach, and Tommy. Swearing to himself, Ed struggled to his feet.

But Zach turned toward Tommy and spoke before Ed had a chance. "I'm not white. My mother's Cree," he said, his voice strong and steady.

Kid's got spunk, Ed thought.

"Yeah?" Tommy said. "What about your old man? Or do you even know who he is?" The boys with Tommy hooted.

"Tommy," Ed said, and everyone fell silent. "This is not our way. This is not how we greet guests."

"He's not our guest," Tommy shot back. "We didn't invite him here."

"Here, in this place, he is *my* guest," Ed said. "Just as you are. If you cannot act like one, then leave."

Tommy glared at Ed. He looked at the other boys around him, but no one was willing to disrespect an elder. "Screw this shit," Tommy said. He stalked out of the room. A couple of the older boys followed him, but to Ed's surprise, most of them remained. Bonnie whispered something to Zach. Zach smiled and said something back.

Ed sat down again. "Well, *I'm* glad you're here, Zach. And I'm sure I'm not the only one." He stared hard around the circle, prompting several kids to greet Zach and welcome him. "And I better see all you newcomers here again tomorrow, or you're going to make me think I was boring." The kids laughed, and most of the tension left the room.

"Time to start," he said. "Today, I will tell you more stories of Nanabush, the Trickster."

Several of the younger kids squealed in delight and clapped. Martha, one of the older girls raised her hand. "Are these new stories, Mr. Two Rivers?"

"No," he said, grinning. "These are very *old* stories." The kids laughed again. "But they aren't stories I've told you before, if that's what you mean. It will take me a very long time before I run out of Trickster stories. Once, many winters ago, when I was a boy, *my* misoomish told stories of Nanabush in our hunting lodge every night for the entire winter. He said that stories of the Trickster are endless, for Nanabush is as old as the world itself. Older even, because Nanabush remade our world after the great flood."

He shifted his position. His back was already killing him. "Today, I will tell you of how Nanabush tried to get his supper by teaching some birds the 'eyes closed' dance...."

AFTER THE EXCHANGE with Tommy, Zach was wishing Colin had never mentioned the storytelling session. He was used to feeling different, but he'd never felt hated for being different before.

Then Bonnie whispered to him. "Tommy's the one who doesn't know who his dad is, if the stories about his mom are half true. Forget about him. *I'm* glad you're here." She squeezed his hand again.

Any thoughts about Tommy vanished, shoved out by Bonnie's presence. He turned in her direction and smiled. "Thanks. Then I'm glad I'm here, too."

The man Bonnie called Ed Two Rivers also made him feel welcome. Then Ed started his story.

He'd heard the name Nanabush before, but couldn't remember where. When Ed started telling about the "eyes closed dance," a chill run down his spine. He waited until Ed finished the story, which had all the kids howling with laughter, before he raised his hand.

"Yes, Zach?" he heard Ed say.

What was he doing? He swallowed. He could feel everyone waiting for him to talk. "Is Nanabush...does he have any other names?"

"Good question, Zach. The Trickster—well, he's kind of universal. He shows up in stories of all native people. And each people, they have a different name for him. Coyote. Raven. We, the Ojibwe, call him Nanabush or Nanabozho or Wenabozho. To the Blackfoot, he is Napi. To the Assiniboine, Iktomi. You're part Cree, right? Well, your people call him Cahkapes or Ayas...."

Some of his fear left him. Cahkapes. Ayas. Not Wisakejack.

Then Ed went on, "...but usually, the Cree call him *Wisakejack*."

Zach swallowed. That chill spread into his gut. The strange being of his dreams—the creature who was acting as his guide, who was preparing him to face some unrevealed coming danger—was the Trickster.

ED FINISHED FOUR TRICKSTER stories in the hour, all well received by his audience. Well, almost all his audience. Zach Morgan hadn't seemed to enjoy them. But he hadn't been bored either. If anything, he paid closer attention than any of the kids.

As the other kids filed out, Zach walked up to where Ed was boxing up his books. Bonnie had hung around, too.

"Mr. Two Rivers?" Zach asked.

"Hi, Zach. Did you like my stories?"

"Uh, yeah. They were great. I wanted to ask another question, though."

Something about this kid. Something *different*. He couldn't put his finger on it. Maybe it was just how eerily accurate the boy was in positioning himself to face him. Good ears? "Shoot."

"Is Wisakejack always like that? I mean, like, you can't trust him?"

He wondered about how Zach had phrased the question in the present tense, but he shrugged it off. "Well, he *was* tricky, for sure. He was a shapeshifter. He could change into any animal, person, or thing he wanted to. And he could *talk* with animals and plants. Other spirits, too. But he was also a powerful being and did lots of good. Kitche Manitou himself gave Wisakejack the power to recreate the world after the flood. Not like Noah in the Bible. Our flood story is quite different. Have to tell you that one sometime. Wisakejack recreated all the animals and plants and people after the flood."

"That's why he greets everybody as 'little brother' or 'little sister' in his stories," Bonnie added. "Because we're all related to him."

"Everything's connected," Zach whispered.

Ed considered Zach. This kid knew more than he was letting on. "That's right. That's one of our strongest beliefs. Everything in the world shares a common spirit connecting us all." He turned to his boxes. "Got a couple of Wisakejack books on CD. Maybe you'd like to borrow them?"

Zach hesitated, then nodded. "Sure. I'll dump them to my iPod from my mom's computer. Thanks."

Ed considered the boy as Zach put the books into his coat pocket. "I've got a feeling, Zach, these weren't the first Trickster stories you've heard."

Zach didn't answer right away. "A friend told me some," he said, quietly. "At least, I thought he was a friend."

"Yeah," Bonnie piped up. "I used to think Sarah Red Hawk was my friend, until she copied my environmental studies paper and told the teacher I'd copied hers." She bit her lip, looking at Zach. "I can, uh, walk with you back to the motel if you want, Zach."

"Sure," Zach said, and she beamed. He held out his hand to Ed. "Thanks, Mr. Two Rivers."

Ed shook his hand. "Hope to see you here again."

"I can bring you tomorrow," Bonnie said quickly. Then she reddened. "I mean, I know you don't need 'bringing' but we can walk over together."

"Sure, Bonnie," Zach said. They started to leave, then Zach stopped and turned back. "So, Mr. Two Rivers? Wisakejack—he's really a good guy, right?"

Again, Ed noticed Zach's use of the present tense. Kid's definitely *different.* "Well, that's a hard one to answer," Ed said, with a laugh. "Wisakejack tended to mess things up a lot, even when he was trying to help. And he *was* called the Trickster."

Zach nodded, but Ed could have sworn that Zach looked scared as he walked away. But thoughts of the boy disappeared as he remembered that, in less than two hours, he was burying his granddaughter. Fighting to keep his grief from showing, he locked up the hall and walked back to the store.

CHAPTER 23

THE SPIRIT ROAD

JUST BEFORE DUSK, an hour before Mary Two Rivers was to be buried, the snow began to fall, as if Mary's death had called winter not only into the hearts of those who had loved her, but into the town where she'd lived her short life as well.

Scrunched between Ed and Gwyn, Caz stared out the window of Ed's truck as Ed drove to the cemetery on the reserve. She watched the thick flakes falling as the small houses on the outskirts of town gave way to the occasional diner or gas station, and finally to thick bush. Ed didn't talk, and Gwyn was never chatty.

The silence suited her mood. She and Ed had spent a fruitless day scouring the town for anyone with the Mark. If another Heroka was in Thunder Lake, they were keeping well hidden.

The day of searching for one of her kind in a town of strangers had had an unexpected effect on her. She'd been barely over a year old when the Tainchel had murdered her parents and her brother. Her life since their deaths had been an endless series of foster homes, none of which had lasted for more than a year. She knew she could be difficult, but she didn't think she was any worse than most kids were. But even Mitch, her legal guardian, had only ever spent time with her long enough to pawn her off on the next set of foster parents.

The simple truth, to her, was that no one *wanted* her.

Until the last couple, the Martenenkos. They'd been nice. She'd even begun to trust them, to try to get along with them.

Then they were dead. Murdered. By the Tainchel again, if Gwyn was right. Murdered because of her. Now Mitch himself was dead, again at the hands of the Tainchel.

All she knew was that through her entire life, the only people who seemed to want her were the Tainchel, and that wasn't the kind of wanting she wanted.

So here she was, still alone in the world and still being hunted. The hours she had spent today becoming a hunter herself, searching for another of her kind in the faces of strangers in a strange town had only deepened her sense of loneliness and fear.

Was this all her life was ever going to be? Always an outsider, feared and hated? Always alone? Always hunted?

Ed turned at the sign, "Thunder Lake Ojibwe First Nation." The roughly paved road ran through bush for another mile before they passed a gas station beside a cabin with a sign declaring, "Trading Post—Authentic Indian Handicraft." A mile in, the bush ended, and they entered the main part of the reserve.

The reserve contained about thirty homes spread around a small lake. Most were tiny box-like bungalows, with the occasional wooden cabin, all on closely spaced lots, the bush running up right to the back.

Ed parked on the road in front of a small bungalow with white siding. A black hearse sat in the driveway, a layer of white flakes building on it. "This part," he said, not looking at them, "it's really just for family...." His voice trailed off.

She saw Gwyn's jaw muscles tighten, but he just nodded. "We'll wait here."

Ed looked relieved. "When we come out, we'll walk to the cemetery, behind that thing." He nodded toward the hearse. He got out of the truck without another word and went inside.

Gwyn got out, leaving the door open. She shivered at the cold. "Hey!"

"I don't like being cooped up," Gwyn growled. Tail wagging furiously, Gelert jumped down from the truck bed to rejoin his master.

She got out too, flipping up her hood against the cold. She'd have to find a winter coat somewhere in town. Rizzo poked his nose out of her pocket, sniffed, then disappeared again. "You know, most of my totem hibernates through the winter."

Gwyn stared at the house. "I'm tired of being treated like a leper. Mary was important to me, too."

She swallowed, feeling again her sense of isolation in this human world. She looked at Gwyn. She was, she admitted, in major awe of him. Gwyn Blaidd was a thing of legend in the Heroka. The man who had fought the Tainchel—and won.

Or not. Now even he was on the run. And even before the Tainchel's resurrection, he'd been living in isolation himself. If Gwyn Blaidd could only know a life of being alone and hunted, what more could she expect?

A life with Gwyn as her new guardian? She'd never tell him that, but ever since he'd told her Mitch's plan for her, she'd secretly prayed for it to come true. Yeah, right. Like that was going to happen. Gwyn had never said so, but she knew he'd brought her along only because he'd had no other choice. She sighed. It wasn't as if she *tried* to pick fights with him. It just seemed to happen.

The sound of a single drumbeat rolled down to them from an open window in the house. Another followed, then two more. She looked at Gwyn.

"The sacred water drum of the *Midewewin*," he said. "Four beats, one for each day that it will take for Mary's spirit to reach the Spirit World. The ceremony's begun." Voices inside joined together in a low chanting. Gelert perked up his ears, staring at the house.

"The Meeday—what?"

"Mee-day-way-ween. The Ojibwe Society of Medicine, their main order of shamans. Really old. Predates the Europeans coming to this country. Ed's an elder in it."

"What do they do?"

Gwyn shrugged. "They're the practitioners of traditional medicine, the custodians of tribal knowledge and lore. And they lead most ceremonies—namings, marriages, burials. Ed might tell you more. Or not. They don't talk about it with outsiders much."

"You said the Midewewin is their main shaman order. Are there others?"

"Used to be another called the *Waubunowin*. The Society of the Dawn. Their ceremonies mostly took place at night, ending at dawn. No idea if it still exists anywhere. They're even more closed-mouthed about the Waubunowin than they are the Midewewin."

"Why?"

Gwyn hesitated. "The Society of the Dawn supposedly dealt with more of the darker magics and spirits."

She considered that. "So, like, they're the Sith to the Midewewin's Jedi?"

Gwyn glared at her. "Do *not* say that to Ed."

"Darker magics? Like the Windigo spirit?"

He just shook his head. "Don't you start on that idea, too."

After about twenty minutes, the chanting stopped. People began filing out. Pallbearers loaded Mary's coffin, and the hearse eased out of the driveway. Charlie, Ed, Vera, and a short, squat Ojibwe woman fell into step behind, with others from the house following. As the hearse rolled slowly past, Charlie glared at them, but the woman gave Gwyn a sad smile. Gelert whined.

"That's Elizabeth, Mary's mom. She's good people," Gwyn said as he and Caz fell in behind the last of the procession, a few paces back. Several in the crowd cast nervous glances over their shoulders at them.

The cemetery was a half mile from the house at the end of a dirt road in a large cleared area surrounded by bush. A mound of snow-covered earth stood beside an open grave, and beside the grave stood an ancient Ojibwe man. Caz looked at Gwyn who shrugged. "Probably the elder who'll lead the ceremony."

The pallbearers laid Mary's coffin beside the grave, and the grievers formed a circle around the elder and the grave. Gwyn and Caz stayed outside the circle. The drumming and the chanting began again, and the elder started to speak in Ojibwe in a song-like rhythm. "Do you know what he's saying?" she whispered.

"Some," Gwyn replied quietly. "Mary will travel the Spirit Road, the path from this life to the Spirit World. Her spirit will have four days to make that journey and safely reach her new home in the Spirit World where all her ancestors live. He's giving her instructions on how to overcome obstacles she'll encounter on her journey."

The elder finished. The drumming stopped. The pallbearers lowered Mary's coffin into the grave. They picked up their shovels.

The sound of the dirt striking the coffin hit Caz like a drumbeat from beyond the grave. Some of Elizabeth's strength left her then, and she broke down. Charlie took her in his arms as she sobbed into his chest.

When the grave was covered, the grievers came forward to lay tokens on the ground beside it and to touch the soil. Soon flowers, cards, ribbons, feathers, and offerings of tobacco ringed the mound. The elder placed a small, round pot on the grave mound and dropped a match into it. Flames leapt up. Gelert growled but settled at a touch from Gwyn.

"They'll keep that fire burning for the next four days," Gwyn said, "lighting Mary's journey along the Spirit Road. Friends will keep vigil, speaking to her, guiding her."

Elizabeth, Charlie, Vera, and Ed spent a quiet moment alone beside the grave, and then began to make their way out of the cemetery, receiving condolences as they moved through the crowd. After they left, the mourners filed out behind them.

The gravesite was now empty except for her and Gwyn, and the elder who had given the ceremony, who was now moving the farewell tokens to the foot of the grave.

"The Spirit World lies to the west," Gwyn explained, "the same direction the grave faces. He's placing Mary's gifts where she'll find them as she begins her journey along the Spirit Road." Gwyn began walking out of the cemetery, Gelert beside him.

Caz followed. "Now what?"

"Charlie and Elizabeth will give a dinner for those who came to the ceremony."

"And we're going? Sure we'll be welcome?"

Gwyn shrugged. "Probably not. But I need to talk to Ed about something Leiddia mentioned."

"So that's it for the funeral?"

"Four days from now, there'll be a bigger feast," Gwyn said, "celebrating Mary's arrival in the Spirit World, where she will live in happiness forever in the traditional ways of her people, waiting to meet her loved ones when they make their own journeys there."

Gwyn kept walking, but Caz stopped to stare back at the gravesite. The flames from the pot flickered in the deepening darkness, reminding her too sharply of Mitch's funeral pyre.

Happily ever after—yeah, right. She wondered where the spirits of all the people she'd lost in her short life were right now. Her parents, her brother, the Martenenkos, Mitch. Walking the Spirit Road themselves? Or were they still here, watching her, waiting for her to avenge their deaths. She wiped her cheek, suddenly wet and not from the falling snow. Pushing away the memories of those she'd lost, she turned her back on the grave and ran to catch up with Gwyn.

MARY TWO RIVERS stood at the edge of a path winding west into this dark primal forest. Dusk had crept up quickly and what light remained would soon fail—as the strange pull in her heart that had drawn her this far had suddenly failed her. She had no idea how she had come to be here. She was supposed to be doing something. But what?

This forest before her was so very different from the bush of her home. These trees were taller, thicker, more closely spaced. With the fading light, she couldn't even see where their tops disappeared into the night sky.

She began to cry. She didn't want to be here. She wanted to go home.

Home.

The thought called like a soft voice, pulling her, promising to fill the emptiness that now lay inside her where her heart used to beat. And then she realized that it *was* a voice, a voice calling to her, calling her home.

Home, the voice chanted in Ojibwe, lay beyond these strange, dark woods. The voice was telling her what she must do. She must follow the path that she was on, for this was the Spirit Road, the path that would lead her home. As it spoke, the path she'd been following began to glow slightly. But the voice brought warnings, too—warnings of the dangers in this journey.

You will be afraid, but you must walk alone.

You will be hungry, but you must eat alone.

You will be tired, but you must sleep alone.

Your spirit will become weak. It is then that the tests will appear.

Tests. The smell of the creature that had killed her still lingered in this place. Was that the test? Would it pursue her even here? Did she have to escape that thing? She hoped not, because that really hadn't worked out too well the first time.

"You know," she said out loud, "being dead shouldn't be this much work." With a shiver and a sigh, Mary stepped onto the glowing path that was the Spirit Road, and the dark trees swallowed her.

THE SHAMAN now called Comdowtah lay curled on the floor, shivering and wracked by hunger.

You must feed the Hunger, the voices said.

"So soon?" Comdowtah cried. "It's been only two days."

The Hunger grows stronger as the time approaches. We grow stronger, too. As do you.

Comdowtah laughed, and then cried out in pain. "You call this strength?"

You deny the power. The Hunger is your power, your strength.

"This is not what I wanted."

It is too late.

"Too late for me?"

For the Boy. The Wolf. This world.

Comdowtah wept. From the pain, the hunger. The despair.

Feed the Hunger!

CHAPTER 24

TRICKS AND TREATS

W HEN KATE ARRIVED back at the motel after her day at the dam, she found a note from Macready about taking Zach to an Ojibwe storytelling session. Still shaken from her experience at the dam, she crumpled up the note and threw it in the garbage, angry with Macready for taking Zach without her permission, and fearful over Zach being in a strange situation.

She checked her email, finding a confirmation from Jonas that the DNA results on Mary Two Rivers would be ready tomorrow morning, and that both Leiddia Barker's DNA samples and Rick Calhoun's clothes had arrived at the CSIS lab. She emailed him a summary of her day, omitting her strange vision, and then signed off just as a knock came.

Zach, Quincy, and Macready stood outside, along with a pretty Ojibwe girl, who Zach introduced as Bonnie. As Macready excused himself, Kate started to say something about taking Zach, but with Bonnie there, she bit her tongue.

She turned to Bonnie. "Zach and I are going to have dinner at The Outfitter. Would you like to join us?"

Bonnie looked crestfallen. "Oh, I'd love to, Ms. Morgan, but I have chores and homework to do." She turned to Zach. "So I'll meet you here tomorrow, and we'll walk over to the storytelling?"

Kate started to protest, but Zach gave Bonnie such a big grin, she didn't have the heart. "Sure, that's great," he said.

Kate smiled as Bonnie left, but groaned inwardly. From the way Bonnie looked at Zach, she could tell the girl was quite taken with her son. Kate was in no way ready for the "girls" stage in Zach's life.

Over dinner, as she listened to Zach talk excitedly about the storytelling session, she admitted to herself that she'd not really been worried about his safety.

Between Macready and Quincy, Zach had been safe. The truth was that she was resisting Zach's interest in a culture she'd left behind.

Later, as she lay in bed, she allowed herself a smile of pride. Zach was growing up, becoming comfortable on his own and in new situations. And attracting the opposite sex. She sighed, thinking about all the changes that would bring in both their lives.

But the same thought reminded her of why she was here—to find out if Zach's Heroka blood might bring other changes for him, changes much more serious than suddenly noticing girls in a different way. She'd tried searching the Tainchel databases for answers to those questions after she'd returned from the dam, but without success. Maybe tomorrow....

When sleep finally took her, her dreams were troubled, filled with images of Zach that morphed into wild animals hunting people beside a dark lake, a lake where strange words whispered to her from the water.

THAT NIGHT, Zach lay in bed listening to Ed's Wisakejack stories on his iPod. They weren't clarifying anything about Wisakejack beyond the ambiguous picture that Ed's storytelling had painted, or beyond the one he'd already formed himself.

He had no doubt that he was in contact with another mind during his nightly encounters with Wisakejack. These were not regular dreams. He'd learned early on how to control his dreams. And there was one thing he knew about these dreams.

He wasn't the one in control.

The next story started. Maybe this one would answer his main question: should he trust Wisakejack?

"Wisakejack is a central figure in many Cree stories," the narrator began.

"Hey, turn it up," a familiar voice said.

Zach opened his eyes and sat straight up in bed. Except he wasn't in bed anymore. He was lying on the ground inside the teepee again. A fire burned in the middle. Beside it, Wisakejack sat cross-legged. The tent flap was open, and outside, a starry night sky rested on a dark forest.

Zach groaned. "I don't suppose I could have a night off from you?"

"No time," Wisakejack said. "Too much to learn. Now shush! I want to listen."

"I don't have my iPod here, so you can't—" Zach stopped. The narrator's voice seemed to be coming right out of the air.

Wisakejack chuckled. "You're still lying in your bed with your talky thingy playing. And if you can hear it in your head, then I can hear it."

"Oh."

"Now, please be quiet. They're talking about me, so naturally this is important."

"Wisakejack," the narrator was saying, "was often an object of humor in stories."

"Always leave 'em laughing, little brother," Wisakejack said with a grin.

The disembodied voice continued. "He is a mass of contradictions. Sometimes, he is powerful, magical, wise, heroic, and altruistic. In other tales, he is pathetic, helpless, stupid, vain, and morally ambiguous. Modern Cree regard him with a mixture of respect, contempt, and affection. He is a teacher and a fool—"

"Hey, this guy's good," Wisakejack said, nodding.

"He called you a fool."

"A teacher *and* a fool. Being a fool was *how* I taught. Want kids to learn what *not* to do? What's dangerous? What's not acceptable by the People? Best way, show 'em somebody doing something stupid or bad—and paying the price. Make it funny too, and the kids'll enjoy learning."

"He was always hungry," the narrator continued.

"Well, duh," Wisakejack snorted. "My *people* were always hungry. My stories reminded kids how close starvation always was. Just a bad hunt away—just one mistake—if they didn't use everything Kitche Manitou gave them—treat it all with respect—learn that everything is connected. If they didn't—well, the Hunger was always waiting."

Zach thought he was beginning to understand the Wisakejack stories. Maybe he'd been wrong. Maybe he could trust his strange visitor after all.

"When Wisakejack recreated the world after the flood," the narrator said, "he put up a barrier between man and the animals, so that man could no longer talk to them."

"Okay, so why'd you do that?" Zach asked.

Wisakejack's grin disappeared. "Of all of Kitche Manitou's creations, only humans are capable of greed. I didn't want all my newly recreated, beautiful, pure animals to be contaminated. So now, people can't teach animals greed. All they can do is hunt them, kill them, destroy their homes, lock 'em in cages…." He shook his head.

"It would be cool to talk to animals," Zach said.

A sly smile crept onto Wisakejack's face. "Some still can. There are those who never forgot the ancient compact with the animals. Those who remembered that we depend on the earth, the plants, and the animals. Remembered that everything's connected. To those, I left the gift."

"Who are they?"

"They're called the Heroka. But shush. He's still talking."

"But others," the narrator continued, "say that Kitche Manitou later took away Wisakejack's power over people and animals, leaving him only the ability to flatter and deceive. A trickster."

Zach stared at Wisakejack across the fire, suddenly afraid. The flames threw dark shadows on the spirit's face, making it hard to read his expression. But he was certain of one thing—Wisakejack wasn't smiling anymore.

"Probably should have hit the 'pause' button before that part," Wisakejack said quietly.

"You're the Trickster," Zach whispered.

Wisakejack sighed. "Little brother, I'm here to help you."

Zach jumped up. "Prove it!"

Wisakejack shrugged. "I already saved you once. You gotta trust me."

"Trust the Trickster?" Zach yelled, backing away. "Get out of my head! Stay away from me!" His fear seized him. Ducking through the teepee flap, he ran into the cold night air and plunged into the black forest. He ran as fast as he could, stumbling in the darkness and falling several times. He ran and ran. Finally he stopped, sinking to the ground, leaning against a pine tree, gasping.

"Okay, you want a night off?" came a voice from above. Jumping to his feet, Zach looked up. Perched like a bird on a thick branch twenty feet over his head, Wisakejack shrugged. "So be it. You're on your own tonight, little brother. But you better wear this." He tossed something down.

Zach caught it. It was a deerskin jacket, beautifully soft, and fringed and decorated, like the one Wisakejack wore, with a matching leather pouch on a long strap.

"Put it on, kid." Wisakejack sniffed the air. "Because winter's coming early—and it's going to be a killer."

Zach looked up again. Wisakejack had vanished. As he searched the branches above for his strange dreamtime visitor, something cold and wet hit his face. Turning to a clear patch of night sky, he could see snowflakes falling against the stars and blackness behind.

He shivered, suddenly feeling very cold—and very alone.

CHAPTER 25

THE SMELL OF THE SPIRIT WORLD

MARY'S FUNERAL DINNER took place at the reserve's ceremonial grounds. Gwyn sat beside Caz on a set of three-row wooden bleachers, close to the warmth of one of the many bonfires, but apart from the other guests. Caz had been silent since the cemetery, which was fine with Gwyn. He didn't feel like talking, so they sat watching the festivities.

Overlooking the Rez's small lake, the ceremonial grounds were simply a flat area cleared of bush a hundred yards in diameter. In the middle stood an open structure, fifty feet across, resembling the framework for a circular tent built entirely of pine tree trunks. Another circle of timbers on the ground marked a boundary around this structure.

Inside this area, two lines of men wove between the bonfires to accompanying drumming and singing in a traditional Spirit Road dance. Others were eating and talking, standing in small groups or sitting on the other bleachers outside the circle.

Ed made his way through the crowd to climb up to where they sat. "You okay?" Gwyn asked quietly as he sat down beside them.

Ed seemed to consider this. "My granddaughter is traveling the Spirit Road. Soon she will be with her people again. Soon she will be happy again." He nodded. "Yes, I'm okay."

Gwyn couldn't think of anything to say, so he just nodded, too.

"You talk to her?" Ed asked.

"Leiddia? Yeah." He swallowed, remembering her smell, the taste of her lips. "She doesn't know anything about Mary's death. I'm sure of it."

"I never thought she did," Ed said. "But you knew her best."

"She doesn't know of any other Heroka around here, either."

"And we've found no one with the Mark. So what does that leave?" Ed asked.

"Windigo?" Caz offered.

Ed stayed expressionless. Gwyn snorted, but then remembered something that Leiddia had mentioned that morning. "Wasn't Walter Keejek kind of the expert on windigo lore? Can we talk to him?"

Ed just stared at the bonfires.

"Ed?" Gwyn asked.

"You don't believe it's a windigo," Ed said, still staring at the fires. "Walter won't change that."

"No, but Leiddia reminded me that there is such a thing as windigo psychosis. Someone might be convinced they've turned windigo, and are acting out their psychosis."

"By killing and eating people?" Caz said. "Again, yuck." Then she seemed to remember about Mary and fell silent.

"Shouldn't we still talk to Walter?" Gwyn asked. "He might know something."

Ed hesitated again, then pointed to where the elder who had led the ceremony at Mary's graveside was leading a line of dancers. "That is George Ozawamik, an old friend and a Midewewin elder. He knows much about the windigo legends. More than I do. He'll join us after this ceremony."

Gwyn sighed. "All right. So what's the deal with you and Walter? Leiddia said you two had a big fight."

Ed just nodded.

"What about?"

"Things he wanted to do with the Midewewin. Things he was teaching Mary."

Caz perked up. "Gwyn was telling me about the Midewewin. So it's a society of medicine men?"

"Women too," Ed answered, turning to Caz, probably glad to change the subject. "It is so old, no one even knows where the name came from. Some say it means 'The Good-Hearted Ones,' from *mino dewewin*. Some say it comes from *midewe*, which means 'The Resonance,' for the drums we use in the ceremonies. The government and the priests almost wiped it out when they forced all the kids into residential schools. Entire generations were never taught in its ways. But many bands have brought it back, teaching the old ways of healing. George and my grandfather taught me those ways when I was young. Walter and I helped reestablish the Midewewin here."

"So what kind of things do they teach?" Caz asked.

"An initiate learns the ways of the plants and their powers, which ones to use for which illness, how to gather each plant, which parts to use, how to prepare it, how to administer it. An initiate must also learn the ceremonies, the petitions to the spirits, the chants. It is a way of life. And you learn more at each level."

"Levels?" Caz asked.

"There are four levels of the Midewewin...."

Ed continued explaining as Caz listened. Gwyn listened too, knowing better than to try again to get Ed to talk about Walter when he clearly didn't want to. But as the warmth of the fire and the hypnotic rhythms of chanting and drums washed over him, he succumbed to a desire to close his eyes. Flickering against his eyelids, the shadows thrown by the flames began to suggest shapes—shapes of beasts that moved, not in the random flicker of fire, but in the steps of a dance that had been old before humankind walked this Earth.

The dance was important. Once, he had known why. Once, he had known the dance. Maybe he still knew it. Maybe if he focused hard enough on the flickering shapes, he could recall the steps, remember the dance.

Step. Turn. Jump. Jump.

Remember the dance....

Step. Turn. Jump. Jump.

Remember....

GRANDSON.

Pine scent, sweet and sharp, stung his nostrils. He blinked his eyes opened. The last thing he remembered was closing his eyes at the ceremonial grounds. Now he lay face down on a carpet of pine needles in the dark. He looked up.

The ceremonial grounds and the bonfires were gone. Those who had come to grieve and remember Mary were gone, including Ed and Caz. He was alone in a dark forest under a clear night sky and full moon shining above a lake as black as a pit and as still as a corpse. He shivered. He remembered this place— the trees taller, the woods thicker, the smells sharper than in any forest he'd ever known—the sense of something primal, older than the very Earth itself, and yet somehow still virgin. Eternal but untouched.

He'd been here before. The night Mitch had died.

No. The night Mitch had been *allowed* to die. Allowed to die by....

Grandson.

By Mahigan, the silver wolf. The fury that Gwyn had felt that night erupted in his belly like a flame catching on dry tinder.

Grandson.

Behind him. A bit to the right. His wolf senses seemed sharper in this place. In one smooth motion, he turned and leapt.

He had the momentary satisfaction of sensing surprise from Mahigan as his fist connected hard against the beast's head. In the next eye blink, the wolf—suddenly impossibly huge, larger than the dark forest itself—seized him in great jaws and tossed him like a chewed bone. He hit a pine tree the size of a redwood ten feet up, then fell to the ground, his impact only slightly cushioned by the thick carpet of moss and needles.

Groaning, he pushed himself to his hands and knees. Pain flamed in his left side. He looked up, expecting Mahigan to be moving in to finish the job.

Instead, the wolf sat on its haunches several yards away, normal size once more, its great head tilted to one side as if considering him. Gwyn felt a touch in his mind again, and suddenly the pain in his side disappeared. He sensed a mixture of conflicting emotions in Mahigan—pride battling anger, hope fighting despair.

I did not kill your friend, Grandson.

"You let him die," he rasped, pulling himself to his feet.

I could not have saved him. I am a spirit. I may only walk in your world through my wolf children. And those such as you.

"Then why didn't you let me save him?"

You would have died. You could not have faced that creature. You still cannot. You do not have the strength.

"You could've given me some of yours. You seem to have some to spare."

Once, that was true. I could have filled you with my power, the power of your totem.

"Yeah? So why didn't you? Getting old? Can't get the power up anymore?"

The failing lies not with me, but with you.

A chill not borne by the night air shook him. "What are you saying?"

You could not hold my power. You have forgotten what you once knew. All life is connected, and through that web of life, your kind draws its strength. You have removed yourself from that web.

"My kind is dying, along with our animal brothers."

And you accept that fate, your hate feeding your resignation, your resignation feeding your hate.

"I don't hate—"

You hate humans. For the deaths of your people, your totem, your friends.

"That was the Tainchel—"

Yet you see all humans as you see them. Given a choice, you would save your people even if it meant the end of all humans.

"Not a choice I'm likely to be faced with."

You have no idea what choices you will soon face. And you are prepared for none of them.

The chill returned. "What do you mean?"

Tell me, grandson—why are you here?

"To help a friend. Two friends—"

You came here to kill the ones who killed your friend, who hunt you and your kind. Your hate brought you here. Or so you think. You do not know the true reason.

"What do you mean?"

You were drawn here. For a purpose far from any you hold or could imagine.

"Nobody pulls my strings," he growled, but some doubt was growing.

The dark forest was brightening. Flames flickered behind Mahigan, and for a moment, Gwyn thought the forest was on fire. Then he realized that this world was fading, that he was returning to the real world where the bonfires burned and Mary's mourners danced. Mahigan grew fainter. "Tell me what I need to do!" Gwyn cried.

The wolf's final words came as faint as the wind moving the pines overhead. *The boy holds the key. Find the boy.*

SOMEONE WAS SHAKING HIM. "Gwyn!" That was Caz's voice.

He opened his eyes. Gelert was licking his hand, whining. The dog's fear for him was almost overwhelming. Sending calming thoughts to the hound, he tried to orient himself.

He was back at the ceremonial grounds, lying on the same bleachers, and part of him understood that he'd never physically left. From the faces around him, though, he guessed he wasn't the only one aware that something strange had just occurred.

Ed stood beside Caz, staring at him. It was one of the few times he could recall Ed looking worried. An aged Ojibwe man, his eyes wide, stood behind Ed—George Ozawamik.

"What happened, Gray Legs?" Ed asked.

Gwyn ran a hand over his face, trying to focus. "You tell me. One minute I was here, the next…." His words trailed off. Where *had* he been? He'd now met Mahigan twice, and he still had no idea of where that strange primeval forest was.

Leaning in closer to Gwyn, George sniffed at him. Turning to Ed, he said something in Ojibwe. Ed frowned. "He says you smell of the Spirit World. What happened?"

Gwyn had no intention of relating his encounters with Mahigan, especially in front of a stranger. He began to say something, to make up some story, but suddenly, a sensory river flooded his mind. Smells of the bush, of warm animal musk, of the blood scent of prey. Sounds of softly padding paws on moss and pine needles, fur whispering against fur. Feral emotions, the adrenaline rush of the hunt, the bond of the pack.

"Gwyn," Caz said, "have we lost you to la-la land again?"

"Wolves," he whispered. "They're back. I can sense a pack again."

Ed and George started talking in Ojibwe, and he felt their eyes on him.

"He's brought them back," he said, as much to himself as to anyone.

"He?" Caz said. "Who he?"

He didn't answer her. As the wolves' minds continued to merge with his, he sensed that Mahigan had called this pack back from wherever they had disappeared to. He felt another shock as he realized how far away these wolves were, miles beyond what he would have guessed based on the strength of his contact with them.

You smell of the Spirit World.

That was it. His contact with Mahigan, so recent and powerful, had left its mark on him, a mark that the wolves could sense even from a great distance. An old memory returned, a memory of how strong his link with his wolf brothers had once been, when the wolves ran thick and wild over this land. A pang of loss stung him, but he savagely thrust the feeling aside when he caught the scent the pack was following.

The smell of rotting wood and mushrooms and corruption.

"They're tracking it," he said. "That scent I found where Mary was killed. And where Mitch was killed." He stood. "We need to go. Now." Else, he risked losing his link to the wolves, and through them, the trail they were following.

Or rather, had *stopped* following.

Searching the minds of the pack, he found the alpha male. Distraught, the wolf had halted the chase, torn between obeying the will of Mahigan to follow the trail and succumbing to the pack's fear of the thing they hunted.

Now that he'd found the trail, Gwyn wasn't going to lose it. He calmed the animal and coaxed it to follow the scent once again. The wolf whined but complied, probably due to the touch of Mahigan that still permeated Gwyn's spirit. It set out again on the trail, the rest of the pack falling in behind it.

Keeping his link with the pack, Gwyn jumped down from the bleachers. "Ed, I need your truck. I'm going to use the wolves to track this thing down."

"If you're hunting what killed Mary, then I'm coming too," Ed replied.

"Me, too," Caz said, jumping down beside Ed. Gwyn started to protest, but Caz cut him off. "Don't start. You just told me this thing was there when Mitch was killed."

"I don't know—" he stopped, looking at the hard set of both their faces. "All right, let's go. I don't want to lose my link."

George said something in Ojibwe. Ed turned to Gwyn. "He asks if you know what you hunt."

"So what is it?"

George leaned in close to Gwyn. He could smell the old man's breath, sour and tinged with smoke. "*Windigo*," George whispered.

Gwyn snorted. "Him, too?" Ed nodded. Gwyn just shook his head and stalked off toward Ed's truck, not waiting to see if Ed or Caz were following.

CHAPTER 26

THE HUNGER RETURNS

IT WAITED. With its hunger, in the dark woods on that cold night, it waited. All around it, it felt the emptiness, the memory of all the things that had lived in this place but were now gone. These woods now had their own hunger, a hunger that fed its own.

Spitting out the clump of moss it had been chewing, it sniffed the air. It could smell the man now. Smell his sweat. Smell his flesh. He was coming closer.

It waited....

FRANK MUELLER PULLED HIS CRUISER up in front of Walter Keejek's cabin around eight o'clock that night. After calling in his position, he got out of the car. Hitching his pants up under his belly, he walked to the cabin, whistling. Snow still fell thickly, but enough moonlight shone through the cloud cover and reflected off the carpet of white for him to see his way.

Some out-of-town relative had filed a missing person's report on Walter, after not being able to contact him for several weeks. A check at the hunting guide company where he worked occasionally confirmed that he hadn't been in for a month. And no one around town could recall seeing him for quite some time. Thornton had convinced the local provincial court judge to issue a search warrant for Walter's cabin.

Climbing the rickety steps, Mueller rapped on the front door and waited. No answer. He banged more loudly. Still no response. Trying the door handle, he found it unlocked. The door swung slowly inward revealing only darkness.

"Walter?" he called. "It's Constable Frank Mueller, OPP. You there?" Still no answer. Pulling his flashlight from his belt, he clicked it on and stepped inside.

Something brushed against his legs. "Shit!" he shouted, jumping back, stabbing the flashlight down. A black cat stared back, meowing, yellow eyes shining in the beam. Swearing, he kicked at the cat but it scampered out the door. His heart still pounding, he shone the flashlight around.

He stood in the main room of the cabin. A sagging couch and a rough-hewn wooden table with a lamp sat in front of a small stone fireplace. The floor was bare wood. A pot-bellied wood stove stood in a corner off to the right, its exhaust pipe curving up to a hole in that wall. A stainless steel sink, another wooden table and chair, and an ancient refrigerator completed what looked to be the kitchen area.

Two makeshift bookcases flanked the fireplace—just three shelves of rough pine planks resting on cinder blocks. Mueller turned on the table lamp near the fireplace and scanned the books. Most were nonfiction: environmental science—animal behavior—a government report on hydroelectric projects in Ontario—several books by native authors on Cree and Ojibwe ceremonies and stories. He shook his head. Not a fucking decent read in all of them.

A computer monitor sat on the kitchen table. The computer itself—one of the old tower models—sat under the table. He'd take that with him. Maybe the geek who supported their systems in the office could get into it. Keejek's emails might give them a clue as to his whereabouts.

A door at the back led to a bedroom with an air mattress on the floor and a pile of blankets in disarray. The medicine cabinet in the small bathroom held nothing but toothpaste and aspirin. No prescriptions. Healthy old guy.

Fuck this, he thought. *Take the computer back and call it a night.* He stepped back into the small bedroom.

He stopped. What was that?

Standing in the dark, he strained to hear above the wheeze of his own breathing.

There it was again. Something moving outside the bedroom window.

He crept quietly to the window. A small cleared area sat behind the cabin. He could make out a stand of firewood and a rusting mountain bike, both now under a growing blanket of snow. He could see a series of marks in the snow but they didn't look like any footprints he recognized. Farther, the trees formed a dark curtain the dim light couldn't penetrate.

He swallowed. Probably just an animal. Who'd be snooping around here, anyway? Unless it was Walter, finally returning home.

Going back into the main room, he walked to the front door and stepped onto the porch. "This is Constable Frank Mueller," he called out to the night. "Is that you, Walter?" No answer came, and he heard no more sounds of anything moving outside. He shrugged. Must have been his imagination. Or the wind.

He went back inside. He'd take the computer back to the station, file his report, and get some dinner. He disconnected the computer from the monitor, picked it up in both arms, kicked open the front door, and went outside.

A branch snapped in the woods to his left. He stopped, turning in that direction. He stared into the dark bush but could see nothing beyond the vague outline of trees.

"Walter?" he called again. Still no answer.

He stepped off the porch and walked to the cruiser. "Whoever you are, I know you're out there," he called, heaving the computer onto the hood. "*I'm here with a search warrant.*" He opened the front passenger door. "Figure you can't say the same. Unless you're Walter Keejek, you're trespassing. So why don't you just come out, and save me the trouble of looking for you?" he called, not relishing the prospect of postponing dinner to tramp around in dark bush at the end of a double shift.

Still no answer. He hefted the computer off the hood and carried it to the open door. "You make me come find you, I'll charge you with trespassing. Come out now, and I'll let it slide." He bent over, wrestling the computer onto the seat.

Maybe it was bending over like that, exposing his backside to his unseen observer, that brought the thought into his head. Maybe it was the sudden memory that two people had died horribly recently, and right now, he had his hands full, his back turned, and his gun holstered.

Or maybe it was the smell that reached him just then—the sharp, acrid odor of fungus mixed with the sweetness of decaying wood and the stench of something rotting.

Whatever the reason, it occurred to him in that moment that missing dinner was not the worst thing that could happen to him that night.

That thought flitted through his mind and slithered down his spine an eye blink before the worst thing that could happen to him sank its teeth into his butt.

Mueller screamed.

AFTER WISAKEJACK DISAPPEARED from the tree branch above him, Zach stood alone in the dark forest wondering what to do. Trying to wake up wasn't working. He wasn't controlling this dream—Wisakejack was.

He looked at the jacket that Wisakejack had given him. Long, thin needles, dyed different colors and woven into the soft leather, decorated its front. He ran his fingers over them. Porcupine quills.

He frowned. Now, how did he know that?

Wisakejack had been truthful about one thing for sure—it was cold and getting colder as the snow fell even faster, slipping through the canopy above to blanket the forest floor in soft whiteness. He shrugged. No harm in staying warm and dry, even in a dream. He shrugged the jacket on, thrilling to the softness and warmth of the leather. And it fit him perfectly.

He couldn't explain it, but something about the jacket just felt…right.

He slipped the strap of the leather pouch over his head and right shoulder so that the pouch hung at his left side. Again, that felt right. Something rattled inside the pouch. Opening it, he pulled out a polished bone tapering to a sharp point, a rough stone, a smooth stone, and some white parchment.

Wisakejack's strange tale of his escape from his mother came back to him. The medicine pouch in that story had held four things: a bone awl, a fire-flint, a stone to strike the flint on, and birch bark to catch the spark. "Hope this doesn't mean something's chasing *me*," he muttered as he put the objects away.

Even if this was a dream, he was still cold. He needed to find somewhere warm to wait. He sniffed the air. Although he could see in his dreams, he still relied on his other senses, from a lifetime of habit. He smelled smoke. A campfire, perhaps? He walked in the direction of the smell, sniffing as he went, until a light flickered between the trees. Aiming at the light, he weaved his way through the woods, finally emerging into a clearing where a log cabin stood. Smoke rose from an opening in its roof, promising the warmth of a fire inside. He approached.

The cabin was not like any he'd ever read about. Moss insulated the spaces between the logs, and covered the roof. An animal skin formed a door, hanging free with a pole across it about two feet from the ground, heavy enough to hold it in place against the wind, but allowing the lower flap to be sucked in to provide drafting for the fire.

He stopped. Okay, how had he known that? He studied the forest around him. "You're still feeding me lessons, aren't you?" he called to the night.

No answer.

He shivered. The storm was getting worse. Snow pellets bit into his face like icy insects, and the wind groped cold fingers beneath his new jacket. Enough. He lifted the door flap.

Inside, fresh spruce boughs covered the dirt floor in a soft spongy carpet, except in the middle where bare earth surrounded a fire that lit the room in a cozy glow, its smoke rising to an opening in the roof. A small pot hung over the fire from a tripod of three heavy sticks, a wooden bowl beside it. The thick scent of the spruce was sweet and wonderful, mixing with the smell of beaver stew cooking in the pot. Despite the storm outside, the cabin was warm and comfortable.

Scooping some stew into the bowl, he sat down on the cushion of spruce boughs and began fingering the food into his mouth. Delicious.

He stopped in mid-swallow. Again, how had he known it was beaver stew? He looked around the cabin, suddenly feeling that he wasn't alone. Then he shrugged. Even if this was only happening in his head, his head told him he was hungry and cold. The cabin and the food addressed both problems.

Finishing the stew, he sat staring into the fire, letting its warmth soak into him, enjoying the wonderful feeling of a full belly on a cold winter's night. He yawned. Using his arm for a pillow, he lay down on the soft spruce boughs facing the fire.

The flames danced before him, and after a while, he could see shapes in their flickering movements, as if animals or people or creatures were performing for him, telling him a story.

He closed his eyes, listening to the fire crackle. There too, in each pop or hiss, it seemed as if messages whispered. Important messages. The messages were in a strange tongue, but he felt that if he concentrated a little harder, their meaning would become clear. He slowed his breathing, straining to make out the words.

Just before he drifted off, he wondered if it was possible to fall asleep in a dream.

FRANK MUELLER SCREAMED AGAIN. Searing pain stabbed into his buttocks. Blades of agony slashed down his legs. The thing attacking him from behind was dragging him from the cruiser. His fingers, scrabbling desperately for any handhold, found the car's door handle. Grabbing it, fueled by pain and fear, he pulled with all his might, finding strength he didn't know he had.

Something ripped. The pressure on his legs suddenly released, and he dropped hard to the ground beside the cruiser. Rolling onto his left side, he clawed at the release on his holster, looking down at his leg as he did so.

Half of the back of his right thigh was gone.

He tasted vomit, but he fought down the urge to retch. He was still in shock. The real pain hadn't hit him yet. He had to get his gun out before this thing attacked again, before his pain took him. He tugged at his gun. Fucking thing was stuck. He looked up.

All he could make out was a dark shape three feet away, rising from where it had fallen after losing its grip on him. It rose to its feet.

To its *two* feet.

A thought battled through his pain. What the fuck was this? A bear on its hind legs?

The thing raised its head and spread its arms. He could see its outline clearly now. He tugged desperately at his gun. This was no bear.

It was over seven feet tall with a huge misshapen head and wild hair. Its arms were unnaturally long and thin, its hands enormous with long, spindly fingers ending in curved claws. It lunged at him.

With a high-pitched scream like a little child, he gave his gun a final frantic tug. It came free. Swinging it wildly toward the thing, he fired.

The bullet caught the creature high on its left side. It shrieked, an ear-piercing screech like a train whistle. Stumbling back, it steadied itself and charged him again.

But now he had time to aim. Leveling his gun at the thing's chest, he pulled the trigger. The thing screeched again and straightened up. He fired again, and kept firing until he'd emptied the gun into the creature.

Staggering backward, the thing collapsed onto the ground. It spasmed once, twice, and then lay still.

The pain claimed Mueller now, scorching up his spine like a river of acid burning every nerve ending in his body. Collapsing onto his stomach, he puked onto the ground. He swore and swore, long and loudly, spitting out vomit. "You stinking piece of shit. I'm going to cut you into little fucking pieces. I'm going to piss on your corpse. I'm going...."

He stopped. He was almost blacking out from the pain, but something beat its way through to what little remained of his consciousness. He forced himself to raise his head, to turn, to look back to where the thing he'd just killed lay on the ground.

Only it wasn't lying on the ground anymore.

Frank Mueller had time for one final scream.

ZACH WOKE SUDDENLY from his dream within a dream. Sitting up, he looked around.

The cabin had changed. He now lay, not on spruce boughs, but on a wooden floor in a ramshackle modern cabin. A stone fireplace with no fire burning stood on the far wall flanked by makeshift bookcases. An old couch and a wooden table stood in front of the fireplace. A lamp on the table provided the only light. A small kitchen stood on the far side with a wood stove, old fridge, and another wooden table and chair. Clouded moonlight reflecting off snow streamed through uncovered windows.

He reminded himself that he was still dreaming, that he was asleep in his motel room in Thunder Lake. But he remembered falling asleep in his earlier dream, and he was certain that something had awakened him to this different dream. A sound.

A sound of someone screaming.

A new sound snapped his head up—a gunshot, followed immediately by an inhuman screech, a high-pitched whistle more like the howl of a winter wind than anything a throat of flesh and blood could produce. But it was the familiarity of that howl, more than the cry itself, that sent a chill up his spine. He'd heard that cry before. In another dream.

The sounds had come from the front of the cabin. He looked toward the front door, and his heart leapt again. The door stood open.

He jumped again as more shots sounded. Four, maybe five. Then silence.

As he lay there, his heart pounding his chest, a man began swearing a long angry stream of curses. Despite the pain and fury the swearing carried, he found it strangely calming, its rude humanity washing away that earlier inhuman cry.

Until the stream of curses died with another scream. A very human, very final scream.

Silence followed. He lay frozen on the wood floor, hardly daring to breathe, afraid to make any sound. He stared at the open door, half expecting a dark shape to appear in the rectangle of pale light.

But as the silence dragged on, he found the courage to move. Rising on shaking legs, he crept quietly to the door. He peeked outside.

Snow clouds had eaten the moon. The brightest light came from a police car in front of the cabin, about twenty feet away, its front passenger door open, its inside lights on.

Something huddled beside the car, something alive, for he could see a head and shoulders bobbing up and down and hear the sounds of ripping and chewing.

He remembered the familiar whistling cry and knew that this was the same creature from his first dream encounter with Wisakejack. Only this time, the Trickster spirit wasn't around to save him if this thing discovered him.

As if the thing could read his mind, its head snapped up. Sniffing the air, it threw its head back and gave a long piercing whistle.

Then it spun, and its blood-red eyes fell on him.

He jumped back into the cabin. Too late. It had seen him. Outside, the whistling wail sounded again. Only this time, it was closer. Much closer.

The thing was coming for him.

CHAPTER 27

A MISSING SHAMAN

GWYN WRESTLED THE TRUCK around another sharp turn, sending its headlight beams lurching into the dark bush. Trying to maintain his link with the pack while driving was turning the pursuit into a series of near misses with ditches. To make things worse, while the pack could chase the trail straight through the bush, he had to follow the few roads that cut through the area. He swore as the pack changed direction again, forcing him to double back to a road they'd just passed. He wrenched the wheel around.

Ed grabbed at the door handle to steady himself. Caz, sitting in the middle, clung to the dashboard.

Gwyn looked at Ed. "So would Walter Keejek agree with your windigo theory?"

Ed didn't answer right away. "Walter knows more about the Windigo spirit than anyone. All the stories, all the signs."

"So what happened between you two? You said he used to be in the Midewewin."

Ed nodded. "One of our founding elders here."

"So?"

Ed hesitated. "Walter became deeply interested in the Waubunowin—The Society of the Dawn."

Caz looked at Gwyn and mouthed, "The Sith." Gwyn ignored her.

Ed went on. "He wanted us to integrate some of their practices into the Midewewin. The rest of us...didn't share his ideas. Walter kind of withdrew from us after that."

"When was this?" Gwyn asked.

Ed looked at him. "Around when the dam lake was made. George told me that no one in the Midewewin has seen him for over a month."

"So, what?" Caz said. "We have a missing shaman windigo expert who recently started practicing booga-booga magics? Can you say 'suspect'?"

Ed didn't answer. Gwyn made another turn. The pack was slowing.

"So if this thing is a *real* windigo—" Caz began. Gwyn glared at her. "—which, of course, it isn't," she continued, "but, you know, if it is, how will we know? I mean, aside from big feet and it trying to eat us."

Ed shrugged. "My people have as many descriptions of a windigo as we have stories of it. Most say it is over seven feet tall, and grows the more victims it eats. It will be naked, but it does not feel the cold. It *is* the cold, for it is the spirit of winter."

Gwyn looked at the snow falling harder now, white flakes flashing bright in the headlight beams. Winter had come so sudden and early. *It is the spirit of winter....*

Ed went on. "Its body is hard like stone, its arms and legs long and thin, its hands clawed, its head enormous, its face black from frostbite, its mouth huge. It has gnawed its own lips away in its hunger. Its teeth are like broken quartz, its eyes lidless and rolling in blood. Its breath comes in whistles, and its cry freezes its victims when they try to run. And inside...," Ed said, tapping his chest, "...a heart of ice."

"And we're *trying* to find this thing?" Caz said.

"Best time to do it," Ed said. "A windigo only hunts at night."

Gwyn slowed as the road emerged into a clearing. In front of a decrepit wooden cabin, a police cruiser stood with one door open.

"Ed, you recognize this place?" Gwyn asked.

Ed nodded, his face grim. "It's Walter's cabin."

Gwyn got out of the truck. Something—or someone—was lying in front of the cruiser. "Let's go."

PANICKING, ZACH TURNED from the door and the approaching creature, frantically searching for an escape. A door to another room lay at the back. Maybe he could slip out a window.

He'd made it halfway across the room when another whistling shriek froze him in his tracks. A wind swirled into the cabin, sucking the warmth from the room and replacing it with the biting cold of a sudden winter.

As it had in his first dream encounter with this thing, that cold paralyzed him as if he'd fallen into an icy river. Just before he lost all control over his legs, he twisted to face his pursuer. The creature stepped through the door, and Zach finally saw what hunted him.

The thing was a grotesquely stretched parody of a human being, with a large misshapen head and long, spindly limbs. Dark hair covered its naked body in uneven patches. Its feet were absurdly long with one huge toe and pointed heels. Its hands seemed to consist entirely of fingers and claws. Its chest heaved, and its breath came in whistles.

A mane of matted hair framed a nightmare face of blackened skin, bulbous nose, bulging red eyes, and lips pulled back from brown jagged teeth. Something dangled from those teeth. With a sick feeling, he realized those were strips of flesh from whatever—or whomever—it had been eating. Its smell reached him then, and he fought an urge to throw up.

But the sensation that overwhelmed him was the *cold* that flowed from this creature, that *was* this creature, enveloping everything around it. The cold that had frozen his legs, that was slowly rising, paralyzing his hands and arms. Wisakejack's words returned to him. *Winter's coming—and it's going to be a killer.*

The thing's red eyes locked on him. It moved toward him. Frozen to the spot, he could only watch as the creature crept closer. He was going to die.

Wait. He was just dreaming. So what if this thing grabbed him? He'd just scream and wake up, right?

Right?

Wrong. He knew these were no ordinary dreams. Wisakejack was not a product of his imagination. Neither was this monster. This world, these things existed somehow, somewhere. He remembered his first encounter with this creature—falling, cutting his hand—a cut he'd still had when he woke. He didn't know what the rules were anymore in these dreams—if these *were* just dreams—but he could be hurt in them. And that meant he could die in them too. Die, for real.

The thing was three paces from him. For some reason, it was being very cautious. Maybe it could smell Wisakejack on him.

Wisakejack. He cursed himself for running from his strange guide. Then he cursed Wisakejack for not preparing him for this. Him and his stupid stories. Why hadn't he told him a story about what to do when a monster is chasing you?

A monster chasing you....

While he still had some control over his upper body, he forced his hand to move, reaching for the medicine pouch, his eyes on the advancing creature. He pushed his hand inside, searching with his fingers, pulling out what he needed one by one—the fire-flint, the striking stone, and the birch bark.

But he needed to be kneeling. How could he kneel if he couldn't use his legs? The thing crept closer. Two steps away now.

Wait! He didn't need to use his legs—he needed *not* to use them. Closing his eyes, he focused on relaxing every leg muscle he could still sense.

And immediately collapsed to the floor. The creature jumped back in surprise. Sitting up, Zach tossed the birch bark down in front of him. He struck the flint with the stone, holding it over the bark. Sparks flew, but none hit the bark.

The creature dropped into a crouch. Again, he struck the flint. The creature tensed, ready to leap.

He struck the flint one more time. A spark touched the bark. Immediately, a wall of flame erupted between him and the creature, rising to the ceiling and spreading to both walls.

On the far side of the flames, the creature shrieked, pacing up and down, searching for a way through. Strangely, the fire was spreading only toward the creature. The wall of flames had not advanced even an inch on Zach's side. As fire engulfed the room around it, the creature threw back its head, gave another piercing shriek, and leapt out the door. Moments later, he heard it crashing through the woods.

So now, how did *he* get out of here? The flames cut him off from the door.

He realized then that he could sense no heat from these flames, yet the cabin should feel like a furnace by now. Tentatively, he reached a hand toward the flames. A round hole appeared. He stuck his hand through the hole. Nothing— no pain, not even a feeling of heat. He moved closer. An opening formed. He stepped through.

The fire consuming the room seemed indifferent to him, as if he stood in a protective bubble. He walked through the inferno and out the front door.

The police car was gone, and thankfully so was the body. In their place, Wisakejack sat cross-legged in the clearing, grinning as the flames of the fire danced in his black eyes. He stood up as Zach approached. "So you finally found some of the magic in you."

"I found it in a pouch, not in me."

"This is a dream, little brother. It's all in your mind. That's where the magic is, too."

Zach thought about that. "So *I* made the fire appear?"

"Yep. And by the way, you look way cool in that jacket. Like me. Hey! You found our winter hunting lodge too. Good. That teepee was getting chilly." Wisakejack headed past Zach toward the cabin.

"Uh, it's on fire—" Zach stopped as he turned. Instead of the flaming ruin of the modern cabin he expected, he stood facing the older log cabin structure that he'd first found, erect and untouched, surrounded by the dark primal forest. Shaking his head, he followed Wisakejack inside.

AS THE SNOW FELL THICK around them, Gwyn stared down at the remains of Frank Mueller lying ghastly under the stark illumination of the flashlight beam. Somewhere behind him, Caz was violently retching. Gelert growled but stayed well back. The same strange tracks he'd found at the scene of Mary's death led from the body and into the bush.

Ed walked up beside him, holding his rifle. "I called it into Thornton. He's sending another cruiser." He considered the corpse and the tracks. "Snow's not as thick on the body as in the tracks. Would've kept its heat for a while. Been dead about thirty minutes."

Gwyn nodded, sniffing the air and eyeing the dark bush. "I can still smell it."

"Where are your wolves?"

His link with the alpha male was still strong. The wolf had brought the pack to a halt. In its mind, the smell of the thing they hunted threatened to overpower any other sensory input Gwyn could detect. He sifted through the wolf's mind, searching for any visual image.

There. A flash in black and white. Then it was gone. But he'd seen enough. Something crouched before the wolves, grotesquely human, down on one knee.

He pulled his mind back, orienting himself to the mental tug of the wolves. Northeast, less than a mile. Same direction as the tracks. "C'mon. They've cornered it."

Ed was examining Mueller's service revolver with a gloved hand. "He emptied it."

"For all the good it did him," Gwyn said. "So what do your stories say about killing one of these things?"

"So now you believe him?" Caz asked, joining them, wiping her mouth on the sleeve of her hoodie.

Gwyn stared at the strange tracks, remembering the glimpse he'd caught of what the wolves had cornered. "Maybe."

"In its windigo form, no weapon can harm it," Ed said. "Only in human form can it die. And even then, there are things that must be done…." His voice trailed off.

"So how do we fight it?" Gwyn asked.

Ed shrugged. "With a pure heart."

"Ed—"

"What do you want me to say, Gray Legs?" Ed asked, hefting his rifle, a rare edge in his voice. "It doesn't matter. This thing killed Mary, so I am going to do my best to kill it. If it kills me…." Ed gave another shrug.

Mahigan's words came back to Gwyn. *You could not have faced that creature. You do not have the strength.*

We'll see about that, he thought. "All right," he said. "Let's go." Turning their backs on Mueller's grisly remains, they headed into the bush following the strange tracks.

CHAPTER 28

WHERE THE HUNGER CAME FROM

AWAKENED BY THE PHONE, Kate tried to focus on the red digits of her bedside clock. Four thirty-eight in the morning. Groaning, she fumbled the phone to her ear, her head still on the pillow.

"Hello?" she mumbled.

"Ms. Morgan? This is Thornton." Pause. His voice sounded different. "There's been another killing." He paused again. "One of my constables. Frank Mueller."

She sat up in bed, chilled by more than the cold motel room. A cop? Pushing the hair out of her eyes, she switched on the bedside lamp. "What happened?"

"He was investigating a missing person's report. He didn't call in on schedule, and we couldn't raise him." Another pause. "Then we got a call. Someone found him."

"Like the others?" she asked quietly.

"Yeah. Like the others."

She swallowed. "I'm so sorry."

"This thing," he said, "whatever it is, it's killed a cop now. I want to find it. Fast."

So now it's important? she thought.

"We'll be letting Leiddia Barker go as well. This clears her."

"No! Wait, you can't do that," she said. Jonas wouldn't want the only Heroka they'd located released.

"What do you mean? She was in my jail when Mueller was killed."

"What about the cougar? What if these killings were done by a cougar?"

Thornton snorted. "A wild animal she can control? From miles away? While in jail? Give me a break. Some folks may hold with that crap, but not me. And neither would our courts. I can't keep her in jail, Ms. Morgan."

She tried to force her still sleepy mind to work. "Just hold her until we know the DNA test results. I'll have the first set this morning. I'll call you as soon as I hear."

A pause, then a sigh. "Can't see what you could come up with that'll stand up in court, but all right. I'll hold her till noon." He hung up.

She put the receiver back. It wouldn't have to stand up in court. Simon Jonas would be the only judge Leiddia Barker would ever face. And Kate already knew the verdict. She lay back, closing her eyes. An image of Leiddia, huddling naked in a Tainchel cage, came to her. Who were the real monsters here?

The caged figure began morphing to another shape. But it wasn't an animal that replaced Leiddia's tall form. It was the figure of a young boy. The boy raised his head.

It was Zach.

"No!" she screamed. She opened her eyes, her heart racing. She was lying on the bed. She looked at the clock. Five-fifteen. She slumped back on the pillow. She'd fallen back to sleep. It had been a dream.

No. A nightmare. One that could come true—if Jonas ever found out about Zach.

But why was it any less horrible to condemn Leiddia to that fate?

She swung her legs over the side of the bed. Why? Because Zach was her son. Because she would do everything she could to find out what his Heroka blood meant. Had it caused his blindness? What would he become? Was there a cure?

Sorry, Leiddia, she thought, as she booted up her computer, *but my son comes first.*

She established a secure link to Jonas on her laptop. To her surprise, the Tainchel chief's face flashed up on her screen. He was up early.

Or perhaps he'd never gone to bed. His eyes were bloodshot, his face haggard, as if he hadn't slept all night. He wore a dark navy silk dressing gown over similar pajamas. "Good morning, sir," she said. "I didn't expect to see you."

Jonas looked grim. "There have been disturbing developments. But this is early for a report from you as well. What's happened?"

She told him of the third killing. "Thornton plans to release Leiddia Barker today unless the DNA results link her to the Mary Two Rivers killing—"

Jonas interrupted. "Kate, I have the first DNA test results. That's why I've been up."

That didn't sound encouraging. "What did the tests show?"

He stared at her for a moment. "Barker's DNA confirms that she is indeed Heroka. However, the DNA taken from the wounds on the Two Rivers girl did *not* match that of Leiddia Barker—" He paused. "—nor that of a Heroka."

Now she understood his appearance. This was a huge blow to him. "Then the killer was a wild animal, sir, so a Heroka could still be involved. Was it a cougar? Barker could have sent it, even from jail."

Jonas interrupted her with a wave of his hand. "It wasn't a cougar."

Another Heroka? With a different totem? Or had these killings been real wild animal attacks, unrelated to the Heroka all along? "What kind of animal was it, sir?"

At first, she couldn't read what she saw on his face. She would have understood disappointment or anger at his plans coming apart. But what she saw was something else.

It was horror.

"It wasn't *animal* DNA, Kate," he replied quietly. "It was human."

GWYN STOOD SILENTLY beside Ed and Caz, staring at the man who lay before them. The wolf pack and Gelert hovered behind them in the trees. The dark woods stood silent as well, muted by the blanket of snow, as if out of respect for the dead.

The body belonged to an older Ojibwe male, naked, of average size and build, probably in his sixties. Blood smeared his mouth, and strips of bloody meat still hung from half-opened lips. Gwyn counted six bullet holes in his chest. At least two had hit the heart. The man was very dead and, from all appearances, very human.

"Know him?" Gwyn asked Ed.

Ed nodded. "Walter Keejek."

"I don't get it," Caz said. "He's just a guy. I thought this was some kind of unstoppable monster."

"He probably was when Mueller shot him," Ed said. "Took all those bullets, but that couldn't kill him, not while he was windigo. After he finished with Mueller, he ran." He nodded in the direction they'd been following. "He has a small hunting cabin up that way. Maybe he always changed back after he fed, once the hunger was gone. That'd explain the human footprints where Mary died. But this time when he changed back...." He shrugged.

"All those bullet holes suddenly mattered," Gwyn said. His Heroka ears caught the sound of a police siren from the direction of Walter's cabin. "Cops. We'd better tell them about this."

"And probably get arrested for killing Mueller," Caz said.

Gwyn nodded at the body. "We aren't the ones with a cop's bullets in him."

"Not yet," Caz muttered.

Ed stared at the corpse. "They have to give us the body. When a windigo dies, there are things that must be done."

"Like what?" Caz asked.

Ed just shook his head and headed back toward the cabin.

"What was that about?" Caz asked.

"Don't know," Gwyn said, setting out after Ed. "But this clears Leiddia. And the Heroka."

Caz fell in behind him. "So that's it? Mystery solved?"

Gwyn didn't answer. He was thinking of finding the dead Tainchel agent the night Mitch had died—naked, body riddled with bullets, surrounded by partially eaten bodies and that same smell of corruption. Just like Walter Keejek. Something was still missing in this puzzle.

IN ZACH'S DREAM, he sat beside the fire inside what Wisakejack had called his hunting lodge. Across from him, Wisakejack was shoveling beaver stew from a bowl into his mouth with his fingers.

"What *was* that thing?" Zach asked, still shaken from his narrow escape.

"A man—," Wisakejack replied, between bites.

"That was *not* a man."

Wisakejack licked his fingers. "You didn't let me finish. It *was* a man—a man infected by the *Windigo* spirit."

"Windigo?"

"A spirit. A very old, very powerful, and very nasty spirit. That's a lot of 'verys,' and I mean every one of them. It is *The Hunger that Walks*."

"That thing was a man infected by *hunger*?"

Wisakejack wagged a dripping finger at him. "By the *Spirit* of Hunger. Hunger's a powerful force, remember? Especially in winter for our people, when a hunter took his family to their hunting territory. They were alone, isolated, totally dependent on the hunter's skill and respect for Kitche Manitou. And that respect included taking only what they needed. If a hunter killed more game than his family could store and eat, his family paid the price for his gluttony." Wisakejack held up his bowl, now empty. "No more food."

"They'd starve to death," Zach said quietly.

Wisakejack wiped his hands on his jacket. "The *lucky* ones starved."

"You call starving lucky?"

"Better than turning windigo, or being killed by one."

Zach paled. "You mean…."

"The white settlers, they thought those incidents were just people doing what they had to, to stay alive. Some poor Indian getting through a winter by eating their own family. But the Windigo Spirit is real, little brother. And it's back."

"But why is it here? Why now?"

Wisakejack clapped his hands. Zach blinked. They now stood on top of a huge dam. A dark lake lay below, its surface undulating slowly like the chest of a sleeping beast, rising and falling with each breath.

"Under all that water," Wisakejack said, "a forest once stood. Of course, logging companies stripped the trees before they flooded it. Trees, animals, hunting territories, migration routes—gone like that." Wisakejack snapped his fingers. He looked at Zach. "Why's the Windigo Spirit here? Little brother, the Windigo spirit is a hunger that grows the more it feeds, a hunger that can never be satisfied. The Windigo Spirit is the spirit of greed."

Wisakejack clapped his hands again. Zach gasped. He now clung to the back of a huge eagle flying high above the dam and its captive lake. A parade of hydro towers marched from the dam along a clear-cut into the distance. The dam fell behind. A glow grew on the horizon, a glow not from the rising sun but from a huge city that suddenly lay pulsing with light and movement below them, its steel and glass towers turning night to day.

Wisakejack's voice sounded in his head. "A hunger that can never be satisfied, little brother. It just keeps growing the more it feeds. Feeds on the land."

"Our society," Zach whispered.

"Humans have very big appetites," Wisakejack said. The eagle banked sharply, and Zach's vision spun. He clamped his eyes shut to stop the sudden vertigo, and when he opened them, he was standing with Wisakejack, in human form once more, on the dam overlooking the dark lake again.

"So how do we stop it? The windigo?" Zach asked.

"Our problem is actually a little bigger than a single human turned windigo," Wisakejack said. He looked to the east. "Sun's coming up. Meaning you're about to wake up. I'll tell you more tomorrow night. For now, let's just say that the Spirit World and your world are getting closer." Wisakejack and the scene behind him began to grow gray and murky. Zach was waking, not to the morning sun but to the darkness of his blindness. "So? You trust me now, little brother? Won't run off again the next time we meet?"

Zach nodded. "Yeah. Sure. I trust you." He was lying, but he'd decided that his best strategy for now was to go along with this strange creature and learn as much as he could.

Wisakejack eyed him narrowly. "No. You don't."

Zach swallowed. "Yes. I do. Really."

Wisakejack shook his head. "Can't trick a trickster, kid. Especially *the* Trickster. Nope, you're just playing along, figuring that, for now, I'm better than the pointy-toothed alternative." Wisakejack stared at Zach, any hint of mirth gone. Suddenly, he broke into a huge grin. "Good for you! You really *are* learning." With those words, the forest, the morning sky, and Wisakejack all faded to black, and Zach woke up.

From beside his bed, Quincy gave a good morning "whuff," instantly aware of his master's wakefulness. With that familiar sound, a feeling of almost overwhelming relief washed over Zach. Never before had he been so glad to trade his sighted world of dreams for his everyday life of blindness.

"Morning, Quince." He patted the dog, receiving a warm wet lick on his hand. He wiped his hand absently on his pajamas top—and immediately snatched his hand away as if he'd touched a live wire. His heart pounding, he lay unmoving in bed, barely daring to breathe.

His hand had brushed against, not the cotton of his pajamas, but soft leather.

Very slowly, he ran his hand down the garment, his fingers finding a raised pattern, which he knew would be porcupine quills, dyed different colors and woven into the leather.

Somehow, against any logic he could fathom, he was lying in his bed, wide-awake in the real world, wearing a jacket that an ancient Cree spirit had given him in a dream.

Wisakejack's words returned to him. *The Spirit World and your world are getting closer.*

CHAPTER 29

DOGS AND CATS LIVING TOGETHER

GWYN WAS WAITING outside the OPP station with Ed's truck, Gelert in the back, when the door to the station flew open just past noon, and Leiddia bounded out like a wildcat sprung from a cage, her black parka unzipped despite the cold. When she saw him, she stopped and grinned, a hand on one hip, then strode to the truck and got in.

They stared at each other for a moment, then she leaned over and pulled him into a long kiss. She broke it off and sat back, smiling at him. "Hi."

"Hi," he replied, smiling back. "Home?"

"Home. Most definitely, home."

He put the truck into gear and pulled away. She considered him as he drove. "You look like shit."

"You should talk." She was paler than usual, with dark circles under both eyes.

"And you always said I was beautiful in the mornings," she said, running a hand through her long black hair. "Well, being locked in jail with a mob out for your blood and a drunk screaming in the next cell doesn't make for the best night's sleep. What's your excuse?"

He related last night's events surrounding Mueller's death, still omitting his strange encounter with Mahigan.

"Holy shit," she said. "All they told me was that Mueller died like Mary did, and they'd caught the guy, so I was in the clear. Walter? Dead?" She shook her head. "Like I said, I knew he and Ed had a big fight. But this windigo shit's a bit of stretch for me. He *ate* Mueller? Really?"

"It's a stretch for me, too. But I can't explain the tracks we followed or what I sensed the wolves saw. Or how he made it nearly a mile with six bullets in him."

"It's all too weird." She shook her head, then shrugged. "I'm just glad for Ed and Vera that they've caught Mary's killer, that this nightmare's over."

He didn't reply. Given the similarities between Mary and Mueller's deaths, he was ready to admit that Walter Keejek was Mary's killer, windigo or not. But that still didn't explain the similarities between what had happened at Cil y Blaidd and here, nor Mahigan's warnings of some imminent danger.

He pulled up in front of her cabin, and they got out. She unlocked the cabin door, and he followed her in, telling Gelert to stay outside.

Beyond some different furniture and decorations here and there, the place was much the way he remembered it. A love seat, a worn leather armchair, and a low oval coffee table sat facing a large stone fireplace. A big-screen TV sat to the right of the fireplace. The hardwood floor was bare except for a white bearskin rug in front of the hearth. A small open kitchen stood off to the right behind a waist-high wall, with a white table, four matching chairs, and a food and water dish for the cat.

A rush of memories flooded him, most of them good. He swallowed, overcome by a sudden sense of loss, a realization of what might have been between them. He'd been happy here once, with her, and "happy" wasn't a word that he applied to many periods of his life.

The black cat that he'd seen the night of the mob appeared from somewhere and jumped into her arms. "Oh, Poos! Did you miss me?" she asked, rubbing her cheek against the cat. She held it up. "Poos, this is Gwyn."

"Puss? That's original."

"*Poos*. Cree for cat."

"Hmm," he said, keeping his distance.

"Don't mind him, sweetie. He's more of a dog person," she said to the cat. "Start a fire, will you? I want to get changed."

He knelt beside the fireplace and lit some kindling as she disappeared into the bedroom. He threw another log on the fire as the flames caught. When she didn't reappear, he followed her into the bedroom and found her sitting on the bed, hugging her knees to her chest, crying.

He sat on the bed beside her. "Hey," he said, putting his arm around her.

She buried her face into his shoulder. "Sorry. It all just kind of caught up to me. Three people murdered. People blaming me. Being in jail. Poor Mary dead."

He took her in his arms, holding her, and stroking her hair. She turned her face up to him. He looked into her green eyes, then he kissed her. She returned it hungrily, thrusting her tongue deep into his mouth. He pulled her down onto the bed as he felt himself grow hard, but she pushed him away. "No."

Thinking he'd misread her, he rolled back. "I thought—"

She pulled him back into another deep kiss. "Not here. It's freezing. Let's go out by the fire." She winked at him. "I'm sure you remember that rug."

She led him to where the fire now burned warmly. They stood on the white bearskin rug before the fire, slowly undressing between kisses. When they were both naked, she slid down his front, kissing and biting him before she knelt and took him into her mouth, as he wondered why he had ever left her. She pulled him down to the rug and straddled him. He entered her, and she rode him slowly, her breasts swaying, her long hair caressing his chest and face. She brought him to the edge of orgasm half a dozen times, slowing her rhythm just enough each time. They finally came together, and she cried out, arching her back and clawing his chest with her nails.

After, she lay on top of him, both of them panting and sweating. Reaching over, she grabbed the edge of the bearskin rug and wrapped it over her back and around them both. Then she propped herself up on her elbows and stared at him, her long black hair framing her face, her nipples tickling his chest.

"This doesn't settle things between us yet, Dog. This was just sex."

"Just?" he said, running a finger down a breast.

She smiled. "Ok, just great sex." She stroked his hair, and the smile ran away. "But the thing is, you left me. You broke my fucking heart. If I give it to you again, what are you going to do with it this time?"

He took her hand and kissed her wrist. "Cat, I'm sorry I ever hurt you. I'm sorry I left." He looked at her, feeling the truth of the words as he began to speak them. "I loved you then, and I still do."

She considered him for a long time, until a tear grew in an eye. "My god, Poos," she said to the cat, who was lying on the sofa beside them, "I do believe he means it." She kissed him deeply, and he rolled her onto her back.

They made love once more and fell asleep before the fire, entangled together and in the rug. When he awoke, it was getting dark, and the fire had died to embers. She stirred, and the rug slipped from her shoulders. She shivered. "Fuck, it's freezing."

He got up and threw a couple of logs on the fire, poking at it until the flames caught again.

She watched him as he dressed. "So what's the plan?"

"I told Ed we'd meet him at the community center today."

She nodded. "Right. His storytelling."

"You've been to them?"

"Sure. He's a great storyteller. And it makes him happy—doing something to keep the old ways alive."

He grinned. "What do you know about the *old ways*?"

She stood, wrapping the rug around her, and sat on the couch facing the fire. "Just what I've learned from Ed." Poos jumped up and wriggled inside the blanket with her. She scratched the cat's neck.

"So why'd you downsize?" he asked, eyeing the cat. "She's not quite cougar category."

"You just ignore the mean man, Poos. He doesn't know you." She shook her head. "Painter was the last cougar around here. No bobcats this far north, of course. I went looking for a lynx. That's when I found out they're gone, too. And it's not just my totem."

"Yeah, I sensed it. The whole bush area around the town seems to be empty."

She nodded. "You won't even find a squirrel."

"When did it happen?"

"Couple of weeks after they flooded the valley. Makes sense. That flooding fucked up the entire ecosystem."

"Yeah, but every species wouldn't disappear overnight. It'd take months, at least a migration season."

She shrugged. "All I know is that one day, the animals were here. The next, they were gone." She frowned. "Hey! You said that you used a wolf pack to track that thing last night. Where'd you find them?"

He hesitated. No, if they were going to start again, he had to tell her everything. He related his two encounters with Mahigan, and the strange warnings the wolf spirit had given.

She shook her head. "Stranger and stranger. It said you were *drawn* here? But you came back because of Mary's death—"

"And to help you."

She smiled and kissed him. "My point is that—if your wolfie spirit is right— then Mary was killed just to bring you here." She shivered. "That makes it even more awful."

"God," he muttered, as that sank in. "That's horrible."

She stood up, dropping the rug to the floor, and began dressing. "So you mean finding Walter last night doesn't solve the mystery after all."

He shook his head. "I don't think it does." He related the events with the bodies being eaten during the Tainchel attack.

"You need to tell Ed about Mahigan," she said, zipping up her jeans. She grinned at him as she finished getting dressed. "Well, on the upside, it means you'll definitely be hanging around for a while." He smiled back at her, surprised at how good that made him feel.

Outside, Gelert jumped up from the porch, tail wagging, and then ran and leapt into the back of Ed's truck at a command from Gwyn. Leiddia got in the passenger side.

Gwyn opened the driver door, and then stopped. He reached out with his mind, searching. Nothing. Gelert whined, ever sensitive to his master's moods.

"What?" Leiddia asked.

He got in, started the truck, and put it into gear. "The wolves from last night. The ones that Mahigan had brought back. They're gone again."

Leiddia stared into the bush as he drove the narrow road from her cabin. "Makes you wonder where they go, doesn't it?"

CHAPTER 30

SECRETS REVEALED

JUST BEFORE FOUR O'CLOCK** that afternoon, Zach found himself walking arm-in-arm with Bonnie through lightly falling snow on their way to the community center for Ed's storytelling session.

"So, did you hear there was another animal attack last night?" Bonnie asked, leaning closer, her voice dropping to a conspiratorial whisper.

He shook his head, thinking more about how nice she smelled than about her question. She then began relating, with more enthusiasm than he would've expected, the grisly details she'd heard about the brutal murder of a local OPP constable.

As she talked, an image from last night's dream rose unbidden—an image of the creature crouched over something lying beside a police cruiser. The image faded but a chill unrelated to the cold weather remained.

Had the killing in his dream last night really happened? Could his strange dreams be showing him events in the real world? Was a real windigo running loose around Thunder Lake? His leather jacket had crossed over from the dream world to this one. Maybe other things could as well.

He shivered. He'd considered wearing the jacket today, but ultimately decided against it, not knowing how to explain it to his mom. But thinking again of the windigo, he wondered if he should have worn it, since Wisakejack had hinted it could provide some sort of protection. Too late now.

Bonnie finished her story. "Gruesome, eh?"

He remembered then his first dream encounter with the windigo. The creature had been feeding on something in that dream too. "You said *another* animal attack. Has this happened before?"

"Well, *yea-ah*. It's been *all* over town," she said, sounding surprised.

"Kind of new here, remember?"

"Oh, right. Yeah, twice in the last two weeks. Same thing. Body eaten and stuff. The last one was three nights ago. Mary Two Rivers. Ed's granddaughter." Bonnie paused. "I liked her." She fell silent.

Three nights ago. The night of his first dream. He shivered. Both the killings he'd seen in his dreams had actually happened. His Wisakejack dreams *had* been mixing with the real world all along.

He swallowed. He'd been right. Wherever he went each night, whatever he experienced—these were not just dreams. But then, what were they?

WHEN GWYN WALKED into the community center with Leiddia, Ed was just setting up for his storytelling session. Ed greeted Leiddia warmly, and she broke down when she told him how sorry she was that she missed Mary's funeral.

Caz came in, weaving through the kids hanging around the doorway like an otter chasing a fish. Gwyn introduced her to Leiddia.

"You were at my cabin that night with Gwyn. Thanks," she said, giving her a hug and a kiss.

"Hey, you know, whatever. Nothing much," Caz said, blushing a little.

Gwyn turned to Ed and Caz. "I need to tell you both something." He related his two encounters with Mahigan, finishing with the wolf spirit's claim that something had drawn him to this town.

"Man, you're just a weirdness magnet, aren't you? Drawn here for what?" Caz asked.

He shook his head. "I don't know, but I'm guessing that it's something beyond clearing Leiddia's name and finding Mary's killer."

"And finding the Tainchel," Caz said, her young face setting into hard lines. "Right? That's why we came, remember? To find the Tainchel. At least that's why I came." She shot a look at Leiddia, who was now holding onto Gwyn's arm.

"Shit, the Tainchel. I just remembered something," Leiddia said. "When Thornton brought me into the station, there was a woman there." She paused. "I think she had a scanner."

"Tainchel?" Gwyn asked. "You sure?"

"Not positive, but I'd put money on it."

"But that's *good* news," Caz said. "We *want* them to be here. They're the ones who killed Mitch. And my parents. And the Martenenkos."

Gwyn didn't say anything. Part of him agreed with Caz. The Tainchel were still his enemy, and he *had* come here to....

The words of Mahigan came back to him. *You came here to kill. Your hate brought you here.*

The kids were now sitting in the storytelling circle, talking loudly and laughing. Ed checked his watch. "Time for my show. You're welcome to stay. We can finish talking after."

The three Heroka nodded. As Ed sat down in the circle, Gwyn ran his eyes idly over the kids. His gaze froze on one boy, probably about twelve or thirteen. The boy was blind, with a beautiful black Labrador for his seeing-eye dog. But that wasn't what caught his attention.

Around the boy, a silver aura flickered, as if he were lit from inside with an ethereal fire.

"Caz," he said, nodding in the boy's direction.

"Shit, the kid has the Mark," she whispered. "Uh, doesn't he? I've never seen a silver one before. Have you?"

Leiddia shook her head. Gwyn thought of Mahigan's silver aura, but he said nothing. "So you don't know him?" he asked Leiddia.

"Nope. New kid in town, I'd say."

The boy's black Lab had sensed Gwyn and was standing now, eyes locked on Gwyn. Gwyn sent calming thoughts, and the dog sat back down, tail wagging. Gwyn looked back at the boy, only to find the boy's dark glasses staring directly at him. After a moment, the boy turned back to Ed.

"Pretty good eyes for a blind kid," Leiddia commented.

Gwyn shook his head. "Some other sense is working here." He suddenly remembered last night's encounter with Mahigan and the silver wolf's parting words.

The boy holds the key. Find the boy.

"So who—or what—*is* he?" Caz asked. "And if he's Heroka, who are his parents?"

"No idea," Gwyn said quietly. "But I'm going to find out."

WHEN ED'S STORYTELLING session ended and the kids were milling around in groups, Gwyn approached the boy. The young Ojibwe girl who sat with him paled when she saw Gwyn and whispered something in the boy's ear. Gwyn sighed. His reputation was again preceding him.

As Gwyn came over, the boy's black Lab stood up, whining, tail wagging furiously. Gwyn was about to calm the dog again with a thought when the boy simply touched the dog's head. The dog sat back down immediately, as placid as if Gwyn had done it himself.

"Hi there," Gwyn said.

The boy turned and seemed to lock his sightless eyes on Gwyn. "Hi. I'm Zach," he said, extending a hand. The Ojibwe girl moved a few steps back, out of the conversation circle but close enough to hear the exchange.

Gwyn shook his hand. "Hi, Zach. My name's Gwyn Blaidd. That's a beautiful dog."

Zach gave a big grin. "He's the best. His name is Quincy."

"Hi, Quincy." Gwyn stroked Quincy's head, linking with the dog's mind as he did so. Love flooded him from the dog, normal for any canid he met, but this time mixed with equally intense feelings for Zach and a stream of dog memories of their times spent together. The dog adored the boy and would give his life to protect him.

"I can tell that you're a good master for Quincy, Zach," Gwyn said, scratching the dog behind both ears. "He loves you a lot."

Zach looked puzzled. "How can you tell that?"

"Let's just say I'm good with dogs."

Gelert came up behind Gwyn, and Quincy's ears snapped back, his fear of the huge wolfhound so sharp Gwyn could smell it. Gwyn introduced Gelert to Zach.

"Easy, Quince," Zach said, stroking his dog's head, as Quincy tried to back away. "He's not good around other dogs."

Gwyn reached out to Quincy with his mind, reinforcing it with the touch of his hands, sending the dog the shared racial memory of the wolf totem and the trust for their brothers that this brought. The change in the Lab was immediate. Quincy stopped trying to hide behind Zach, and approached Gelert cautiously, wagging his tail.

"How did you *do* that?" Zach asked.

And how could you tell that I did, without seeing it? Gwyn thought. "Like I said, I'm good with dogs." The kid was very sensitive to his dog's emotional state. He definitely had Heroka blood. "So, Zach, what brings you to town?"

PULLING UP AT the community center, Kate jumped out of her car and ran up the steps. She'd told Zach that she'd pick him up at five, and it was now almost five-thirty.

She'd just lived through another day from hell. The OPP had found the bullet-riddled body of a local Ojibwe man at the end of a trail leading from Frank Mueller's partially eaten corpse. And since she couldn't provide any evidence linking Leiddia Barker to the killings, Thornton was attributing all three deaths to the dead man and had released Leiddia.

She shook her head, still trying to process what Jonas had told her. Human DNA? A human being had killed these people, and then….

She shuddered. A human killer was one thing, but someone eating their victims as they lay dying wasn't something she could even begin to accept.

Nor, she sensed, could Simon Jonas. He hadn't been pleased about Leiddia Barker's release, but he could do nothing about it. The DNA testing on the clothes of the first victim, Rick Calhoun, would be completed by tomorrow, and a chopper would pick up the DNA samples from Mueller's body tonight, but Jonas didn't expect the evidence from either body to reveal anything more than what Mary Two Rivers's remains had provided.

So now they had no Heroka in custody, and she was no closer to accessing the Tainchel's records on the Heroka to learn about Zach's future as a half-blood version of those—

Those what?

Monsters.

That's what she'd been thinking. Did she really think her beautiful loving son was a monster?

Part of her did, the same part that feared Zach and what he might become. She shook her head. It didn't matter. She loved Zach and would do what she must to make sure he stayed human.

Inside the community center, she stopped in front of the doors to the main meeting hall. She could hear a muffled ringing. Fear clutched at her throat as she realized its source. Clawing open her purse with shaking hands, she pulled out the scanner as it rang again. The display showed three flashing icons, indicating positions inside the room directly ahead of her. Inside the room where Zach was waiting.

Waiting with three Heroka monsters.

Panic seized her. Shoving open the door, she flew into the hall.

GWYN WAS LISTENING to Zach explain about his mom's work on the dam project, when the doors to the hall burst open, and a woman exploded into the room.

She was short, stocky, with brown hair. There was something familiar about her. Her eyes, wide and frightened, flashed from Zach to Leiddia, and then locked on Gwyn. Her mouth opened and closed, but no sound came out. She took a half step back. "No!" she cried. Her face hardened, and she ran forward.

Zach had turned to face the doors as soon as they'd opened. "Mom?"

Gwyn was chasing a face through a forest of memories. He finally caught it. A name came with it, as the woman grabbed Zach by an arm. "Kate?" he said.

Kate Morgan jerked Zach toward the door, almost pulling the boy off his feet, throwing herself between Zach and Gwyn. "Get away from him!" she screamed. "Don't touch him!"

Zach kept his balance only by grabbing onto the lead handle on Quincy's back, who yelped and whined. "Mom, what's wrong?" he cried, fear and confusion straining his voice as Kate pulled him toward the door.

"Zach, we have to get out of here. Now!" Kate cried. They reached the door as Gwyn and the others in the room stood stunned. Kate turned back to face him. "Stay away from him, Blaidd! Do you hear me? Stay away from my son." The door slammed shut, and they were gone.

Caz came up to stand beside Gwyn. "Uh, what just happened?"

"You know her, Gwyn?" Leiddia asked.

He turned. Ed, Leiddia, and Caz were all looking at him, waiting. He swallowed and nodded. "Her name's Kate Morgan," he said quietly, as memories of their short time together rushed back to him. "We were…close."

"How close? Because that kid," Leiddia said, "he kind of looks like you."

He didn't answer. He stood staring at the open door of the hall, the image of Kate dragging Zach from the room burnt into his brain.

He'd been thinking exactly the same thing.

CHAPTER *31*

AFTERMATH—MOTHER AND SON

KATE PULLED UP IN FRONT of their motel with Zach and Quincy, having no memory of driving from the community center. At first, she couldn't make her hands release the steering wheel, and when they finally obeyed, they shook so badly she had to clutch them in her lap.

Gwyn Blaidd. Here. In a little town that didn't even show on most maps. How could this be happening? Her quest to save Zach from being Heroka had brought him face to face with the very man who had caused this.

She caught herself. Caused this? Caused *Zach*. Gwyn was Zach's father. Zach wasn't a *thing*, something that had been *caused*.

"Mom?" Zach's voice beside her was such a tiny thing, she barely recognized it.

Quincy whined from the back seat, sensitive as always to his young master's mood. Zach hadn't said a word since she'd dragged him from the hall. She must have frightened him terribly, especially with him not being able to see what was happening. Taking a deep breath, she tried to speak as normally as she could. "I'm sorry, sweetheart. I didn't mean to scare you—"

"I wasn't scared."

"—but we had to get away from there as quickly as possible." She got out of the car. Zach let Quincy out and walked with him to his room door.

"But why?" he asked. "What's wrong with Mr. Blaidd?"

Mr. Blaidd. She'd held out a hope that he hadn't learned Gwyn's name. How long had they been talking? And what about? Her hands still shaking, she fumbled with the key in the lock to his room. "He's just not someone I want you around," she said, finally opening the door. She held it open as Quincy led him in.

"But why?"

She started trembling again. Why? How could she answer that? This wasn't supposed to happen. She had planned to have answers before she told Zach about Gwyn, answers about what Gwyn was, about what Zach might be. She pressed her hands to the sides of her head. "Zach, please. I can't talk about this right now. Not tonight. Tomorrow, I'll try to explain—"

"But why? He seemed really nice. And Quincy really liked him. Quincy can tell when people—"

"Zach!" she yelled. "I *don't* want you to see him!"

He jumped as if she'd slapped him, and she felt that she had. She'd never raised her voice to him before. He swallowed and took a step back from her. Quincy whined and licked his hand.

"Zach, I'm sorry. I didn't mean to—"

"How do you know him?" he asked, his voice cracking. "Did you meet him here?"

Still ashamed for yelling at him, she answered quickly. "No. We met a long time ago."

"When?"

"Before you were born," she said before she could catch herself. Oh god, why had she said that?

He sat down on the bed, still wearing his parka. Quincy laid his head on his knee, and he stroked the dog absently.

Maybe he wouldn't figure it out.

He turned his sightless eyes to her, in that eerie way he had of finding her. "Is Gwyn my father?"

The sound that escaped her was a frightened thing, the whimper of a beaten animal. She reached a trembling hand towards his lips, as if she could still close them in time, could still stop the question. But it was too late. The question crouched before them now, a beast waiting to tear her and Zach and their life together into pieces.

She looked at him, tears brimming in his sightless eyes. She couldn't lie to him. Not about this. "Yes," she said, her voice a lifeless thing. "He's your father."

"Oh."

She stood there, trying to read the emotions playing across his face, waiting for him to say something else because she didn't know what to say. She sat beside him.

"Why didn't you ever tell me?" he asked finally.

"It's complicated."

"Are you're afraid of him?"

She nodded, a pointless gesture for him, but it helped her say the words. "Yes," she said, part of her rejoicing in finally saying it out loud. "Yes, I am. I'm afraid of Gwyn Blaidd."

"Why?" His jaw muscles tightened. "Did he hurt you?"

Memories danced back to her, of days together, nights together, of laughing and loving, of just being able to be herself and him accepting her for that. She swallowed, suddenly ashamed. "No," she said softly. "No, he never hurt me."

"Then why are you afraid of him?"

So many good memories in that short magical summer. But then she remembered their last night together. The night he had shown her what he really was. The night she'd run away. Run from him in terror. "Because of what he is."

"What do you mean? What is he?"

Good question. What were the Heroka? When she'd met Jonas, she'd called them an *infection*. A beast infecting a human form. Was that what they were? In truth, she didn't know. She just knew she didn't want Zach to be one of them.

"I'm not sure you'd believe me. I'll try to explain tomorrow, but please, stay away from Gwyn. I don't want you seeing him."

"Does he know about me?"

She swallowed, ashamed again. "No."

He nodded. "I always wondered why my dad never wanted to see me. Makes sense now. He never even knew I existed."

The accusation stung her. "I was protecting you. I did it for you." *Liar*, she thought.

"Protect me from what? He seems really nice—"

She jumped up from the bed, unable to control her fear. "Zach! I don't want you seeing him. I don't want you near him. Do you understand? *You are to stay away from Gwyn Blaidd!*"

He stood too, facing her. She couldn't remember him ever looking this angry before. "You want me to stay away from my father because *you're* afraid of him? But you won't tell me *why*?"

"I *can't* tell you, Zach," she said, her voice breaking. "Not now. Tomorrow, we'll talk. I'll try to explain—"

"Are you afraid of *me*, too?"

She swallowed. Was she? "No, honey. No," she said. "No. Zach, I love you." She tried to hug him, but to her shock, he pushed her away and took a step back.

They stood there, mother and son, together, but now for the first time, apart. A gulf had just grown between them, sudden and wide, wider than the step back that Zach had just taken.

Unable to hold her son, she wrapped her arms around herself instead. "We'll talk about this tomorrow," she said. "I'll...I'll explain everything then." When he didn't answer, she walked to the door to her adjoining room. "I'll order in pizza for dinner, okay?" she said, ashamed at the banality of her words. She turned to go.

"I know you're afraid of me," he said quietly, freezing her in the doorway. She looked back. He sat on the bed again, stroking Quincy's head. "Not all the time. But sometimes. I can feel it."

"We'll talk tomorrow, Zach," was all she could bring herself to say. Closing the door behind her, she threw herself on her bed, burying her face and the sounds of her sobbing in the pillow.

AT SOME POINT, sleep took her, and she began to dream. In her dream, she was begging Zach to stay away from Gwyn, and he was growing increasingly agitated, his words becoming slurred, until they resembled more the growls of an animal than the speech of a human. Finally, throwing back his head, he let out a feral howl...

And changed into a gray timber wolf.

She screamed, and the wolf that was her son leapt through the motel room window, shattering the glass. Running to the broken window, she watched him bound across the road to the trees on the far side. There, a larger black wolf waited for him. Kate cried out Zach's name. Both wolves looked back at her, then slipped silently into the bush and disappeared.

She awoke, soaked in sweat. She lay shaking on her bed as the words she'd heard whispered on top of the dam returned to her, their meaning finally and frighteningly clear.

You are no longer needed in this.

Zach. The voice had meant that she was no longer needed in Zach's life. Gwyn was going to take him from her, make him a Heroka, one of the beasts in the night. He would no longer be human.

He would no longer be her son.

Near to panic, she stumbled to her laptop and began recording a message for Jonas. She'd just explained about encountering two Heroka accompanying Leiddia Barker, when Jonas's thin, pinched face appeared.

"Kate, this is excellent news," he said, excitedly. "Do you have pictures or names of these subjects? Or a description?"

She swallowed. A description? If she'd wanted to, she could describe every contour, ever scar on Gwyn's body. "I don't know who the younger female is yet, sir, but the male...." Her voice trailed off. Why did she hesitate?

Did he hurt you?

No, he never hurt me.

"Kate?"

You are no longer needed in this.

She would lose Zach unless she did this. "Sir," she replied, her resolve returning. "The male's name is Gwyn Blaidd."

She hadn't expected any sign of recognition by Jonas. She certainly hadn't expected him to suddenly pale, or to leap up and begin pacing back and forth, muttering to himself.

His face filled her display again as he sat back down, typing. An image flashed up on her screen—a night scene, showing a tall man, dressed in black, leading a group of similarly clad people out of a forest. Flames lit the trees from behind. She looked at the man. Dark, shaggy hair framing a square face above a square jaw, a long straight nose splitting sharp cheekbones and eyes the color of midnight.

Gwyn. The picture showed a date from seventeen years ago, yet the Gwyn she had just left looked exactly as he did in this picture. He hadn't aged in all that time. Somehow, that just fed her resolve.

"Is this the man?" Jonas asked, expectation written in the tense lines of his face.

Why did he have a picture of Gwyn? Why was Gwyn so important to him? But she just nodded.

The coldness in his eyes belied the smile that leapt onto his face. "Well done, Kate! Well done, indeed. You have found the most dangerous Heroka of all, the man behind the ambush I described when we first met. The man responsible for the death of twenty agents."

She fell back in her chair as if he'd punched her. She'd been right all along. Gwyn *was* dangerous. A killer. And yet….

Did he ever hurt you?

"Twenty agents, Kate. Including my own son."

She remembered. Was her son in danger, too? Her resolve returned. "What now, sir?"

"I will organize an extraction team to capture Blaidd and the others. We have enough evidence of his role in the ambush to arrest him. He was certainly involved with your local murders as well. Finding him there explains so much. No doubt he killed that unfortunate police officer last night to exonerate the Barker woman while she was in custody."

She hadn't considered that. Had Gwyn killed Mueller? And then *eaten* the body? She felt a growing horror. She had to get Zach away from here. "Sir, I'm concerned for my son's safety."

Jonas nodded. "As am I. And for your own as well. Mr. Lessard will accompany the extraction team. He'll escort you and Zach back to Ottawa, separately from the captured Heroka, of course. You've accomplished your mission. There's no need for you to remain."

You are no longer needed in this....

She pushed the thought away. "When will they arrive, sir?"

"In forty-eight hours. Until then, both you and Zach should stay in your motel."

The delay surprised her, given Jonas's eagerness to capture Gwyn. And how would she keep Zach safe from Gwyn for two days? But she just nodded. "One more thing, sir. What about the DNA testing from the first victim, Rick Calhoun?"

"Those results will be available late tomorrow, along with those for the murdered OPP officer. We picked up his samples this morning, and I've expedited those tests as well," he replied. "Further testing had seemed pointless, given the results from the Two Rivers girl, but now I'm hoping for proof of Blaidd's involvement."

She hesitated. "But the Two Rivers girl's results indicated a human killer, not a Heroka."

Jonas gave a dismissive wave. "No doubt some error. Or perhaps Blaidd infected that poor man with his tainted blood, turning him into a monster."

Or perhaps you just know the answer you want, she thought.

"Good work, Kate," Jonas said, signing off. The screen went black.

Good work. She slumped in her chair, remembering the videos of caged Heroka. The Tainchel had killed them all. And now Jonas would have the Heroka who had killed his son. The father of *her* son.

She swallowed, the guilt over what she'd just done to Gwyn battling her fear for Zach. Was Gwyn really a killer? She had only Jonas's word for that. But then the words from the dam came back to her.

You are no longer needed in this.

She would lose Zach to Gwyn if she didn't do this. She wouldn't let that happen.

Turning off her notebook, she got up to order the pizza for her and Zach.

CHAPTER *32*

AFTERMATH—CAT AND DOG

O N A SNOW-COVERED picnic table in a small park behind the community center, Gwyn sat beside Leiddia, both bundled in their parkas watching the river flow past black and sluggish in the early darkness. Ed had driven Caz back to the store.

"So, you going to tell me about her?" Leiddia asked quietly.

He stared at the river, its water as murky as the memories he sifted through. "It was after the Ambush. After Stelle and I broke up. I was having trouble dealing with what happened." He stopped. "With what I did."

She squeezed his hand. "I know."

"I moved around for a while. Mostly up north. I met Kate in Waskaganish. She's Cree and was from there, back for a visit or something." He paused, remembering. "We were both lonely. Things happened. Things ended."

"If Zach's your son, then yeah, I'd say things happened."

He shook his head. "She never told me about him."

"When was this?"

He thought for a bit. "Fourteen years ago this past summer."

She nodded. "That fits. Kid looks about thirteen."

"He's my son. He has the Mark."

"That's a weird kind of Mark."

"He's my son," he said, surprised at the certainty he felt. Or how much he wanted it to be true?

"Ok," she said, shooting him a look, "let's say he is. So why didn't she tell you?"

"We were together just one summer. She might not have even known she was pregnant when she…when she left."

"But why wouldn't she tell you after? Why'd she leave?"

He didn't answer. She'd figure it out.

She looked at him. "She found out you were Heroka."

He nodded. "And made her exit pretty much the same way she did just now."

"Why hadn't you told her before that?"

He grimaced. "Not the best ice breaker with humans, is it?"

"So how'd she find out?"

He sighed. "She was getting suspicious that there was something different about me. Little things, like the way Gelert and dogs were around me. She's not stupid. Then we're in a bar one night, and some guy starts about them serving Indians, meaning Kate. I go outside with him, Kate telling me to forget it because he's a lot bigger than me. Fight starts. Fight ends, him face down. Then three of his buddies jump me. Same result. I look at her, and I can see it in her face. She knows."

"You told her?"

He hesitated. "I showed her. Later that night."

She stared at him. "You shifted? In front of a human?"

His anger fought with his guilt as he remembered Kate's face. "I thought she should know who I really was." He stopped. "At the time, it seemed important."

Leiddia looked away. "You loved her."

He stared at the cold water slipping by. "It was a long time ago, Cat."

Neither of them spoke for a while. Then she turned to him. "So what about Zach? Are you going to wake him?"

He'd been asking himself the same question. "I don't know. I'm still dealing with having a son. And I have Caz on my plate right now, too."

But the Mark of the Heroka that colored Zach now colored all of his thoughts about the boy, too. He didn't have just a son—he had a son who could become Heroka. Maybe his race wasn't dying after all. Maybe there was hope.

"But you're thinking of it, aren't you?" She made it sound like an accusation.

"Why not? Why shouldn't Zach have a chance to be one of us?"

"Depends, Dog," she said, standing up and brushing the snow off the seat of her jeans. She faced him, arms crossed. "You going to be around for him? Or are you going to disappear on him like you did on me?"

He got up too, flinging a piece of ice from the tabletop into the river. "You survived."

Anger flared in her face, and she shoved him hard enough to almost send him sprawling. "Did you hear *anything* I said in the jail? I went through *hell*, Gwyn. He's just a kid—and a blind kid, too."

"So I'll be there for him," he said. "Why wouldn't I be? He's my son," he added, instantly regretting the words.

"And I was just another woman in your life, was that it? Easy to leave them behind, apparently."

"That's not fair."

She turned away. "You're right. Stelle died. Kate ran off. *I'm* the only one you left behind."

"Cat," he said gently, but she wouldn't look at him, so he stared at the black river flowing by, unstoppable, disappearing around the next bend, never to be seen again, like those moments in his life he wished he could change.

She wiped a wet cheek with a mittened hand. "There's something else. About Kate. I didn't mention it at the community center, because your young Caz would have gone after her."

"What?"

She hesitated. "She's the woman I saw at the police station. The one with the scanner."

"What? She's a Tainchel agent? With a Heroka son? That makes no sense."

"Maybe the Tainchel don't know about Zach."

He considered that. "Their scanners don't detect sleepers—or at least they didn't used to—so that's possible. But why would she put Zach in that kind of danger?"

"Maybe I'm wrong about her being Tainchel. Or maybe Zach's *not* Heroka. His Mark *is* pretty weird."

"He's one of us," he said, but he knew the reason for his stubborn certainty. If Zach wasn't part Heroka, then Zach also wasn't his son. And he suddenly wanted very much to have a son.

"Well, there's something *different* about him," she said.

"All the more reason to tell him about his heritage."

"Maybe. But what would waking him do to his life? Kate's afraid of us. She's probably afraid of Zach too, afraid of something exactly like this happening. You wake him, and he may lose her. And as a full Heroka, he won't be able to hide from Tainchel scanners. Either way, you damn well better be there for him." She looked at him. "Just promise me that you'll let *him* make the choice."

He nodded. "I'd never force it on him."

"I know," she said. They both fell silent, staring at the black water flowing by. "I really do love you," she said suddenly.

"I love you, too," he said. He kissed her, and they held each other for a while, then walked to her car.

"Can I drop you at Ed's?" she asked. When he hesitated, she shook her head. "You're not staying with me, stud. This all happened too fast. These killings. You and me again. Now…," she said, waving a hand, "…this. Your old girlfriend showing up. Finding out you have a son. I need some time, Dog."

He swallowed his disappointment and nodded. "Yeah, okay. I get it. No, I'll walk. Need some time to think."

They kissed goodbye. He stood on the street watching her drive away, then walked back into town. And as he walked, in all his jumble of thoughts of Leid-dia, of Kate, of the strange happenings in this town, one thought continued to rise above them all.

He had a son.

CHAPTER *33*

DIFFERENT

ZACH LAY IN BED, angry and frightened and confused, none of which were good things to be, he was finding, if you were trying to fall asleep. And falling asleep was exactly what he wanted to do, because for the first time since his encounters with Wisakejack had begun, he wanted to see the strange spirit. No, he *needed* to see Wisakejack.

His ear pressed against the paper-thin motel wall and his blindness-tuned hearing had let him overhear his mother's conversation with her boss, and to learn to his horror that she was turning his newly discovered father over to Gwyn's enemies.

He needed help, and he needed it *tonight*. That meant Wisakejack.

At some point, he finally fell asleep. He remembered his clock announcing midnight. The next thing he knew, he was in the hunting lodge from last night's dream, wearing the leather jacket again, and sitting cross-legged on the floor before the fire beside Wisakejack.

Grinning, Wisakejack held out a cardboard box. "Pizza?"

"Uh, no, thanks. Just finished some. Pizza?"

"Like I said, our worlds are drawing closer together. Just another example."

"Look, I need your help—"

Licking tomato sauce off his fingers, Wisakejack held up a hand. "Let me guess. You just met your dad for the first time but your mom is scared shitless of him and won't let you see him and now she's turning him over to some strange people that you don't think have the nicest intentions toward him and you want to save your dad and ask him why your mom is scared shitless of him and why he left in the first place and will he stick around this time and be your dad for real assuming we can figure out how to make these bad people not take him away." Wisakejack took a breath. "Right?"

"Uh, yeah. How—"

"This is just a dream, remember? I'm in your head, so I know what's in here with me."

"These are *not just* dreams!" Zach cried. "They can't be! I get hurt in them for real. Stuff in the real world happens here. Stuff from here comes into the real world. They *can't* just be dreams! If they're just dreams, then...." His throat choked off his words.

Wisakejack squeezed his shoulder. "Hey, I get it. If they're just dreams, then I can't help you help your dad." He smiled, but with a hint of sadness. Then he grinned. "Well, then, obviously I'm wrong. Let's see what we can do."

Zach rubbed his eyes. "Like what?"

Swallowing his last bite of pizza, Wisakejack wiped his hand on his jacket. "Okay, so your dad's in danger. Two parts to that problem—your dad and the danger. Let's start with your dad. First off, he isn't human. And neither are you."

Zach was suddenly too frightened to speak. As a blind kid, he was used to feeling different. But *inhuman*? Was Mom right to be afraid of him?

"Your pop's a full-blooded Heroka—remember them? The only ones that I left with the power to speak to animals. A very old race of beings who were once married to the animal spirits. Heroka means 'those without horns.' I'll explain that part later."

"And they're not...human?" Zach asked, afraid of the answer.

"Superhuman, really. Human, with extras. Look like people, can mate with people. But they're still connected to the original animal spirits. That gives them *powers*, little brother."

Wisakejack described the Heroka and their powers, and Zach's fear faded, partly because Wisakejack obviously respected the Heroka, and partly because, once Zach got past the weirdness of shapeshifting, they just sounded really cool. But mostly he was thinking of how he'd always felt less than a whole person, not as good as sighted people. Now he had superpowers.

"So if each Heroka is tied to an animal totem, what's Gwyn's—" He stopped. No, he was going to start saying it. "What's my *dad's* totem?"

"He's the grandson of my brother, Mahigan, the wolf spirit. Wolves, coyotes, foxes, dogs—all of them honor the spirit of Mahigan in your father."

Wolves! Even cooler. Dogs too. That explained Quincy's reaction to Gwyn. "Is that my totem, too?"

"Who said *you* had a totem?"

"But you said that I'm Heroka."

"No-o-o-o, I said that you're not human. You're a half-blooded Heroka. Sometimes called a mongrel in less polite company. And you're currently sleeping."

"Well, duh, I'm dreaming."

"No, I mean you haven't been *awakened* to your Heroka powers. And a sleeper is just another human, unless a certain *thing* happens."

Zach felt as if Wisakejack had slapped him. He wasn't human, and he wasn't Heroka. He really *was* different. "What thing?"

Wisakejack leaned in closer. "Blood."

Zach swallowed. "What?"

"For you to become Heroka, your blood must mix with the blood of a true Heroka."

"And then I'll be a Heroka?"

Wisakejack scratched his chin. "Maybe. Thing is, I can't be sure. You're different."

That word again. "What do you mean?"

Wisakejack explained about the Mark and how Zach's was different. "Which means all bets are off," Wisakejack said. "A blood mix with a Heroka might awaken you or do nothing. Or do something else."

"Something else? Like what?"

Wisakejack shrugged again. Zach swallowed. Like make him into a monster. Suddenly the fears that his mom must have held about him all these years became his fears. His hopes of becoming something special, of becoming a Heroka, had died as soon as they'd been born. He wasn't special. He was just different. Horribly different.

"But I thought we were trying to help your dad," Wisakejack said, "not make you Heroka."

"Oh. Right," Zach said with a guilty nod, trying to push his fears for himself behind his fears for Gwyn.

"So now you know about your dad. That brings us to the danger part of your problem."

Zach nodded. "Those men that my mom's working for."

Wisakejack waved that away. "They aren't the *real* danger."

Zach swallowed. "The Windigo? I thought it'd been killed."

"*A* windigo was killed—a man infected with the Windigo spirit. But you can't kill the Windigo spirit. That's still around. But as far as I can figure out, the Windigo's just a symptom of the disease. Something bigger's going on. Like I said, the Spirit World and your world are somehow getting closer. I think other spirits, even more powerful than the Windigo, are involved."

"*Evil* spirits?"

"Hmm. Good and evil's not really a concept we spirits focus on."

"How can you *not* have a concept of good and evil?"

"Because we think of the world differently. Take Kitche Manitou. All life force flows from him. Without him, *everything* would cease to exist. But we don't think of even *him* as good. He's simply the one who made this world and its rules. Respect his rules, and you can live in his world quite nicely, thank you. Break the rules, and trouble starts."

Zach nodded slowly. "Our hunger for water and trees and power. We've upset the balance. We've broken the rules."

Wisakejack nodded. "Spirits aren't evil, but they'll sure make you pay for breaking the rules."

"So what other spirits are involved here? And what's the real danger?"

"Slow down. Before I can explain, you need to *understand* about spirits, including yours truly."

"Anything that would help me understand *you* would be great."

"I *am* very complex, you're right. Anyway, we were the *original* beings of Earth created by Kitche Manitou. We prepared the Earth for the coming of humans. When the world was ready, we changed part of ourselves into everything you see around you, from the stars to the rocks and plants and animals. That's why *everything's connected*, because everything—*everything*, even the rocks— has a spirit, one that is a part of the Great Spirit, Kitche Manitou."

"So that's where you spirits live?" Zach asked doubtfully. "In rocks and animals and stuff?"

"*Part* of us does. We dwell in the Spirit World, which sort of overlays your world." He looked around the cabin. "That's where we are right now."

"That's why there were two cabins here last night," Zach said. Wisakejack nodded. "So what do the spirits have to do with the danger my dad is in?"

"Part of a struggle as old as the Earth—the struggle to create the ideal world."

"Why would there be any struggle over that?"

"Let's just say opinions differ on how you define 'ideal.' Like, for instance, does it include humans? You see, we spirits are kind of in two camps: those like me who are benevolent to humans, and, uh, well, the other kind. The People-friendly spirits dwell in the sky—the home of the sun and air and rain—the sources of life and nourishment. The spirits not so keen on humans dwell in the deep places of the world." Wisakejack nodded to his right.

Zach turned. The hunting lodge had disappeared. They now sat on a stony beach beside the dark lake of his dream in which he had first encountered the windigo. The lake lay like a restless beast, its waves clawing at the pebbled shore as if reaching for him. Shivering, he moved back, his eyes on the black water. "The Great Water Lynxes."

Wisakejack nodded.

"But why do the Lynxes hate humans?"

Wisakejack shrugged, eyeing the lake. "Remember—humans came last. None of Kitche Manitou's other creations need your kind to survive. The Lynxes and some other spirits of the deep places think that the easiest way to protect the world from human greed would be to cut out the humans."

"You mean kill us?" Zach said, shocked.

Wisakejack raised a hand. "Not saying I share that view. Just that it's out there."

"So that's the real danger?"

The spirit shrugged. "What I hear from my brothers, the animals, is that something big's going to happen, the Lynxes are involved, and it's somehow tied to this place," he said, nodding toward the lake. He looked back at Zach. "And to your dad and you."

"What?" Zach cried. "What do you mean?"

Wisakejack shrugged. "All the whispers mention the Wolf being involved— that certainly means your dad—and a boy. And since you're the only non-adult male I've found who's mixed up in all this, I'm figuring they're talking about *you*."

Something heavy suddenly seemed to crouch on Zach's chest, making it hard for him to breathe. He stared at the dark lake. "You're a spirit. Can't you just, well, *ask* the Lynxes?"

"Remember the part where I killed them after they killed my wolf brother?"

"If you killed them, how are they still alive?"

"Immortal spirits. I just sent them back to the Spirit World." He waved a hand. "Anyway, I can't just stroll into their deep places and ask 'wassup?' Nope, we have to find out how you and your dad fit into this."

Zach swallowed. "But how?"

Wisakejack looked thoughtful. "That dog you have—"

"Quincy?"

"He's your guide in your world, right? Because your world's a big, dangerous place, and it's hard to find your way around safely if you don't know what's out there."

"Yeah, I get it. I'm blind. Kind of figured that out."

"Just trying to explain something." Wisakejack looked at the lake. "If you're going to tangle with these spirits, you'll need to find your way around the Spirit World. And the Spirit World is even bigger and more dangerous than your world. So you're gonna need a guide here as well. A *spirit* guide."

"How do I find a spirit guide?"

Wisakejack raised a finger. "Not *a* spirit guide. *Your* spirit guide. This is no small thing. Finding your spirit guide is like entering into a long-term relationship. You'll have your guide your whole life if you believe in it. Your spirit guide will come to you in dreams and show you visions of what you need to do."

Zach frowned. "That sounds a lot like *these* dreams. Aren't *you* already my spirit guide?"

"Wish I could be, little brother. But I don't do one-on-one on a regular basis. The only reason I'm here now is because you're involved somehow in whatever's coming."

"Great. So I'll have *two* spirits telling me what to do," Zach said, sighing. "Well, maybe my spirit guide will actually tell me something useful."

"Ouch. That hurt." Wisakejack shrugged. "But, yeah, that's pretty much what I'm hoping for, too. If it's *your* spirit guide, then it should know what *your* role is in all this."

"So what will this spirit guide look like? How will I know it's *mine*?"

"Spirits are part of everything, remember? So you could end up with a spirit of the moon or the sun or the wind, even the rocks or water." Wisakejack stroked his chin. "But, given your Heroka blood, I'd bet a month of meals that you'll get an animal spirit as your guide."

Zach brightened. "Maybe it will be the spirit of my Heroka totem," he said. "Maybe it will help me become Heroka."

Wisakejack's face was unreadable. "Maybe."

Zach's earlier hope of becoming a Heroka returned. His fight with his mom came back to him too, along with his anger at what she was doing to Gwyn. If he acquired Heroka powers, maybe he could become less dependent on her, maybe even leave home and be on his own.

Or be with his father. Another idea formed. If he were a full Heroka, wouldn't Gwyn *want* to be with him then, to teach him how to be a Heroka? Sure he would. He'd *have* to.

That meant finding his spirit guide might be the best way to keep his father in his life, to make sure Gwyn didn't leave again.

"And my spirit guide will help us figure out the mystery, right? Tell me how to save my dad?" Zach asked. Wisakejack nodded. "Okay, I'll do it. I'll find my spirit guide," Zach said, surprising himself with the conviction he felt.

Wisakejack gave a big grin, and Zach caught a momentary flash of the coyote overlaid on the spirit's face. Then it was gone. "That's great, little brother. You're doing the right thing." He sat staring at Zach, grinning.

"Uh, Wisakejack? *How* do I do it?"

"Oh, right! Forgot that part," Wisakejack said. "You have to go on a *vision quest*. You're the right age for it, at least. Boys usually do their vision quest sometime between ten and sixteen. And you're sexually, uh, inexperienced, shall we say. So that's all good. But you're going to need some help, and we'll have to make some compromises to tradition. Here's what you have to do...."

Zach listened, wondering how he was ever going to accomplish this. But one thought chased away any doubt that tried to creep in. He could save his father.

CHAPTER 34

THINGS THAT MUST BE DONE

CAZ LOOKED UP as Ed poked his head into the store's back room where she lay reading on her cot. "I just gotta give George a ride…somewhere," he said. "You okay on your own for a while?"

If Gwyn had said that, she would've snapped something about not being a child. With Ed, she just nodded. "Sure."

"Don't go wandering off," he said. "Gwyn'd kill me."

She shook her head, and he left. After she heard his truck drive away, she got up, slipped on the old parka that he'd loaned her, and stepped out the back of the store.

Snow was falling again. The river that wound lazily through town lay just twenty yards behind the store. Tugging her parka hood up over her head, she walked down to its banks, sat on a big rock, and rolled a joint. Lighting it, she took a deep toke and held it in.

If she hadn't already felt like a leper as a Heroka before Kate Morgan's explosive exit at the community center, she certainly would now. Yet another human who hated and feared the Heroka, even when her own child was one.

And Gwyn now had a son, which would make it even less likely that he'd want to become her guardian. She took another toke.

She had to *do* something. Something to prove to Gwyn that she wasn't as useless and helpless as he obviously considered her. Something more than wandering around town looking for some mystery Heroka. A Heroka hadn't killed her family or Mitch. A windigo hadn't killed them either.

The Tainchel had.

But so what? She didn't know where the Tainchel were, and even if she did, she couldn't go up against them herself. She was no Gwyn. She felt useless.

Play to your strengths, Caz. That's what Mitch had always said. Yeah? So what were her strengths?

She stared at the river flowing by black and sluggish in the darkness. Ed had told her streams and ponds crisscrossed this whole area, creating a network of watery roads for guides and hunters. And animals.

She smiled. *Play to your strengths.* Flicking the roach into the water, she walked back into the storeroom. She took Rizzo out of her pocket, gave the rat a kiss, and put him into the paper-lined cardboard box Ed had provided. "Ed'll take care of you for a while, buddy. I'll be back in a couple of days."

After leaving a note for Gwyn, she shrugged off her parka and took off all her clothes. With a last peek at Rizzo, she stepped outside and closed the door behind her. Standing naked and shivering on the doorstep, she began to focus her mind in the way that all Heroka know.

A few moments later, a sleek brown otter scampered across the snow-covered ground to the river and slipped silently into the cold dark water.

SIMON JONAS PUT DOWN the phone and eased back into the big leather chair in his home office, having arranged for Kate and Zach's return to Ottawa, as he had promised.

But there the truth in his promise ended. The boy was too unique to leave free and unprotected any longer. Jonas had no further need for Kate, but he wasn't yet sure what to do with her. He probably could rely on her silence as long as he held her son. And besides, who would believe a crazy woman spouting nonsense about government conspiracies and shapeshifting monsters?

Or he had other options. She had cut off contact with her family long ago and had no friends. No one would miss Kate Morgan.

His gaze fell on the picture of Daniel on his desk. The woman was a minor concern. He was about to capture three Heroka. And one of them was Gwyn Blaidd.

Turning out the lights, he went upstairs. He could hear Patricia singing along to a song on the radio in the bedroom. He stopped outside the door.

She would ask him about Daniel, as she always did, never remembering that their son was dead. And he would tell her the truth and comfort her, as he always did, never failing to curse the monsters who had done it.

But tonight would be different. After all these years, all these nights. Tonight he would tell his wife that he had found their son's killer. Opening the bedroom door, he went in, humming the song that Patricia was singing.

KATE SAT HUDDLED on her bed hugging her knees to her chest. She'd been like this since she'd said goodnight to Zach. He hadn't said a word to her since they'd fought over Gwyn.

She'd wanted to explain everything to him. To explain all she'd done, explain how it was all for him and would always be for him. But she hadn't been able to find the words. So she'd said nothing.

All this *was* for him. But what had she accomplished? She'd found no information on the Heroka in the Tainchel databases. Either the Tainchel kept that information well hidden, or she didn't have the required security clearance. She was no closer to getting answers on Zach's fate than when she'd joined. Instead, she'd brought Zach into a murder investigation and face to face with the last person on Earth she wanted him to meet, and alienating him from her by doing so. And now she'd done something terrible, turning three people over to a man like Simon Jonas.

Just who was the monster here? Feeling more alone and miserable than she'd ever been in her life, she hugged her knees tighter and rocked back and forth.

Her notebook announced new mail in a singsong voice far cheerier than her mood. She got up to check it. It was a note from Lessard, confirming that he would pick her and Zach up the day after tomorrow. Out of habit, she paged down through the email trail, hoping to find some tidbit of information concerning the Heroka or the Tainchel.

An earlier attachment had been deleted, but its filename still showed on the original message: RQ-T2317771. "RQ" meant a requisition. Maybe her low-level clearance didn't let her into the Tainchel's Heroka and DNA databases, but she could access the requisition system. Opening the database, she typed in the RQ number.

The requisition had been submitted that night, shortly after her conversation with Jonas. It appeared to be for transportation and equipment for the extraction team. She scanned the list.

One helicopter. She wondered about that. Jonas had said he'd arrange to bring her and Zach back separately. Maybe Lessard would just drive them back in her MNR car. The rest of the order listed several sub-items under one main item labeled "Heroka Containment Units." She scanned the sub-items—cages, restraints, tranquilizers. She swallowed, her guilt rising again. They were shipping Gwyn and his friends back like animals.

Something else caught her eye: the quantity field beside "Containment Units." A field representing the number of Heroka that Jonas expected to bring back. A field that should say three, a unit each for Gwyn, Leiddia Barker, and the teenage Heroka she'd seen with them.

But it didn't say three. She stared at the screen.

Quantity: Four (4).

A chill settled on her as the implication of that single extra unit sank in.

The Tainchel knew about Zach.

WITH ONLY TWO MOTELS in town, it hadn't taken Gwyn long to find where a Cree woman from out of town and her blind son were staying. Now he sat in The Outfitter watching the blue and white hotel from across the street as he sipped on a single malt and sifted through his thoughts and feelings.

Just a few hours ago, he'd been making love with Leiddia. She'd been cleared of suspicion in Mary's death, Mary's killer had been caught, and they'd found no sign of the Tainchel that he'd expected to find here. So he had allowed himself to believe. To believe that maybe he and Leiddia could have a life together again. Hell, maybe he could become Caz's guardian. They could all settle down here, and live happily ever after.

Yeah, right.

Now Kate had reappeared, a woman who feared and hated him, a woman who might be working for the Tainchel.

He'd loved Kate once and was certain that she'd fallen in love with him that summer fourteen years ago. But that had ended the night she'd run from him in terror.

And why? Because he'd shared the truth of what he was with her. And when she'd learned that truth, she'd become just another human who feared the Heroka.

But now, Kate had given him something else. A son. A son who could be like him. A Heroka.

He thought about Leiddia and their reawakened love. He thought about Kate's face as she ran from him, about his hate for the Tainchel, and about his hopes for Zach. Those thoughts kept running through his head, until finally they all met in a dark glade in a primeval forest where the words of a strange silver wolf echoed.

You were drawn here for a purpose far beyond any you hold or could imagine.

A chill settled on him. It occurred to him in that moment that the likelihood of arriving in a small northern Ontario town at exactly the same time as Kate and Zach and the Tainchel was an event not explainable by any stretch of coincidence. Why was Kate here? Why now?

You were drawn here....

Leiddia, Kate, Zach, himself. All tied somehow to a series of brutal murders and, if Mahigan was right, something much, much larger.

The boy holds the key.

Suddenly, amid all his feelings for his newfound son, another intruded.

Fear for Zach.

IN HIS DREAM, Zach listened as Wisakejack explained a vision quest.

"Now, the most important part is picking the spot where you'll sleep to receive your vision. And that depends on the kind of spirit guide you want to attract."

"What do you mean?"

"Well, we need a very powerful spirit to help you. The most powerful spirits, remember, live in two places—the sky and the deep places of the world. To attract a spirit of the deep places, you sleep near deep water. Or trees, whose roots reach down into the earth."

"But I thought those spirits don't like humans," Zach replied, puzzled.

Wisakejack shrugged. "Well, then, if you want a spirit of the air, you'll need to sleep in a tree platform." He stopped. "Hmm, blind kid in a tree. Not a great idea. Ok, then in some high place or near tall trees."

Zach thought of Gwyn. "What if I want to attract the wolf spirit?"

"The wolf is associated with the earth and the forest, so you'd want to sleep on the ground near trees. Your ideal spot is somewhere high, near tall trees, beside water. That puts you close to all the spirits." Wisakejack winked. "You're bound to attract *something*."

Something, Zach thought. *But what?*

THAT NIGHT, ED stood beside George Ozawamik on the receiving dock behind the Thunder Lake Community Hospital. They'd hidden Ed's truck off the highway and walked through the bush behind the hospital to get here. Ed carried a heavy canvas bag. He gave three short raps on the receiving door. They waited.

"You do not think that this thing died with Walter Keejek, do you?" Ed said.

George shook his head. "A shaman can send the Windigo spirit into another. Make *them* windigo. Walter had that power. He was Waubunowin. He could have taught another."

"If that is true, we must find them and stop them," Ed said. "We should tell Thornton."

George shook his head. "The police, the whites, they won't believe any of this."

The door opened. Billy Ozawamik, George's son and a maintenance worker at the hospital, stood inside. Blinking against the sudden brightness, Ed stepped in, followed by George. Billy led them silently past cartons tattooed with medical supply logos and down a hallway to a stairwell, avoiding any other night staff.

Descending the stairs to the basement, they stopped before a set of metal double doors. A handwritten cardboard sign taped to the wall read "MORGUE" in big block letters.

Ed hesitated. *When a windigo dies, there are things that must be done.*

"Old friend," George said softly. "The hunger that took your Mary must not walk again."

Ed shook his head. "If the Windigo spirit is truly here, it is stronger than two old men."

"Then," George replied, "we will make sure that it does not walk again in this one."

Ed sighed and nodded. He pushed open the doors. Billy flicked a light switch. The room contained two metal tables. One was empty. A black body bag lay on the second, concealing the body inside, but not the fact that it contained one. "Thirty minutes," Billy said, then left.

Putting the canvas bag on the empty table, Ed laid out its contents: rubber gloves, a hunting knife in a leather sheath, a wooden-handled chisel, a heavy rubber mallet, a big metal bowl, a can of lighter fluid, a box of matches, and finally a black marker.

Opening the body bag to reveal the bullet-riddled corpse of Walter Keejek, George drew a dashed line with the marker on Walter's chest roughly outlining where the heart lay. Ed looked at George from across the body. "Ready?" George asked. Ed nodded.

And they began.

Later that night, as Ed lay in bed, unable to sleep, Vera snoring softly beside him, what haunted him wasn't that crude surgery. He'd butchered his share of game. No, it wasn't the blood or the desecration of the corpse that kept him awake.

It was the memory of what they'd pulled from the body—the heart they had burned in the metal bowl. No, not burned.

Melted.

For what they'd pulled from the corpse had not been a thing of flesh. It had been a heart-shaped block of solid ice. He shuddered. The Windigo spirit *was* here in their town. And it was *strong*.

CRYING OUT, COMDOWTAH dropped to the floor. The hunger had returned, suddenly and stronger than ever.

"Why?"

The voices spoke. *The windigo man is dead. The Windigo spirit can no longer feed through that one. It returns to you.*

"Help me!"

You know what you must do. Send the Windigo spirit into another.

The shaman slumped against a wall. "No! I won't do that to another person. Not again."

Then the Windigo will feed through you as it did the first time. You or another. It makes no difference. The Windigo will feed.

Comdowtah remembered that first time, the boy on the top of the dam. Trapped inside the monster, unable to stop it as the thing ripped the boy apart. The boy's screams. The taste of sweet flesh and warm blood.

"No," the shaman whispered. "Not that."

Then find another.

MARY TWO RIVERS leaned against the trunk of the largest birch tree she'd ever seen. She'd been walking the glowing path through the dark primeval forest ever since the voice had told her this was the Spirit Road, the path that she must walk until she reached her spirit home where all of her ancestors waited for her.

"Better be a big house," she muttered. And she had only four days to do it, one of which she'd already used. She wondered what would happen if she didn't make it in four days. Probably nothing good. What else had the voice said?

You will be afraid, but you must walk alone.

You will be hungry, but you must eat alone.

You will be tired, but you must sleep alone.

"Okay, so let's see how I'm doing," she said aloud. "Afraid? Check. Hungry? Check. Tired? Check." She stopped and looked around her in the dark forest. "And I'm definitely alone. Well then, so far, so good," she said, suppressing a hysterical giggle.

She began to cry. She'd had plans for her life, starting with continuing to live it. This totally sucked.

A branch snapped. Choking off a sob, she held her spirit breath. Another snap and the sounds of heavy feet. Whoever was approaching was not concerned with hiding their presence. Another sound came to her then, a high-pitched intermittent whistling. It took her a moment to realize it was the sound of something breathing. She hid behind a tree as a memory began to stir. A few seconds later, the intruder passed by, no more than five yards from where she hid.

And she remembered.

She jumped out from hiding. "You *killed* me, you son of a bitch!"

The Windigo stopped. As its bulbous red eyes fell on her, it occurred to her that, even though she was dead, there might be fates that could befall her spirit she should probably try to avoid. Swallowing, she stepped back.

But the Windigo made no move toward her. Its voice was a thing of ice cracking in the middle of a frozen lake. "I have eaten your flesh already, child. Your spirit is of no use to me. I need fresh meat and hot blood." Turning away, it continued through the forest.

"What? That's it? Take my body, then forget about me?" she yelled after its retreating back. "Obviously a guy," she muttered.

She remembered the final Spirit Road instruction she'd received. *Your spirit will become weak. It is then that the tests will appear.*

This, she was sure, was one of those tests. But what was the answer? Ignore the Windigo and keep walking the Spirit Road? Follow the creature?

She looked to where the Spirit Road lay before her, glowing faintly in the dark, beckoning with the promise of warmth and family, of love and home, of final rest. She took a step in that direction.

I need fresh meat and hot blood.

She stopped. That thing was going to kill again, going to end someone else's life in Thunder Lake just as it had ended hers.

"Oh no, it won't," she said. "Not if I can help it."

Turning her back on the Spirit Road, she stepped off the glowing path and set out through the dark forest after the Windigo.

PART III:

The End of the World All Over Again

"To you, Kitche Manitou has given the book. To us, he has given the Earth."
—*Red Jacket, orator of the Seneca Nation in the Six Nations*

CHAPTER *35*

YOU CAN RUN, BUT...

RISING EARLY THE NEXT MORNING, Kate packed as much as possible without waking Zach, then loaded their suitcases into the car. After discovering Jonas's deception, she'd spent a sleepless night trying to think of a plan. She'd finally decided to leave town that morning, to get Zach away from both Gwyn and Jonas. Once Zach was safe, she'd figure out their next step.

She slipped behind the wheel, planning to drive to the Valu-Mart to stock up on supplies before leaving. She turned the key. Nothing. Not even a growl. She popped the hood, but could see nothing obvious. Going back inside, she called the only garage in town.

An hour later, shivering in the early morning cold, she watched as the burly Ojibwe mechanic closed her hood. The name on his grimy overalls said "Bernie." He shook his head. "My best guess? Your on-board computer. I'm not reading anything. It's like something's wiped all of its settings."

Or someone, she thought, conspiracy theories spinning in her head. "What could cause that?"

Bernie shrugged. "Never seen it before. Could be a short. Or a bad board."

"Can you fix it?"

He nodded. "If the board's not fried. Just need to download the factory settings from the manufacturer's site."

"How long will that take?"

"Got a couple of jobs ahead of you. Should be ready tomorrow night. Unless I need a new board. Then you're talking couple of weeks."

Weeks! She ran her hand through her hair. "Where's the nearest car rental?"

He laughed. "You're not from around here, are you? There isn't one." He wiped his hands with a rag and stuffed it back in his coveralls. "So? You want me to work on it?"

She pulled her wallet out. "Yeah. And look, I'll pay you double if you work on it first."

Bernie looked at her. "You Anishinabe?"

"Cree."

He eyed her for a moment. "You in trouble?"

"I need to get my son back home," she said, folding her arms. "For school," she lied.

He considered this. "Okay. I'll work on it today. Drop by about six tonight. Either I'll have fixed it, or I'll know if I need the part. That work?"

"Tonight is fine," she said. If he could fix it, they'd still be able to leave before Lessard showed up tomorrow evening.

"And forget the pay double crap. You're one of us," he said, as he started to hook the car to the tow truck.

She swallowed. *One of us.* Was she? But as Bernie pulled away, she pushed those thoughts aside.

Walking toward her was Gwyn Blaidd.

AFTER A SLEEPLESS NIGHT at Ed's, the morning found Gwyn back at The Outfitter. He still didn't know what he planned to do about Zach, or even how to approach Kate. And despite the conviction he'd expressed to Leiddia, he still didn't know for certain that Zach was his son. He needed Kate to confirm that. And to confirm that she worked for the Tainchel.

But after an hour of bitter memories and worse coffee in The Outfitter, he'd decided this was a bad idea and was about to leave when Kate emerged. When he saw her loading suitcases into the car, he made up his mind. If she left town, he might never learn the truth. Kate wouldn't make herself or Zach easy to find. He waited until the tow truck left, then crossed the street.

When she saw him approaching, her eyes widened. She looked back at the motel, as if torn between fight or flight, and then turned to face him, her arms crossed. *The mother defending her cub*, he thought, with grudging admiration.

"Did you do that?" she snapped, pointing after the disappearing tow truck and car.

This was starting well. "I didn't touch your car, Kate."

"Then what do you want? I told you to stay away from him."

"I came to see you, not Zach."

She hesitated at that. "I have nothing to say to you."

"I need to know. You owe me that."

"I owe you nothing. Not after what you did."

"What did I ever do to you, Kate?"

"Have you forgotten that night? I never have. God knows, I've tried."

"I showed you the truth."

"That I'd been sleeping with some kind of monster?"

"We're not monsters—"

"You're not human. Then I find out that I'm pregnant—"

"So Zach *is* my son!" He hadn't truly let himself believe it until now.

She paled. "You didn't know?"

"How could I have known? You never told me."

She looked away. "He's blind."

"I noticed."

She looked back at him. "Well?"

"Well, what? You blame *me* for that?" he said, his anger now rising.

Kate dug both her hands into her hair. "I don't know what I believe. I just know that Zach is not going to be like you."

"Is that what this is about? You think I'm going turn Zach into one of your monsters?"

"You won't get the chance," she said, managing to sound both frightened and threatening.

"Maybe I don't need to."

She paled. "What do you mean?"

"I mean, he's got my blood in him," he said, unable to control the anger driving his words. "I'm not human? What do you think Zach is? Maybe he's already one of your monsters, Kate. You ever think about that?"

Her mouth worked, but no words emerged. Turning, she ran to the door of her motel room. "Stay away from us!"

"Do you even know what Zach is?" he yelled after her. "Do you even know your own son?"

"Stay away from us!" she screamed, slamming the door behind her.

AN HOUR LATER, Kate sat in a booth in The Outfitter, staring out the window, lost in a forest of dark thoughts and darker fears. Across the table, Zach sat slumped, listening stone-faced to his iPod. They might as well be at separate tables. He hadn't initiated a single conversation with her since their fight, responding to anything she said with one-word answers or shrugs. She looked at him. How had she managed to screw things up this badly? Again, she longed to explain everything she'd done and why, but didn't know where to begin.

The waitress brought corn flakes and orange juice for Zach and the Number 2 special with scrambled eggs for Kate. Scrambled like her life.

She was convinced that both Gwyn and Jonas intended to take Zach from her, and they both knew where to find him. She needed a place to keep Zach hidden until Bernie fixed her car, hopefully by tonight. But where? Who could she ask? Thornton? He'd hand them both over to CSIS as soon as Jonas asked. The only other people she knew in town worked at the dam, and they'd be the first people Jonas would check on when he found her and Zach gone from the motel.

"Mom?"

She looked up, her problems momentarily forgotten in the hope that Zach had forgiven her. She swallowed. "Yes, honey?"

"I was wondering…," he began, stirring soggy corn flakes with his spoon.

"Yes?"

"I was wondering if I could stay at Bonnie's tonight," he said in a rushed mumble, the expectation of rejection underscoring every word.

"That girl you met at the storytelling?"

Zach nodded. "I mean, we're going home, and I won't get to see her again."

An idea formed. "She lives on the Rez, right?"

He nodded, not looking at her.

The Rez was out of town. This would solve her problem. "Well, we'd have to ask her parents—"

Zach's expression morphed from hopeful to an excited grin. "Oh, I emailed Bonnie. Her dad says it's okay. He'll even pick me up." He stopped. "I mean, if you say it's okay."

"Sure. Why not?" she said, relief and hope washing over her.

Zach beamed at her. "Really? Oh, wow! I thought you'd—I mean, thanks, Mom."

"You're welcome, honey," she replied, hating herself for being a hypocrite. If it weren't to keep him safe, she probably *would* have said no. She swallowed. "Zach? I'm really sorry we fought last night."

His smile slipped away. "Me, too."

She bit her lip. "I love you."

He sat back, his head bowed. "I love you, too," he said quietly.

The waitress came to refill Kate's coffee, ending the awkward moment. They ate in silence, Kate enjoying her breakfast far more than its quality justified, smiling both at Zach's happy face and the thought that she'd found a place to hide him.

And maybe this would take his mind off his father.

ALL ZACH COULD THINK ABOUT as he sat happily slurping mushy corn flakes was that he was going to save his father. After his dream last night, he'd convinced himself that finding his spirit guide was the key to saving Gwyn, becoming Heroka, and solving the mystery of what was happening in this town, a mystery that somehow involved him.

Listening to his mother's knife and fork scraping against her plate, he felt a pang of guilt about lying to her. Well, a part lie. He *was* going to Bonnie's. He just didn't plan to spend the night there. Then he remembered that his mom was handing Gwyn over to those government people, and his anger shoved any guilt aside. He would do his vision quest. He would save his father.

AN HOUR LATER, Kate stood with Zach and Quincy in the motel parking lot as a battered pickup truck pulled up. Bonnie jumped out, and she and Zach immediately started talking excitedly about how they'd spend the day. A big man climbed out of the driver's side, and Kate felt a jolt of recognition. It was Joe Makademik, from the protest at the dam on her first day.

"Morning, Kate," he said with a grin. "Remember me?"

She nodded. "Of course. Nice to see you again, Joe. I didn't realize Bonnie was your daughter." They shook hands, and she noticed he held on a little longer than he needed to.

He nodded at Zach and Bonnie. "They've become fast friends. Bonnie hasn't stopped talking about Zach."

"It's been great for Zach, being new here. And Bonnie's a wonderful girl. You and your wife have done a great job," she said, forcing both her smile and the small talk.

His smile ran away. "My wife passed away five years ago. But you're right—Bonnie's a great kid. More credit to her than me. Not sure I know what I'm doing." Joe looked at the size of Zach's duffel bag. "You planning to stay for a month, Zach?"

Bonnie shot Zach a look. Zach shrugged. "We're not sure what we're going to do, so I thought I'd just bring a bunch of stuff. Plus I brought my sleeping bag, uh, because I'm used to it."

Joe shrugged. "No problem." He put Zach's bag in the back of the truck. Quincy jumped up and lay down with his head on the bag, while Kate hugged Zach goodbye. Joe gave her directions to their house on the Rez, and they exchanged cell numbers.

"I'll pick Zach up tomorrow morning," she said. *Tonight, if they fix my damn car.* She was getting Zach away from here as soon as possible, but she didn't say that.

Joe gave her a wink as he pulled away. She watched the truck disappear around a corner.

"Looks like Zach will be missing his lessons today."

Startled, she turned to find Colin Macready behind her, staring after the truck. He smiled.

"Oh, Colin. Good morning," she replied, trying to gather her thoughts. She didn't think the tutor was with the Tainchel, but he might still unwittingly pass along information on Zach's whereabouts to Jonas. The less he knew, the better. "Zach's just spending some time with Bonnie today."

Macready nodded. "Glad they've become such friends." He looked at her. "Where are they going?"

"The library," she lied.

He shrugged. "Guess I can take the day off."

"Yes. Sorry for the surprise, but Zach just asked me this morning."

Macready waved a hand. "No problem at all. I can catch up on paperwork." He looked around. "Say, where's your car?"

She explained, and he nodded. "I'm sure they'll get it fixed. Well, I think I'll grab some breakfast. Have a good day." With that, he headed across to The Outfitter.

Have a good day. Sure, if Bernie fixed her car, if she could keep Zach hidden from his werewolf father, if they could get out of this goddam town before her whack-job boss arrived to take them prisoners. Sure, no problem. She headed back into the motel to finish packing.

SEATED AT A WINDOW in The Outfitter, Macready sipped black coffee and considered a GPS display on his phone. A blinking icon appeared on the screen. The tracker he'd attached to Quincy's harness was still working perfectly. He watched as the icon traced the truck's route through Thunder Lake. When the icon passed the library and headed out of town, he nodded to himself. He'd been right. The bitch had lied to him.

He continued to watch the screen, unconcerned. The tracer had a range of a hundred miles, and that truck probably couldn't top fifty miles per hour. He'd be able to catch up in his car—the car Kate Morgan didn't know about—if they were making a run for it, and could alert Jonas to intercept. Twenty minutes later, the icon showed the truck stopping inside the Ojibwe reserve. Smiling, he set the unit to alert him if the tracer moved more than a mile from its current location, and put it away. Everything was under control.

Still, Kate's lie indicated that she felt she needed to hide the boy. But from whom? Blaidd most likely, especially after that argument he'd watched from his motel room. She hadn't seemed to be wary of him when they'd talked just now, and he couldn't figure out how she could possibly have stumbled onto Jonas's plans for Zach. No, it must be Blaidd.

He shrugged. It didn't matter. They'd never fix the damage he'd done to her car before Jonas arrived with the extraction team. And the tracker would let them find Zach whenever they wanted.

Kate Morgan and her freak son could run, but they couldn't hide.

CHAPTER 36

THE THINGS IN THE LAKE

ZACH TIGHTENED HIS GRIP around Bonnie's waist as she gunned the four-wheel ATV up a rise, negotiating the thick bush outside the Rez. The snow had started again. Not the fat, fluffy flakes that he'd felt on his face that morning, but tiny hard pellets that stung his cheeks. He buried his face into the back of Bonnie's parka, enjoying the feel of her girl body against him, trying to focus on why he was here and not on the reaction in his crotch.

He felt the ground level out again. The ATV slowed to a stop, and Bonnie cut the engine. The ringing in his ears from a half-hour of engine drone slowly faded, replaced by a cold silence broken only by Bonnie's breathing.

"Uh, Zach, you can let go now."

Embarrassed, he let go, but leaned back too far. Losing his balance, he fell off the ATV, landing on surprisingly soft ground.

Bonnie laughed. "Sorry, but that was funny. You okay?"

He grinned up at the direction of her voice. Probing underneath him, he found a thick carpet of pine needles and leaves under two inches of snow. "Well, at least you picked a comfy spot for me to sleep," he said. Her hand gripped his as she helped him up. "Where's Quincy?" he asked.

"He's coming. I got a little ahead of him." She sighed. "I can't believe you talked me into this."

Neither could he. They'd chatted online last night. He'd told her everything—his dreams with Wisakejack, Gwyn being his father, what Gwyn was. And what he himself might be. He hadn't told her about his mom and the government people, just that his dad was in danger and needed his help.

To his surprise, Bonnie had accepted the news about Gwyn and the Heroka without question. Many Ojibwe knew the Heroka, and her dad had suspected Gwyn of being one when Gwyn lived there before.

She was less accepting of his strange dreams with Wisakejack. But that changed when he described his encounter with the windigo. She asked him for visual details, and he'd described the scene, including the cabin, the police cruiser, and its car number.

That had done it. *That's Walter Keejek's cabin*, she wrote back, *where Frank Mueller was killed that same night. And that's one of the cruiser numbers, too.* She couldn't explain how a blind boy could know visual crime scene details that were never made public, unless his strange story was true.

Convincing her to help him do his vision quest was another matter. But one by one, he eliminated all of her concerns. *You'll take me there and pick me up the next morning*, he'd written. *You'll pick out the spot. I won't be wandering around, so being blind's no problem. I have winter clothes and a sleeping bag rated for forty below.*

What about food?

I'm not supposed to eat on a vision quest.

No! she replied.

Okay. I'll bring water and some energy bars.

What about bears?

Wisakejack says that whatever's happening here has driven all the animals away.

There've been three killings here in the past week, she protested.

They caught the killer last night.

My dad will kill me!

He won't even know.

The plan was that once Bonnie's dad left for work, Bonnie would take Zach by ATV to find a spot to camp for his vision quest that night. When her dad came home that evening, she'd tell him there'd been a change of plans and that Zach's mom had picked him up already. Bonnie would then pick Zach up the next morning and take him into town. With any luck, neither Bonnie's dad nor Kate would ever find out.

And besides, he'd finished, *I'll have Quincy with me.* With that, she'd given in.

Zach heard Quincy "whuff" a greeting as the dog padded through the snow, happy to have caught up with his master and enjoying being away from buildings and roads and cars.

"No, Quincy!" Bonnie cried.

"What's he doing?"

"He was going to pee on the ATV."

Zach laughed. "He doesn't like it. Too noisy and smelly. Good thing your dad has one, though."

"He's a guide, and they're the best way to get around in the bush."

"Where are we?" He could hear water slapping a stony beach nearby, somewhere below them.

"A place like you asked for—somewhere high, near tall trees, beside water. We're on a hill overlooking the dam lake in a stand of jack pines."

Zach nodded, remembering how Wisakejack had described the ideal site to help a dreamer attract a spirit of the air, or even the Wolf spirit. "Great! It sounds perfect."

"Think it'll work?" Bonnie asked.

He shrugged. "Wisakejack said we're breaking a lot of traditions, like you should do this in the spring, when the spirits are most active in our world."

"Not to mention warmer. Brrr."

"Oh, and you're supposed to take off all your clothes."

"Well, if you're planning to do that, I'm taking you back right now," she replied. "Let's get you set up. I've got to be back before my dad comes home."

With Bonnie's help, they laid spruce boughs at the base of a huge jack pine overlooking the dam lake. They'd brought two sleeping bags, which they zippered together to form one large one to make room for Quincy as well. "I want my head pointing north," Zach said.

"Towards the lake? Why?"

"Wisakejack said that I should point towards one of the four compass points, to help me contact the spirits of the four winds. He said North was my best choice."

Bonnie hesitated. "I don't know. North is where the winter spirits live, like the Windigo."

He swallowed, his suspicions of Wisakejack returning. He shook his head. "Let's point it north. I either have to trust Wisakejack, or forget about saving my father."

Finally, after feeding Quincy, he was ready for the night. Bonnie gave him a hug, which he readily returned. "Now, don't wander around. Stay warm and covered up. I'll pick you up in the morning as soon as my dad leaves."

"Thanks, Bonnie. You don't know how much this means to me."

"I think I do. You take care of him, Quincy, you hear? Don't let anything happen to him," she said. Zach was surprised at the real concern in her voice. Quincy whined in reply.

"I'll be fine," he said, trying to make himself believe it.

"Better be," she replied, "for both our sakes. See you tomorrow."

The roar of the ATV drowned out his goodbye. He listened as the sound grew fainter and fainter until it died away completely, and he and Quincy were alone in the bush.

MACREADY WAS COMPOSING an email report to Jonas in his motel room when a high-pitched beeping from his GPS unit brought his head up. He checked the device—and cursed. The alert that he'd set had been triggered. The Morgan kid had left the reserve.

Grabbing his coat, he headed down the street to the car he kept behind the hardware store. He roared out of town toward the location of the flashing icon on the GPS screen.

An icon that suddenly disappeared just as he hit the highway. Startled, Macready pulled off to the shoulder and stopped. He checked the unit, but it appeared to be working properly. The boy's signal had simply vanished.

Pulling back onto the road, he sped toward the last location the tracker had shown for Zach Morgan, deep in the bush surrounding the reserve. He would go to that point and then follow the vector the kid had been on before the signal disappeared—toward the new dam site.

The closest he could drive was five miles from the kid's last location. Parking on the side of a logging road, he changed into warmer clothes and boots from his trunk, and set off into the now darkening bush by foot, flashlight in hand, fighting down a growing panic.

Simon Jonas was arriving that evening with a Tainchel extraction team, and his prized half-breed Heroka brat that he'd entrusted to Macready had just vanished. As Macready struggled through thick bush and deep snow, he nursed his anger with thoughts of what he was going to do to the little freak when he caught up with him.

EAGER TO RECEIVE his vision and meet his spirit guide, Zach wasted no time in settling down for his night beside the dam lake. He took off his boots before getting into the sleeping bag, but kept his parka on with the hood up. It was still snowing, but with his head turned away from the wind blowing in from the lake and with Quincy huddled beside him, he felt quite toasty.

He lay there, breathing in warm dog smell and listening for animals. But Wisakejack seemed to have been right about the animals disappearing. It sounded as if he and Quincy were the only things alive for miles. The sole noise was the wash of waves against the shore. The shore must have been stony, as each wave brought a crunching sound. As he listened, the crunching grew louder, as if the lake was moving closer.

Or something from the lake was walking toward him.

He sat up, suddenly afraid. And blinked against cold moonlight shining down bright and clear through the trees onto a blanket of snow.

He could see. He was dreaming.

And he was alone. Quincy and the sleeping bag were gone. This place didn't seem as cold, which was fortunate, since his deerskin jacket had replaced his parka. He stood. The layout of the forest and lake was similar to what Bonnie had described, except he saw no sign of the dam. These trees were huge, with an ancient feel to them, as if they had always been here and knew in their woody hearts that they always would be.

He felt more than knew that he was now in the Spirit World, the realm of his vision quest. "Well, if I'm on a quest, I guess I'd better start questing," he said aloud, wishing Quincy was with him. Picking out the most obvious landmark as his first destination, he started down the slope through the trees toward where the lake lay dark and suddenly still.

A ripple out on the black water caught his eye. In the middle of the lake, something had just broken the surface. Another ripple appeared beside the first. They were too far away to make out any details, but he could tell that both things were large. Assuring himself that this was all part of his vision quest, he continued down the slope as the things in the lake swam toward him.

CHAPTER *37*

OMENS AND OTTERS

SIMON JONAS STARED from the CSIS helicopter at the dark forest passing below. In the rear of the chopper rode his extraction team and the containment units. They would arrive in Thunder Lake by six-thirty that evening, a full day ahead of what he had told Kate Morgan. There they would capture the three Heroka along with Zach Morgan, and return the four specimens to the Tainchel facility. He still hadn't decided how best to handle the Morgan woman.

Leaning back, he closed his eyes. He hadn't slept for two days. Fatigue and the steady drone of the chopper's blades soon overwhelmed him, and he slipped into a restless sleep that drifted into dream.

In that dream, he felt cold, a cold that defied the blazing sun and clear blue sky overhead. He stood in a field of coarse grasses and moss-covered rocks. In the remote distance rose a forest of pine trees. He began moving toward the forest, and in the way of dreams, found himself suddenly before it. A figure stood in the shadows near its edge. A figure that looked vaguely familiar. The figure stepped forward into the sunlight.

Jonas let out a cry. "Daniel!" He rushed forward to embrace his son. Daniel returned his embrace, and Jonas wept into his shoulder. His son felt solid, felt warm, felt like Daniel. It *was* Daniel. For a second, Jonas caught a scent of something bitter, and yet, at the same time, sickly sweet, but then the sensation and the fleeting feeling of unease it had brought were swept away in his overwhelming joy at being reunited with his son.

Jonas stepped back, gazing at his son, desperately wanting to believe this was more than a dream. "Is it really you?" he asked.

"I am the immortal soul of Daniel Jonas, who was your son."

There was a soul. There was an afterlife. "And this place?"

"A place I constructed in your mind. A mortal could not withstand gazing upon the full beauty of Heaven."

Heaven. There was a Heaven. And his son was there. All his beliefs were true. But of course they were.

"I'm sorry, father," Daniel said, "but we have little time. I bring you a message from our Lord."

A message from God? For him?

"He knows you hunt the abominations that mock His creation of man in His own image." Daniel said. "You do His work, father."

A cry escaped Jonas. God himself knew of his work against the Heroka.

"And now, father," Daniel continued, "our Lord has more work for you."

Jonas looked at Daniel, amazed. *He* had been *chosen*. "Anything. What must I do, my son?" he whispered, desperate to hear how he could serve.

His son smiled at him. *"Bring to Him the Wolf and Boy."*

For a heartbeat, Jonas heard something else hiding behind those words, something other than the warmth and love that Daniel had projected up to then. Something that whispered of places deep and dark and cold. But that thought disappeared as the implications of the words sank in.

"You mean…Gwyn Blaidd? Zachariah Morgan?"

Daniel nodded. "You must bring them to the hydroelectric dam powerhouse at Thunder Lake, by noon of the last day of October. There the secret for destroying the Heroka forever will be revealed to you."

Jonas blinked, wondering at the strangeness of the request. But the Lord worked in mysterious ways. October 31. That was tomorrow.

The sunlight was dimming. Daniel began to blur. Jonas was waking up. "Will you do this, father?" Daniel called, his voice fading. "Will you do this to avenge me? Will you do this for our Lord?"

"Yes!" Jonas screamed, panicking that he would wake before answering. "Yes, I will. I love you, Daniel."

The light faded to black as Daniel's final words reached him in the darkness. "I love you, too, father. You are His terrible swift sword."

He awoke. For several minutes, he sat unmoving, slumped as he had slept, fighting against the sounds of the chopper and the conversations of the Tainchel agents that tried to pull him back to the mundane. He longed to return to his dream, to see his son once more.

Then the full import of the dream struck him. He had been vindicated. His crusade against the Heroka was God's work. A tear ran down his cheek. God was helping him avenge Daniel's murder. He had been chosen.

You are His terrible swift sword.

He thought of the team he had assembled and swore a silent oath. He *would* be swift. He *would* be terrible. And God have mercy on anyone who stood in his way.

THE SHAMAN COMDOWTAH awoke from a self-induced trance. The man called Jonas had proven to be surprisingly malleable. A few images and memories pulled from the man's own mind, and he had believed immediately. What Simon Jonas thought to be his strengths—his beliefs, his desire to avenge his son's death—were really his weaknesses.

Is it done? the voices asked.

Comdowtah nodded. *He will bring us the Wolf and Boy.*

And we shall bring a new world!

The shaman didn't reply, suddenly envying Jonas his unwavering sense of righteousness.

BENEATH THE DARK SURFACE of the river, Otter Caz swam easily with the sluggish current, oblivious to the icy chill that flowed over her sleek waterproof fur and layers of winter fat. She surfaced to take air, sniff the wind, and check riverbanks lit by moonlight on snow. Staying on the surface now, she swam on, continuing to follow the thing that called to her, the thing that had tugged at her feral mind since she had shifted.

Somewhere in her otter brain, she knew she was supposed to be searching for the humans who had killed her friend and her parents, who hunted her kind. But something called to her, as it was calling to all the animals in the bush around this human town. She couldn't tell what it was, but she could feel the weight of years that lay on that touch, could smell the scent of an age when spirits walked this world, spirits like *Amik* who ruled her totem.

She swam on, following the river and the pull on her mind, leaving the small town behind, until only dark bush flanked the banks. Just as her strength was nearly spent, the river poured itself into a small dark lake. On the far side, her night-sharp eyes made out the long flat outline of a human-built wall of some kind. This lake was the place that had been calling to her. The pull was stronger here but now seemed directionless. Confused, she swam to the middle and floated there, resting, sensing.

The lake looked small, but she sensed much water here. This lake was deep, deeper than a lake this size should be. Deeper....

There. She felt it now. Deep was where it was, the thing that called. No, the *things*. She sensed two minds, linked as one. Taking a gulp of air, she dived straight down.

The pale moonlight above died to stygian darkness beneath the surface, and she now swam blind with only the pull of the things below as her guide. Every stroke of her tiny webbed hands and feet drove her deeper, deeper than she had ever gone before, but on she went, answering the call of what lay below.

She stopped, suspended in darkness and cold. She had air and strength enough to continue, and the pull was stronger than ever. But a memory had stopped her.

She had felt the touch of the things below before.

As if they read her thoughts, their pull suddenly grew greater, calling to her to dive deeper, to come to them. Their call was strong, but her fear was stronger. Twisting upright in the water, she drove with all her might for the surface, fleeing as if from two predators. Still the things below pulled at her, slowing her muscles, tightening her chest, until each stroke was agony, a struggle against opponents whose strength was much greater than her own.

But finally, she broke the surface and gulped in air. Exhausted, struggling to stay afloat, she looked around, sensing a change. The forest seemed thicker, the trees taller. The human-built wall was gone, replaced by a long ridge of land. She sniffed. This air held no trace of gasoline or human waste, no scent of humans at all. This place was old, primal.

She felt something else, too, something that had been missing from the human world. Here she could sense again the touch of many familiar minds, those of her totem—beavers, squirrels, rats, muskrats, and other otters.

The call of the things below returned, and with it her fear. Ignoring her exhaustion, she swam for the river mouth, calling to her totem brothers and sisters to follow her.

Reaching the river, she looked back on the lake. The human-built wall had returned. The trees had shrunk, and the stench of the human town upriver hung acrid in the air again. But she could sense that many of her totem had followed her from that primal place back to these woods. No longer alone, she turned her sleek brown body toward the town, away from the lake and the things that lived beneath it, the things she now remembered encountering before.

She had sensed their presence once, sensed them at some subconscious level in her human mind, not understanding it until now. She swam faster, calling her clan to follow. She wanted to put distance between herself and the lake and to return to her human form as soon as possible.

For she had smelled the touch of the things in the lake before. She had smelled it here, on someone in this town.

CHAPTER 38

IF YOU GO OUT IN THE WOODS TODAY...

KATE SAT AT A WINDOW BOOTH in The Outfitter, eating fish and chips, and using her satellite link to download email onto her laptop. She had only one new message, from the Tainchel lab, marked "Urgent" with a subject heading "Case File T12054: DNA lab results, Thunder Lake subjects 1, 3."

Subject One would be the first murder victim, Rick Calhoun. Subject Three was Frank Mueller. Jonas had said both results would be ready today. At least he hadn't lied about that.

She was about to open the email when three black SUVs pulled into the motel's parking lot across the road. Ten men got out, all in identical white parkas. Darkness had fallen two hours ago, but the light from the motel sign was enough for her to recognize the spindly figure that unfolded itself mantis-like from the first vehicle. Simon Jonas.

Almost gagging up her last mouthful, she grabbed her laptop, purse, and coat. Tossing a twenty on the table, she slipped out the back of the restaurant, heading for the garage on foot, praying that Bernie had fixed her car.

Jonas had lied, of course. He'd probably planned all along to arrive early. She wondered again about her car. Was someone in town working for him? Macready? She hadn't seen him all day. At least Zach was safe. If he hadn't asked to stay at Bonnie's, Jonas would have him now. She tried to calm herself. If Bernie had fixed her car, she'd pick up Zach, and they'd be gone. That man wouldn't get her son.

She swallowed. No, but he'd get Gwyn and Leiddia Barker and that teenager. She slowed to a walk. What had Gwyn ever done to her? He wouldn't be easy to capture, but Jonas's men would have guns. She had to warn him. But how? She had no idea where he was staying and didn't know anyone she could ask. And she didn't have time to search for him.

Joe Makademik. When she picked up Zach, she'd tell Joe to find Gwyn and warn him. That way, Gwyn couldn't follow her and Zach, either. Her son still came first. By the time she reached the garage, she'd convinced herself she was doing the best thing for both Zach and Gwyn.

The garage was at the back of a lot shared with a Tim Horton's and a herd of pickups, ATVs, and snowmobiles in various states of disassembly. A small metal door stood beside a higher wider one. Bernie answered her knock.

Two cars filled most of the place. One was up on the hoist. The second was Kate's, and it had its hood raised. "Well, I was right," Bernie said as they walked to her car. "The problem's your motherboard."

"So," she said, trying to keep her voice calm, "were you able to reset it?"

Wiping his hands on a rag, he eyed her. "Nope." When she started to protest, he held up a hand. "I couldn't reset it because it's not there. Somebody's pulled it." He eyed her again. "Somebody doesn't like you."

Tell me about it, she thought. Her mind raced. She needed a car. "It's because I work at the dam. I've been getting threats since we arrived here. Phone calls. Notes slipped under our motel room door," she lied. "I…I can't take it anymore. I'm scared. For my son, more than for me. We're going home. I have to get him away from here."

Bernie wagged his finger at her. "Thought you were in trouble. Yeah, that dam's really stirred things up. Lot of our people lost their hunting territories, their trap lines…you know."

Our people, she thought. There it was again. "Look, is there any way you can help me? I'll pay. I just want to get out of here."

He considered her, and then he nodded at the car up on the hoist. "That there? That's my cousin's. Different model from yours, but same make. Same motherboard. Denise—that's my cousin—she don't hardly use it. She can live without a car for a week. I'll swap her board into your car, and order her a new one. That work for you?"

"Yes," she said, realizing she'd been holding her breath. "Yes, thank you. Thank you so much."

Bernie shrugged. "Hey, we gotta stick together, eh? 'Sides, want to show you not everybody here's an asshole." He hit a button to lower the hoist. "Gimme twenty minutes, and you'll be outta here."

Bernie was good to his word, and a half hour later, she was on her way to pick up Zach. She had a car, she'd slipped past Jonas, and soon she and Zach would be safely away from here. Maybe her luck was finally beginning to turn.

SIMON JONAS STOOD in Kate Morgan's now-empty motel room. Kate was gone. Her son was gone. Macready was missing. He had no idea where Gwyn Blaidd or the other two Heroka were. And yet, he felt surprisingly calm.

Lessard came in. "Sir, the manager says she paid her bill this morning and checked out."

Jonas simply nodded. "And the tracker on the boy's dog?"

"We're not getting a signal. And Macready's not answering his cell." Lessard shifted on his feet. Jonas just nodded again. "Uh, sir," Lessard said, "what are your orders?"

He's nervous, Jonas thought. He had never seen Lessard nervous. The agent probably expected an explosion of fury from him.

But he felt neither anger nor concern. Far from it, he felt at peace, as he had since his dream on the helicopter. God had chosen him. God would send him a sign. But how? He smiled. Of course.

"Cancel Ms. Morgan's CSIS ID and network access, Mr. Lessard. Search the town for her and the boy. And for our truant Mr. Macready. Keep your scanners on in case you encounter these Heroka that Morgan reported. Have the OPP issue warrants for their arrest. Call me if you make contact with any of our quarry."

Lessard frowned. "Aren't you coming with us, sir?"

"No, Mr. Lessard," he said quietly. "I am going to get a room in this rustic establishment and go to sleep." With that, he turned his back on a stunned Lessard and left the room.

To sleep, he thought as he walked to the motel office, *perchance to dream.*

READING THE SCRAP of paper with Joe Makademik's directions, Kate turned at the second street of small, closely spaced bungalows on the Rez and pulled into the rutted, dirt driveway of the "seventh house on the left."

Parking behind Joe's battered pickup, she walked to the door, turning her parka's collar up against the cold and the blowing snow. She knocked, allowing herself a small smile. It had been close, but she and Zach were going to escape this nightmare, escape from Simon Jonas and the Tainchel, from Gwyn Blaidd and the Heroka, and from the murderous events in this dark little town.

The door opened, and Joe's big frame filled the doorway.

She smiled up at him. "Hi Joe. Sorry, but I've had a change of plans. Bernie fixed our car early, so Zach and I are going to head out tonight."

He looked puzzled, but then grinned. "And Zach wanted to say goodbye to Bonnie. Sure, c'mon in." He peered past Kate. "Is Zach in the car?"

That thing that now seemed to live permanently inside her awoke at his words, sinking sharp cold claws into her gut. "What do you mean? He's here with you."

Joe's smile disappeared, and his jaw muscles tightened. "He was gone when I got home. Bonnie said you'd picked him up." He turned to look behind him.

Bonnie stood in the doorway to a small kitchen, looking like a startled animal desperately wanting to leap into the safety of the bush but too afraid to even move.

"Bonnie," Kate cried. "Where's Zach?"

COLIN MACREADY WAS COLD and tired and frustrated. But mostly, he was angry. Very angry. If that bitch hadn't lied to him, if that little freak had just stayed put, he wouldn't be cold and tired and frustrated.

And lost. After reaching the tracker's last location stored on the GPS, he'd headed into the bush, following the boy's last vector by the GPS compass. But after about a hundred yards, the GPS had suddenly refused to identify even his own current location. He backtracked, and the unit started working again. He tried several routes with the same result—once he got within about a mile of the dam, the GPS lost its satellite signal.

Some electrical field caused by the power station? But he'd understood the dam wasn't operational yet. It didn't matter. He had to find the brat before Jonas arrived. Shoving the useless GPS into his parka, he set out again in the direction the kid had been following, toward the dam and the lake, swearing to himself.

He'd make the kid pay for this.

MARY TWO RIVERS chased the Windigo for the entire day through the primal forest of the Spirit World. Now daylight was fading. The creature had quickly outdistanced her, but since it preferred to knock trees down rather than walk around them, she'd had no trouble following its path.

Until that path disappeared.

She stopped. Ahead, the forest stood calm and unbroken, not a leaf or branch disturbed. Where had the Windigo gone?

There. To the right. A window seemed to hang shimmering in the air, a window showing a much different forest than the one in which she stood. The trees beyond this window didn't reach as high. The air that wafted through to her had lost its freshness. And in the distance lay a dark brooding lake contained by a huge dam.

Recognizing the bush outside Thunder Lake, she cried out in joy. She rushed forward, overwhelmed with sudden homesickness, but as she did, the window shrank in on itself, disappearing with a loud "Pop!"

She sank to the ground in front of where the window had been. She'd failed. The creature had returned to her hometown to kill someone else, somebody she probably knew. Now she had only two days left to travel the Spirit Road to reach her ancestral home and final rest. And she didn't even know how far away that home was.

Or where. She looked behind her in the darkening woods, unable to see any trace of the glow of the Spirit Road. She was lost. She'd always figured that your problems ended when you died. Hers had only got bigger.

Suck it up, girl, she thought. She still had two days. She'd just follow the trail of broken trees back to the Spirit Road. Turning, she started to retrace her steps.

"At least," she muttered, "things can't get any worse."

She stopped. Ahead, shapes moved toward her through the trees. Many shapes. She swallowed. "Okay," she whispered. "I guess they can."

GWYN SIGNALED THE BARTENDER for another scotch. Ed sat on the stool beside him. They'd been there since dinner, and Gwyn did not intend to leave until he was good and drunk. Unfortunately, it took a lot to get a Heroka drunk.

Ed took a sip of his coffee. He'd stopped trying to keep up an hour ago. "Maybe I could talk to her. Tell her, you know, some of your, uh, good points."

"Won't help," Gwyn muttered. "She made it clear. I'm some kind of monster. Not fit to be near my own son. A son she never even told me about." He was hurting, and part of it was the resurrection of memories of how a woman he had once loved had run from him in fear fourteen years ago, and the realization that she still feared him, simply because of what he was.

The bartender poured him another, and he took a deep swallow. Maybe the Heroka *should* die off. Maybe they *were* monsters. This world held no place for his race. Or for him.

But he had a son!

Ed was talking. Something about how he should have tried to stop Walter Keejek when he'd found that Walter wanted to resurrect the Society of the Dawn. Ed kept talking, but his words were lost on Gwyn, who suddenly felt a familiar touch on his mind.

Grandson!

He looked up from the bar, as the voice of Mahigan sounded in his head. It seemed to be coming from outside.

Grandson!

He stood up, grabbed the bar to steady himself, and walked to the door. Looking back, he was only mildly surprised to see himself still sitting at the bar, apparently listening intently to whatever Ed was saying. He looked down. His body had a translucent look and a silver glow. With a shrug, he stepped outside.

The silver wolf stood in a strangely empty and silent street. The streetlights were dead. No light shone from any window. Only the cold wash of the moon, full and high in a clear night sky, and Mahigan's silver aura gave light to the scene. Except tonight had been cloudy and snowing, and the moon only half full.

He walked up to Mahigan. "You called, Fluffy?"

The wolf growled. *You shame me with your disrespect. You shame your totem. I am your grandfather.*

"So go play with another grandkid, Pops. What do you want with me anyway?"

I told you to find the boy.

"Been there. Done that. Give me my gold star so I can get back to drinking."

You were to keep him near!

"You kind of left that part out. His mom doesn't want me anywhere near him." But an unease stirred in him.

I said that you and the boy were drawn here for a purpose.

"Uh, huh. A purpose you never explained."

Because it is hidden from me, but I sense that its time is near. Our two worlds grow closer together. I too have been drawn to this place. Whatever is happening, you and the boy are the key. And he is in danger.

A fear leapt into his chest. "What do you mean?"

Here. See.

He sensed the minds of wolves, and recognized the same pack he'd used to track the windigo two nights ago. "You've brought them back. Where the hell do they keep disappearing to?"

To the Spirit World.

"Why? How?"

Our worlds grow closer. Those who still remember their grandparents can now find their way into the Spirit World from this world. And they are being called.

He recognized the scene in the minds of the wolves. They were near the dam lake. "So what does this have to do with Zach?" Then he caught the scent the pack was following—the sweet pungent smell of rotting wood and mushrooms. "Shit. I thought that thing was dead. How—?" He stopped as he caught another scent from the wolves.

Zach.

The windigo was back. And it was hunting his son.

His fear for Zach broke the spell that Mahigan had cast. The silver wolf and the strangely empty street faded away, and he gasped himself to consciousness, seated at the bar again—or still—beside Ed.

Ed looked at him. "Gray Legs, you okay?"

Without answering, he jumped off the stool, suddenly sober. He sent a mental command to the pack, ordering them to protect the boy with their lives until he got there. Pulling a startled Ed with him, he headed for the door with Gelert at their heels. "C'mon. I need your truck."

KATE BRACED HERSELF against the door as Joe slid his truck around a curve. The headlight beams bobbed and slashed through the darkness of the encircling bush, flashing white on birch and gray-brown on pines. Bonnie sat between them, still sobbing. "I'm sorry, daddy," she said for the hundredth time.

"We'll talk about this tomorrow," Joe said, tight lipped.

Bonnie sobbed more loudly, and turned to Kate. "It was just so important to him, I wanted to help him. I'd never want him to get hurt. I really like Zach."

Kate had calmed down somewhat, once she knew where Zach was and that Bonnie could lead her right to him. She was now more angry than frightened, but her maternal instinct took over. She wrapped an arm around Bonnie's shoulders. "It's okay. I just don't understand why he wanted to do a vision quest. And why now?"

"It was for his dad," Bonnie sniffed.

Kate pulled her arm back. "What?"

Bonnie looked nervous again. "He said this would help his dad. That Mr. Blaidd was in danger."

Kate swallowed. Had Zach overheard her conversation with Jonas? Heard her betraying Gwyn? Had *she* driven Zach to try this crazy stunt?

"I'm sorry," Bonnie sobbed again.

"Wait a minute," Joe said as the truck lurched over a pothole. "You mean *Gwyn Blaidd* is Zach's father?" He shot Kate a look. She nodded, not trusting herself to speak. He kept looking at her. "You one of them too?" he finally asked.

One of them? She sat stunned as the implication sunk in. He knew that Gwyn was Heroka. Shit, was she the only one who hadn't known? She shook her head.

He seemed to relax at that. He nodded. "Good."

"Why good?" she snapped, surprised that her immediate reaction was to defend Gwyn.

"Because his kind, they're bad news, is all," he said.

A tense silence fell, unbroken until her cell rang. She fished the phone from her parka's pocket, expecting the display to show Simon Jonas's number and ready to let it ring. But to her surprise, the name displayed was "Thornton OPP." She hesitated, then answered.

"Ms. Morgan, we have a problem," Thornton began. "We've found another body. A local Ojibwe man. Same thing, I'm afraid. Partially eaten."

Jonas obviously hadn't talked to Thornton about her yet. "I'm sorry," she said, feeling relieved but puzzled, "but why is that a problem? You've already found the killer, the man you discovered yesterday near where Mueller was killed. This is just another of his victims." Joe and Bonnie both shot her a look.

"I'm afraid not," Thornton replied. "This man was killed tonight. Whatever's killing these people, it's still out there."

As Thornton's words crackled cold and harsh in her ear, the thing that lived in her gut clawed its way up her spine. A monster was still out in this bush somewhere.

And so was Zach.

CHAPTER 39

...You'd Better Not Go Alone

IN HIS DREAM, Zach stood on the stony shore of the dark lake, watching in the cold moonlight as the things in the water drew nearer. They were close enough now that he could make out two large feline heads with tufted ears and blood-red eyes. Red eyes that locked on him.

"You know, little brother, I think you should consider taking your quest elsewhere," came a familiar voice from behind him.

He spun around. Wisakejack was staring hard at the things in the water. He nodded. "Yep, relocation is definitely recommended." With that, Wisakejack leaned close to Zach and blew on him. Zach's head spun. A moment later, they stood high on the ridge overlooking the lake.

Below, the things in the lake now stood on all fours dripping at the water's edge, their red eyes still on Zach. They resembled huge black cats, but heavier and with the slick shiny skin of some sort of water creature. Throwing back their heads in perfect unison, they screamed.

Those screams were like no animal cry he'd ever heard, with a horrible, almost-human quality to them, as if these things had once been people before some nightmarish transformation created what squatted below.

Zach shivered and took an involuntary step behind Wisakejack. "Are those what I think they are?"

Wisakejack nodded. "The Misipisiwas. The Great Lynxes," he said, still eyeing the things. "Rulers of the deep places in the world. Head honchos of those spirits I mentioned, the ones not too fond of humankind."

"Why'd they show up in my vision quest? What do they want with me?"

"Nothing good," Wisakejack answered. "If they're here, things are even worse than I feared. C'mon, I'd like more distance between us and them." He turned away, and Zach followed. "Ah, here we are."

Ahead in a snow-covered clearing sat Wisakejack's hunting lodge. Zach looked back. They'd walked maybe three paces, but he could no longer see the ridge where they'd stood or the lake below it. Shaking his head, he followed Wisakejack inside.

Warmth and the smell of sweet spruce and beaver stew filled the room. He shrugged off his deerskin jacket and sat on the spruce boughs in front of the fire. "Why are you so worried about the Lynxes? You seem to control things here pretty good."

Wisakejack eyed him narrowly. "*This* dream's a little different—you're on a vision quest. You're walking in the spirit world. That makes any spirits you encounter here much more powerful. Best to avoid the ones who aren't friendly to humans. And that goes double for the Lynxes." Dipping his bowl into the pot, he fingered some stew into his mouth.

"Now you're going to tell me a story, right?"

"A story? No time for a story. Right now, we have to deal with the Lynxes being here. Major bad news."

"But I have to find my spirit guide tonight. This is the only chance I'll get."

Wisakejack waved his hand. "Hey, the night's young. You have lots of time for that."

Zach sighed. "Okay, fine. So how do we fight the Lynxes?"

"Good question," Wisakejack said rubbing his chin. For a few seconds, he was silent. Finally, he raised a finger. "To fight those with horns, we need *those without horns*."

Zach frowned. He'd heard that term before. "The Heroka!"

Wisakejack nodded. "So we're back to helping your dad. He's both Heroka and a wolf, which makes him a major player in whatever's going down. Which means you gotta get back to your vision quest." Wisakejack turned his head, as if listening to something. "And you're running out of time."

"What?!" Zach cried, leaping up. "You *just* said I had lots of time."

Wisakejack and the lodge grew hazy. The fire died to embers. The lodge's cozy warmth became an icy chill. He was waking up.

"Yeah," came Wisakejack's disembodied voice, "but that was before I knew you had company."

The lodge disappeared, and Zach almost choked on his next breath of sub-zero air as he woke. Pulling his sleeping bag over his head, he reached for the warmth of Quincy beside him. The dog wasn't there. He sat up, shivering. "Quince?" he called in a low voice, suddenly afraid of breaking the cold silence of the bush.

A familiar low growl came from his right. Reaching out, he ran a mittened hand along the dog's back. The animal was standing rigid, every muscle tensed, pointing in the direction that he and Bonnie had taken to reach this spot. Quincy growled again. Zach shushed him and listened.

There. A crunch of snow. Again. And another.

He swallowed. Someone was coming.

Or some*thing*.

TWO MILES INTO THE BUSH, Gwyn stopped running to sniff the air. Panting beside him, Gelert did the same and gave a low whine. Gwyn nodded. "Yeah, we're getting close." Zach's scent was now clear enough that he no longer needed his link with the wolves to follow the boy's trail.

But another scent was also clear. The creature was closing in on Zach.

Ed had dropped him as near to the wolves' trail into the bush as possible. He'd then sent Ed back to find Leiddia, hoping another Heroka predator in the fight might even the odds. Assuming Ed found her. Assuming she got here in time. Assuming either of them stood a chance against this thing. He remembered Mahigan's words. *You could not have faced that creature. You still cannot. You do not have the strength.*

Guess I'm about to find out if you're right, gramps, he thought, sniffing the air again and adjusting his direction through the thick bush. It didn't matter. He was Zach's only hope, and he'd die protecting his son if he had to.

ZACH CALMED QUINCY with a stroke of his hand, and then tried to calm himself. His just-ended dream encounter with the Great Lynxes had him fearing the worst. The barrier between his dreaming and his waking worlds was becoming thinner and thinner. Could the Lynxes have come through that barrier? But they had walked on four legs, and whoever—or whatever—was approaching was two-legged by the sound of the gait. And he was swearing.

That voice, if not its tone, was familiar—Colin Macready. He heard Macready stop a few paces away and could tell he was catching his breath.

Zach sighed and stood up. So much for his vision quest. "Relax, Quince. It's Colin." But Quincy responded with an even deeper growl, as threatening a sound as he'd ever heard his normally gentle dog make. "Quincy—"

"You little piece of shit," Macready gasped. "I am going to drag you all the fucking way back to Jonas."

Stunned, Zach backed away, suddenly as fearful of this man as he'd been of the Lynxes. He could understand Macready being angry at having to hunt for him, but this wasn't the gentle teacher he knew.

And he'd heard the name Jonas before. That was the man his mom worked for. The man who was coming to capture Gwyn. His fear deepened. Was his mom in danger too? What was going on?

All further thoughts ended as Quincy leapt past him with a snarling roar, knocking Zach down. Macready screamed. He heard the muffled sound of Macready and Quincy hitting the ground, followed by Quincy's snarls, cloth tearing and Macready's cries, as the two struggled in front of Zach.

He started crawling toward them. He didn't know what he could do, but he had to help Quincy. Maybe he could hit Macready on the head with a rock. He searched the snowy ground with his hands as he crawled, trying to find something to use for a weapon.

The roar of the gunshot nearly deafened him, but not enough to cover the terrifying howl of his dog. "Quincy!" he screamed, scrambling forward. He reached Quincy's side. The dog was breathing rapidly and whining in pain. He tore off his mitts. Quincy gave another whine and licked his hand when Zach touched his snout. He ran his hands carefully down the dog's body. His hands came away wet and sticky. "Oh god! No, Quincy. God, no," he cried. Tenderly, he searched again with his fingertips, trying to find where the wound was so he could press on it to stop the bleeding.

But two hands grabbed him by the shoulders and hauled him roughly to his feet. "You little freak! Look what your fucking beast did to me!"

The side of his head exploded in pain. Half stunned, he stumbled sideways and fell. Macready had hit him with something. Probably the gun. It didn't matter. Ignoring the pain, he began crawling back to Quincy, something warm running down his cheek.

Only to have Macready pull him upright again. "You are so fucking lucky Jonas wants you alive, or I would gut you like a fish. I'm going to enjoy watching him experiment on you."

Zach didn't understand and didn't care. "Please, Colin, help my dog," he sobbed.

Macready shook him so hard his teeth banged together, biting into his tongue. He could smell burnt powder and knew Macready still held the gun in his hand. "Your stinking mutt's dead."

"No!" Zach cried, twisting in Macready's grip as the man dragged him away from Quincy.

"You're coming with me if I have to—" Macready broke off. "What was that?"

Zach had heard it too, probably more clearly than Macready. A whistling shriek, long and eerie and cold, like a winter wind howling through dead trees. Only this wasn't the wind. He knew that sound.

The windigo was coming.

But it was dead! How could it be here?

Another whistle sliced the cold night. How didn't matter. The thing was here and getting closer. Farther in the distance came the lonely cry of wolves. A thought of Gwyn flashed through his mind.

The windigo must have been close now, for Macready gasped. "Jeezus god, what is that thing?"

Macready threw Zach roughly to the ground, and Zach heard him stumble away. Another whistle froze Zach where he'd fallen. He lay there, listening as the thing passed by him, leaving the stench of corruption hanging sweet and sickly in the cold air. The windigo's cry must have had the same effect on Macready. Zach could hear the man whimpering nearby, apparently unable to move.

Macready managed to regain some control though, for the bark of his gun again shattered the night. Four more shots followed. The windigo gave another whistling shriek, then a roar. Macready screamed once more, a frightened desperate thing that died in a gurgling sound. Zach heard the ripping of clothing and then the sickening crunch of bones, and he knew. The thing was eating Macready.

Able to move again, Zach began to crawl back to where Quincy lay. He couldn't escape. He knew that. The thing would feed on Macready, and then on him. But he would comfort his dog to the end, and die beside the best friend he'd ever had.

A whine helped him find Quincy. The dog's side was slick with blood, his breathing ragged and painful. Cradling Quincy's head in his lap, he sat in the cold waiting to die, wanting only to be home with his mom. Listening to the windigo feed, he tried to decide if he wanted Quincy to die first or if he wanted his friend with him to the end.

The horrible sound of feeding suddenly ended. He heard an icy creaking as the creature stood. The howl of the wolves rang through the trees again, and he knew with a strange certainty that they were coming to help. The pack was close now, but closer still was the icy whistling breath of the windigo. Helpless, Zach lay cradling Quincy as the crunch of the creature's feet in the snow drew nearer.

CHAPTER *40*

WOLVES AND WINDIGOS

GWYN WAS STILL A MILE from the dam lake when he felt a mental touch from the alpha male of the wolf pack. He stopped running. Ahead, Gelert turned and looked back, whining. Quieting Gelert with a thought, he opened his mind to the wolf.

And cried out in pain, dropping to his knees in the snow. The link with the wolf was so intense that each sensation was like a hot needle shoved into his brain. Pushing through the pain, he fought to understand what the wolf was sending him.

Sounds—growls and snarls, the crunch of breaking bones, yelps of pain. Smells—the creature's stench, Zach's scent. And the smell of blood. The windigo had found Zach, and the wolves were fighting to protect him, but they were losing.

The visuals were just as chaotic, but he caught one flash that turned his blood cold: white snow stained black with blood and littered with the bodies of wolves. And something else—a body, face down and deathly still.

Zach!

Throwing off his parka, he quickly stripped off his clothes. Naked but oblivious to the cold, he focused his mind in the way that only the Heroka knew. Crying out, he fell to the ground. His body shuddered, spasmed.

The change began.

Man shape melted into the lupine. Ebony fur flowed feral over pale skin. Black eyes blazed to twin emerald fires. Teeth lengthened, sharpened. Hands became paws. Feet became paws.

Moments later, a huge black timber wolf, twice normal size, raised its head and howled. With a snarl, the animal bounded into the bush. Gelert howled, too, and then followed on the heels of his transformed master.

"THERE!" BONNIE SAID, pointing to a stretch of bush at the side of the log-ging road that looked, to Kate, like any of the hundred other stretches they'd passed. Joe slammed on the brakes, almost sending the truck sliding down the banked side of the snowy road.

"Those are the tracks of our ATV," Bonnie said, pointing to a twin set of vague indentations in the snow leading into the trees. New snow had almost filled the tracks.

"So let's go," Kate said, reaching for the door handle. They'd loaded Joe's ATV into the back of the truck before they left.

Joe had been silent since Kate's call from Thornton. Now he turned to her. "Kate, I can't take Bonnie into the bush if a killer's still around here. And I can't leave her in the truck alone."

"So what are you saying?" she asked, her panic rising. "I have to find Zach, and Bonnie's the only one who knows where he's camped."

"Call Thornton. Get some cops up here."

"We'd still need Bonnie. She has to show us."

"It's not far, Daddy," Bonnie offered in a timid voice.

"I'm sorry, Kate, I can't put my daughter in danger."

"What about my son?" she snapped. "What about the danger he's in?"

Joe didn't answer. Lights suddenly glared from behind them. She turned to look. Headlights bobbed along the snow-covered road toward them. "That's Ed Two Rivers's truck," Joe said, as the truck pulled up behind.

An older Ojibwe man got out, and she recognized him from the community center. Another figure emerged, and Kate's gut tightened even more. Leiddia Barker.

At this point, she didn't care. She just wanted to find Zach. She jumped out and ran to Ed. "Zach, my son, he's out there—"

"We know," said the man Joe had called Ed Two Rivers. "Don't worry. Gwyn's out there too. He'll find him." He and Leiddia began unloading two ATV's from his truck.

Gwyn! How had he known? It didn't matter. "That creature's still out there, too. Or another one. Or something. The police found a fresh corpse."

"We know," Leiddia snapped, straddling an ATV with her long legs and kicking it into gear.

They knew? How?

"I can still see the tire tracks," Ed said. "Won't for long, though, the way this snow's coming down."

"And I can smell Gwyn," Leiddia said. "So let's go, damn it." Gunning her ATV, she headed into the bush, following the trail.

Ed got on the other machine and called to Kate and Joe. "You coming?"

Joe looked back at his truck where Bonnie watched them. "Kate, I need to get Bonnie home. I'm sorry."

Get your own kid safe, she thought, *and forget about mine.* No, that wasn't fair. She nodded. Joe looked relieved. "I'll come back once I get her to my brother's place." He looked at Leiddia's retreating back. "You sure you want to do this?"

"Yes," she said, getting on behind Ed. He shifted it into gear, and they lurched down the banked side of the road and into the trees following Leiddia's tracks, leaving Joe standing beside his truck.

She tried asking Ed questions, but the engine noise and their parka hoods and the strengthening wind made conversation impossible, so finally she just focused on not falling off and praying that Gwyn had found Zach.

The irony of that wish did not escape her.

WOLF GWYN SPED THROUGH dark bush, the primal hunter once more, his now feral mind consumed by a single thought: *protect the pup.*

The pup's scent trail was strong, but so was something else: the stench of meat no longer fit to eat, mixed with fungus and the rot of tree stuff. His wolf brain had never encountered the smell before, but a still-human part of him told him the thing that owned that scent was a predator. His pup was in danger.

Another raced behind him. Not a wolf, but of his totem, with a warm familiar smell. A friend and one who would do his bidding. Even to the death.

The minds of his brothers and sisters that fought the beast called to him. He reached out. Agony and rage poured back, blood lust, and the hunger for the kill. But in their minds, above all else, fear now ruled. The pack had been eight strong when they'd attacked the thing, five males, and three females. All young and fit. Now four lay dead in the snow, and another was dying. The remaining three, the alpha male among them, drew back in fear of this strange prey they could not bring down.

With a snarl, Wolf Gwyn sent them to attack again. Protect the pup. The pup was all. Their pain was nothing. Their fear was nothing. Their deaths were nothing. Protect the pup.

But still they cowered. He roared at them with his mind. Never before had any of his totem refused him. As if in answer, the words of his grandfather Mahigan came back to him: *You cannot defeat this thing. You do not have the strength.*

Where his human form had refused to believe those words, the black wolf felt their truth. So be it. He would die, but he would die defending his pup.

He broke from the trees into a clearing filled with the scattered bodies of wolves. Ahead, a sole remaining wolf, the alpha male, fought a monster of ice and bone. Wolf Gwyn bounded past a partially eaten human corpse, sniffing it as he passed. Too big. Wrong smell. Not the pup. Where was the pup?

Behind the wolf and the creature lay one of his brothers. Not wolf. Dog. Hurt. Beside the dog lay another human. Small. Right smell. The pup! Alive!

The alpha male stood between the creature and the pup, fangs bared, head lowered. Unfazed by this display, the creature advanced.

With a snarl, Wolf Gwyn closed the remaining distance. At that sound, the creature turned to face its newest attacker. Gwyn leapt, hitting the thing full in its chest. The creature fell, and Wolf Gwyn closed its great jaws on its prey's throat.

But his teeth did not find warm flesh and hot blood. Instead, they bit ice harder than steel and colder than the grave, glancing off harmlessly.

The creature struggled to rise. At Gwyn's command, Gelert and the alpha male each seized a wrist of the creature in their jaws, holding it down. The thing gave a whistling shriek that to his wolf ears was like a knife slicing his skull. Gelert and the other wolf both whined in pain but held on. Shaking the screech from his head, the black wolf lunged for the thing's throat, determined to find a weakness.

Again and again, he struck. Again and again, he found only impenetrable ice, and every attack brought his own throat within range of the creature's jaws. He was tiring, and bleeding now in several places where the creature's teeth had torn him. Narrowly escaping a snap at his throat, he paused before trying another attack.

Seizing its chance, the thing gave another ear-piercing shriek and then heaved its chest, throwing Gwyn off. Lifting Gelert into the air from where he still clung to its wrist, the thing tossed the huge hound hard against a pine tree. The dog leapt up, but then gave a yelp and fell back down, whining. With its freed hand, the thing wrapped long icy fingers around the neck of the wolf still clinging to its other wrist. Bones snapped with a sickening sound, and the wolf fell to the ground dead. The creature stood.

Wolf Gwyn leapt again. But the creature swung an arm like a club, striking him hard on the side. He landed on his back on a rocky patch of ground, and the air whooshed out of his wolf lungs. Fighting pain and gasping for air, he struggled to stand but collapsed again. The thing closed on him.

In his wolf form, he was almost indestructible, able to withstand damage that would kill an ordinary wolf or his own human form. But he knew he was badly hurt. Bone ground against bone in his side, making each breath agony, and the blood staining the snow where he lay was his own.

He watched helpless as the thing looked down at where he lay panting in pain. It looked at the dead wolves and the injured Gelert. Then it looked at the human pup, who still lay protecting a big black dog. With another whistling scream, it moved toward the boy.

Somewhere beneath his pain, deep in his animal brain, the small part of him that was still Gwyn Blaidd looked past the horror of what was happening and understood. The windigo was ignoring a feast of flesh that lay before it in the eight dead wolves, in Gelert, in Gwyn's injured wolf form. It wanted only the pup.

It wanted *human* flesh.

Then he would give it what it wanted.

The windigo bent over Zach.

"Hey!" Gwyn shouted. His call came more as a cry of pain than the gruff growl he'd planned. But it had the intended effect. The creature turned its grotesque head toward him. Red bulbous eyes stared from a face of blackened frostbitten skin to where Gwyn lay in the snow, human again, naked, shaking uncontrollably from pain and cold.

"Y-yeah," he stuttered in a croaking rasp, "I'm t-talking to y-you, stinky. M-more meat on m-me than th-that little g-guy."

The windigo looked down at Zach, then back to him. Apparently coming to the same conclusion, it turned and stalked toward him on long spindly legs and feet the size of snowshoes.

He lay shivering as the thing approached, its stench stronger with each step, knowing he was about to die. He could have stayed in wolf form and survived. When the windigo finished with him, it would still turn on Zach. So what had he just spent his life for? A few more moments for the boy? Maybe that would be enough. Maybe someone would come. Leiddia. Ed. Someone. All he knew was that for now, his son was still alive.

The windigo loomed over him. Pulling back blackened lips to reveal sharp jagged teeth, it reached a long, clawed hand toward him.

CHAPTER 41

CHOICES

THE VOICES OF THE **G**REAT **L**YNXES stabbed into Comdowtah's mind like claws into flesh. *The Hunger walks in your world again.*

I had no choice, the shaman replied, caught off guard by the sudden intrusion. *I had to send it into another. You knew that.*

But it has found the boy! the Lynxes cried. *The Wolf fights to protect him but he cannot win. The Hunger will feed on them both. All our plans stand at the edge of a precipice.*

I know, Comdowtah replied. *I'm dealing with it.*

A scene of carnage flashed bloody into the shaman's mind. The location was familiar. Near the dam site, southwest shore. Comdowtah reached for the mind of the windigo.

NAKED, **BLEEDING, SHAKING** uncontrollably from pain and cold, Gwyn lay helpless as the windigo reached for him. Its stench filled his lungs, and he puked onto the snow, each spasm of retching shooting fresh daggers of agony into his injured side.

The thing grabbed him, sinking icicle claws deep into his shoulder, and he realized that the cold he'd felt until then on his naked skin was a warm summer breeze compared to the winter this creature carried. Flipping him casually onto his back, exposing his belly, it raised a clawed hand.

And stopped. It turned its lopsided head, as if listening to something. Straightening, it looked down to where he lay helpless and shivering. Its words crawled like icy worms into his brain. *Spawn of the Dog, the Horned Ones have another purpose for you and your whelp. You will not die tonight.*

With that, it turned and with huge strides disappeared into the thick bush.

Not understanding why he was still alive, he knew he wouldn't remain so if he didn't find warmth right away. Twenty feet away, Gelert lay where the windigo had tossed him. He reached for the hound with his mind, fearing what he might find.

Immediately, love flowed back to him, mixed with fear and pain. Thankfully, the dog wasn't seriously hurt. Dampening his pawakan's pain, he directed the animal's healing processes. A moment later, Gelert managed to stand. Surveying the scene, Gwyn sent the dog a command.

Gelert dragged Zach's sleeping bag to him, helping him wrap both of them in it. As Gelert's body warmed him, his strength began to return and with it, a full awareness of his injuries. Any deep breath brought another shooting pain in his side, and he guessed he'd cracked a rib. But any bleeding had stopped, and none of his injuries appeared serious. Pain he could handle.

"Zach!" he called to where the boy still huddled beside his big black lab.

The boy's head came up, and relief washed away his pain. His son was alive. "Gwyn?"

"Yeah. Are you okay?"

A sob followed. "Quincy's hurt. Mr. Macready shot him."

He felt a touch of pride. His son had just faced a windigo, but his first thoughts were for his dog. He assumed this Macready was the half-eaten corpse that lay not far away. He'd seen a pistol in the snow. If the man had managed to hit the windigo, the creature would die once it transformed back to human form.

He touched Quincy with his mind. The dog was injured, but he couldn't tell how badly. "I'll look at Quincy in a second," he called. "Are *you* okay? Are you hurt?"

"I'm okay," Zach called, his voice more under control. "Is it gone? The windigo?"

How had he known it was a windigo? "Yeah, it's gone. Stay where you are. I'll be there." Once he could feel his hands and feet again, he sent Gelert out to inspect Macready's body while he stayed wrapped in the sleeping bag. Most of the man's clothes were shredded, but his boots, socks, toque, and gloves were still intact. He had Gelert bring those to him, along with the other remnants.

The sleeves of the man's parka had survived. He pulled one onto each of his legs, followed by the socks. The boots were a tight fit, but unlaced and without an insole, he could squeeze into them. Putting on the toque and gloves, he stood up, wincing against the pain. With the sleeping bag around him, he was sheltered from the cold, but felt ridiculous. He looked at Gelert. "You tell no one of this." The hound tilted his head and whined. Gwyn walked over and knelt beside Zach.

The boy threw himself against him, hugging him and sobbing. "You gotta help Quincy."

The big Lab feebly lifted its tail then dropped it. Gwyn calmed the dog with a thought, and then touched its mind, locating the source of its pain—left side and the back left leg. The bullet seemed to have missed any organs, but he sensed muscle damage in the leg. He focused the dog's healing functions. Quincy would recover, but couldn't walk right now.

He related all of this to Zach. The boy hugged him again. "Thanks, Gwyn."

Kneeling in the snow, he held Zach, his only thought in that moment being that his son was alive. Zach leaned back, and Gwyn could now see that the side of his face was badly bruised and covered in blood. "You *are* hurt! What happened?"

"Mr. Macready hit me. With his gun, I think."

Gwyn looked back at Macready's corpse. If the man hadn't been dead, he would have killed him. "Let me look at that." He pulled Zach's hood back. Blood matted his hair, and the scalp wound was still bleeding.

The snow was falling thicker, and the wind blowing harder. The temperature was dropping too. "Zach, we have to find some shelter. The storm's getting worse, and I need to look at your wound."

The boy just nodded. Gwyn peered through the blizzard. In breaks of swirling whiteness, he caught glimpses of the black surface of the dam lake and, about a half mile to the east, the long curve of the dam wall itself. He couldn't make out details, but remembered visiting where Mary had died and seeing the dam in the distance and small buildings on top of it.

"Zach, we're going up to the dam. I think we can find some shelter for the night there."

"What about Quincy?"

"He can't walk, and I can't carry him that far. Gelert will stay with him, and we'll wrap them both in the other sleeping bag." Gelert walked over to lie beside Quincy, nuzzling the smaller dog, who whined and thumped his tail. "We'll come back for them in the morning. Gelert will keep him safe and warm, and he'll have a chance to heal." He looked around the clearing at the bodies of the wolves, slowly disappearing under a blanket of snow. And tomorrow, he would bury his brothers who gave their lives for his son.

Zach stroked Quincy, and then nodded. "Okay."

Gwyn covered the dogs, instructed Gelert, and then he and Zach set out toward the dam, Gwyn hugging the sleeping bag around himself, and Zach holding onto him. Below them, the black lake blinked in and out of visibility through the storm, like a giant dark eye watching them in the night.

ON GWYN'S THIRD KICK, the Quonset hut door gave way with a screech of metal. He led Zach inside. Finding a Coleman lantern and matches, he lit the lamp and then wrestled the door closed again.

It had taken a half hour to guide Zach through the bush and deep snow to the dam road and then to climb that road to the locked gate. Smashing the window of an MNR van parked outside, he'd used a tire iron from its trunk to lever open the gate's padlock.

Inside the hut, a battered couch sat along one wall, with a mini-fridge in one corner and a chemical toilet in another. A dented metal desk held dog-eared magazines and a first-aid kit. Most importantly, a small space heater stood on the floor, and an MNR guard's uniform and parka hung behind the door.

He sat Zach on the couch, then changed into the uniform and parka, both small on him but wearable. Clothed again, he went outside to start the generator he'd seen. The wind was stronger up here, clutching at him as if it was trying to pick him up and toss him into the black waters below. Fighting his way back inside, he switched on the space heater.

"There. Downright cozy. Now let's look at that head of yours." Sitting down beside Zach with the first-aid kit, he looked at the boy's wound. The blood flow had stopped, at least. He began to carefully clean the wound.

"Gwyn?"

"Yeah?" The storm had prevented any conversation on the way here.

"Were you a wolf when you fought the windigo?"

That surprised him. "Yeah. Your mom tell you about me?"

Zach hesitated. "No. She's never talked about you. I didn't even know who my dad was until the other day."

Gwyn frowned, puzzled. "Then how'd you know about me being a wolf?"

Zach shook his head. "You won't believe me."

Gwyn smiled. "Listen, after the last few days, I'll believe quite a bit."

Zach shrugged. "Okay, here goes."

Gwyn listened as Zach recounted his recurring dream encounters with the spirit Wisakejack, including eerily accurate visual details about Frank Mueller's death. Well, he knew one sure way to test the boy's story. "The windigo you faced in your dream the night the policeman was killed—what did it look like?"

Zach described in detail the creature Gwyn had just faced. As far as he knew, no one beside himself had seen this thing and lived to tell about it.

"Okay, I believe you," he said, explaining why. "Plus, you're not the only one who's been visited by spirits lately." He related his encounters with Mahigan.

Zach nodded. "Wisakejack said the same thing—that the spirit world and this world were drawing closer. And that a wolf and a boy are involved."

"You and me," Gwyn said. "The windigo said the 'horned ones' want us both alive. I'm guessing that they're those Great Lynxes you saw in your dream tonight."

"But why us?"

Gwyn shook his head, and then realized Zach couldn't see that. "I don't know, but Wisakejack told you that human greed for electrical power brought the Windigo spirit here, and these Lynxes are associated with deep water. I'm guessing it's something to do with this dam."

"But what?"

"No idea. My turn. What the hell were you doing out here alone?"

Zach explained how he'd managed his vision quest. "But why?" Gwyn asked. "What made you think you needed to do a vision quest?"

Zach swallowed. "To save you."

"And, uh, why do I need saving?"

Zach bit his lip. "First, you have to tell me something."

"Shoot."

"Why'd you leave my mom?"

Gwyn sighed. "Do you ever ask easy questions?" But the boy—his son—had a right to know. "I didn't. She left me." He described events on the night that Kate had run away.

Zach was quiet for a moment. "That's why she's so frightened of you. And of me sometimes. She's afraid I might change too. I think that's why she did it."

"Did what?"

"Started working for that man, Mr. Jonas."

Gwyn's guts tightened as old memories rose. "*Simon* Jonas?"

Zach nodded. "I think she's trying to find information on the Heroka. What it means for me."

Inside Gwyn, anger battled guilt. Leiddia had been right—Kate *was* working for the Tainchel. And for his old enemy. But he'd driven her to that choice. She'd fled from him in terror, and then, alone with her fear, discovered she was pregnant.

What had that been like? Wondering what was growing inside her as each day passed? Then wondering for years what her son might become? Somehow, she'd learned of the Tainchel and joined them, searching for answers to "save" her son. Because of him.

"She's told them," Zach said. "About you being here. That's why I had to save you. They're coming for you. For your two friends as well."

Gwyn swore. They had to get out of town, all of them. But the storm was still raging. He'd have to wait until Ed and Leiddia came—if they came.

Zach's sightless eyes found Gwyn in that eerie way he had. "Do you hate her? My mom?"

He thought about that. He certainly had reasons to hate Kate Morgan. But he understood why she'd done this—a cornered she-wolf protecting her pup. "I did, for a while," he said quietly. "Mostly I was hurt. But I gave her reasons to be afraid, to do what's she's done." He sighed. "No, I don't hate your mom."

Zach nodded. "I'm glad." They both fell silent, listening to the wind howling outside and their own thoughts.

"So how was this vision quest supposed to help you save me?" Gwyn finally asked.

Zach shrugged. "Wisakejack said my spirit guide could explain what's going on here."

"Well, let's hope your spirit guide knows more than mine does," Gwyn said, thinking of Mahigan.

Zach hesitated. "And he said a spirit guide would help me become a Heroka."

Gwyn stared at Zach as a hope returned. His son *wanted* to be a Heroka. "The only way to do that is to mix your blood with the blood of a full Heroka."

"Like you."

"Yep. We could do it right now. You're bleeding. I'm bleeding."

Zach swallowed.

"Don't worry, Zach. It's *your* choice, not mine." *And not your mom's either*, he thought.

"And then I'd be a real Heroka? With all your powers and stuff?"

"Yes." He waited, watching his son, praying to his wolf spirit that Zach would accept his heritage and become like him. But the boy remained silent. "Well, Zach," he said finally, "do you want to become a Heroka?"

CHAPTER 42

DECISIONS

KATE PEERED AROUND ED as the roar of Leiddia's ATV ahead of them died. The snow was blowing harder, but she could see that the trail they'd been following ended in a clearing. Dark forms lay everywhere, partially draped in shrouds of snow. Leiddia knelt beside something. A bloody corpse.

"Oh, god. No!" Kate cried, throwing herself off the ATV and stumbling to where Leiddia knelt.

Leiddia held up a hand. "It's not Zach. Some guy. Don't know him." She stood. "And it's not Gwyn either, in case you were worried."

Enough remained of the corpse's face for Kate to recognize Colin Macready. "That's Zach's tutor. I don't understand. Why was he here?" Then her fear for her son returned. She looked around frantically. "Where's Zach?"

A muffled "whuff" made her turn. A huge gray form was struggling from beneath a blanket of snow covering a bright red sleeping bag. Zach's sleeping bag. A moment later, Gelert limped toward them. Behind him, Quincy's head poked out from the bag.

"Quincy!" she cried, running to the dog. The big Lab tried to stand, but collapsed back down. Blood caked the fur on his side. "He's hurt!" she cried. "Oh, god, where's Zach? Why isn't he here?"

Leiddia moved from one fallen form to another. "Lot of dead wolves."

"Are any of them…? I mean, could any of them be…?" Kate struggled to frame the question.

"Be what? Gwyn?" Leiddia snapped. "No. He'd have changed back if he'd died as a wolf." She knelt again. "But he was here. Only one wolf could make a print this big." She sniffed a partially covered print. "Yep, that's him. And in quite a fight, by the looks of this place. He would've brought these wolves."

"And they're all dead," Kate said, trying not to think what that meant.

Ed called from the far side of the clearing. "Tracks here. Man and a boy." Kate's heart leapt.

Leiddia sniffed the tracks, then looked up. Kate had never seen the woman smile before. It completely transformed her face. "These smaller prints are Zach's. The bigger ones aren't Gwyn's boots, but they have his smell. Probably stripped that dead guy." She smiled at Kate. "Your son's alive, and he's with Gwyn."

Kate covered her face with her mittened hands. "Thank you. Thank you both so much."

Leiddia stood up. "You can thank Gwyn when we find them. *He's* the reason Zach's alive," she said, shooting Kate a hard look. Kate swallowed.

Ed was following the tracks. "Gwyn's hurt, though. From the way he's walking."

"Let's get moving," Leiddia said. "The storm's getting worse. These tracks will fill in soon, and then I won't be able to track them by smell, either." She ran back to the ATVs.

Gelert crawled back into the sleeping bag beside Quincy. "What about the dogs?" Kate asked.

"Quincy can't walk," Ed said, getting on his ATV. "I'll bet Gwyn's left Gelert to keep him warm and safe—and that's what he'll do. We'll come back for them once we find Gwyn and Zach." Kate got on behind him.

As Ed followed Leiddia, Kate could only hang on and think. All her fears about Zach now seemed so senseless in the face of nearly losing him. And now the man she'd feared would steal Zach from her was the reason he was still alive. And another Heroka was leading her to them both.

So what was her part in all of this? What had she done to save Zach tonight? Nothing. She was useless. Worse than useless. She'd brought Zach into this nightmare. Her betrayal of Gwyn had made Zach pull this stunt. As they emerged from the trees, she caught a glimpse of the dam ahead, and the words she'd heard there came back to her.

You are no longer needed in this.

Apparently, she thought, *I never was.*

Then another thought occurred, and the old fear returned. She still didn't know if Gwyn could change Zach into a true Heroka, but if he could, then tonight was providing him with the perfect opportunity. Would she lose her son after all?

ZACH SAT BESIDE GWYN in the little hut, the storm howling outside dwarfed by the storm raging inside him as he struggled with the biggest decision in his life.

But why the struggle? Wasn't this what he'd wanted? To become a Heroka?

Yes, it had been. So why was he hesitating? What had changed?

His vision quest. He'd hoped to find guidance. And he had. Not in the way he'd expected, but he *had* received a vision from a spirit.

The windigo. The windigo had shown him what it meant for a human to change into something inhuman. To be truly, horribly *different*.

"Gwyn, I think it'd be great," he said slowly, "you know, to have Heroka powers." Gwyn shifted on the couch beside him, but said nothing. "The thing is, I've felt different most of my life. I don't...." He hesitated, then blurted out the rest. "I don't want to be any more different than I already am."

"What are you saying?" Gwyn said. "That you *don't* want to be Heroka?"

Zach could feel the disbelief and the pain in those words. But he still knew his answer. He shook his head and closed his eyes against his tears.

"No, I don't," he said. "I want to stay *me*."

GWYN PACED THE HUT like a caged animal as Zach slept. They hadn't talked much after Zach had made his decision. The boy had fallen asleep on the couch shortly after.

To him, Zach's decision had not only been a rejection of his Heroka heritage, but a rejection of the Heroka themselves. Given the choice between staying human or turning Heroka, Zach had chosen human. Final proof that the Heroka did not belong in this world, that they were truly a dying race.

Zach stirred on the couch. Gwyn stood looking down at his son's sleeping form. The bandage he'd applied to the cut above the boy's eye had come unstuck. Blood beaded along the wound. He looked down at his own arm, where blood beaded from his own cuts.

It would be so easy. Just reach out. Mix his blood into Zach's wound.

Then it would be done. Zach would be Heroka. His son would be what *he* was, more his son than Kate's. There would be a future for his line, for the wolf totem. He would have a reason to keep on living. He would have hope.

The blood trickled down Zach's forehead. So easy. Just reach out....

He reached out. His arm hovered above Zach's wound.

Then, with a loving touch, he wiped the blood away from the cut with an antiseptic wipe, and reapplied the bandage. Zach stirred but didn't wake.

He stared down at the sleeping boy. His son had chosen, and he would respect that choice. It didn't matter if Zach was Heroka or human—he was still his son. He pulled the sleeping bag up to cover Zach, and then settled down on the floor beside the couch and tried to fall asleep.

PRETENDING TO SLEEP, Zach lay curled on the smelly couch, sensing Gwyn standing over him. When Gwyn gently reapplied his bandage, Zach knew that a critical moment in his life had just passed, knew it in the same way he sometimes knew where Quincy was even when the dog was not near.

Quincy. He prayed that his friend was still safe. He felt so alone. And he'd just turned his back on being a Heroka. All he'd wanted to do was to talk with Gwyn about being father and son, but other stuff had got in the way. Somehow, he'd managed to get both his mother and newfound father mad at him. He had gone on a vision quest but felt more lost than ever. He didn't even know who he was anymore.

Gwyn settled down on the floor and was soon snoring, while Zach lay awake, feeling as if he stood swaying at the edge of a cliff. His old life, safe and familiar, lay behind him. Ahead, in the depths below that cliff, an unknown future waited, dark and dangerous, like the lake in his dreams.

Dreams. He closed his eyes, hoping to dream. Maybe Wisakejack had some answers.

He awoke sometime later from a dreamless sleep. As he lay listening to Gwyn's snoring and the snow tapping against the hut, he realized that this was the first time since he'd met Wisakejack that he had *not* dreamed of the spirit.

Had Wisakejack abandoned him as well? His mom, his new dad, and now his strange dream visitor? Was he going to lose everyone from his life?

He stopped. What was that sound? Not daring to breathe, he lay perfectly still, listening.

There. Again.

He swallowed. Someone—or something—was outside the hut.

GWYN WOKE TO ZACH gently shaking his shoulder. Groggy with sleep, he raised himself on one arm, instantly regretting the movement. Every cut and muscle screamed its protest. "What's the matter?" he groaned, rubbing his eyes.

"I heard something outside," Zach whispered.

Instantly awake and oblivious to his pain, he sat bolt upright and listened. Then he smiled, recognizing the voices he heard.

CHAPTER *43*

KATE AND CAT

IN THE LITTLE QUONSET HUT, just past 6:30 a.m., Gwyn watched a reunited Kate and Zach talk quietly together on the couch. When they'd arrived, Zach's first question had been about Quincy. Ed had assured him that Quincy was recovering, still guarded by Gelert. Gwyn had changed into his clothes that Ed had brought and now stood with Ed and Leiddia, as they exchanged their stories about the prior night's events.

"Thanks," Gwyn told them both.

"Sounds like you had the tougher night," Leiddia said, as she kissed him. "Sorry we took so long to find you. That storm filled your tracks, and I lost your scent. We went up the west shore before we backtracked and found your trail again."

"Any word of Caz?" Gwyn asked. Ed shook his head. The note that Caz had left at the store had simply said she needed some time in her otter form and would return the next evening. That would have been last night, but neither he nor Ed had been back to the store since they'd started searching for Zach. "Do either of you have a phone? I'll call her."

Pulling out her phone, Leiddia frowned at the display. "No signal."

Gwyn swore. He had to tell Leiddia what Zach had told him—that Kate had turned them all over to Simon Jonas and that they all had to get out of Thunder Lake right away. But he had to find Caz before they could leave.

"Thank you, Gwyn," Kate said.

They all turned to her. She sat with an arm around Zach, her face tear-streaked. "Thank you for saving Zach."

Gwyn swallowed, unsure of what to say, happy for the reversal in her attitude toward him since their last meeting, but still furious with how she'd betrayed them to the Tainchel.

"And thank you for giving him the choice," she said, then hesitated. "About becoming...you know, one of you."

"And you said no?" Leiddia asked Zach.

Zach nodded. "I decided I wanted to stay me."

Leiddia gave Gwyn a look, but he couldn't read it. Was she thinking that Zach wouldn't have to worry about Gwyn being there to teach him about being a Heroka, the way he should have been for her? Well, that no longer mattered, given Zach's decision. Besides, they had other concerns.

"Kate," he said quietly, "Zach told me what you did."

Kate paled. She looked at Zach.

"What?" Leiddia said.

"You were right," Gwyn told her. "Kate works for the Tainchel. And now, she's reported finding us to them. They're on their way to Thunder Lake."

Leiddia's eyes widened. "You fucking bitch!" she swore, trying to push past Gwyn to get to Kate. Kate jumped up from the couch and backed away from the taller woman.

Stepping between them, Gwyn grabbed Leiddia by an arm. "Hold on."

Leiddia twisted free from him and stepped back, glaring at Kate. "You were handing us over to those monsters? Do you know what they do to our kind?"

Kate looked at Gwyn, her face pleading. "It was for Zach. It was all for him. I knew they had information about the Heroka. I needed to know what he might become, how to stop it—"

"Stop it?" Leiddia snarled. "Like we're some disease to be cured?"

Kate turned to Gwyn. "After that night when you changed...then I found out I was pregnant. I was frightened. I didn't know what he'd be, what he was—" She stopped. She turned to Zach. "Zach, I didn't mean to say—"

"I'm just me, Mom. That's all I've ever been," he said, his voice breaking.

She hugged him to her. "I know that now. I'm sorry." Turning back to Gwyn, she hesitated. "There's more. They're after Zach now, too. And...." She shot a frightened glance at Leiddia. "And they're already here. I saw them at our motel last night. That's why I left town to pick up Zach. They didn't see me—"

"How many?" Gwyn snapped as Leiddia swore.

"Three cars, ten men, including Jonas," Kate said, not meeting his eyes.

"*Simon* Jonas?" Leiddia said, looking at Gwyn. He nodded.

"Mr. Macready was one of them, too, Mom," Zach added quietly.

"Jonas knew all along," Kate said, looking at him. "About you. He was just using me to get to you. To use you as bait." She buried her face in her hands. "I've done everything wrong."

"Duh," Leiddia muttered. Gwyn stayed silent, still angry with Kate. But that anger now battled his guilt for causing the fear that drove her to do this.

"So what do we do now, Gray Legs?" Ed asked, peering out the door. The snow had stopped, and the sky was brightening. "The guards start at eight-thirty. We've got maybe an hour and a half to get out of here."

"And go where?" Leiddia asked.

"Away from here," Kate said. "Zach and I have to leave town. Both of you, too. And that teenage girl. They're looking for all of you."

"I *live* here," Leiddia snapped. "This is my home. This is all I have."

"Cat," Gwyn said, putting a hand on her arm. "She's right."

She pulled her arm away. "Not like you to run, Dog."

"First, I get you, Zach, and..." He paused. "...and Kate to safety. Caz, too, wherever she is. And Gelert and Quincy."

Leiddia started pacing like a caged tiger, swearing to herself. "Fuck it, al-right," she said finally. "But where? You said the Tainchel knows about Cil y Blaidd."

"Just away from here for now," he said. "We'll figure out the next step later."

"How?" Leiddia asked. "That's five people, plus two dogs."

"My plane's at Deer Lake. It can hold all of us if I take out a seat. But we'll need a car as backup, in case they're watching the plane."

"They'll be looking for my Ministry car," Kate said. "We can't take that."

Ed shook his head. "My truck won't hold all of you."

Leiddia sighed. "My van. It's big enough."

"Okay," Gwyn said, "I'll take Ed's truck and come back with the van."

"I have to go, too," Kate said. "Our things are at Joe Makademik's. He won't give them to you. And I'm not leaving Zach here." She shot a look at Leiddia.

Leiddia snorted. "Brilliant. So we send the three people that Jonas can rec-ognize on sight?" She shook her head. "Gwyn, Zach is safest here with you protecting him. Anyway, I have to get stuff from my cabin if I'm leaving town."

"Less suspicious if I drive you," Ed said, "in case the cops stop my truck. We'll ride the ATVs back to my truck. Pick up the dogs on the way. And while Leiddia's getting her van, I can pick up your stuff from the store, and check to see if Caz is there."

Gwyn didn't like it, but it made sense. "Okay, but call Caz as soon as you get a signal."

Ed nodded. "And if she doesn't answer? And she's not at the store?"

Gwyn swore. Why couldn't Caz have just stayed put? "Tell Vera what's hap-pened. If Caz comes back, have Vera warn her and tell her to stay in her otter form. Tell her I'll pick her up at Deer Lake one week from today."

He looked at all of them. "So? Are we agreed?"

Kate bit her lip, and he wondered whether she was worried about leaving Zach with him, or about going with Leiddia herself. Probably both. Finally, she nodded. She turned to Zach. "I'll be back as soon as I can. Your—" She glanced at Gwyn. "Your father will stay with you." She hugged Zach goodbye.

"Don't forget about Caz," Gwyn called as they left. Where was she?

And where was Simon Jonas?

IN HIS ROOM in the same motel that Kate Morgan had recently fled, Simon Jonas was dreaming. He'd left Lessard instructions to wake him only if his men located their quarry. He didn't expect them to have any success, and he didn't care. He was expecting guidance from another source.

Before going to sleep, he'd knelt beside his bed on the worn carpet and prayed for God to come to him again in a dream, to show His terrible swift sword where to strike. Dreams filled his restless sleep, but none were the one for which he'd prayed.

Right now, he was walking through a dark forest, a full moon floating bright and cold in a star-blazed sky. Ahead, something shone through the trees, floating wraithlike and always, no matter how he pursued it, sufficiently obscured by trees and distance to remain a tantalizing mystery, pulling him deeper and deeper into these ancient woods. It seemed as if he had been following it all night in this place where night lasted forever. He trudged on. No snow lay here, and yet a numbing cold still gripped him.

The light ahead suddenly loomed larger. Had it stopped? Was he getting close?

He stepped into a clearing, brilliantly lit by the glow of the moon. The glow increased. He looked up and gasped. At first, he thought the moon was descending to Earth. No—not the moon. A luminous white globe hovered above the clearing, and in that sphere—

Crying out, he prostrated himself, averting his eyes from the angel.

A voice seemed to emanate from the heavens above. "I am the archangel Michael," it cried, each word a symphony. "I am the messenger of your Lord."

Huddled on the ground, Jonas wept in joy. Of course. Who else would the Lord send to direct his Sword but the commander of His army in heaven? The angel spoke, and Jonas listened, reciting back his strange instructions when ordered.

The scene faded. He awoke, still enraptured but feeling strangely cold. The bedside clock glared 7:20 a.m. in blood-red digits. Grabbing his cell, he called Lessard. "Gather the men immediately," he rasped, and then cut off the agent's protests. "I don't care. I know where Blaidd and the boy are. Never mind how. Just get the men back here. Now, dammit." He hung up.

Shivering as he dressed, he checked the thermostat. *Must be broken*, he thought. *It's freezing in here.* Pulling on his coat, he went outside to wait for Lessard and his men.

AT ZACH'S CAMPSITE from the previous night, Kate watched as Ed checked on Quincy. Gelert, taking their arrival as his release from babysitting duties, immediately bounded off, presumably in search of Gwyn. Ed proclaimed Quincy to be recovering, but too weak to leave town with them, so he offered to care for the dog until he healed enough for Ed to send him to Zach. Leiddia helped Ed make an improvised travois from the sleeping bag and strapped-together tree boughs, and then attached it to the back of Leiddia's ATV. They placed Quincy carefully on top, and drove the ATVs back to Ed's truck.

No one answered at Joe Makademik's house, so Kate transferred their luggage from her car into the back of Ed's truck alongside Quincy, and they headed for Leiddia's cabin. Leiddia sat slumped against the passenger door, fast asleep. Kate wasn't surprised. When the snow had filled the tracks last night, Leiddia had followed the trail on foot by her sense of smell, walking miles in the storm, while Ed and Kate followed on the ATVs. Even being a Heroka, she must be exhausted.

Kate was grateful for Leiddia's help in finding Zach, but the female Heroka remained hostile to Kate for having betrayed them to the Tainchel. Kate couldn't blame her, but she didn't relish being alone with Leiddia once Ed dropped them off at her cabin. Her alternative was to accompany Ed into town, but she feared encountering Jonas and the Tainchel more than waiting with Leiddia until Ed returned.

Leiddia awoke just as Ed pulled up in front of her cabin. She got out of the truck, stretching her lithe body in a very catlike manner. Climbing out after her, Kate grabbed their bags from the back and said goodbye to Quincy.

Ed tried calling Caz's cell again. Shaking his head, he put the phone away. "Still no answer. If I find her, I'll bring her to the plane. If we're not there in an hour, leave without us. Call me when you know where you're heading, and I'll bring Caz to you. Quincy, too."

He drove away, leaving Kate alone with Leiddia. Still apprehensive, she followed Leiddia to the cabin. A black cat scurried up as they entered. Leiddia ignored it. Kate set their bags down. "Thanks, by the way. For helping to find Zach."

Leiddia stared at her, and for a moment, Kate thought she wasn't going to answer. "No problem," she said finally. "He's Gwyn's son. Besides, I know what it's like to lose someone close to you. The hole it leaves inside you. The emptiness. I wouldn't wish that on anyone."

Even me, Kate thought. "You lost someone?" she asked, relieved that Leiddia was being civil.

"Painter. My pawakan. Like Gelert for Gwyn."

The cougar. "Oh," Kate said, uncomfortable talking about the Heroka.

"You don't much like me, do you?"

"What? No, I mean…no," Kate stammered, caught off guard.

"Yeah, right," Leiddia snorted, walking over to stare down at her. "Seems to me it should be me not liking you. Bringing the Tainchel here, handing us over to them."

Kate swallowed, again very aware of her vulnerability. She took a step back.

Leiddia shook her head. "Don't worry. I'm not going to hurt you. To be fair to you, Gwyn didn't pick the smoothest way to introduce you to our, uh, talents." She sat on the arm of the sofa.

"He told you about that night?" Kate said, feeling vulnerable again but in a different way.

Leiddia nodded. "We're not that different, you and me. For one thing, we seem to have the same taste in men. I mean, he *is* something we both share, right? Or rather, shared." She gave a little smile, spreading her legs.

Kate felt herself reddening, but smiled too. "How long were you together?"

Leiddia looked out the window. "Too long. Not long enough. Not sure which. I was tough to live with after I changed. And he was still in love with a dead woman. Stelle." She turned back to Kate. "He ever mention her?"

Kate shook her head.

"He would've met you not long after she was killed. Probably why he opened up to you the way he did. Showed you what he was. He was hoping you'd fill the hole she'd left in him."

And I ran from him, Kate thought.

"Anyway, as for you and me," Leiddia said, standing up, "the enemy of my enemy and all that crap." She held out her hand. "So, friends?"

Kate shook her hand, relieved beyond words.

"More girl talk later. Right now, I gotta pack some things." Leiddia looked at the black cat, which stared at her and then ran to jump up on a front windowsill. "Poos will warn me if we have visitors, but keep an eye out, will you?" She disappeared into the bedroom.

Kate's fear of the Tainchel pushed thoughts of Leiddia from her head. She kept pacing the room, acutely aware of every sound outside. Needing something to occupy her mind, she sat on the sofa facing the fireplace and booted up her laptop. Through the bedroom door to her right, she could hear Leiddia opening and closing drawers.

The email from the Tainchel lab she'd downloaded in The Outfitter still sat unopened in her inbox—the email containing the analysis of the DNA samples from Rick Calhoun and Frank Mueller. She opened it.

It had two attachments, one for each victim. She clicked on Mueller's file. As expected, the cop's killer had been Walter Keejek, the same man who had killed Mary Two Rivers—human, not Heroka. She sighed. This was a waste of time.

"Another five," Leiddia called from the bedroom.

"Great," Kate answered. Since she had to wait anyway, she clicked on the second attachment, the one for Rick Calhoun, the killing that had first drawn Jonas's attention to this town and ultimately had led to her and Zach being here. She scrolled through the report, skimming it quickly until one word caught her eye.

Heroka.

She stopped scrolling. That couldn't be right. Paging back up, she began reading again, her fear growing.

The lab had identified Heroka DNA in hair samples found on Rick Calhoun's clothes. Her finger trembled on the touchpad as she scrolled down. A Heroka *had* killed the first victim. Jonas had been right all along.

Further, the report read, *we can confirm a positive match of the foreign hair samples found on Subject One with the DNA—*

A loud thud made her jump. Leiddia stood at the doorway to the bedroom. A large duffel bag crammed to bursting lay at her feet where she'd dropped it. "Ready?"

"Uh, yeah. Just need to finish this email," Kate said. She kept reading.

…with the DNA taken from—

"You okay?" Leiddia asked.

"Yeah, yeah. I'm fine," Kate said, glancing at her.

Leiddia's gray-green eyes were locked on Kate. "You look kinda pale."

"Rough night," Kate said, her hand shaking on the touchpad as she read.

…with the DNA taken from the captured suspect….

Oh god, no. She wanted to scream as she read the next words.

Leiddia Barker.

"Something wrong?" Leiddia asked.

Kate swallowed. "No. Nothing. I'm, uh, all done." As she reached to close the laptop to hide the incriminating email, she glanced up nervously, expecting to find Leiddia's eyes still on her.

But Leiddia was watching something behind Kate. Kate turned.

Perched on top of the sofa looking over her left shoulder was Poos. The cat was staring at Kate's laptop screen, its head moving back and forth, as if it were reading.

As if it were reading....

Too late, Kate slammed the laptop closed. She turned, only to find Leiddia standing right beside her. She hadn't even heard a floorboard creak.

"Looks like the cat's out of the bag," Leiddia said, her face sad.

Kate threw the notebook as hard as she could at Leiddia, then leapt from the sofa. If she could make it to the van....

She was halfway to the door when Leiddia slammed into her from behind, sending her sprawling to the floor. She tried to rise, but Leiddia threw her back down.

"Sorry, Kate. I really am," Leiddia said.

Kate opened her mouth to scream, but Leiddia's fist hammered into her temple. Lights exploded behind her eyes, and the room faded into darkness.

CHAPTER 44

BE CAREFUL WHAT YOU WISH FOR

LEIDDIA SAT SLUMPED against the door of her cabin. Beside her lay Kate Morgan's unconscious form. Leiddia was crying, and she couldn't stop.

She had cried a lot when this began, when she discovered the mistake she'd made, how she'd been tricked. When the thing inside her had taken over, and the hunger began to grow.

She'd cried when she killed Rick Calhoun, or rather, when the thing she'd been forced to become killed him. More than cried. She threw up for two days, and couldn't eat for a week. She'd cried and cried when Mary Two Rivers died. Mary had been her friend. She'd watched her grow up. She and Gwyn had taken her camping.

And she'd killed her.

Not the way she'd killed Rick Calhoun, but she had killed her nonetheless. Her Heroka ability to control animals had made it easy to control a human. The Lynxes had taught her shaman ways, taught her how to send the Hunger into another, so that it didn't use *her* to feed, didn't make *her* change.

Make her a windigo.

Poos leapt onto her lap, mewing softly. She stroked the cat gently. "I wish you really were my pawakan, Poosie. Wish I'd settled for you."

But she hadn't. When Painter had died, the cougar's death ripped out a piece of her heart, of her soul. Left her empty. Left her hungry for the bond that only a Heroka can know and that only a pawakan can fill.

Painter had been her first pawakan, and after bonding with the life force of the cougar, untamed and untamable, a house cat like Poos could never fill the hole inside her.

Gwyn had taught her what he could about being Heroka, but he'd left too soon, driven away by her. She sobbed harder. She'd been so frightened by her new powers and the animal urges they'd brought, so afraid of living this new life alone that she'd driven him away by trying to hold him too tightly.

With Gwyn gone and knowing no other Heroka, she had faced her search for a new pawakan alone. So she set out on a vision quest. She'd done vision quests for years, whenever she had a problem she couldn't solve. Ed had taught her, and she'd often found guidance in the dreams that came when she was part of the wilderness where the Heroka were most at home.

Finding a new pawakan was just another problem, wasn't it? Why shouldn't a vision quest help with that, too?

Depends on what you meet in those dreams. She remembered that night....

Camped by the dam lake, under a crescent moon in a star-shot sky, waiting for sleep. Warm summer breeze wafting bush smells to her, the scent of animals who were closer to her than any person she'd ever met. Except for him. Except for Gwyn.

Waves lapping, crickets chirping, the howl of a wolf—the bush's symphony finally summoning sleep.

And with it, dreams.

In her dream, she stood where she slept, but the dam and its lake were gone. She looked down into a river valley surrounded by dense bush under a full moon.

Below, on the near riverbank, about where the middle of the dam lake now lay, a man stood watching her, brown-skinned with long white hair. He wore the traditional outfit of an Ojibwe shaman. As she stared, in the way that happens in dreams, she found herself suddenly before him. The river murmured beside them, and it seemed that voices hid in those murmurs.

"Boozhoo, noozhis!" he greeted her, with a smile that didn't reach his night-black eyes.

Now that she was closer, she could see he was old. Very old. "I'm not your granddaughter."

The shaman spread his hands. "Who knows for sure? I am Comdowtah. Do you know me?"

She shook her head. The shaman looked disappointed. "I am forgotten already?" He shrugged. "No matter. I can help you on your quest."

"What do you know of my quest?" she asked, trying to suppress her excitement.

He spread his hands again. "I know that you are Heroka, that you are *Bizhiw's* clan, and that you seek a spirit companion."

Bizhiw meant lynx in Ojibwe. "None of my totem lives in my home anymore. No lynx. No cougar. The lake that now lies in this place in my world has driven them away. How can you help me?"

Comdowtah smiled. "I was a great shaman and can put you in touch with the most powerful spirits."

"You *were* a great shaman? Past tense?"

"I am dead now for five hundred winters. We stand on my grave."

She suppressed a shudder. "Who are these spirits?"

"They are called the Great Lynxes."

Lynxes! Perfect. "Show me."

"As you wish." Smiling that cold smile again, Comdowtah pushed his face close to hers, puckering as if to kiss her. Revolted and suddenly afraid, she tried to step back but found she couldn't move. *It's only a dream,* she thought. His lips moved closer, but not toward her mouth.

He breathed on her eyes. His breath was sour and smelled of rotting meat. And it was cold. The cold of the grave. The cold of a killing winter. Her eyes closed.

And she saw.

She was underwater now, but able to breathe. Moonlight trickled down from the surface, cold and faint, just enough to reveal two large shapes, black with the slick shiny fur of an otter or muskrat, but with fat feline bodies and heads. And the tufted ears of the lynx.

Noozhis, you seek us? The voices sounded in her mind, not her ears. The two creatures spoke together, as if one.

She swallowed. "I seek my pawakan, a creature from the totem of my kind. Of *our* kind. Of Bizhiw's clan."

Both great heads nodded in unison. *You hunger for a spirit to fill your emptiness. We know of hunger. And of emptiness.*

"Can you help me?" she asked, barely containing her excitement.

Again, the heads nodded as one. *This is what we offer.*

Both creatures pointed a black paw at her. A current swirled from their claws, and chill water struck her face. The water seemed to flow through her, not around her. The coldness numbed not only her limbs, freezing her immobile, but also her thoughts. She was powerless to move her mind away from what the Lynxes showed her. But once she realized what they offered, she did not wish to turn away.

For the Lynxes offered power. Power over not only her totem, but all totems, all animals. With strength and vitality no Heroka had ever known. She could rule the animal world. All animals would be her pawakans. She would never be alone again. She would never feel empty again.

Is this your wish? the Lynxes asked.

The scene began to fade. She was waking up. The dream would end, and with it, her chance for this power. "Yes! Yes!" she gasped.

Then here is your companion.

Something stepped between the Lynxes and moved toward her. Large, grotesque, and misshapen, it resembled no animal she'd ever seen. She'd given her answer without thinking, afraid of losing this power. Too late, she realized there'd be a price. There was always a price.

The thing in her dream reached for her. Screaming, she twisted away in the water, trying to wake up. Too late. The Windigo spirit touched her.

She'd awakened that night shivering despite the warm summer air, feeling a cold and a hunger that had never left her since. A cold in her heart. A hunger in her soul. Her dream had ended. And her nightmare had begun.

Kate Morgan stirred on the floor, bringing her back to the present. She had dreamed that dream to end her loneliness, her emptiness, to find a life of companionship. That dream would never be. The Lynxes had plans, and she could only obey. There were things she had to do.

She got up. She moved toward Kate.

CONSCIOUSNESS LIMPED BACK into Kate's brain like a whipped dog afraid to return home. Shooting pain stabbed her temple. She opened her eyes. She was lying on her back, staring at the ceiling in Leiddia's cabin.

Leiddia.

It all rushed back to her. She had to get away, to warn Zach and Gwyn. She tried to roll onto her side, but a hand grabbed her and threw her roughly back down. Her head smacked against the floorboards, and she cried out.

Leiddia leapt onto her chest, straddling her. Kate swung a feeble punch, but Leiddia slapped her fist aside. Locking both of her wrists together in a one-handed grip, Leiddia pinned her arms over her head.

Kate twisted and writhed, struggling to break free, but she was no match for the Heroka's strength. She started to scream, reduced to a final hope that someone passing by the remote cabin might hear. That hope died in a gurgling sound as Leiddia's other hand closed around her throat.

"I'm sorry, Kate," Leiddia sobbed, tears streaming down her face, "but you've brought Zach to them. They don't need you anymore."

Zach? They? Even as panic seized Kate, she remembered the voices from the dam. *You are no longer needed in this.*

Leiddia's hand tightened like a metal band about her throat. Blood pounded in her head. Her ears began to ring. She couldn't breathe. She was going to die.

There came the sound of breaking glass.

Leiddia's head snapped up. The grip around Kate's neck and wrists disappeared as Leiddia's hands flew up to ward off small gray forms that leapt chattering at her face. Gasping in a breath, Kate shoved Leiddia off her and rolled away. Pushing herself up on an elbow, she tried to take in the scene with still-blurred vision.

A sea of tiny dark shapes—brown, gray, black—swarmed squealing across the floor in a straight line to Leiddia. Kate blinked, her eyes finally able to identify her saviors.

Squirrels.

She was being saved by squirrels.

And rats, she noted with a shudder. And chipmunks and mice and weasels. The animals streamed like a furry river into the cabin through a window by the door, where a large tree branch protruded through the smashed pane. Once inside, they leapt to the floor and made straight for Leiddia. Poos the cat arched its back and hissed, then retreated into the bedroom.

Leiddia was on her feet now, screaming in rage and pain, flailing at her attackers, who tore at her clothes and bit into any exposed flesh they could find. Bleeding from cuts on her arms, neck, and face, Leiddia flung herself across the room, tearing two squirrels from her as she ran. Wrenching open the door, she dashed outside, the rodents still in pursuit.

Kate struggled to her feet, having to force each breath in and out. Outside, an engine roared. By the time she reached the door, Leiddia's van was fishtailing onto the road away from the cabin.

A young woman, skinny and taller than Kate, picked herself up off the ground, brushing off snow. She looked somewhere mid-teens. She wore a dark brown parka over torn black jeans and a wrinkled Springsteen t-shirt. Her spiked hair was dyed a dark blue. Two silver rings pierced her right eyebrow, and she had a stud in her right nostril.

Seeing Kate, she strolled toward her, accompanied by a parade of Kate's little rescuers. It took Kate a moment before she remembered this girl from the community center when she'd found Zach with Gwyn. She noticed—with less shock than she would have had a few moments ago—that a gray rat poked out of the girl's parka pocket.

The girl hooked a thumb in the direction of the departed van. "Now, *that* was fun." Walking up to Kate, she stuck out a hand. "Hi, I'm Caz."

KATE LEANED HARD against Caz as Ed slid his truck around a snowy bend in the logging road, almost dropping a wheel down the steep bank as they raced back to the dam to warn Gwyn. The trank gun and dart case in her parka pocket dug into her ribs. She'd retrieved them from her luggage before they'd started their pursuit. She just hoped she'd get to use the gun.

Caz had called Vera, telling her to send Ed back to Leiddia's cabin right away. Ed brought other news. He'd just dropped Quincy at the vet when Willie Burrell pulled him over. The OPP had issued warrants for Gwyn, Caz, Leiddia, Kate, and Zach.

"Wanted to know if I'd seen any of you. Told her no, of course," Ed said. "But it means we can't go to the cops."

"Jonas did that," Kate said. "He's used his CSIS credentials on Thornton." She was barely controlling her panic. A Heroka *had* been behind the killings, and she'd left Zach with another of them. "We have to get to Zach," she said for probably the twentieth time.

"Yeah, we got that," Caz said, clutching the dashboard.

"She murdered my granddaughter," Ed said, his face grim. "She killed Mary."

Kate shook her head. "She killed Rick Calhoun, but her DNA didn't show up on Mary or Mueller."

"She is windigo," Ed said. "A shaman can send the Windigo spirit into another. Somehow, she has learned to do that, and that is how Mary died." He slammed the truck hard around another bend. "She killed Mary."

Kate looked at Caz, trying to ignore Rizzo sniffing at her from Caz's pocket. "How'd you know to show up at Leiddia's?" While they'd waited for Ed, she'd filled Caz in on recent events. She hadn't heard Caz's story yet.

Caz related her encounter in otter form with the two presences at the bottom of the dam lake.

"And you'd encountered these…things before?" Kate asked.

Caz nodded. "I'd sensed them before. The same way I sense my totem animals. But I didn't remember until I sensed them again in the dam lake. It was so strong there. After I escaped from them, I remembered. It's like a smell they leave behind. And Leiddia has that same smell on her. So I brought some friends back and headed for her place."

"You sensed their spirits," Ed said, nodding. "Two, you said?"

"Yeah," Caz said. "I mean, I think so. It was weird. I'd feel two minds one moment, then only one the next. Like they were a single being, yet separate, all at the same time."

"Glad I'm not the only one hearing voices," Kate said, then related her own strange experience at the top of the dam. "It felt as if the voices were coming from deep in the lake."

Ed looked even grimmer. "*Mishi-bizhiwag.*"

"Mishi-whosit?" Caz said.

"The Great Lynxes," Ed said. "Bad spirits. They rule the deep places. The way to their realm in the spirit world lies in the deepest waters. They don't like humans."

"Then why are they messing with Leiddia?" Caz asked.

"That is how they gain power in our world. They come to you in dream, disguised as someone you want to meet. Or with something you want. They seduce you. Once they touch you in dream, you are theirs."

"Something else," Caz said. "After Otter-me escaped from them under the dam lake, I surfaced—but it wasn't the dam lake anymore. I mean, it was still a lake, but it was different. Older, you know, wilder." She described it.

Ed muttered something in Ojibwe. "You were in the Spirit World. Mahigan, the wolf spirit, told Gwyn that the Spirit World and our world are drawing closer. You crossed over somehow, there in the lake."

"Sounds like the lake's the center of the big bad around here," Caz said.

"There's more," Ed said, glancing at Kate. "Mahigan told Gwyn that whatever's happening, it involves the wolf and a boy."

Kate swallowed. "Gwyn and Zach."

"Uh, so basically," Caz said, "you guys left the two people Leiddia needs most at the exact spot where she needs them."

"She planned this," Kate whispered. She slumped in the seat. Leiddia had a head start. They wouldn't get there in time. Only Gwyn Blaidd—the Heroka that she'd been fleeing all these years—stood between her son and a killer. Again, the irony did not escape her.

GWYN SAT ON THE COUCH in the hut beside Zach, waiting for Leiddia and Kate to return with their getaway van. The boy had been quiet since the others had left. "You missing Quincy?" Gwyn asked, trying to guess the boy's thoughts.

Zach nodded.

Gwyn squeezed Zach's shoulder. "I know what that feels like, to be that close to an animal. I miss Gelert already. If a Heroka and their pawakan are apart for too long, we feel it like an ache, an emptiness. That's why Caz carries that damn rat with her everywhere." He grinned at a memory. "I remember when Leiddia first showed up in town with her cougar...." His words trailed off, as something occurred to him.

Leiddia. Her new pawakan, Poos, the black cat. It hadn't been with her this morning.

He shook his head. So what? He didn't have Gelert with him right now. But without wanting to, he thought back over the past few days.

The night Thornton arrested her at her cabin, she'd left the cat behind. Then spent two days in jail without asking for it. She'd left it behind again when she accompanied Gwyn to the community center. And then again last night. And she hadn't mentioned Poos as a reason for needing to go back to her cabin before they left. Or counted the cat in the number of their escape party.

He stood up, a sudden fear taking him. He couldn't explain it, but one thing he knew for sure: that cat was not Leiddia's pawakan. But then what was? And why had she lied to him? He didn't know the answers to those questions, but he did know one thing.

Something was not right with Leiddia.

"Gwyn?" Zach asked.

He pulled on his parka. "Zach, we have to get out of here. I think you're in danger."

Zach stood. "What's wrong?"

"I'll explain later. Do up your coat." Gwyn shoved Zach's toque on the boy's head as Zach fumbled with his parka. Taking Zach's arm, he opened the door and stepped outside.

Pain stung his shoulder—once, twice. Too late, he saw the figures in white parkas. Figures with rifles. Shoving Zach back in the hut, he pulled two black darts from his shoulder. Tranks. He didn't have much time.

He dove for his nearest attacker. The man fired but missed, and Gwyn drove a fist into his jaw, feeling bones crunch. Two more rushed him. He grabbed each by the throat, slamming their heads together. Another dart bit into his leg. A man swung his rifle at him like a club. Dodging it, he buckled his attacker's knee with a kick, and the man fell screaming.

His arms and legs moved as if he were underwater. The tranks were taking hold. But he wasn't done yet. Four attackers were down. Maybe he'd get out of this. Get Zach out of this. He dropped the nearest man with a punch to the throat.

"Stop!" cried a male voice from behind him.

Yeah, right, he thought, ripping the rifle from the next man's hands and slamming it butt-first into his face.

A gunshot rang out. "I'll kill the boy, Blaidd. Damn you, beast, you know I will."

He turned. He knew that voice.

In the door of the hut, a man had Zach's arm twisted behind his back and a pistol pointed at the boy's head.

"Jonas," Gwyn growled, and took a step toward his old enemy.

Jonas shoved the gun barrel hard against Zach's temple. Zach cried out. "I mean it, Blaidd," Jonas shouted. "I'll kill him. Surrender or he dies."

A familiar howl sounded from the direction of the gate. A man screamed. Gwyn turned to the sound. Twenty yards away, Gelert bounded toward them. Behind him, a Tainchel agent lay dead in the snow, his throat ripped out.

Jonas threw Zach to the ground. He swung the gun toward the dog. Gwyn shouted a silent command, ordering Gelert to stop. But the great hound was already in the air, huge jaws open, ready to snap the life from the man who dared to threaten his master.

Jonas fired.

"No!" Gwyn screamed as Gelert twisted in mid leap, and then hit the snow-covered concrete hard in front of Jonas. Whining, the dog tried to rise, but fell back, his chest shuddering with each breath.

"Gelert!" Gwyn cried, wracked with his pawakan's pain as if he'd been shot himself. He stumbled forward, trying to reach his fallen friend, but the tranquilizers finally took hold, and he fell to his knees. Jonas stepped toward Gelert and raised his gun again.

"No! Please, don't!" Gwyn rasped.

Jonas turned to him. "*Don't?! Please?!*" he snapped, his lips quivering. "Have you forgotten, beast?" He pointed the gun at Gelert's head. "This is for Daniel. This is for my son."

He pulled the trigger.

Gelert spasmed then lay still. Screaming his name, Gwyn tried to crawl to the dog, but the drug was too strong. Collapsing onto the cold surface of the dam road, he could only watch as Jonas walked past Gelert's body toward him. The tranks took hold completely. The last thing he saw was Jonas's booted foot swinging toward his face.

CHAPTER 45

SIMON SAYS

SIMON **JONAS STARED DOWN** at an unconscious Gwyn Blaidd. "Vengeance is mine, saith the Lord," he whispered. But today, vengeance was finally his, too. Lessard knelt beside Blaidd, checking for a pulse.

"He's alive, Mr. Lessard," Jonas said. "It takes more than that to kill one of them. Report."

Lessard stood up. "Two men dead. Three unconscious, probable concussions. One can't walk. Two others, plus myself, ready for orders, sir."

The two other Tainchel agents stood beside the Morgan boy, who knelt sobbing in front of the hut. A movement caught Jonas's eye. Framed in the hut's doorway behind the boy, something had just appeared. A dog? No....

A coyote.

The coyote walked up to the boy. Jonas raised his gun. The coyote...disappeared. Jonas blinked.

Seeing Jonas raise his weapon, Lessard and the other agents spun around, rifles ready. Seeing nothing, Lessard looked back at Jonas. "Sir?"

Ignoring the question, Jonas pushed past him. He looked behind the boy. Nothing. He looked inside the hut. Empty. He stepped outside again.

Lessard cleared his throat. "Sir?" The other agents exchanged glances.

Jonas shook his head. An animal couldn't disappear into thin air. In the excitement of capturing Blaidd, he must have imagined it. Now was not the time for distractions—he was serving the Lord. "Nothing. Secure the prisoners. Get the cars. We are to take them to the powerhouse at the base of the dam. We will be met there."

Lessard raised an eyebrow. "You've received orders, sir?"

Jonas glared. "Those are *my* orders to you. Now get moving." He watched the men turn away. He *had* received orders, but these fools would never understand. He would keep his own counsel with his Lord.

ZACH LAY SOBBING on the snowy ground where Jonas had shoved him before shooting Gelert. He'd heard the gun shot, but more, he'd *felt* the dog's pain. He prayed that Gwyn was unhurt. He prayed for his mother to save him. When would this nightmare end?

What was that? His eyes—his *blind* eyes—detected light. Shock fought through despair. He looked up.

A coyote was walking toward him, glowing silver against the darkness of his blindness. When it reached him, it just kept on walking.

Right *through* him.

Then things got *really* weird.

He turned around, expecting the coyote to emerge glowing behind him. No coyote, but his own hands now had the same silvery radiance. As he stared, light flowed from his fingers like streams of sparkling water, covering the ground. Wherever the water touched, he could see. The light spread until he could see the entire landscape as he did in his dreams, and the landscape he saw was the dark lake of those dreams, but lit now in daylight.

His head swam as his perspective changed. He stood now barefoot on the lake's stony beach, wearing his deerskin jacket and matching breeches. Knowing he needed to do so, but without remembering why, he began walking along the beach, gathering an armful of weathered, bark-stripped tree branches.

Carrying his bundle of sticks, he waded into the surprisingly warm water until it rose to his thighs. Just below the murky surface, indistinct shapes swam past. Selecting a stick, he waited, searching.

There. A huge frog stroked by, legs splayed, its rounded back just breaking the surface. He touched the frog with the stick. The stick disappeared. The creature shuddered, its stroke slowing. Swimming in a lazy circle, it returned to lay motionless before him.

Spots painted the frog's back in a random scatter, each a different size and color. Pulling another stick from his bundle, he touched a large brown spot. The spot and the stick both vanished.

A bellow trumpeted from the marshy end of the lake. A huge bull moose emerged from the trees. Staring at him, the moose dropped to one knee, then stood again, head lowered.

Selecting another stick, he touched another spot on the frog, smaller and black. A sleek otter surfaced, flipped onto its back, and swam a circle around him.

Another stick, another spot. A beaver appeared from below, slapping the water with its flat tail.

More sticks, more spots. And for each, a new animal.

A hawk swooped to drop a dead mouse before him in the water. A black bear lumbered from the bush and rose on its hind legs. A gray timber wolf appeared and raised its head in a mournful howl.

Finally, he touched the last spot remaining on the frog with his last stick. A coyote trotted from the bush onto the beach. Sitting beside the wolf, it tilted its head to stare at Zach.

Mammals of all sorts, predators and prey, now lined the shore around him. Birds of every feather whirled above him. Water creatures, cold-blooded and warm, circled him in the water. All were watching him, waiting.

But waiting for what? What was he supposed to do?

"Go," he said, suddenly not wanting to be in this dream. Still they remained. Then he noticed he still held the last stick. Unlike the others, this one had not disappeared.

The frog still floated before him, its bulbous eyes locked on his face. Extending that final stick, he touched the frog one last time.

The stick disappeared. With a flip, the big frog slipped below the black surface, followed by the other lake creatures. Above, the birds broke from their circling and winged away. On shore, the animals slipped into the dark bush, until only the coyote remained. Taking one last look at him, it too turned and padded away.

And he was alone. He waded back to shore. The scene was darkening. The strange dream was ending—the second in a row in which Wisakejack had *not* appeared. What did that mean?

He awoke to the blindness of his everyday world, expecting to be still lying on the cold concrete outside the Quonset hut. But instead, he found himself riding in a warm vehicle, with cold metal around his wrists and no memory of getting here. Where was he? Was Gwyn okay?

He opened his mouth to ask his captors. Or rather, he tried to. His mouth wouldn't open. His lips wouldn't move. A fear as great as when he'd met the windigo gripped him. He tried moving his feet, a finger, anything. Nothing worked.

He no longer had control over his own body.

The car stopped. He heard the door beside him open. A man barked at him to get out. He sat there, helpless. Suddenly, he felt himself moving, getting out of the car, standing up. A strong hand grabbed his arm. His legs moved by themselves as his captor pulled him along. What was happening?

A familiar voice sounded in his mind. *Sorry, little brother*, Wisakejack said, *but I'm taking charge of you for a little while.*

What have you done to me? Zach screamed in his mind.

Think about the dream, little brother. Think about the dream.

LEIDDIA PUSHED OPEN THE GATE leading to the powerhouse at the base of the dam. Walking back to her van, her eyes ran to the pile of branches under the trees hiding the body of the guard she'd just killed. The small part of her that was still Leiddia Barker felt the bile rise in her throat. Dropping to her knees, she puked onto the ground beside the corpse, until the things that lived inside her seized control again. The Lynxes.

Get up. We are almost there.

Wiping her mouth on her parka sleeve, she rose shakily. Trying to resist was useless. Here, beside the lake, their hold on her seemed absolute. She got back into her van, wincing from the myriad wounds inflicted by Caz's swarm of rodents. After her escape, she'd stopped to patch herself up using the van's first-aid kit. She covered the cuts on her face as best she could with makeup, cursing Caz every minute while the Lynxes exhorted her to get to the dam site. *Bring us the Wolf and Boy.*

Driving through the gate, she parked near the powerhouse. And waited.

About twenty minutes later, two SUVs drove into the lot, stopping about thirty feet away. A tall thin man got out of the first car—Simon Jonas, arriving as she'd instructed him in his dream with the "angel." Three more Tainchel agents in white parkas emerged, rifles ready, followed by Zach. Finally, a familiar figure appeared, hands cuffed behind him.

Gwyn.

Her heart fell. She'd held out hope that her wolf man would overcome the Tainchel, that he'd escape with the boy. Now it was truly over. This scene would play out as the Lynxes planned. Just four Tainchel, though. Kate Morgan had said she'd counted ten. Leiddia felt a tinge of pride. Gwyn hadn't gone down without a fight.

One agent pointed his rifle at her, but Jonas motioned for him to lower it. He approached her alone, and they faced each other out of earshot of his men. He considered her. She waited, praying that Kate Morgan had not lied about never sending her picture to Jonas. She was also betting that the Tainchel would not have their scanners turned on, since Gwyn's presence would cause them to be constantly ringing.

"Who are you?" he asked finally.

"I am the one called 'Lynx,'" she replied, repeating the name the "angel" had given Jonas in his dream. "Our meeting was foretold to you."

He hesitated. "Why should I trust you?"

She could almost smell how much he wanted to believe. "Do you think *He*," she said, glancing heavenward, "would lie to you?"

His eyes widened. She held his stare until he gave a curt nod. "And you can show me the secrets of the Heroka?"

She nodded. "We need access to the dam's control room." She held up Kate's security card. "This will get us into the powerhouse. Your CSIS credentials will do the rest." She looked at Zach. He seemed fine, almost strangely calm. Gwyn stared at her glassy-eyed. Blood and bruises covered his face, and one eye was swollen nearly shut. They'd pay for that. "Can he walk?"

Jonas nodded. "Yes. He's just sedated."

She realized then that Gelert was missing. "Where's his dog?"

"I killed him," Jonas replied.

She swallowed. *Gwyn, I'm sorry.* This had started with the death of a pawakan, and it was ending the same way. It didn't matter. It was too late to stop this. "Bring them both," she said, walking to the powerhouse door.

AT THE EDGE of the parking lot, Kate crouched with Caz and Ed in thick spruce trees, watching Leiddia face Jonas and his men. They'd hidden Ed's truck in the trees up the road after following Leiddia's tire tracks here. They'd only just hidden themselves when the two black SUVs arrived.

"Zach!" Kate gasped, seeing a small figure emerge from the first SUV.

Leiddia turned suddenly, scanning where they hid.

"Quiet!" Caz whispered. "She'll hear you." When Leiddia turned back to Jonas, Caz peered through the branches. Her Heroka eyes saw farther than Kate's or Ed's. "I don't see Gelert, but Zach seems okay. They've beaten the crap outta Gwyn, though. Who's Leiddia talking to?"

"That's Jonas," Kate whispered.

Caz shook her head. "What gives? Gwyn and Zach are cuffed, but Leiddia and the Tainchel are like best buds."

"I don't know. I don't care," Kate said. "We have to save Zach."

"Gwyn too," Caz muttered.

"Except we're outnumbered and outgunned," Ed said. "Wish we could hear what's going on."

"Maybe we can," Caz said. Pulling Rizzo from her pocket, she put the rat down on top of the crusted snow. The two stared at each other, the rat's whiskers twitching. Then it turned and scampered off toward Leiddia and the others. The rat had covered only half the distance when Leiddia opened the powerhouse door. Jonas and his men followed her, hauling Zach and Gwyn with them.

"Caz!" Kate cried.

"I know," Caz muttered, focused on Rizzo, who was still five yards from the door. The last Tainchel agent stepped into the powerhouse. The door began to close. With a final burst of rodent speed, Rizzo dove at the narrowing crack. The door closed, but not before Rizzo scooted through at the last second.

Caz grinned. "In!"

"Great," Kate said, forcing a smile. Zach's fate now depended on a rat.

INSIDE THE POWERHOUSE, Rizzo paused to catch his breath. He felt exposed but his orders from Mistress Caz were clear.

Follow the humans. Stay close. Listen.

At least in here, he was warm. The humans had already crossed the floor of the strange building and were climbing metal steps to a smaller room inside this bigger room, enclosed with clear walls. Rizzo scurried after them, past huge metal domes. Reaching the stairs, he struggled up one by one until he reached the door to the glass room, which had just enough space at the bottom for him to squeeze under.

Hiding behind a wastepaper basket in a corner, he focused on the noises the humans made. Their sounds meant nothing to him, but Mistress Caz would hear them in her head and understand. Rizzo twitched his ears up and listened.

AS THE TRANK DARTS wore off, Gwyn's head slowly reconnected to his body, and every part of that body reported in with screams of pain. Jonas must have beaten him after he passed out. He didn't remember taking this much damage in the fight.

His hands cuffed behind him, he sat on the floor of a small room dominated by a large instrument panel. Beside him sat Zach, head down, eyes closed, hands cuffed in front.

"Zach," Gwyn rasped, his throat raw and burning. "Are you okay?"

Zach did not respond. The boy seemed unharmed, but his silence worried him. Was it shock? He'd been through so much. His strange dreams, Macready shooting Quincy, facing the windigo, the Tainchel's attack, Gelert....

Gelert. The scene on the dam rushed back to him. Gelert leaping. Jonas swinging his gun toward the dog. The shot. The impact of the bullet, the pain, the dog's collapse on the cold concrete. Through their connection, Gwyn had felt it all. Now, he felt...nothing. He reached with his mind trying to establish contact with his pawakan. No response, no sense of the dog's presence anywhere.

Gelert dead? A void inside Gwyn yawned opened. He shook his head, trying to focus through his pain and the emptiness. He had no time for grief now. He had to get Zach out of here. But the emptiness remained.

Leiddia, Jonas, and a dam worker Leiddia addressed as Vickers stood before the instrument panel. Light from the panel lit their faces in a bloody glow. Vickers looked very nervous. The three Tainchel agents stood with their backs to Gwyn. He tried to bring his feet under him. If he could stand up....

Turning at the sound, Jonas kicked him back down. "Stay down, beast, or my men will hurt you again. And don't bother trying to shift. We've pumped you with something to prevent that abomination."

Ignoring Jonas, he glared at Leiddia. "Why are you doing this, Cat?"

Jonas looked at her suspiciously. "You know each other?"

She shrugged. "Small town."

"We should put another trank in him," Jonas muttered, eyeing him, fists clenched.

"If you want to get inside their secret lair," Leiddia replied, "then you'll need him able to walk. He can barely do that now."

"I thought *you* could show us."

"I can lead you to it. You'll need a Heroka to get you inside. Biometric security."

What was she talking about? What secret lair? What was she up to?

Jonas considered her with narrowed eyes. "Then show me."

Leiddia turned to the panel. "This facility isn't producing power yet. That means they're routing the lake's entire outflow through the control dam, not the main dam."

"What's the difference?"

"Water flow through the main dam drives the generators. The control dam simply controls the water level in the lake, and right now, it's set to keep the reservoir level constant. Inflow to the lake from upstream flows out at the same rate through the control dam."

"So?"

"So the control dam outflow forms a spillway, a river that never existed before the dam was built. A river that now hides something."

Jonas's eyes widened. "The secret lair of the Heroka!" he whispered, as if he'd found the Holy Grail.

She nodded. "So all we need is for Mr. Vickers to close the control dam gates, stopping the outflow. The spillway level will drop, revealing the entrance."

Vickers paled. "I can't do that. I'm responsible—"

"Mr. Vickers," Jonas snapped, "this is a matter of national security. You've verified my CSIS credentials. Close the gates."

"But that will raise the lake," Vickers protested.

Jonas looked at Leiddia. She shrugged. "The lake's quite low. It can handle more inflow for the time we need."

Jonas turned to Vickers. "Do it."

Vickers hesitated, then with a glance at the rifles, he swallowed and turned to the control panel. From the floor, Gwyn couldn't see what the man was doing, but a few seconds later, Vickers turned back. "All right, it's done."

Leiddia studied the panel, then nodded. "Good."

Gwyn saw it coming—the way she lowered her stance, shifting her weight. She dropped two of the Tainchel with punches to their throats before Jonas and the one called Lessard even reacted.

Lessard raised his rifle, but Leiddia easily wrenched it from him and cracked it across his forehead. As he collapsed, she hammered the rifle butt against the side of Jonas's head, dropping him to the floor too.

Vickers screamed and ran for the door. Leiddia grabbed him by his collar and slammed his head down onto the panel. He slid limply to the floor to join the others.

"Leiddia," Gwyn rasped, "what are you doing?"

Ignoring him, she considered the men at her feet. "Caz is bound to have called Ed—"

"Caz! She's okay?"

She smiled almost gently at him. "Yeah, she's okay. Tried to turn me into squirrel food, though. Your mom's okay, too, kid," she added, but still Zach gave no response. "But I'm sure they'll have followed me. So, I need some backup." She turned to the unconscious men on the floor.

With the exception of Jonas, the three other Tainchel along with Vickers began to convulse. Their limbs spasmed. They began to change. Gwyn watched in horror, recognizing in each of them the beginnings of the thing he'd fought last night. She was turning these men into windigos. "Cat, what's happened to you?"

She looked at him, her face wet with tears that ran like blood in the red glow of the control panel. "Sorry, Dog. I'm not your Cat anymore." She turned away, her eyes on the panel. "And now," she whispered, "we wait."

CHAPTER *46*

WATER, WATER EVERYWHERE

"**W**AIT?" KATE ASKED, as Caz related the events in the control room through Rizzo's eyes and ears to her and Ed. "Wait for what?"

"Dunno," Caz replied, "but now we're even more screwed. Gwyn can't shift, Gelert's missing, and Leiddia's got a windigo army."

At least, according to Caz, Zach still appeared unharmed. "*Is* there a secret Heroka lair around here?"

Caz shook her head. "News to me. Sounds like a line for Jonas."

"Then why did she need to close the control dam?" Kate asked. "That will empty the spillway, but why—" She stopped, remembering the voices that spoke to her at the dam. "The lake will get deeper. *That's* what she's waiting for."

Caz looked at Ed. "Those things at the bottom of the lake."

Ed nodded. "The Great Lynxes. They rule the deep places. Deep lakes lead to their realm in the spirit world. I bet the deeper that lake gets, the closer the spirit world gets to ours. And the stronger the Lynxes get."

"Great," Caz said. "So now what?"

Silence fell. Kate bit her lip, thinking. "There's a spare pass card in the trailer. Once she leaves, we'll go in and open the control gates again. I can work the board. Then we call Thornton."

Ed and Caz could come up with no better plan, so they settled down under the spruces to wait. Caz considered her. "So why are you with the Tainchel? You don't look evil."

Kate tried to explain that night with Gwyn, how she blamed him for Zach's blindness, how she feared the Heroka, feared what Zach might become. How she hoped the Tainchel held the secrets to Zach's future.

Caz shook her head. "Heroka and humans mate all the time. I've never heard of blindness being a problem. I think that was just fate. I really don't understand why humans are scared of us. I mean, yeah, our powers make us different, but really, we're just like you. Some of us are good, some not so much." She shrugged. "Leiddia tried to kill you. I saved you. And Gwyn saved Zach. Gwyn growls, but he doesn't bite. He's one of the good ones." She stopped. "Do *not* tell him I said that." Caz turned back to watching the powerhouse, leaving her with her thoughts.

Caz was right. Gwyn had never harmed her. Her fear of him had become a fear for Zach, not just of him becoming Heroka, but of him becoming more different that he already was. She remembered being persecuted growing up for being different, for not being white. She'd run from that too, just as she'd run from Gwyn. She'd left her home behind and tried to become white by denying her own heritage, her own culture. Denying who she was. Just as she was trying to deny who Zach was.

"Shit," Caz said, straightening up. The young Heroka's eyes were distant, and Kate knew she was focusing on her link with Rizzo. "So much for your plan. She just smashed the control panel." She paused. "They're leaving."

A few minutes later, the powerhouse door opened. Kate gasped at the four things that emerged first. "God, what are those?"

"Windigos," Ed said, as casually as a guide pointing out a moose to a tourist.

Zach, Gwyn, and Jonas appeared next, trailed by Leiddia holding a gun. Jonas lurched along more than walked, as if he wasn't in control of his own body. Leiddia marched Gwyn and Zach to the nearest Tainchel vehicle. Jonas got in the front seat beside her.

"Looks like she's saved Jonas for something special," Caz said. "Wonder where she's going?"

Kate knew, with a certainty that surprised her. "You said it yourself. The lake's the center of all this. She's going to the top of the dam."

"Shit!" Caz whispered. "They'll drive right by us. Duck."

They huddled down, Kate praying the spruces were thick enough to hide them. The SUV roared by without slowing, heading back to the main road, followed by the windigos, on foot and moving with astonishing speed. The bizarre parade disappeared down the road.

"Guess they weren't hungry," Caz said, peering after them. A small gray form scampered across the snow-covered parking lot toward them. Caz picked up Rizzo and gave him a kiss. "Good work, Rizz."

"Ok, let's go," Kate said, anxious to follow Zach and his captors.

"Wait," Caz said. She held out Rizzo for Kate. "Here."

"What? Why?" she said, eyeing the rat, but making no move to accept him.

"I've got an idea, but it means I have to leave you guys. If you have Rizzo, I'll be able to track you and catch up later."

"What are you planning?" she asked, warily taking Rizzo into her gloved hands.

Caz frowned. "Gonna work the problem from the other end. You just keep track of Gwyn and Zach." Leaving the cover of the trees, she ran across the parking lot to the remaining Tainchel car. She fumbled under the steering column until the engine roared to life. A few moments later, she drove by them on the way back to the road, waving as she passed.

Ed stood up. "C'mon. Let's get my truck." He started up the road.

Kate looked down at Rizzo cradled in her hand. Leiddia had guns, super strength, and man-eating monsters. They had a rat. Rizzo wiggled his nose at her. Shaking her head, she tucked the rat into her inside pocket and headed after Ed.

HIS HANDS CUFFED BEHIND HIM, Gwyn could only glare at Leiddia as she opened the door of the SUV. She'd stopped just inside the gates on the top of the dam. Jonas stood zombie-like behind her. She'd left the four windigos outside the gates, presumably as guards. Gwyn had tried calling any wolves in the area, but once again, they seemed to have disappeared.

Leiddia pulled Zach from the car. He still hadn't said a word. He followed commands from Leiddia but otherwise seemed completely unresponsive.

"Get out, Gwyn," she said, motioning with Jonas's gun. A knife sheath now dangled from her belt. A length of cord lay draped over her left shoulder.

He got out slowly. If he could knock her down, land a kick to her head....

As if she'd read his mind, she took a step back and aimed the gun at Zach. "He'll be the first to die, Gwyn, so be good. Now turn around." Pushing him against the car, she used the cord to tightly bind his already cuffed hands. Why was she doing that?

"Hold onto Gwyn's arm, Zach," Leiddia ordered. "Gwyn, get moving." She pointed along the dam road.

He started walking, Zach a silent companion on his arm, Jonas lurching like a Frankenstein marionette beside them. As they passed the Quonset hut, he saw Gelert's body, lying broken and bloody on the snow, and the emptiness that had been growing inside him, the emptiness that his pawakan had once filled, opened like a chasm beneath him. He dropped to his knees, overcome by grief.

Leiddia stopped beside him, looking at Gelert. "Hurts, doesn't it?" she said, as she hauled him to his feet again. "It'll get worse, trust me." She pushed him forward.

"What happened to you, Cat? Why are you doing this?" he asked, as he started walking again. How could this be the woman he loved?

She gave a mirthless laugh. "You left me—that's what happened. If you'd stuck around, lover boy, I doubt we'd all be here right now."

He listened with a growing horror as she related how her search for a new pawakan had brought her under the control of the Great Lynxes.

"You weren't here for me, Gwyn, so I tried to find my own way. And I got lost."

"You could've fought it," he said, trying to convince himself. Was he really the reason this had happened to her? The reason that Zach was in danger?

"Think so?" she said sadly. "Well, you'll soon have a chance to prove you're stronger than me. You've just lost your pawakan, and you're about to meet the Lynxes. Just like I did."

"Screw you," he said, but a fear rose in him, from that empty space where Gelert used to live. What would *he* do to fill that emptiness? Would he become like Leiddia?

They walked in silence, then she suddenly spoke again. "I'm sorry about Gelert, Gwyn. Mary, too. I really am. Sorry for all of it."

He looked back at her. Tears streamed down her face even as she held the gun on him. She seemed to be two different people, one the Leiddia he loved, the other a puppet of these spirits. "So what do they want?" he asked. "These Great Lynxes of yours?"

"To come home. They ruled the deep places of our world once, until the Trickster killed them."

He glanced at Zach, remembering Zach's story of his strange dream companion. "Trickster?"

"Nanabush. Wisakejack. Iktomi. Raven. Coyote," she said. "He has lots of names. Ages ago, the Lynxes killed his brother, the Wolf, so he killed them, exiling them to the Spirit World where they've stayed...until now."

He didn't like the part about the Wolf dying. "So how do they plan to come back?"

"By recreating the events that led to their exile, with some changes—like them not dying this time around. And the first step is to bring the main players together again—here in this place." She nodded at the lake's dark surface rippling below them.

"What's so special about this place?"

"Comdowtah, the shaman I met in my dream, the son of a bitch who so kindly introduced me to the Lynxes—his remains lie at the bottom of this lake. Turns out he's the guy who formed the Waubunowin, the Society of the Dawn, centuries ago."

"Ed says they dealt in dark magics."

She shrugged. "Let's just say they didn't shy away from dealing with the less-friendly spirits, like the Lynxes. As near as I can figure it, the lake rising above Comdowtah's grave awakened his spirit, and through him, the connection he had with the Lynxes. They rule the deep places. As that water rises, so does their power in this world. Thus our side trip to the control room."

They'd reached the middle of the dam, where an observation platform extended twenty yards along the dam and twenty yards out over the lake. "Far enough. Sit down," she said, motioning with the gun. Gwyn sat, Zach beside him, their backs against the safety barrier on the lake side of the road just before the observation platform started. Jonas stood unmoving to their right.

"What do you mean by 'the main players'?" Gwyn asked.

She stared out at the dark water as if listening to something. "The Lynxes, the Wolf, and the Trickster."

He considered that. "So the Lynxes are out there," he said, nodding at the lake, "and I'm guessing I'm substituting for the Wolf. So where's the Trickster?"

She looked at him, tears running down her cheeks. "He's right beside you."

Startled, he turned to Zach, who still sat head down and silent. "Zach, what's she talking about?" he asked, not expecting any response. To his surprise, Zach turned to him.

But it wasn't Zach who grinned mischief at him with those sightless eyes. "Sorry, wolf brother," spoke a voice from Zach's mouth that wasn't Zach. "Zach can't come to the phone right now. Can I take a message?"

ZACH LISTENED TO THE EXCHANGE between Leiddia and Gwyn, felt his head lift, heard Wisakejack speak through his mouth. Through it all, he remained a prisoner in his own body, an audience for his senses, but unable to control even the smallest of his actions.

He remembered the coyote walking into him at the dam and disappearing, He remembered his strange dream of the lake and the animals. At the time, he'd wondered where Wisakejack had gone. Now he knew.

The spirit was inside him.

Yes, came a familiar voice in his head. *Yes, I am.*

You lied. About the vision quest, Zach replied in his thoughts.

Little brother, which part of Trickster *do you not understand?*

But why make me do a vision quest? You said it would give me my spirit guide.

And so it did. I was in your dream, wasn't I? Count yourself lucky. You met other spirits last night. The Lynxes. The Windigo. You could've ended up with them.

Zach shuddered. *But I've dreamed of you lots of times. Why didn't you become my spirit guide before?*

I didn't just need to be your spirit guide—I needed to come through.

Through?

To your world. If you're gonna survive what's coming, you need me with you all the time, not just in your dreams. And the situation wasn't right until this morning.

What do you mean?

The Spirit World and your world are getting closer, remember? And guess where they're closest?

The dam lake! You needed me near the dam lake, so you could come through.

Yep.

Zach fell silent. The end of the world was coming, and he'd just helped the ancient spirit who'd destroyed the world once before cross over into this world at the exact place where the catastrophe was supposed to occur again.

Zach, you do know that I can hear what you're thinking, right?

Zach stiffened, a chill running up his spine. *Let me go!* he screamed in his head.

Think about that last dream.

Tell me!

Can't, little brother. You have to figure it out yourself. It's the only way you'll truly understand.

Understand what?

Who you are.

KATE SAT BESIDE ED as he drove, trying to ignore Rizzo wriggling inside her parka. Leiddia's tire tracks and the windigo footprints in the snow were easy enough to follow. She was definitely heading for the top of the dam.

As the road emerged from the trees, the dam and its captured lake swung into view. Once again, she had the sensation of the massive dam as a fragile thing, incapable of containing the lake should it decide that it no longer wished to be contained.

Decide? *Yes,* she thought, finally accepting what she'd known but refused to believe since the strange voices whispered to her that day on the dam. She didn't know if Ed's Great Lynxes were real, but something was down there under that black surface.

You are no longer needed in this.

She pulled the trank gun and the dart case from her parka. Nine darts lay inside the case: three black, three red, three green. Black for unconscious—heavy-duty tranks. Green for safety—to prevent a Heroka from shifting. And red for danger—to force a Heroka to shift.

She selected a black dart, then hesitated. She'd get just one shot. Would a single trank bring Leiddia down?

Or....

Returning the black dart to the case, she selected a red dart, hesitated for a breath, and then loaded it into the gun. She shoved the case and gun back into her pocket. No longer needed? She'd see about that.

They were close enough now to spot Leiddia's stolen SUV parked inside the gate. On this side, the four windigos shambled back and forth, blocking access to the dam road. Ed stopped the truck fifty yards back.

Up until now, her only thought had been to follow Zach. Now what? "Can you shoot them?" she asked.

Ed shrugged. "Bullets can't touch them."

She swallowed. "So now what?"

Ed considered the windigos. "We get to Leiddia. She's the one we need to stop."

"Great idea. But how do we get by those things?"

He shifted the truck back into gear. "We drive through them."

"Through?"

"Through."

Ed floored the gas, and she braced herself as the truck bore down on the windigos and the gate.

"**WHAT HAVE YOU DONE** with Zach?" Gwyn snarled at Leiddia, as a Zach who wasn't Zach grinned at him.

"He's still in there," she said, staring sadly down at the boy. "The Trickster's riding him, just like the Lynxes are riding me. Zach's a pawn in this as much as I am."

Gwyn's feeling of helplessness grew. Until now, he'd told himself that at least Zach was still safe, that somehow he'd find a way to protect his son. But he'd already failed. Zach had been in danger all along.

Zach's grin faded. His eyes closed, and his chin fell to his chest again.

Gwyn swallowed. "Will he be okay?"

She shrugged. "Define 'okay.' Once this starts, nothing's going to be the same anymore."

"What do you mean? What's going to happen?"

"The end of the world, as we know it. Thing is, the Lynxes aren't fond of humans. So before they return to this world, they want to make some improvements. Like wiping people off the face of it. Just leave the animals."

He stared up at her. "Destroy all human life?" She couldn't mean that.

She nodded, tears flowing again.

"How?"

"A flood." She nodded at the dam lake. "When the Trickster killed the Lynxes all those ages ago, he released their power over the deep waters, triggering a flood that destroyed our world. Yeah, that really happened, just not the Noah version. Our big reunion here means all the original powers are in place to do it again. The Lynxes will open a path to the Spirit World, right here in this lake, and all the waters of creation will flow from their realm into ours. The Trickster recreated the world after the first flood. This time the Lynxes will do the redesign. And it won't include people."

"That'll kill the animals too."

She shook her head. "Remember wondering where all the animals around here have gone? The Lynxes opened the way into the Spirit World for them. When the flood begins, animals around the world will sense the coming danger and escape into the Spirit World. But humans can't sense the way. There'll be no escape for them."

"So how does this flood start?"

She knelt beside him, her face sad. "That's where you and Zach come in."

The empty place inside him yawned wider, and the chill from that place spread through him. "What do you mean?"

"The Lynxes don't have the strength to open the portal for the flood themselves—the lake isn't deep enough. They need the power of the Trickster and the Wolf. Two ways they can get that power. Door number one, you and Zach willingly offer the power of the spirits you carry, adding it to the Lynxes' power."

"And door number two?" he asked, already knowing the answer.

"The Lynxes release your power the same way the Trickster released the power that caused the original flood—by killing two powerful spirits. Only this time, the spirits that die will be the Wolf and the Trickster—you and Zach." She stroked his hair, sobbing hard now. "So you've got a choice, lover."

"Nice choice. Help destroy the world or die along with my son," he said, looking at Zach.

"Not the world—just the humans," she said. "They'll open a path for the Heroka as well as the animals. We can sense the way. You can save our race and all our totem species." She stood, looking down on him. "C'mon, Gwyn. You hate humans for what they've done to this world, to our animals, to us. They killed your woman. They killed Mitch. They killed Gelert. They hunt our animals. They hunt *us!* Without humans, our totem animals would flourish again. The full strength of the Heroka would return. We could rule this world."

He swallowed, hating himself for having the same thoughts. Suddenly, Leiddia stared out at the lake. "And you don't have much time to decide. It's beginning."

He started to ask what she meant, but then he felt it. Sensed it the way animals sense a change in the weather. Smelled it rolling in from the lake. Tasted it on the breeze.

A change was coming, hard and fast.

Chapter 47

Changes

THE TRUCK WAS TWENTY YARDS from the windigos when the change hit. Ed smelled it even before it arrived. It smelled the way spring wafts up wet and earthy from the ground after a long hard winter, or the way a thunderstorm hangs coppery in the air before it breaks.

It smelled old, this change. But young too. Old and young, all mixed up together. A smell from a world that no longer existed. Except suddenly, on that day, in that moment, on top of a dam in his little town, it did exist.

The change boiled up from the center of the lake and rolled across the black water like a wave, washing away the stain of the here and now, leaving in its place a world born when time began, a world that would live until time ended.

The change rushed toward him and Kate as their truck rushed toward the windigos. The dam disappeared, replaced by a huge ridge of land separating a dark lake from a deep valley below. The dam road became a rutted trail atop that ridge. The maintenance buildings on the dam became shrub-tufted hillocks. And everywhere, winter gray vanished, replaced by spring green of a dark primal forest of trees taller and thicker than Ed had ever dreamed possible.

The change hit the security gate. The gate vanished, because steel didn't exist in the Spirit World.

The change hit the truck. The truck vanished, because trucks didn't exist in the Spirit World. Ed had already begun to brake, but the change still left him and Kate absurdly hurtling through the air as if seated on invisible chairs until gravity caught up to velocity and sent them tumbling head over heels.

A snow bank, rapidly melting in the sudden primal spring, cushioned their landing. Groaning, Ed struggled to his feet, his back screaming at him. They'd landed about fifteen yards past the windigos. As one, the creatures turned toward them.

"Ed," Kate said, backing away.

"I liked you boys better in my stories," he muttered, backing away as well. Something felt different. He looked down at his feet. He now wore deerskin moccasins, the kind that his *nookomis*, his grandmother, used to make for him. He also wore deerskin leggings and a beautiful beaded jacket. At his waist, a beaded medicine pouch hung from a strap around his shoulder.

Kate was also now dressed in traditional garb. She grabbed at her side where a similar pouch now hung. "My dart gun! It's gone!"

No guns in the Spirit World, he thought, knowing in his heart more than his mind where they now were. The windigos were ten paces away. "I think we should run," he said. But even as he said it, each windigo threw back its head and gave an ear-piercing whistle that froze Ed's feet to the spot.

"Ed?!" Kate cried. "I can't move my legs."

As the cold crawled up his own legs, his hand brushed against the medicine pouch. Jamming his hand inside, he pulled out a bone awl, a fire-flint, a stone, and a burnt piece of birch bark.

He smiled, remembering a story he'd often retold to his class. "Looks like someone's already used you," he said, tossing the birch bark away. "Well, let's try this." Returning everything to the pouch except for the bone awl, he began a singsong chant in Ojibwe, slapping his empty hand against his thigh to substitute for the drumbeat.

The windigos were five paces away. As they raised their arms, reaching for him and Kate, he hurled the awl down in front of them.

Immediately, huge thorn bushes sprang up, twice their height, thick and twisted, with needle spikes as long as his arm. The bushes raced across the ridge in both directions toward each edge, forming an impenetrable barrier cutting off the windigos from him and Kate. On the far side of the thorn forest, the windigos cried out in pain and frustration.

Kate stared, mouth open. "What just happened?"

He grinned at her. "Magic."

"How?"

"I think we're in the Spirit World."

She nodded slowly, surprising him. "It looks like the vision I had on top of the dam. Old and young, all mixed together. And magic works here?"

He nodded, hooking a thumb at the thorn barrier proudly. "Not bad for an old man, eh?"

But the thorns also cut off any escape for them. They looked along the ridge. He could make out a cluster of figures in the middle on the lake side, one with long black hair—Leiddia. Gwyn and Zach would be with her for sure.

"Guess we go this way," Kate said, her face grim.

They set out along the ridge. Kate slapped her own medicine pouch as they walked. "My dart gun. It was right *here*." She shoved a hand into the pouch. "What the hell is this? Lunch?" She held out the contents—three blackberries, three mint leaves, and three plump strawberries.

Ed shrugged. "Medicine."

"How do you know?"

"It came out of a medicine pouch. Don't know how we can use it, though." Unlike what he'd found in his own pouch, Kate's items didn't trigger any story memory.

Kate jumped as Rizzo poked his head out of a pocket on her dress. "Great, no gun but I still have a rat. What are we going to do?"

"We'll think of something," he replied, hoping he sounded more confident than he felt. What could an unarmed woman and an old man do against a murderous shapeshifter and two powerful malevolent spirits like the Lynxes?

Mahigan had told Gwyn that the Wolf and Boy were somehow involved. He remembered Zach's fascination with Wisakejack. Only one story he knew of with a wolf, the Lynxes and the Trickster.

And that one had not ended well.

DESPITE HIS SITUATION, as the change rolled over them, the wolf part of Gwyn reveled in the scents carried on the sudden summer air, remembering the smell of this primal world from his encounters with Mahigan. The silver wolf had said that the Spirit World was drawing closer. Gwyn guessed it had finally arrived.

The roadside barrier against which he and Zach had been sitting was now a row of low boulders. The dam had become a huge ridge of land, dropping away sharply on this side to the lake that still lay below, darker and even more foreboding.

Beside them, the observation platform had shifted into a rocky promontory jutting out from the ridge, a stone finger suspended over the water, pointing to the middle of the lake.

Zach remained asleep or in a trance beside him, but was now dressed in a deerskin jacket, decorated with beadwork. Gwyn looked down to find that he wore a similar outfit.

He now understood why Leiddia had tied his hands earlier. The cold metal of the handcuffs had disappeared, but the ropes remained. He tested his bonds. With time, he could break loose, but she'd done a good job.

Leiddia stood beside them, staring out over the lake. She was dressed in a calf-length leather dress, also decorated with intricate beadwork patterns, patterns that seemed to shift whenever he stared at them. She no longer had Jonas's gun. He figured guns didn't exist in the Spirit World anymore than handcuffs. The knife sheath still hung at her side. Jonas stood statue-like beside her, dressed in ill-fitting animal skins, as oblivious to this transformed world as was Zach.

Leiddia spun to stare back along the ridge. He followed her gaze. Where the dam road gates had stood in the real world, a brown-green barrier now rose. On this side of that barrier, two figures approached. His Heroka eyes could make them out, even at this distance. Ed and Kate. Where was Caz?

"Your friends may be few, wolf man," Leiddia said, smiling a sad smile, "but they are loyal."

"Leiddia, please. Leave them out of this."

"I'm sorry, Gwyn. I don't have a choice." She turned to Jonas and raised a hand. The man fell to his knees, quivering, and a now-familiar transformation began, as Jonas's humanity slowly disappeared inside a flesh-eating monster.

Gwyn watched with mixed emotions. Jonas had killed Gelert, but he wouldn't wish this fate on anyone. "Another windigo? Ed and Kate didn't seem to have much trouble with the ones you left behind."

"Fool. We stand now in the Spirit World." The words were echoey, distant, and strangely formed. They came from Leiddia, but the voice was not hers, as if two voices had spoken together from her mouth, forming words using human lips and tongue that were strange to them. He swallowed, realizing that he'd just heard the Lynxes themselves. Her eyes had changed, too, from Leiddia's deep green to a sickly yellow. With the shift to the Spirit World, had Leiddia lost the last piece of control over her own body?

"So what's the difference—" He stopped.

Jonas was already larger than the other windigos—and he was still growing. This creature was enormous, four times the height of a man, with claws as long as Gwyn's arm and a face that seemed all twisted mouth and pointed teeth. Its transformation complete, the thing threw back its head, and a whistling shriek sliced into Gwyn's skull like a jagged blade of ice, freezing his muscles so that he had to fight to even breathe.

The Lynxes laughed at him through Leiddia's mouth. "Not *a* windigo, dog. *The* Windigo. The Hunger-That-Walks itself. None can stand before it." Lynxes-as-Leiddia whistled three discordant notes. The Windigo dropped to its knees before her, and the ground trembled. She pointed along the ridge toward Ed and Kate. "You hunger for meat. There it walks. Kill. Feed. But whatever you do, stop the old man. He has shaman power."

The thing gave another shriek, then lumbered away. When Leiddia spoke again, it was with her own voice, her eyes green again and wet. "I'm sorry, Gwyn."

"IT'S HUGE," Kate said, as she realized the size of the monster bearing down on them. "Why's it so much bigger than the others?"

"It's the Windigo Spirit itself," Ed answered. "That's what killed my Mary."

We can't stop that thing, she thought. *We're going to die.* The Windigo was covering twenty feet with every stride.

Reaching into his medicine pouch, Ed pulled out a gray stone. He began to chant again, slapping his free hand against his leg in a matching rhythm. The Windigo was only five giant strides away. Four strides. Three....

"Ed!" she cried.

Ed flung the stone down in front of the monster. The entire ridge shook, throwing her, Ed, and the creature to the ground. Somewhere deep below them, a rumbling grew. Where the stone had landed, the earth suddenly cracked open. Out of this crack, rock walls erupted skyward on all sides of the creature, surrounding and enclosing it completely.

The rumbling died. She blinked. A miniature mountain, thirty feet high, now stood where the Windigo had been.

Ed grinned. "Told you we'd think of something."

She hugged him. "*You* thought of something." *I'm just along for the ride*, she thought.

He nodded at the figures in the distance. "Let's go."

They'd gone only twenty yards when a sharp cracking sound from behind made them turn. The flint-gray mountain was now a glassy blue. The cracking grew louder. Dark lines appeared in the rock, running in zigzags up and down its surface. The lines widened into fissures, and then with a final ear-splitting crack, the mountain exploded into a thousand pieces, pelting her and Ed with pieces of rock. No, not rock, she realized, as a piece shattered on the ground in front of her. The Windigo had turned the stone to ice.

Released, the creature threw back its great head and gave another piercing shriek, freezing Kate where she stood. Unable to move, she could only watch as the Windigo clambered from the shattered remains of its prison.

Ed shook her, breaking the thing's spell. "Run," he said, his voice calm. "I'll deal with this."

"Ed, you can't—"

"This thing killed my Mary. I will face it." His smile, so incongruous with the situation, was calm and certain. He pushed her behind him and stepped forward. "Now go. Save your son."

With one last glance at the monster, she turned and ran, ashamed to be running, knowing that she was leaving Ed to die. Behind her, he began to chant. The Windigo shrieked in reply, but she didn't look back. She kept running, toward the figures ahead, toward her son.

She could see them more clearly now. Leiddia stood looking out over the water. Gwyn sat on the ground, his hands behind him. Zach sat beside him, head down and strangely still, as if waiting for something.

Waiting for what? For his mother to save him? How? No weapon. No ideas. No hope.

She ran on. It didn't matter. She wouldn't quit until she was dead. *Dead. Yeah, Kate. that's the spirit*, she thought. *Think positive.*

Think positive. Think about better times. Think about Zach and their life together.

She slowed. A memory surfaced from somewhere, of a morning when Zach was eight, when he'd brought her a tower of building blocks he'd made, wanting to know their colors. She'd told him, and he'd nodded. She still remembered that little nod, that simple tiny movement. Remembered how it had terrified her, as if he'd already known the colors, as if her blind child could somehow see. She remembered those colors to this day.

Black, green, red.

Colors....

She stopped, remembering other colors. The colors of the darts for the gun she no longer carried. Black, green, red.

She examined again the contents of her medicine pouch. Blackberries, mint leaves, strawberries. Black, green, red.

"Okay," she muttered to unseen spirits, "I get it. But now what?"

An idea formed. But she'd need help. Pulling Rizzo from her pocket, she held him on her palm at eye level. Rizzo stared back, whiskers twitching. "Caz," she said, feeling ridiculous talking to a rat. "I need your help. If you can hear me, have Rizzo turn in a circle, clockwise."

Her faint hope began to die as Rizzo just sat there, sniffing. Suddenly, he lowered his head and twirled once on her palm, looked at her and then repeated the motion.

"Okay," she said, hoping Rizzo hadn't just wanted some exercise, "here's the situation and what I need you to do. I mean, what I need Rizzo to do." She talked, while Rizzo stared and twitched. "Got it?" she asked when finished. Rizzo did another spin on her palm.

Returning Rizzo to her pocket, she began walking again. At least she now had a plan. A plan, she reflected, that depended on a handful of fruit and instant messaging via a rat.

FOR A MOMENT, Ed feared the Windigo would chase after Kate. He had no idea what Kate could do against Leiddia, but he knew she was a mother defending her son. She had strength within her. He could feel it. All he could do was to give her the chance to find that strength.

But the Windigo ignored Kate's retreating figure and instead stopped to tower over Ed. "Old one, I smell your blood. I smell your flesh. I fed from one of your own five nights past."

Ed looked up at the thing that had killed his Mary. "She was my granddaughter."

The spirit's cry was like chalk screeching on a blackboard in that residential school classroom so many years ago. A sound of coldness and pain and loss. It was laughing at him, laughing just as the priests and nuns had laughed at his ways, his culture, his people. "She died. Now you die."

Just as the ways of my people are dying, he thought. He shook his head, trying to dislodge the old memories. "No. This time it will be different."

The Windigo laughed again. "Different? Yes. She was girl—you are man. She was young—you are old. She ran—you stand. Different, yes—but the same. Same blood. Same death. You will feed my hunger as she did."

Chanting under his breath, Ed pulled the final item from his medicine pouch. "Yeah? Well, feed on this." Raising his arm, he flung the flint down before him.

The earth shook, throwing him to the ground again, and sending the Windigo stumbling backward. A huge fissure ripped the ground between them. Within the fissure, a raging river appeared, wider and deeper than the Windigo could cross, racing from the lake to his right across the entire ridge until it plunged finally over the opposite edge in a roaring cataract into the valley below.

He called to the Windigo standing on the far side. "Looks like you're going to stay hungry. I'm emptying your masters' lake, too. They aren't going to be very happy with you."

The Windigo swung its misshapen head from left to right, considering the river. Then, reaching down, it dipped a single, spidery, claw-tipped finger into the water. The river's flow slowed, grew sluggish, until finally it stopped completely, each wave frozen in mid-ripple.

The Windigo stepped onto the frozen surface, the ice screaming crackling protests under its weight. "Now, old man, I eat."

His medicine pouch empty, Ed watched it approach, trying to remember any other magic. But Midewewin magic was mostly of the healing variety. Not too much in the way of attacking giant flesh-eating monsters. He knew a few spells to ward off diseases and a couple more to stop someone sending bad medicine your way. He chanted every one he could remember.

The Windigo stepped onto his side of the river. It reached for him. And stopped. It tried again, but it couldn't seem to get any closer. Ed grinned. Something he'd done had thrown up some protections.

The Windigo stared at him with eyes as cold and deep as the dark lake but utterly empty. Two voids that would never be filled. "Old man, do you know what drew me to your town? To your granddaughter?"

Ed felt a chill he couldn't explain. "Don't know. Don't care."

"You know. You care. The hunger of the whites called me. The same hunger that stole your land, your culture, your way of life. Your world."

Ed shook his head, but that chill inside him grew, flowing out of some deep darkness within. For a moment, he was back in that classroom in the residential school.

The Windigo stepped closer. "Your people are empty. The whites have stolen it all. But the whites are empty too. Their hunger is as mine—it can never be satisfied. They will always want more. And they will take it from you, the little you have left."

"We survive," Ed said, but the coldness had spread. His skin was ice. He couldn't move his legs.

"Like your granddaughter survived?" the Windigo whistled. "The emptiness of her death fills you. Not just her death. Your people are dying. Why resist me? Join your granddaughter."

The Windigo stepped even closer, and Ed realized that his magical protections had disappeared, sucked into this black hole inside him. A shaman couldn't hold healing barriers in place when he was sick inside himself. His legs gave out. He collapsed on the ground, unable to move.

As he lay there, a calm settled on him. His death was near. Soon, he would be walking the Spirit Road. Perhaps his granddaughter, Mary, would be his guide. He could almost see Mary now, walking toward him, with others behind her.

The Windigo stretched out a clawed hand, reaching for him.

CHAPTER 48

FULL CIRCLE

STILL STRUGGLING WITH HIS BONDS, Gwyn watched as Leiddia stared unmoving at the black lake. Something was happening. When they'd arrived, the inky waters had lain as still as death. But moments before, the water had begun to swirl counterclockwise around a point directly below the rocky promontory that jutted out over the lake. A giant whirlpool was being born.

Suddenly, breaking off from her contemplation of the rotating waters, she turned and strode rapidly across the narrow ridge to the valley on its far side. Before the change had hit this place, that side had overlooked the spillway.

She considered the valley for a moment, then returned to glare down at him with the yellow eyes of the Lynxes. "What have you done, wolf spawn?" the Lynxes snarled from her mouth. "No water flows out, yet the lake does not deepen. The whirlpool does not grow. Our *power* does not grow."

"Good to know," he growled. "Wish I could take credit."

Ignoring him, she stared out over the lake again, her gaze unfocused, searching for something that even Heroka eyes could not find.

She nodded slowly. "Ah! We see! Clever little Otter."

ON A BANK OF THE RIVER about a mile upstream from where it flowed into the dam lake, Caz was hard at work, although that might have escaped the casual observer. She was sitting on a rock, smoking a cigarette. But her mind was working overtime keeping her construction crew organized.

Thirty-two beavers and muskrats were busily putting the final additions on a dam that stretched the narrowest width of river she'd been able to find in the short amount of time she knew she had. Large stands of birch trees on both banks—stands that were no longer standing—had finalized her choice.

She lit another cigarette from her last one. Her lighter had disappeared on the shift to the Spirit World, but her smokes had remained. Apparently, the Spirit World approved of tobacco.

"A bit more on the left, Chip Tooth," she called to the nearest beaver, watching as Chip Tooth's family responded by patting more mud into a final gap between the logs. Standing up on the rock, she surveyed her totem's handiwork. Behind the dam upriver, the water was already pooling, spilling over the river's banks and flooding the low-lying bush. The river's flow toward the lake had slowed to a trickle.

"Not bad, my sisters and brothers. Not bad at all." She thought of Mitch. "Play to your strengths, you said." She grinned. "Otter girl to the rescue."

"BAD NEWS? I hope," Gwyn said, as the thing that looked like Leiddia stared across the lake.

"Caz has dammed up the river," she said.

Caz! She was safe. He smiled. He'd underestimated the kid. "Guess I haven't run out of friends yet." Then he realized she'd spoken in Leiddia's voice, and when she turned to him, he could see Leiddia again behind her green eyes, eyes that were crying.

"You soon will, I'm afraid," she said, and a chill ran down his spine. Gazing over the lake again, she began chanting in a singsong voice and tapping her foot. With each tap, a drumbeat rhythm trembled through the ground.

IT SLEPT. Deep in another lake in this world of spirits, it slept, a spirit itself, its great heart shuddering out the slow rumbling rhythm it had kept for eons.

Until now.

Now, another rhythm reached down through these dark waters, a distant thrumming calling it from cold slumber. The slow throb of its heart quickened until it finally matched the drumbeat rhythm.

An eye as tall as a man winked open. Flames flickered inside. The other eye opened. A huge horned head rose from where it had lain buried in the lake bottom, throwing ages of primordial muck into swirling eddies. The head kept rising, pulling a long, black, scaled body undulating serpentine behind it.

Its masters were calling.

"WHAT HAVE YOU done?" Gwyn asked.

Blinking, she shook her head, as if coming out of a trance. She looked at him, yellow-eyed again. "We have killed the Otter," said the Lynxes' voices.

"You're lying," he said, fearing she wasn't, fearing for Caz.

"We are not." She came to stand over him. "We gave you a choice before: join us and rule the world—or die with your son."

"Yeah, I remember. Hard conversation to forget," he said, staring up at the thing who looked like Leiddia. "The lake's not deep enough yet, is it? You're not strong enough on your own. That's why you still need the power that Zach and I hold."

Anger flared in her yellow eyes, but then they flickered back to green. She knelt beside him, his Cat once more. "Gwyn, if you don't surrender the power you hold, they'll just take it anyway, by killing you and Zach."

He looked at her. He shook his head. "I won't kill billions of people."

"They're going to die anyway. My way, you save Zach, yourself. The Heroka, too."

He looked at Zach who still sat head down, chin on his chest, seemingly oblivious to the life-and-death scene playing out around him. His people, his only son—or the human race that hunted his wolves, hunted his kind. Hunted him. The race that had killed Stelle, Mitch, Gelert. He swallowed and shook his head. "Even then. It's too high a price."

The green of her eyes flowed to yellow again, and the hardness returned to the lines in her face. "Then watch the price you choose to pay, Wolf," the Lynxes said from Leiddia's mouth. She drew the knife from the sheath that hung from her belt. The blade was long and carved from some black stone, its surface uneven, its edge jagged and sharp. "Watch your son die." She stepped toward Zach.

Twisting to his side, Gwyn tried to stand, but she kicked his legs out from under him, and he fell hard to the ground. Grabbing Zach by the collar of his deerskin jacket, she began to drag him toward the rocky promontory that jutted out over the lake below.

"Hey!"

The voice came from behind Leiddia. She halted and looked back. Gwyn, too, turned to the sound of the voice.

Ten paces away, in traditional Cree dress, stood Kate, unarmed and empty-handed, her eyes locked on Leiddia. "Take your goddam hands off my son."

Gwyn stared at Kate. What was she doing? The Lynxes laughed through Leiddia's mouth. "The Wolf is bound, trapped in human form, woman. The old shaman has fallen to the Hunger that Walks…."

Gwyn swallowed. Was that true? Was Ed dead?

Throwing Zach to the ground, Leiddia advanced on Kate, knife in hand. "… and you have no weapons. How can you stop us?"

Kate shrugged. "Rat."

Leiddia stopped. Her body stiffened, and she screamed in pain. Dropping the knife, she clawed at the inside of her thighs, shrieking.

Kate rushed past Leiddia to Gwyn. He opened his lips to ask what was happening, but before he could speak, she shoved something red into his mouth.

"Chew!" she cried. "Chew and swallow! Fast!" She pushed his jaw up, forcing him to bite down on whatever she'd put in his mouth.

Strawberries. The freshest, juiciest, sweetest strawberries he'd ever tasted. He chewed and swallowed even as he wondered if Kate had gone mad. How could this help?

Then he felt it. Felt the power returning.

The power to change.

The Lynxes were screaming at Leiddia in her mind, but at that moment, her only concern was stopping the white-hot agony in her crotch. Insane with pain, she fell to the ground and yanked up her deerskin skirt. Blood flowed from a dozen places where flesh had been torn from her thighs—torn by a rat who still clung to her by its teeth.

Screaming in fury, she snatched at her tormentor, but the rat dropped to the ground and scampered away. With her jaw clenched against the pain, Leiddia leapt up.

Zach lay unmoving where she'd dropped him, but Kate crouched beside Gwyn. She had untied his hands, and he seemed to be convulsing. His limbs twitched, and their proportions seemed strange. Leiddia stopped mid-step, recognizing the beginnings of a shift. She had seconds before she faced Gwyn in his powerful wolf form.

The Lynxes cried out in her mind. *The Wolf is coming!*

Kind of figured that out.

Kill them both! The Wolf and the Boy. Kill them where they lie. Kill them now!

The spirits again reasserted their power over her. Her legs moved against her will, walking her forward. Stooping to retrieve the stone knife, she looked up. Beside Kate, a huge black wolf was beginning to rise.

We're too late, she warned. *Gwyn's too tough to kill in wolf form.*

Take the Boy to the spot above the whirlpool. Kill him there, and we will gain the power he holds within himself but does not realize. Then we will deal with the Wolf.

Powerless to resist, she ran to Zach. As she bent to lift the boy, out of the corner of her eye, she saw something moving toward her. She turned, hoping it was Gwyn, hoping that the wolf would stop the Lynxes. That he'd stop *her*.

But no, it wasn't Gwyn. The black wolf was still struggling to stand, thirty yards away. The remnant of the Tainchel drug must have been slowing his shift. No, it wasn't Gwyn.

It was Kate. Alone, unarmed, running to stop her. The mother defending her pup to the death.

In her mind, Leiddia heard the command from the Lynxes, the command to kill this woman, to plunge the stone knife deep into Kate's chest. She tried to resist that command, but even as she screamed silently inside, she felt her hand obey, watched the knife blade flash forward, straight toward Kate's heart.

But the little part of Leiddia that was still Leiddia begged her hand for mercy. Her hand twitched, dropping slightly, and slid sharp and cruel into Kate's belly, not her heart. Gasping, Kate slumped to the ground.

Still holding the knife that now dripped Kate's blood, Leiddia grabbed Zach and slung him over her shoulder. Sobbing but enslaved to the Lynxes, she ran toward the end of the rocky promontory that overhung the lake.

And there, she knew, the Lynxes would make her slit this boy's throat.

KATE LAY BLEEDING on the ground, clutching her belly, feeling her own warm blood seep from her, watching Leiddia carry her son away. She knew she was probably going to die. But the seconds she'd bought Zach might be enough. Enough for Gwyn to finish his change. Enough to save Zach.

Perhaps she deserved to die. She was to blame for all of this, for bringing Zach into it, for bringing him to this town. She, not Gwyn, had been the greatest danger to Zach.

And as she lay there, a coldness filling her as her life drained away, she reflected with an odd calm that she'd come full circle. Her journey, which had begun with fleeing Gwyn when he turned into a wolf, had ended with her helping him become one.

And in the end, as in the beginning, her purpose had remained the same. To save her son.

Something black appeared above her. The head of a huge wolf, the creature she had feared for so long. With a shaking hand slick with her blood, she touched its thick ruff as the wolf licked her face and whined. She looked into its gray eyes. Something passed between them then, human and Heroka. Something like understanding, long delayed.

"Go," she said to the wolf who had been her lover. "Save our son."

She watched the beast bound away. Pain and weakness took her. She closed her eyes.

CHAPTER 49

AND THE BLIND SHALL SEE

LEIDDIA LOWERED ZACH GENTLY to the rocky ground, just steps from the tip of the promontory that jutted out over the lake. The boy lay unmoving, eyes closed, showing no sign of consciousness. For that, she was grateful. It would make it easier. She wouldn't have to look into his eyes when the Lynxes made her kill him. Not like with his mother. With shaking hands, she used her dress to wipe Kate's blood from the stone knife.

The skies had darkened, and a chill wind now blew. A thunderhead cloud now hung above the lake, strange lightnings flashing purple inside it. Directly under the rocky tip, the whirlpool had grown, its outer edges now roaring past below her with frightening power and speed, sloping downward to a blackness in its center, fifty feet lower than the surface of the lake.

When the Lynxes gained their full power, that vortex would consume the entire lake. The blackness deep in its center would open, and through that dark hole, the waters of creation would flow from the Spirit World to flood the Earth.

But the lake did not deepen. The Lynxes' power did not grow. They needed the power of Wisakejack. They needed this boy to die. And if the boy's power was not enough, then the Wolf would die next. Speaking of which....

A feral snarl made her turn. A huge black wolf stood beside where Kate Morgan lay. Baring its teeth, it lowered its great head and bounded toward her.

Step aside, child, cried the Lynxes. With a sob, she dropped the stone knife beside Zach, as she felt the Lynxes reach for that place in her mind where a Heroka began a shift. Once, her animal form had been a black leopard. After her encounter with the Lynxes, a shift meant becoming a windigo. But in this place, once she shifted, she knew Gwyn would face something altogether different.

Two somethings.

She felt the change begin. At least, she wouldn't be the one who killed him.

SAVE THE PUP.

That single thought flamed inside Wolf Gwyn, burning all else from his lupine brain as he raced up the sloping finger of rock. Near the promontory's edge, the pup lay deathly still, but Gwyn sensed life in the boy. Beside the boy, a woman stood naked, her leather dress on the ground. He knew her smell, had loved her in his man form. Overlaid on her human image, he saw another—feline and black. He remembered her animal shape as he remembered her smell, but this shape was different, larger, stranger.

The woman faded, replaced entirely by this creature. The thing shimmered, separated, became two. The wolf stopped, head lowered, teeth bared at the twin creatures that now stood between him and the pup.

Their feline heads sprouted horns like the tufted ears of a lynx, making them resemble huge black cats. But they were as large as bears, with flickering yellow eyes and slick shiny skin. He sniffed. They smelled like fish.

Simultaneously, both creatures opened fanged mouths and gave, not a feline roar, but a near-human scream, like the cry of a drowning man just before he slipped beneath the surface for the last time. It was the sound of despair, echoing in the empty place inside him where Gelert used to live.

The Lynxes' words sounded in his mind. *Wolf Brother, join us. Together we will rule the humans' world.*

No, he growled.

Then you will die. You cannot defeat us. You do not have the strength. Do you not feel the emptiness inside where your pawakan's spirit once dwelt?

He felt the truth of their words. He could not win. But still he advanced. He would not leave his pup to die. Where were his wolf brothers and sisters? He had called to them to join him. An image flashed in his mind from the pack leader—a huge wall of thorns stretching across the entrance to this ridge of land, blocking access for the wolves.

Your totem cannot reach you. You are alone. Your pawakan is dead. You are empty. Empty and alone.

So be it, he said.

The nearest Lynx leapt at him. Dodging its jaws, he charged past it, attacking instead the second creature circling to his other side. Surprised, it left its throat exposed for a split second. Lunging at this opening, his wolf jaws snapped closed, missing the Lynx's throat but closing on thick muscle between its neck and shoulder. He sunk his teeth deep and pulled with all of his strength, tearing free a chunk of black, greasy flesh. The Lynx screeched and twisted away.

He bounded past them to the human child. He sniffed at the pup and smelled warm breath. Still alive then. Perhaps there was hope—

He turned back too late. They were already on him. The needle teeth of one Lynx sank into his left shoulder while the second creature bit deep into his right flank. Snarling, he snapped at the front beast. It jumped back. He turned on the second Lynx, only to have the first beast attack again, its jaws closing on the back of his thick neck. With a pained roar, he tried to shake his attackers off, but they both held fast. Rolling, he managed to dislodge them, but as soon as he stood, they attacked again.

He fought on, but he was weakening. Bleeding from a dozen wounds, his right rear leg unable to bear weight, he snapped at one Lynx and missed. The other leapt into the opening and seized him in its jaws. Raising him into the air as easily as if he were a stuffed animal, it slammed him down hard onto the rock.

Bones cracked. Pain flooded his brain. His hold on his shift slipped away. His wolf body spasmed. Seconds later, he lay naked and bleeding, human again and too weak to move, a few paces from Zach.

The Lynxes shimmered, melted together, and became the naked form of Leiddia. She was crying, and her words were almost lost in the rising roar of the whirlpool below. "Maintaining that shift takes too much of their power, so they're going to let me finish this. Nice of them, eh?" She turned to where she'd dropped the stone knife. "Sorry, Gwyn."

His pain meant nothing to him. All that mattered was that he'd failed. Zach would die. They all would die.

A movement caught his eye. He managed to turn his head.

Zach, his blind eyes closed, his young face grim and determined, was crawling towards him.

SINCE WAKING TO FIND HIMSELF a prisoner of the Wisakejack spirit now inside him, Zach had struggled desperately—and failed—to regain control of his own body. He could still hear, and so had been very aware of his mother's bravery in helping Gwyn shift. He'd heard her cry out when she attacked Leiddia, but hadn't heard her voice since and was horribly worried for her.

He was aware, too, of Gwyn's battle against the Great Lynxes, of his defeat, and of the rapidly approaching deaths of himself and everyone that he loved. Not to mention the end of the world.

Through it all, as he lay trapped in his own body, he'd spent his time thinking, both because this was the only activity available to him and because he had a lot to think about. He had started by thinking about Wisakejack's last words to him.

Think about the dream. Figure out who you are.

So he'd thought about his strange waking dream of the lake and the procession of animals bowing before him. He thought and thought, but was still no further along when Leiddia laid him down on cold hard stone above the sound of roaring waters, just before her change to the Lynxes.

As Gwyn battled the twin spirits, Zach gave up trying to wrestle a meaning from that dream. Instead, he turned to the question that had bothered him right from the start, from that first dream where he'd met Wisakejack.

Why *him*?

Why had powerful spirits needed *him* to play a part in the end of the world? And no matter how he came at the question, he kept arriving at the same unpleasant answer.

He was *different*.

But how? He was blind. He was part Heroka. So what?

His vision quest was supposed to have answered his questions. Instead, it had almost got him killed. He hadn't even been able to finish it. And his only dream since then had been that strange dream with all the animals that he couldn't figure out.

He stopped. His only dream since....

That dream had been his vision. *That* had been his answer. An answer he still didn't understand.

Back to square one. Back to trying to understand what a bunch of animals bowing down to him meant. Too bad he wasn't a Heroka or Wisakejack. They had the power to talk to animals.

They had the *power*....

And in that moment, he knew what his vision meant. He knew what his power was and what he had to do to release it. Yes, he was different. The problem was that he wasn't quite different *enough*.

Not yet.

He ordered his hand to move and was not surprised in the least when, this time, it obeyed. He felt on the cold stone until he found where Leiddia had dropped her knife. He did not cry out as he cut himself. Dropping the knife, he crawled toward the sounds of Gwyn's labored breathing.

LEIDDIA IGNORED ZACH as he crawled to Gwyn. The boy could do nothing. None of them could do anything to stop this. It would soon be over. She picked up the stone knife, unable to stop herself, a slave to the Lynxes.

Below the rocky finger on which she stood, the whirlpool roared, but it had not grown. The Lynxes still needed the power of the spirits of Wisakejack and Mahigan to open the portal completely. And to release those spirits, Gwyn and Zach had to die.

Knife in hand, she walked slowly to where Zach now hugged a naked, bleeding Gwyn. Standing over them, tears streaming down her face, she looked down at the man she still loved and the young boy who was his son. *Which one?* she sobbed.

The Boy! Kill the Boy! the Lynxes screamed. *Take Wisakejack's power, and give us our revenge.*

Shaking, she grabbed Zach by his deerskin jacket and hauled him to his feet. His sleeves were up, his forearms smeared in blood. *From cradling Gwyn,* she thought.

No. A crisscross of ragged cuts covered Zach's arms. Where had they come from? She looked at the knife. Blood stained the blade. But she'd wiped it clean of Kate's blood before. Then she noticed something else.

The boy's Mark of the Heroka had changed. The silver glow was gone, and he now showed the image of a gray timber wolf. The mark of a full Heroka. Understanding dawned on her.

He's mixed his blood with Gwyn's, she cried to the Lynxes.

Kill him now! they screamed.

Zach's sightless eyes found hers. "So you want my power? No problem. Here, take this."

She felt the tug of the Lynxes in her head. Her knife hand started toward his throat. Too late. He kicked her hard in the chest. She flew backward, landing hard on the stony ground near the promontory's tip. Her breath whooshed out, and she lay gasping.

He stood grinning at her. "Nice outfit, by the way, naked lady."

She jumped up, snarling. "Child," spoke the Lynxes through her, "even as a Heroka, you are no match for us."

Zach's smile became sly. "But can you fight all of my totem animals, too?"

"You show the totem of Mahigan. No wolf can reach us here. You are all alone, child." Driven by the Lynxes, she advanced on the boy, gripping the knife.

Zach chuckled. "They don't call me Trickster for nothing, lady." His Mark shimmered. His wolf image vanished, replaced by the image of a large hawk.

Again, understanding came too late to the Lynxes who controlled her—understanding of who it was they faced.

She spun around, eyes skyward, a wing beat before the first eagle slammed into her.

CHAPTER 50

LETTING GO

WHEN ZACH HAD RUBBED the blood from Gwyn's wounds into the cuts he'd made on his own arms, he expected his transformation to a Heroka to be both sudden and painful.

Instead, he'd experienced a strange calm and a slowly building feeling of strength. And a sense of wonder. Wonder at the beauty of this world. Wonder at the immense and intricate web of life of which he was now aware. Everything *was* connected. And he was part of it.

Reaching into that web, he had tugged a thread here, a cord there, calling to the creatures of creation, to all that could hear him, to all that could reach him. And they had answered.

The eagle had been the first. He'd felt a soft brush of an alien mind, a sense of vertigo, then he was seeing—actually *seeing*—through the eyes of the great bird as it plummeted toward a rocky finger jutting above a roaring whirlpool of black water. Two humans faced each other there—a young boy and a naked woman. He sent the bird on its dive toward the woman, and then stepped out of its mind. He had others to summon.

Eagles and ospreys, hawks and owls. Robins and jays, sparrows and swallows. Bats, too. All creatures that flew, feathered and leathered, were answering his call and descending in a cloud of wings on the rocky promontory.

For his was the power to talk to *all* animals. For he was the Recreator. He was the Trickster.

He was Wisakejack.

LEIDDIA LAY STUNNED, gasping in a breath. The eagle's attack had sent her tumbling head over heels to the end of the rocky finger and almost over the edge. She struggled shakily to her feet, only to fall again, screaming as an osprey raked her shoulder.

The air about her swarmed with winged creatures. She stood again, lashing out wildly with her knife as they dove at her. Bleeding from a myriad of wounds from talons and beaks, she snatched a look at the whirlpool below. It had not grown, and the dark portal at its center was still not large enough to open.

Even through her pain, the part of her that was still Leiddia rejoiced at this. If the Lynxes couldn't open the portal, the world would live. The boy would live. Gwyn would live.

But the Lynxes still controlled her. Perhaps they heard her thoughts, for the chill voices spoke again in her head. *Fight them off! Hold them back!*

I can't! she cried, slashing at her attackers again and again.

A moment longer—

A moment longer for what? What were they waiting for?

And then she felt it.

CAZ'S FIRST CLUE that something was very wrong came from her construction crew. One moment, she was trying to check in with Rizzo. The next, she was leaping to her feet as a rush of panic from the beavers swept over her like a tidal wave, in tandem with the sound of their tails slapping the water, signaling danger. En masse, on either shore, the animals were scrambling out of their newly formed pool. She looked upriver.

A wall of water thirty feet high was barreling downstream straight for the beaver dam, overflowing both banks, ripping up towering pines and spitting them ahead of it like toothpicks.

With only seconds to escape, she turned and ran, scrambling up the forest slope from the riverbank, grabbing at any handhold, desperately trying to reach high ground. To her frightened ears, the roar of the oncoming torrent seemed like the bellow of a hungry beast.

Still far from safety at the top of the rise, she chanced a look back. The wall of water was an eye blink from the dam. And in that eye blink, in the sunlight that seeped through the canopy of trees, a cavernous mouth emerged from the wave, rimmed with teeth the length of her arm and framed by a reptilian face with eyes of fire under two curving black horns.

The mouth and the wave smashed into the dam, and the structure exploded. She dove behind a nearby pine as a spinning log slammed into the ground where she'd been standing. She peeked around the tree.

The previously contained water, carrying the swirling wreckage of her dam, rushed downstream toward her, overflowing the banks of the river, drowning the small valley where she crouched on its way to refill the dam lake. Upstream, something long and black undulated in the opposite direction just below the water's surface. Helpless and unable to escape to high ground now, she could only cling to the tree where she huddled, hoping she could hang on when the wave hit.

ZACH'S BLINDNESS-HONED ears caught it first—a slowly rising rumble like an approaching thunderstorm. As his winged squadrons battled Leiddia on the rocky ledge, he linked with a red-tailed hawk soaring above and, through its eyes, looked across the lake.

A wall of water surged down the river that flowed into the lake. At the river's mouth, the wall turned as if with a mind of its own and roared along the far shore toward them. In only moments, fed by the river's release, the whirlpool grew to a swirling maelstrom of black water and white froth, encompassing almost the entire lake and filling the air with a thundering roar. The rocky finger where he stood facing Leiddia trembled, and below, the rising waters seemed to reach for him, as if they were trying to drag him down into the growing vortex.

The black circle in the whirlpool's center was now fifty feet across and eighty feet below the surface of the lake. Its darkness had paled, becoming almost translucent. Gaps appeared and disappeared in that circle, and through those gaps, the hawk's eyes glimpsed, not deeper water or the lake bottom, but cityscapes and landscapes from another world. Zach's world. Earth.

A familiar voice sounded in his mind. *The lake's rising again!* Wisakejack cried. *The Lynxes' power is growing.*

What is that thing? Zach cried, his mind still focused on the center of the whirlpool.

The door to your world. And it's opening. When it does, the Lynxes will send the waters of the Spirit World from here to flood the Earth.

How can I stop it?

Keep attacking her. She's their link to your world and to the doorway.

Zach turned the hawk's eyes back to Leiddia. Above her and around her, his winged army swirled and whirled, dipped and dove at her. Naked and bleeding, she now held a dead eagle by its feet in one hand and the stone knife in the other, and flailed at her attackers with both. But with each attack, she seemed to be slowing. Maybe they had a chance. Maybe....

But something was happening. Around Leiddia, a yellow, undulating glow had appeared. It grew and coalesced until it enveloped her like a watery bubble. A horned owl, diving at her, struck that bubble and bounced off, falling to lie crumpled on the stony ground, as if it had flown into a window.

Oops, Wisakejack said.

What's happening? I can't get at her anymore.

Yeah. The lake has deepened. The Lynxes' power is almost full. They're shielding her.

What can we do? No reply came. *Wisakejack!* Zach cried.

Nothing, little brother. There's nothing we can do. Wisakejack's voice carried a sadness that Zach had never heard in it before.

What?! What do you mean?

I mean it's the end of the world.

No! Zach screamed.

AFTER THE LYNXES slammed him to the ground, Gwyn had lain where he'd fallen, naked and in human form once more, helpless in his broken body and wracked by pain, forced to merely watch events unfold. He watched as Zach mixed their blood together. He watched as his son and his feathered forces battled Leiddia. In Zach's face, Gwyn recognized the distant look of a Heroka linked with his totem, and knew that his blind son was now seeing through the birds that filled the air. In Leiddia's eyes, he saw no trace of the woman he loved, only the cold yellow glint of the Lynxes.

And he felt the sudden surge of power in the whirlpool below, and saw the strange bubble form around Leiddia. She now stood ten paces away, almost at the very tip of the promontory, encased in a sickly yellow glow and protected from the attacks of Zach's squadrons. Zach faced her, his brow furrowed, his young face slick with sweat. Above, in a slate-gray sky, an immense thunderhead cloud towered to the heavens, hanging black and low over the whirlpool, lightnings flashing gold and purple inside it as the first drops of rain fell cold on his naked skin.

He felt something else—the touch of another mind, a touch he recognized.

Grandson, Mahigan said.

He remembered their meetings and felt ashamed. *Grandfather, forgive me. I should have listened. I've failed my totem. I've failed my son.*

The Lynxes offered you power. You rejected it. They offered the lives of the humans that you think you hate. This you rejected too. I forgive you, grandson. You make me proud.

He swallowed, still ashamed. *What's happening?*

The lake rises, and with it, the power of the Lynxes. Soon the doorway in this lake will open, and these waters will flood your world. Once opened, that doorway cannot be closed.

What can I do?

You must stop her, grandson. She is the link for the Lynxes to your world. Only with her death will the portal close. It is down to you.

My body is broken.

I will heal you.

I'm too weak.

You are stronger than you know. I will give you my strength, for now you are ready to receive it.

He felt a warmth rise in him, as if Mahigan's words had struck a fire in his heart. Each breath he took fanned its flames higher, until it blazed within him, lighting and warming the empty place inside that had been dark and cold since Gelert's death.

In that place, he felt the touch of all the wolves in the world. He pulled their strength into him, too, feeding on the vitality of his kind. He felt his broken bones knit, his pain disappear. He was young again, stronger than he'd ever been. He was not *a* wolf.

He was *the* Wolf.

He stood, feeling Mahigan's power still growing in him. *The lake!* cried Mahigan. *The doorway opens!*

With a snarl, he charged Leiddia.

The birds above must have sensed him first, for Zach turned as he rushed by. "Dad!" Zach called. Then he was past Zach and a step from Leiddia.

He struck the barrier.

Wet. Cold. The cold of deep water. A cold that plunged its fingers into him, trying to squeeze the air from his lungs. He couldn't breathe. He was drowning.

But Mahigan's strength pounded in his heart, burned through his veins, fired his muscles. Calling on that strength, he fought like a drowning man clawing for the surface. He pushed for his son, for his friends, for all the people in the world. His vision began to dim. White lights flashed staccato before his eyes. Summoning all his strength, he gave one final push.

And broke through. He gasped in a breath as the barrier fell around him and around Leiddia like a cold hard rain. He caught a glimpse of her still-yellow eyes opened wide in surprise before he slammed into her with all his new strength, lifting her off the ground and sending her hurtling backward through the air toward the tip of the precipice.

She landed hard, then bounced and rolled. Screeching, she slid toward the edge, flailing helplessly at the rocky ground. Her legs slipped over the edge, but one hand found some purchase. She hung there, clinging by that one hand. The hand began to slip. She screamed.

In that scream, it was Leiddia's voice he heard, Leiddia's face he saw. He flung himself toward the woman he still loved. He landed and slid. His hand flashed out, catching her wrist just as she fell.

Her weight dragged him to the edge and almost over, but he held on hard, scrabbling for a hold on the bare surface with his free hand. He lay there holding tight to her wrist as she swung beneath him.

The world changed. Again.

Suddenly, his and Leiddia's modern day clothes were back. And so was the cold. Cold on his face, cold in his nose from each breath, cold where his hand now clung to the edge of the safety wall of the observation platform. He looked over his shoulder. Winter was back. The dam was back. The real world was back.

"Gwyn!" Leiddia called.

He looked down to where she hung in his grip. Her deep green eyes stared back into his. The yellow glint had vanished. The hard coldness of the Lynxes had melted from her face. Her lips, the lips he knew so well, twitched up in a tiny smile. "You did it, Dog. You beat them."

"Leiddia?"

She nodded. "The Lynxes are gone. Back to the Spirit World."

But below them, the whirlpool still roared like an injured beast. The blackness in its center had become a translucent gray through which came a clear view of another world—impossibly tall trees, a dark lake, a towering thunderhead cloud. The Spirit World they had just left. Even as he stared, the scene became clearer still.

The voice of Mahigan sounded again in his mind. *The doorway is opening. Once open, it cannot be closed.*

But the Lynxes are gone—

She is the link for the Lynxes to your world. Only with her death will the doorway close.

No!

"Gwyn," Leiddia called.

He looked down at her. Her eyes were wet, and her smile was now a sad one. "Gwyn, you have to let go."

"No!"

"It's the only way, lover boy. You did good. Now you have to finish it."

"I won't kill you."

"It's me or the rest of the world. Not really much of a decision."

He tightened his grip. Below them, the last touch of gray was fading from the doorway. The Spirit World showed through with almost perfect clarity. He felt cold water strike his face. A rain seemed to be falling, falling *up*, rising from the opening.

Grandson, the portal! The flood begins!

"Cat," he cried. "I love you."

She laughed. "And you know what? I finally believe you." She looked down at her free hand. So did he. Only it wasn't her hand anymore. It was now the huge paw of a black leopard, her shifted form, its claws extended.

"No, Cat. Don't!"

She was crying now. "I love you, too, Dog." The paw flashed up. The claws sank into the back of his hand that gripped her wrist. His muscles spasmed. His hand opened.

She fell.

HE LAY THERE, waiting for it to end, praying for it to end. But it wouldn't. Leiddia kept falling. Falling and falling and falling, as if the water she fell toward was impossibly distant. He lay there, watching her fall, the memory of her face as he let go burning him, as he knew it would burn him forever.

Finally, she struck. The portal shuddered.

Leiddia disappeared.

The view of the Spirit World through the doorway darkened, faded, vanished, until finally the original blackness of the portal at the bottom of the whirlpool returned. The swirling maelstrom in the lake slowed. The wind's roar dropped to a whisper.

He struggled shakily to his feet. He felt a touch on his arm. Zach stood beside him.

"Is it over?" Zach asked.

All he could do was nod. He felt numb, dead inside.

Zach suddenly cried out. "The birds!"

He looked up. The birds that had filled the sky above them were now forming a rapidly expanding circle, as they flew madly away from the lake in all directions. Flew until they stopped. He blinked. Every bird had stopped flying—in mid wing-beat—and now hung immobile in the sky, frozen in flight.

Below, the scene in the lake lay frozen too, the waves poised in mid-swell, the walls of the whirlpool caught in mid-whirl and sloping unmoving down to the black surface far below that now lay mirror-still. No sound came, no air moved, as if the world was holding its breath, waiting....

Waiting for what?

Then he sensed it. "Get back!" he cried. With a roar, the lake suddenly exploded upward, like the hand of a watery giant, reaching for them. He leapt back from the edge, pulling Zach with him. The ground heaved, bouncing them on the observation platform like dice, threatening to throw them over the edge of the dam and down to whatever waited below.

And then it stopped. The roaring sound, the trembling ground, everything.

Standing on still-shaking legs, he helped Zach up. He walked back to the edge of the observation platform and looked down. The portal was gone. The whirlpool was gone. The dam lake lay below them once more, calm and strangely normal. It may have been his imagination, but the water didn't seem as black as it had before.

A flutter of wings brought his head around. A red-tailed hawk settled onto Zach's shoulder. As Gwyn looked at the bird, the realization truly struck him. His son was Heroka. His son was alive. The world was safe.

All it had taken was for the woman he loved to die.

The hawk's head swiveled to look back along the dam. Zach suddenly spun around to stare in the same direction, and Gwyn realized that he was seeing through the hawk's eyes.

"Mom?" Zach said, his voice a small and frightened thing.

Back where she had fought Leiddia, Kate Morgan lay on the snow-covered road. Lay slumped where she had fallen. Lay very still, a dark redness staining the snow around her.

"Mom!" Zach cried. Running to Kate, Zach dropped to the ground beside her still form. "Mom, Mom, Mom," he cried as he shook her. "Wake up, Mom."

Kneeling beside him, Gwyn gently pushed him aside. He opened Kate's blood-soaked parka. He listened for a heartbeat. He felt for a pulse. He looked at Zach. "Zach, I'm sorry."

Zach shook his head. "No. No, she can't be." He broke down then, throwing himself to lie sobbing on top of Kate's body.

Gwyn laid a hand on Zach's shoulder, attempting some small comfort, but the boy gave no indication of noticing him. Sirens sounded. Feeling numb, Gwyn looked back to the entrance to the top of the dam where two cruisers and an ambulance were driving through the gate. *Just in time*, he thought bitterly.

Ahead of the cruisers, two figures walked beside each other. One had hair that was long and gray, the other spiked and blue. A wave of relief swept over him. At least the price they had paid this day would not rise any higher.

CHAPTER 51

ONE LAST STORY

THAT NIGHT, ED AND VERA made up a bed for Zach on their couch. Gwyn did his best to comfort him, as did the others—Caz, Ed, Vera—but mostly Zach wanted to be left alone.

"Give him space, Gray Legs," Ed had said. "Let him grieve. This isn't something that you can fix."

Gwyn knew he was right, but he should have been able to do something for his own son. He felt helpless and more certain than ever that he wasn't fit to be a father. He checked in on Zach throughout the night, finding him awake every time. Whenever Gwyn asked if he could do anything, Zach would just shake his head.

As the eastern sky began to lighten, Gwyn found him still awake. He didn't think the boy had slept at all. But this time, when he asked if he could do something, Zach sat up and nodded. Gwyn sat down on the edge of the couch. "Sure. What is it?"

Zach hesitated, his head down. "I'd like…." He stopped. He swallowed. "I'd like Mom to be buried here. In Thunder Lake."

Last night, Gwyn and Ed had talked about sending Kate's body back to either Ottawa or to her family in Waskaganish. They'd postponed making a decision until they felt that Zach was ready to talk about it. Zach must have overheard them.

Gwyn wasn't sure what Kate's family would think, but he didn't really care. "Whatever you want."

"Thanks," Zach said quietly.

They both fell silent. "Can I ask why?" Gwyn asked after a moment.

Zach's brow creased. "Well, Mom left Waskaganish before I was born. She never went back. I don't know why she never did, but I wouldn't feel right taking her back there now. And Ottawa was just a place Mom ran away to. I don't think she was ever happy there."

Gwyn nodded. "I understand. But why here? Why Thunder Lake?"

Zach didn't answer right away. When he did, it was with a question. "She finally accepted you, didn't she? There at the end? Accepted you as a wolf? As a Heroka?"

Gwyn remembered the understanding that had passed unspoken between Kate and him in his wolf form after she'd helped him shift. "Yes. Yes, she did."

"Do you think that she would've accepted me as a Heroka? Understood the decision I made?"

Gwyn smiled. "Yes, I'm certain that she would have."

Zach nodded. "I think so too. So that's why I'd like this to be the place. I think this is where she finally figured out some stuff. About herself. About you. About me," he said. "And it's where she was a hero. She was a hero, right?"

"Yes. Yes, your mom was a hero."

Zach smiled a little at that. "And it's an important place to me, too. It's where I became a Heroka."

Zach's strange Mark had remained and continued to cycle between all animal totems of the Heroka. Zach had said he maintained his link with different animals, a link that let him see through those animals. Gwyn couldn't explain the strange Mark, but he was simply happy that Zach had gained something for what he had lost.

"And this is where I met you," Zach added, "so like I said, it's an important place to me, too." He turned his head toward Gwyn..

Now is when I should tell him, he thought. *Tell him that I want to be his father. That I'll always be there for him.* But all he did was nod. "I'll ask Ed if she can be buried here at the cemetery on the Rez," he said instead. "I'm sure he'll say yes. I'm sure he'll do the ceremony, too."

Zach looked at him with his blind eyes, as if waiting for him to say more. When he didn't, Zach said "Thanks," then rolled over on the couch.

Gwyn stood up and walked out, leaving the room, leaving his son alone, leaving so much unsaid between them.

THE NEXT EVENING, Gwyn stood with Caz and Zach in the small cemetery on the Rez as Ed led the ceremony for Kate's burial and the start of her journey on the Spirit Road. The early winter had suddenly retreated, and the snow that had covered the cemetery was now a mix of mud and slush. Vera, Bill

Thornton, Willie Burrell, and Bonnie and Joe Makademik joined them for the ceremony, and they all brought gifts to lay on her grave.

Quincy stood beside Zach. Once reunited with his master and with Zach's new Heroka abilities, the dog's recovery had been remarkable. But seeing the dog and Zach together made Gwyn miss Gelert even more. He had buried the great hound that morning in a secluded glen deep in the bush.

After Kate's ceremony, additional people began to arrive in preparation for the final stage in Mary Two Rivers's journey on the Spirit Road. Gwyn walked away as the mourners once again began to ring Mary's grave where flames still flickered feebly in the small pot from the fire lit four days ago. Caz and Zach followed him.

"You not staying for this?" Caz asked.

Gwyn shook his head. "I'm guessing that Heroka will be even less welcome here now, considering Leiddia's role in Mary's death."

Inside the circle, Ed, Vera, Charlie, and Elizabeth stood facing the grave. Vera was scanning the crowd. Her eyes fell on Gwyn, and she frowned. Stepping through the mourners, she strode toward him. Sighing, he steeled himself for a confrontation.

She stopped in front of him, hesitated, and then wrapped her arms around him in a hug. She stepped back. "Last night, with all that happened...." She glanced at Zach. "...I didn't get a chance to thank you, Gwyn. Thank you for finding who did it. Thank you for all of us, and for Mary." She looked down. "Ed tells me it wasn't her fault. Leiddia." She looked at him, tears in her eyes. "He's forgiven her. I don't know if I can."

"No," he said. "No, it wasn't Leiddia's fault. In the end, she gave her life to save us all."

She nodded. "I know you loved her. I know how horrible it must have been for you." She shook her head. "Anyway, I'm sorry."

He swallowed. "Thanks, Vera."

She hooked her arm through his. "C'mon. All of you. I want you to stand with the family. Mary would've wanted that."

Stunned, he let her lead him, Caz, and Zach to stand beside her inside the circle, oblivious to the whispers around them. Elizabeth smiled warmly, and even Charlie gave him a nod.

Ed winked at them and then stepped to the foot of Mary's grave to address the crowd. "This is the fourth day of our Mary's journey along the Spirit Road. The last day. Tonight, she reaches the Land of Souls, and so we gather here to say our last goodbye." He paused, as a little girl raised her hand. "Yes, Debbie?"

"What if she got lost?" Debbie asked.

Some people laughed quietly, and Ed smiled. "She could have, but I happen to know she found some help," he said. His eyes twinkled. "Let me tell you a story...."

I HAD A DREAM. In this dream, I stood in the Spirit World, beside a dark lake, much like the lake that the new dam has made, which has taken so much from us.

I felt a cold wind and heard a whistling shriek. I saw the Windigo spirit coming toward me, covering a hunting territory with every stride. The Windigo stopped, towering over me like the tallest jack pine.

"Old man," said the Windigo, "I am the Hunger that Walks. Hunger for land. For trees. For power. I have flooded your hunting grounds. I have chased away the animals. I have killed your Mary. And now I will kill you." It reached for me.

I tried to use my medicine, but I was frozen. I couldn't move. But then, the Windigo stopped. It stepped back, waving its hands like it was swatting flies. Then it fell to the ground, squirming as if tied in invisible ropes.

I turned. Many people stood behind me, men and women, young and old, all dressed in our traditional way. Some looked familiar. But one I knew for sure. I grabbed her in a hug. It was our Mary.

When I finally let her go, she introduced me. These people were our ancestors, going back generations. Mary had left the Spirit Road to stop the Windigo from hurting our town again. When she didn't show up in the Land of Souls, our ancestors sent out a hunting party. They found Mary, and together they followed the Windigo. When it attacked me, they used all their medicines, which had grown strong over hundreds of winters.

I thanked our ancestors and praised their strong medicine. We all knew what we must do next—cut out the Windigo's heart and burn it in a fire, sending its spirit back to the far North. Mary handed me a long knife, but I shook my head. "This thing took your life," I said. "You should be the one."

"Unless you're squeamish," someone called.

"I cut up my first moose when I was nine." Mary said, nodding at me. "My misoomish taught me."

I watched proudly as Mary walked to where the Windigo lay helpless, its eyes wide with fear. "Oh," she said, "I am *so* going to enjoy this."

ED PAUSED IN HIS STORY. "Maybe that's a good place to stop." The crowd laughed. "So that's how I know that our Mary reached her spirit home. And that, because of her, our town is safe again from the Windigo spirit. Now I'll let you say your goodbyes to Mary." He wiped his eyes. "I've already said mine."

As the mourners came up to talk to the family, Gwyn slipped away, motioning to Caz and Ed. Zach stayed behind, talking to Vera.

"So how *did* Jonas die?" Caz asked when they were out of earshot.

"Well, no giant hole in his chest like in Ed's story," Gwyn replied, "but the coroner *is* guessing massive heart attack." He wouldn't mourn Simon Jonas, but his death wouldn't bring back Gelert or Mitch, or any of those Jonas and the Tainchel had killed. He did wonder whether Jonas had any family. He'd check into that.

"How'd it go with Thornton this morning?" Caz asked.

"Apparently, I didn't give him enough credit," Gwyn said. "When Jonas showed up and started ordering people arrested, Thornton contacted CSIS. They told him that Jonas had gone rogue and to arrest him and his men. Too late to help us, though."

"So he's cancelled the warrants for us?"

Gwyn nodded.

"What did you tell him about what happened on the dam?" Ed asked.

He shrugged. "As little as possible. Seems that the shift to the Spirit World was restricted to where we were. The Tainchel and that Vickers guy from the dam project don't remember a thing after becoming windigos, so we're the only ones who know what happened up there. All Thornton's official story needs to explain are the killings, the damage in the control room, and Leiddia's... disappearance."

"So what *is* the official story?" Caz asked.

"That the original killings were animal attacks. That an environmental activist named Leiddia Barker killed several CSIS agents, trashed the control room. And that Leiddia, while attempting additional sabotage on top of the dam...." He took a breath. "...fell into the lake. Missing, presumed drowned. Given the CSIS involvement, I doubt any of this will hit the media."

"Seems unfair," Caz said. "I mean, I know Leiddia was the big bad in this, but in the end, she kind of saved the world."

Ed shook his head sadly. "I faced the Windigo. I could not resist it. Leiddia carried it inside her for months, and the Lynxes too. She had no choice in what she did."

"She had chances to kill all of us," Gwyn said quietly. "I think that we're alive because she fought those things as hard and as long as she could."

Vera was waving at Ed. "Talk to you later," he said, heading back to the group of mourners.

Gwyn looked at Caz. *Say something, dammit,* he thought. He cleared his throat. "Listen, Caz...."

The young Heroka turned to him. Rizzo poked his head out of the pocket of her hoodie, his ears perked up as well.

"I mean, what I wanted to say, is…you know, about what you did…." He stopped again. *God, I suck at this.*

"God, you suck at this," she said with a grin. He glared at her, and she laughed. "Sorry. Please stumble on."

He laughed himself, then sighed. "Look, I wanted to say that you did good. I was ready to give you hell for running off, but you figured it out about Leiddia, then saved Kate. And your move with the beaver dam gave us enough time to stop the Lynxes. So, anyway, I just wanted to say that I'm proud of you."

Caz reddened and looked down. She gave a little smile and kicked at the ground with one boot. "Thanks," she said quietly.

"And, look, I know you weren't big on Mitch's idea, but I'd like to become your guardian. I mean, I'm not sure where I'll be living, because I can't go back—"

"Okay," Caz said, still kicking the ground, but now with a bigger smile.

"—to Cil y Blaidd. Wait, what did you say?"

Caz laughed. "I said okay."

"Oh," he said, then grinned. "Okay. Great." He moved to hug her.

She stepped back. "Two conditions. One, we don't hug."

He put up his hands. "Right. No hugs. And the other condition?"

She nodded to where Zach stood with Quincy inside a small grove of trees at the edge of the cemetery. "Go talk to your son."

ZACH SAT ON A ROCK with Quincy, watching from a distance as the last of the mourners paid their respects to Mary Two Rivers. He sat watching and sorting through his feelings. Some of those feelings were terrible and sad, while others were happier. The terrible and sad ones were about his mom. The happier ones included having Quincy by his side again and having their bond stronger than ever now that he was Heroka.

His feelings about being a Heroka were mostly happy ones. For one thing, he could see. Well, he could see whatever the animals and birds he linked with saw, which meant a lot of different color variations, but that was still cool, especially being able to get a bird's-eye view of the world, literally.

But some of his feelings of being a Heroka were scary. He didn't know what it would mean to him. He didn't know what his real totem was, or what he would shift into. Or even if he could shift. He guessed that Quincy was his pawakan, but he wanted to ask Gwyn about that. He wanted to ask Gwyn so many things.

But mostly, he wanted to ask if Gwyn was going to be his father. And that, he decided, was his scariest feeling of all.

"So ask him," came a voice from above his head.

He looked up through Quincy's eyes. Wisakejack was sitting on a branch in a tree. He jumped down, landing lightly, then stood up, grinning as always.

"I thought you'd gone away," Zach said, surprised at how happy he was to see the spirit.

"What? Leave without saying goodbye to my little brother?"

"Well, the doorway is closed, so I figured you'd returned to the Spirit World."

"Not yet, but soon. Our worlds are moving apart again."

Zach swallowed. "So, I'll never see you again?"

Wisakejack tilted his head, coyote-like. "Would that be so bad?"

Zach nodded. He'd lost enough from his life already.

Wisakejack's face softened. "Well, never's a long time. And I *am* your spirit guide. Assuming you trust me now."

"Trust the Trickster? No way," Zach said, grinning.

Wisakejack grinned back. "Smart kid." He took Zach into a warm hug. "Take care, little brother. I'm proud of you. Oh, and you can keep your cool jacket." He turned to leave.

"Wisakejack?" Zach called, a final question in his mind.

The spirit stopped and turned back. "Yeah?"

"Why me?" Zach asked. "I mean, did you come to me in my dreams because the Lynxes had picked me? Or did the Lynxes pick me because you came to me?"

Wisakejack rubbed his chin. "Now *that* is a good question." With one last grin, he slipped into the dark forest and disappeared.

"Remind me," Zach said to Quincy, "why am I going to miss him?"

Footsteps were approaching. He turned and watched through Quincy's eyes as Gwyn walked up to them.

"Hi," Gwyn said.

"Hi." Zach swallowed. Oh, god! He had so many questions, but he didn't know how to start. What should he say? What should he ask first?

"Zach," Gwyn said, "I want to be your father, if you'll let me."

Staring at his father through his dog's eyes, hearing those words, Zach realized that of all the questions in his head, only one had really mattered. He threw himself at Gwyn, and they stood there, hugging each other, father and son.

LATER, AS THE LAST of the mourners had left, Gwyn asked Ed to drive Caz and Zach back to the store. "I'll walk back. There's something I need to do."

He watched Zach walk out of the cemetery flanked by Quincy and Caz. *I'll be there for him, Cat,* he thought, remembering his promise to Leiddia. *Caz, too. I'll teach them how to be one of us. And I'll make sure Zach never forgets you, Kate.*

And he would keep them safe. He hadn't mentioned his fears to Caz or Zach, but he doubted the Tainchel had died with Jonas, which meant they were all still in danger. Somebody in CSIS had been tracking either Caz or Mitch. He'd start there, and he wouldn't stop until he'd tracked down whatever remained of the shadowy organization.

But first....

He turned and looked into the dark forest. He felt the touch again. He'd felt it when he arrived at the cemetery, and again when Ed told his story. It was close now and growing closer.

He waited.

A moment later, a large male timber wolf padded from the bush to stand before him. The wolf was larger than most, its coat a silvery gray, speckled with white and black. He reached for its mind. And smiled.

Kneeling down, he ran his hand through the wolf's thick ruff. The wolf licked his face. "You'll do," he whispered. Standing, he left the cemetery, the silver wolf at his side.

KATE MORGAN leaned against a jack pine that was larger and taller than any jack pine had a right to be. She'd been walking through this dark forest since last night, and now stood at the edge of a path winding west through these trees. She had no idea how she had come to be here. She began to cry. She didn't want to be here. She wanted to go home.

Home.

The thought called like a soft voice, pulling her. And then she realized that it *was* a voice, a voice telling her she must follow this path she was on, for this was the Spirit Road, the path that would lead her home. As it spoke, the path before her began to glow slightly. But the voice brought warnings, too—warnings of the dangers in this journey.

You will be afraid, but you must walk alone.
You will be hungry, but you must eat alone.
You will be tired, but you must sleep alone—

"Actually, no, you won't. Not this time," a voice said from the forest. Kate jumped as a young Ojibwe woman stepped from behind a tree. Her face seemed familiar. She'd seen it in a photograph in another world, in another time. "Hi, Kate," the woman said. "I'm Mary."

Kate swallowed. "Can you help me? I'm trying to go home."

Smiling, Mary took Kate's hand in hers. "Don't worry. I know the way."

Together, hand in hand, Mary and Kate stepped onto the glowing path that was the Spirit Road and disappeared into the tall, dark forest.

Author's Notes

"When we understand each other's stories, we understand everything a little better—even ourselves."

—*Someplace to be Flying*, Charles de Lint

I'm including this afterword primarily to address a fear I had about writing this book. I'll cover some other items here, too, but that is my main reason for this section. But before I can get into that, I need to first talk about this tale's genesis.

On the Origin of this Book

The first story I wrote (and sold) professionally was the novelette "Spirit Dance." In it, we first meet the Heroka, as well as Gwyn Blaidd, Gelert, Ed Two Rivers, Michelle Ducharmes, and the Tainchel. We (and Gwyn) also first meet Leiddia Barker in that story, which takes place five years before the events in this book. "Spirit Dance" was my first professional sale. It appeared in the anthology, *Tesseracts6* in 1997, was a finalist for the Aurora Award in 1998, and won the Aurora Award in 2001 when it was translated into French. It's been republished seven times in English and translated another sixteen times. Yes, the story totally rocks, and you should check it out (details at the end of this afterword).

I always planned to revisit the world and characters of "Spirit Dance," so when I finally decided to write my first novel, continuing Gwyn's story was an obvious choice.

On Writing About Another Culture

Now to my fear about writing this book. I'm a white male of European descent (English, Welsh, Irish) who is writing about Cree and Ojibwe culture, traditions, and beliefs. Any author who writes about a current culture other than their own risks being accused of cultural appropriation.

That risk is even greater if the writer belongs to the majority that has tradi-tionally held power in their society and is writing about a minority group in that society. It becomes greater still when that majority has oppressed that mi-nority for nearly a quarter of a millennium, as we have oppressed the First Na-tions people since we first arrived in their land. My ancestors stole their land, broke treaty after treaty, and introduced programs and policies consciously de-signed to destroy their rich and unique culture and way of life.

Perhaps the most egregious wrong perpetrated against our First Nations was the residential school system mentioned by Ed in this book, in which the Canadian gov-ernment and various churches engaged in a premeditated program and formal policy of cultural genocide. The publicly stated goal was to assimilate the "Indian" into Ca-nadian society (meaning white European culture), but the program was designed (in a federal minister's own words in the 1920's) "to kill the Indian in the child."

The residential school system involved the *forced* removal of First Nations children as young as six years old from their parents and homes, and their *mandatory and permanent* residence at boarding schools funded by the federal government and run by various Christian churches including the Roman Cath-olic, Anglican, Methodist, United, and Presbyterian. The abuses perpetrated on First Nations children in residential schools have been documented by the survivors of the system—thousands of cases of horrific physical, mental, and sexual abuse. The system began in 1892 and didn't end until over a century later when the last school run by the federal government closed in 1996.

Amazingly and thankfully, despite the sad history of residential schools and continued government and cultural oppression, our indigenous people have persevered in finding ways to carry on their traditions and to bring their rich heritage to new generations, refusing to have their culture relegated to the past.

If you would like to learn more about this shameful chapter in Canada's his-tory, I'd recommend Basil H. Johnston's book, *Indian School Days*, which relates his personal experiences in a residential school. Johnston is an Ojibwe writer, storyteller, language teacher, and scholar, and has received the Order of Ontar-io and Honorary Doctorates from the University of Toronto. His other books were also a wonderful research source for this novel (see bibliography). I'd also point you to the film "Unrepentant: Kevin Annett and Canada's Genocide," which is available on YouTube. I would also recommend the "Truth and Rec-onciliation" website at http://www.trc.ca.

Additional atrocities continue to be revealed, including the recent exposure of federal research experiments in various communities and residential schools where our government subjected First Nations people to forced malnutrition to study the effects.

So, yes, I'm a tad paranoid that I, as a white man of British descent writing a story that draws from the storytelling traditions and culture of the Cree and Ojibwe, might be accused of cultural appropriation.

I could respond by simply saying that if a writer must only write about characters who are the same as themselves and solely of their own culture, then literature would be a dull and anaemic creature. Shakespeare was not a Danish prince, nor Robert Louis Stephenson a peg-legged pirate. Bram Stoker was not a vampire, nor Isaac Asimov a robot. J. K. Rowling is not an adolescent boy wizard, and Stephen King is not a homicidal car or teenage girl with telekinetic powers.

But I'd be dodging the issue. So first, let me explain *why* I was drawn to Cree and Ojibwe traditions and stories for this book.

It started with my shapeshifter species, the Heroka. I wanted to create something different from a standard werewolf. Writers have been there, done that too many times. For one thing, I wanted the Heroka to include all animals, not just wolves. And I wanted them to be more than just another bunch of shapeshifters. As absurd as it may sound, I wanted my Heroka to be believable.

Well, okay—as believable as shapeshifters can be. For one thing, I wanted to downplay the shapeshifter element. I wanted the primary characteristic of the Heroka to be the bond they hold with their totem species, and to have that bond be complete—physical, mental, and spiritual. I wanted the very vitality of a Heroka to be tied to the vitality of their totem.

Why? Because the bigger message here, the theme of the book if you like, is a warning call about what we're doing to our environment, to our natural resources, to the wilderness that once defined this land—the wilderness the animal species that call this country home depend upon for survival.

So if this story was going to be about environmental exploitation and animal habitat destruction by modern Western society, I needed a contrasting cultural view, one founded on a deep and abiding respect for the relationship that exists and has always existed between humans and nature, humans and animals—a relationship that our modern society has forgotten and forsaken. I wanted a belief system that was diametrically opposed to the European view that places humans and our needs at the top of the pyramid of life on Earth.

And I found it in the stories of our First Nations. The Cree spirit Wisakejack is the voice for those stories in this book, and if I could choose just one of his tales to demonstrate the dichotomy between the traditional beliefs of native people and modern society, and why the beliefs of the Cree and Anishinabe fit so perfectly with the Heroka and the theme of the book, it would be his story of the creation of the world that he relates to Zach in Chapter 10.

First, Kitche Manitou created the four elements—earth, water, fire, and air—and from them made the world—the Sun, stars, Moon, and Earth. Then he created the orders of life. First plants, which needed the sun, air, water, and earth. Then the plant eaters, which need the plants. Then the meat eaters, which need the plant eaters. And finally, he created humans. We came last, because we need everything that Kitche Manitou created before us. Air, water, earth, sun, plants, animals. We are the most dependent of all of the orders of life, making us the weakest of all orders, not the strongest.

The Heroka understand that relationship. They get it. They understand that, as Wisakejack told Zach, everything's connected. Western society has forgotten that. We've forgotten that we are dependent on the land. Forgetting our connnection, we've lost it, too.

Now, I'm not saying these stories encompass all of aboriginal culture. First Nations people are diverse and express their beliefs in varied ways, plus a large number today are also urban dwellers. But many First Nations stories speak of the close connection between humans and animals and the land, and I believe those stories continue to have relevance.

So that's why I chose to draw on the rich and wonderful stories and traditions of the Cree and Ojibwe in this book. But that's only part of my response to any concerns a reader might have about cultural appropriation.

I researched. A lot. I read as much as I could about the ceremonies, beliefs, traditions, and histories of the Cree and Ojibwe. And I read the stories. Ever so many stories. Because, as Wisakejack also tells Jack, that's how the People taught their children. At first, I found those stories very strange, but eventually I came to understand them, appreciate how they both entertained and educated, taught children about the dangerous harsh environment that they lived in, where starvation was only one bad hunt or one greedy hunter away.

I did more research. I stayed at an Ojibwe First Nations Reserve. I interviewed the chief and her mother. I visited three different reserve communities and talked to as many First Nations people as I could. I read more.

In short, I tried to do my homework as best as I could. I've included a bibliography of reference sources that I used in the back of this book. If you're interested, I heartily recommend that you check them out and read the stories yourself, both to enjoy and to learn more about the culture.

Finally, I've treated the Cree and Ojibwe culture with reverence and respect wherever I've used it in this book. That wasn't hard to do. The more I learned of the culture, the more I held it in reverence and respect.

So there's my defence. I fell in love with the stories and the culture, and found in them the same core truth that is the theme of the book and the same vitality that drive the Heroka. I did my very best to make sure I got things right and as accurate as possible. And I treated that culture with respect.

If you're Cree or Anishinabe or of any other First Nation, and you read this book, I'd love to hear from you. Tell me what I got right. Tell me what I got wrong. Tell me what you thought.

On Storytelling

One of the delights of doing the research for this book came from reading as many Cree and Anishinabe stories as I could find. But those stories also caused me some worry. I would read one story, say of Wisakejack and the flood and the recreation of the world, and then read another version of the same story that was significantly different in events and details. For example, in some versions, his wolf brother lives, in others he dies, while still in others, the wolf is not even mentioned.

So back to my fear. I was so concerned about getting the facts and stories right. How could I do that if every version of a story was different? Which version was the "right" one?

I puzzled over that until I realized that these stories were transcribed from versions that people remembered being told when they were young or used to tell to their children. Storytelling for the Cree and Ojibwe was always an *oral* tradition, and each storyteller would tell their own version of a traditional tale. So every version I was reading would naturally be different, varying just as the storytellers varied. Or as we learned about Ed and his storytelling class:

> He never read to the kids from the books. Storytelling was an oral tradition, not a written one. Reading the stories didn't let him change them, adding something each time around to give a slightly different meaning to the story from the last time he told it.
>
> Besides, he liked his versions better.

In the end, I think it's as Wisakejack tells Zach, "a story is true if its meaning is true," and I've tried to stay true to the meaning of all the stories.

On Spelling

Deciding on the "proper" English spelling of Cree and Anishinabe words presented a similar problem. For example, "Ojibwe" is also often written as Ojibwa, Ojibway or Ojibwey, and "Anishinabe" also appears as Anishinaabe, Nishnaabe, or Anicinape.

"Wisakejack" has even more variations, and can appear as any of Wesake-jack, Wisakedjak, Weesageechak, Wiisagejaak, Weesack-kachack, Wisagatcak, Wis-kay-tchach, Wissaketchak, Woesack-ootchacht, and so on.

In the end, I've used the spelling that I found to be most common with native writers (e.g., Ojibwe, Mahigan), and when there did not seem to be a common agreement, I've used the version that gave the closest approximation to a phonetic spelling (e.g., Wisakejack, Anishinabe).

Finally, a "windigo" (not capitalized) is a person who has become infected with the "Windigo" spirit (capitalized).

ON PLACE

My original Heroka story "Spirit Dance" specifically identifies the town where Ed and Vera live as the real town of Wawa, Ontario. In writing this novel, I switched the location to the entirely fictional town of Thunder Lake.

I used the town of Chapleau, Ontario as my basis for research on the bush, flora, fauna, town facilities, characteristics, and police procedures. I chose Chapleau because it's the size I needed (small but big enough to have an OPP detachment) and in the right location (east tip of Lake Superior—north but not too far north). But most importantly, it has three First Nation reserves in its boundaries, specifically two Ojibwe and one Cree. Since I intended to use a mix of both Ojibwe and Cree characters, stories, and traditions, Chapleau was the perfect research location.

That being said, Thunder Lake is *not* Chapleau, nor is it Wawa. Thunder Lake is an entirely fictional small northern Ontario town that I completely made up, using my research only to ensure the details of my fictional town made sense and all fit together correctly. Any resemblance to Chapleau or Wawa is coincidental and unintended. (By the way, there is a lake, not a town, called Thunder Lake in Western Ontario. My Thunder Lake has nothing to do with that one either).

ON OTHER HEROKA STORIES

If you enjoyed this book, I recommend you check out "Spirit Dance," which is available as a stand-alone ebook and is included in my collection, *Impossibilia*. I also have another published Heroka story, "A Bird in the Hand," available as a stand-alone ebook, in which you'll meet my most unique Heroka character, Lilith Hoyl. All of these stories are available from my bookstore at smithwriter.com/store and all major ebook retailers.

Thanks for reading! I'm always happy to receive feedback. You can contact me via my website at smithwriter.com/contact.

BIBLIOGRAPHY

The following are some of the text, film, and other sources that formed part of the research for this novel.

BOOKS

1. Aatiyuuhkaan: Legends of the James Bay Cree, Joanne Willis Newton (text adaptation), James Bay Cree Educational Centre, Chisasibi, PQ, 1989

2. Aboriginal Peoples of Canada, Paul Robert Magocsi (ed.), U of T Press, 2002

3. Cree Legends, Volume 1, compiled by Beth Ahenakew and Sam Hard-lotte, Saskatchewan Indian Cultural College, Saskatoon, 1973

4. Encyclopedia of American Indian Contributions to the World, Keoke and Porterfield,

5. Encyclopedia of Native American Tribes, Waldman

6. Generation to Generation, Edward Benton-Banai, Indian Country Communication Inc, Hayward, Wisconsin, 1991

7. Honour Earth Mother, Basil H. Johnston, Kegedonce Press, Wiarton, Ontario, 2003

8. Indian School Days, Basil Johnston, Key Porter Books, Toronto, 1988

9. Indian Stories from James Bay, compiled by Lillian Small, Highway Book-Shop, Cobalt, ON, 1972

10. Legends of the James Bay Lowlands, stories compiled by David Lightwood, 1974, James Bay Education Centre

11. Medicine Boy and Other Cree Tales, Eleanor Brass, Glenbow-Alberta Institute, Calgary 1979

12. Mythology of the British Isles, Geoffrey Ashe, 1990

13. Mythical and Fabulous Creatures, edited by Malcolm South, 1988

14. Never Cry Wolf, Farley Mowat

15. Ojibway Ceremonies, Basil Johnston, McClelland and Stewart, Toronto, 1982, ISBN 0-7710-4446-1

16. Ojibway Heritage, Basil Johnston, McClelland and Stewart, Toronto, 1976, ISBN 0-7710-4442-9

17. Ojibway Language Lexicon for Beginners, Basil Johnston, ISBN 0-662-10145-6

18. Our Grandmothers' Lives as Told in Their Own Words, Edited by Freda Ahenakew & H.C. Wolfart, Fifth House Publishers, 1992

19. Return of the Wolf, Steve Grooms, North Word Press, 1999

20. Sacred Stories of the Sweet Grass Cree, Leonard Bloomfield, Canada, Dept of Mines; 1993 Fifth House Ltd., Saskatoon; originally published 1930 F.A. Acland, Ottawa

21. Stories of the House People, edited by Freda Ahenakew, told by P. Vandalland J. Douquette, The University of Manitoba Press, Winnipeg, 1987

22. Story Keepers: Conversations with aboriginal writers, Jennifer David, Ningwakwe Learning Press, 2004

23. Tales from the Cree, George W. Bauer, Highway Book Shop, Cobalt, ON, 1973 (James Bay Cree)

24. The Manitous: The Spiritual World of the Ojibways, Basil Johnston, Harper Collins, New York, 1995, ISBN 0-06-017199-5

25. The Orders of the Dreamed: George Nelson on Cree and Northern Ojibwa Religion and Myth, 1823, Brown and Brightman, Winnipeg, 1988

26. A Short History of Indians in Canada, Thomas King, HarperCollins, 2005

27. The Truth About Stories, Thomas King, House of Anansi Press, 2003

28. Wesakejack and the Flood, Bill Ballantyne, Bain & Cox, Winnipeg, 1994

29. Where the Chill Came From: Cree Windigo Tales and Journeys, gathered and translated by Howard Norman, North Point Press, San Francisco, 1982 (Swampy Cree tales)

30. Windigo Psychosis: A Study of a Relationship between Belief & Behaviour among the Indians of Northeastern Canada, Morton I. Teicher, American Ethnological Society, 1960.

31. Windigo: An Anthology of Fact and Fantastic Fiction, edited by John Robert Columbo, Western Producer Prairie Books, 1982

32. Wisdom of the Elders, Peter Knudtson & David Suzuki, Greystone Books, 2006

33. Wolf Country, John B. Theberge, McClelland & Stewart, 1998

34. Wolves and Werewolves, John Pollard, Great Britain, St. Edmundsbury Press Ltd., 1991

35. Zoo of the Gods: Animals in Myth, Legend & Fable, Anthony S. Mercatante,
 . New York, Harper & Row, 1974

FILMS AND EXHIBITS

1. "Cree Hunters of Mistassini," NFB Canada, Directors: Boyce Richardson, Tony Ianzelo; 1974

2. "Inherit the Earth," Producer: Tamarack Productions; 1995

3. "Northern Wanderers: George River Caribou," CBC, David Suzuki, 1990

4. "Power," National Film Board of Canada

5. "School in the Bush," National Film Board of Canada, Producer: Dennis Sawyer, 1986
   a. "Bimaadiziwin -- A Healthy Way of Life": Health
   b. "Gaa Miinigooyang -- That which is given to us": Economic survival
   c. "Gikinoo'amaadiwin -- We Gain Knowledge": Education and learning
   d. "Gwayakochigewin -- Making Decisions the Right Way": Leadership and governance

6. AGO native art exhibit, January 2004

About the Author

"One of Canada's most original writers of speculative fiction." —*Library Journal*

"A great storyteller with a gifted and individual voice." —*Charles de Lint*

Douglas Smith is an award-winning Canadian author who has been published in thirty countries and twenty-five languages.

His collections include *Chimerascope* (2010), *Impossibilia* (2008), and *La Danse des Esprits* (France, 2011). *The Wolf at the End of the World* is his first novel.

Doug has twice won Canada's Aurora Award, and has been a finalist for the John W. Campbell Award, CBC's Bookies Award, Canada's juried Sunburst Award, and France's juried Prix Masterton and Prix Bob Morane.

His website is smithwriter.com, and he tweets at twitter.com/smithwritr.

Join Doug's mailing list to be notified of new books and stories, award news, and events Doug will be attending.

OTHER WORKS BY DOUGLAS SMITH

COLLECTIONS

Chimerascope (ChiZine Publications, Canada, 2010) *Finalist for the Sunburst Award, Aurora Award, and CBC's Bookies Award*

Impossibilia (PS Publishing, UK, 2008) *Aurora Award Finalist*

La Danse des Esprits (Dreampress, France, 2011, translated) *Finalist for the Prix Masterton and Prix Bob Morane*

SHORT STORIES

"Spirit Dance" (1997) *Aurora Award Finalist*

"New Year's Eve" (1998) *Aurora Award Finalist*

"State of Disorder" (1999) *Aurora Award Finalist*

"Symphony" (1999) *Aurora Award Finalist*

"What's in a Name?" (2000)

"The Boys Are Back in Town" (2000)

"La Danse des Esprits" (2001) *AURORA AWARD WINNER (French translation)*

"The Red Bird" (2001) *Aurora Award Finalist*

"By Her Hand, She Draws You Down" (2001) *Aurora Award Finalist; Best New Horrror selection*

"Scream Angel" (2003) *AURORA AWARD WINNER*

"Jigsaw" (2004) *Aurora Award Finalist*

"Enlightenment" (2004) *Aurora Award Finalist*

"Going Harvey in the Big House" (2005) *Aurora Award Finalist*

"Memories of the Dead Man" (2006)

"The Last Ride" (2006)

"A Taste Sweet and Salty" (2006)

"Murphy's Law" (2006)
"The Dancer at the Red Door" (2007) *Aurora Award Finalist*
"Out of the Light" (2007)
"Bouquet of Flowers in a Vase, by van Gogh" (2008) *Aurora Award Finalist*
"Going Down to Lucky Town" (2008)
"Doorways" (2008) *Aurora Award Finalist*
"Radio Nowhere" (2009) *Aurora Award Finalist*
"Nothing" (2010)
"A Bird in the Hand" (2010)
"The Walker of the Shifting Borderland" (2012) *Aurora Award Finalist*
"Fiddleheads" (2013)

SPECIALTY BOOKS

"By Her Hand, She Draws You Down": The Official Movie Companion Book (2010)

A complete list of Doug's published fiction is available on his website along with excerpts and reviews of his work. All of Doug's works are available as ebooks in a variety of formats.

Chimerascope

© Douglas Smith

*Sunburst Award
Finalist*

*Aurora Award
Finalist*

*CBC's Bookies Award
Finalist*

Chimerascope [ki-meer-uh-skohp]—a story of many parts...

Doug's second collection contains sixteen of his best stories, including an award winner, a Best New Horror selection, and eight award finalists. Stories of fantasy and science fiction that take you from love in four-teenth-century Japan to humanity's last stand, from virtual reality to the end of reality, from alien drug addictions to a dinner where a man loses everything.

"His stories are a treasure trove of riches that will touch your heart while making you think." *—Robert J. Sawyer, Hugo Award-winning author*

"A massively enjoyable trek...all filtered through Smith's remarkable imagination and prodigious talent." *—Quill and Quire (starred review)*

"The 16 stories in this collection showcase the inventive mind and immense storytelling talent of one of Canada's most original writers of speculative fiction." —*Library Journal*

"An entertaining selection of stories that deftly span multiple genres." —*Publishers Weekly*

"An engaging and entertaining volume, pieces of whose content resonate after the book is finished." —*Booklist*

"Douglas Smith is an extraordinary author whom every lover of quality speculative fiction should read. Rating: A+" —*Fantasy Book Critic*

"Arrestingly inventive premises in a field where really interesting new ideas are harder and harder to find. ...Smith is definitely an author who deserves to be more widely read." —*Strange Horizons*

"A beautifully diverse selection of short tales...well-crafted, easily digestible; several of the stories are incredibly moving and stick with the reader long after." —*Sunburst Award jury*

"Smith is a master of beginnings...some of the most well-crafted hooks you'll find anywhere...[with] endings that feel satisfying and right." —*Canadian Science Fiction Review*

Look for *Chimerascope* in all major book retailers.

Impossibilia

© Douglas Smith

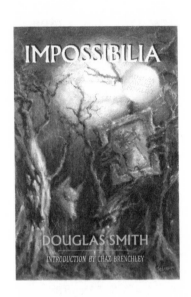

*Aurora Award
Finalist*

Doug's first collection contains three novelettes, including an award winner and an award finalist. Stories of wonder with characters that you won't forget. Characters who, like any of us, have things they hide inside—secrets, fears, aspects of themselves they keep locked away. Or try to. Only their things are a little...different.

A painter who talks to Vincent van Gogh
A shapeshifter hunting one of his own
The secret to being the luckiest man alive

Welcome to *Impossibilia!*

"The finest short-story writer Canada has ever produced in the science fiction and fantasy genres." —*Robert J. Sawyer, Hugo and Nebula Award winning author*

"One of Canada's most original writers of speculative fiction." —*Library Journal*

"A great storyteller with a gifted and individual voice." —*Charles de Lint, World Fantasy Award winning author*

"In the grand manner that harks back to Bradbury and Sturgeon and Ellison."
                                                      —*Chaz Brenchley*

"In my search for the perfect short story, the three in this volume certainly qualify."   —*SF Crowsnest Book Reviews*

Look for *Impossibilia* in all major book retailers.